ONEIROS

MARKUS HEITZ

ONEIROS

Translated by
Sorcha McDonagh

Jo Fletcher
BOOKS

First published in Great Britain in 2015 by

Jo Fletcher Books
an imprint of
Quercus Publishing Ltd
Carmelite House
50 Victoria Embankment
London EC4Y 0DZ

An Hachette UK company

PB ISBN 978 1 84866 529 3
EBOOK ISBN 978 1 78429 041 2

10 9 8 7 6 5 4 3 2 1

Typeset by CC Book Production
Printed and bound in Great Britain by Clays Ltd, St Ives plc

For the people who try to cheat Death every day,
to wrest days, weeks and years from him,
as patients, as doctors, as nurses, as scientists,
as emergency workers and in every job
that I've forgotten.
Just don't give up.

Prologue

'. . . hope that you enjoy your breakfast. We will be arriving at Paris-Charles De Gaulle airport in approximately two hours, at around 10.45 a.m. We will begin the approach for landing in about an hour. There will be more from me about that closer to the time. If you have any questions or requests, my team and I are always happy to help.' Christine finished the announcement in charmingly accented French and English. She stepped out of the way of her colleagues who were beginning to hand out the food.

The 550 passengers in three different classes over two levels wanted their breakfasts. The chief flight attendant was hoping it would perk up the mood on board. They had been delayed by two hours because the staff in JFK airport in New York had been overstretched. Or overwhelmed. Or the technology was outdated. And not for the first time.

Christine's gaze swept around. Flight AF023 was coming back to life seat by seat.

She liked the atmosphere in the mornings. Most of the passengers were more or less cheerful; some still had their sleep masks over their eyes and their seats reclined, dozing away, or headphones in their ears. Elsewhere, she could see someone had a film on already, soft murmurs floated through the air and somewhere in the bright cabin, children laughed. She was reminded of her son and smiled. Oliver, seven years old.

'Could you please deal with seat 81?' Marlène whispered to her as she pushed the first trolley out of the kitchen area. It smelled of freshly brewed coffee, fried eggs, bread rolls and croissants; slowly the smell wafted across the A380-862.

'What's wrong with him?'

'He's being annoying. He's already on his fourth whisky and a while ago he was hanging out at the bar complaining that the dinner had given him diarrhoea.'

'What did he eat?'

Marlène rolled her eyes and paused. 'First soup, then salmon with lemon and saffron rice and salad, then another piece of salmon and two croissants filled with chocolate custard. Two packets of peanuts and a packet of crisps. With a spicy dip. That's as much as I noticed. Claire said that he demolished some free snacks in between. Oh, and he glugged down half a bottle of gin. My stomach would protest too.'

'I'll sort it out.' With a nod of her head, Christine sent her to give out breakfast on the main deck, where most of the low-fare passengers were sitting. On Air France they were called, somewhat cryptically, *Voyageurs*, which sounded classier than third class. There were 340 men, women and children placed in long rows of seats behind and next to each other. The Première – first class in the front of the plane – was completely separate from them.

Christine moved off quickly so that she could help give out the meals afterwards. Being the boss meant more responsibility and no less work. To get to seat 81 and its unruly occupant, she had to go to the higher deck first anyway. There were 106 more *Voyageurs* there, as well as 80 *Affaires*, the business-class passengers.

Christine took the second-best stairs to the upper deck and walked past the rows of *Affaires* on her way down the plane. Her colleagues swarmed around her, delivering the utterly luxurious breakfast to the passengers. She sighed. Right in the midst of this hustle and bustle one of the passengers just had to flex his muscles.

As she went past, she nodded at the flight attendants who had begun giving out the food and were gently waking the last remaining sleepers from their dreams with a whispered *bonjour*.

'Excuse me!'

Christine flinched as cool fingers clasped her wrist and forced her to stop.

'Could I please have a pot of extremely strong coffee?'

She lowered her gaze and looked at the man. He was around forty, in a distinctly average, not very expensive outfit. Christine could estimate the price of clothes incredibly well. Even though he could clearly afford a business-class ticket, his clothes weren't worth more than a hundred euro, including the boots, jeans, checked shirt and neckerchief. A pseudo-cowboy, although judging by the accent of his English he was probably from Scandinavia. He had scruffy blond hair that lay thin and tangled on his head and dark circles under his pale blue eyes. He looked like he hadn't slept in a long time. 'I'll tell my colleagues, Monsieur.'

The man didn't let go of her, his eyes staring urgently. Riveted on her. 'Please let them know that it needs to be very, very strong,' he whispered hoarsely, rubbing his wan face with his free hand. A thin film of sweat covered his large forehead.

Christine could see four empty energy drink cans on the open tray table, and the brownish ring shapes on the otherwise clean plastic surface betrayed the fact he must have drunk coffee already. 'I'll do it right away, Monsieur. Could you please let go of me?'

'Strong! It's important!' His gaze flitted away and focused on the cans. 'Sorry,' he whispered and released his grip on Christine's arm. Then he sank down, mumbling something that was probably meant to be an apology; she couldn't really hear.

Christine went on her way and decided to check the man's name on the plane's manifest as soon as she got back. His behaviour was not normal. He also didn't look like he belonged in business class. Maybe she had a junkie on her hands who couldn't handle his withdrawal any more and was going to lose it just before they started the landing. Or perhaps during it.

As she walked, she straightened her navy blue jacket, as well as the scarf in a lighter shade and the brooch with its Air France emblem, and entered the *Voyageurs'* area where the passengers sat in a two-four-two formation without being too cramped. There was no comparison with the old planes.

Seat 81 was wide awake and in a bad mood, sick bag in hand. He was ranting to the passenger next to him, a young lady with her son to her right and an Asian man to the left, and they were nodding but couldn't say anything in response because he was talking relentlessly. Gesticulating. Getting worked up.

Christine analysed him in a split second. Accent: Italian. Clothes: around five hundred euro, not including the gold jewellery. Category: tight-fisted businessman, show-off and *cazzo*.

'Monsieur?' She showed her teeth as she put on her 'kiss-my-ass' smile, an indispensable part of a good flight attendant's repertoire. An insult that wasn't one.

His black curls shook as he whipped around, his slight double chin wobbled. He was in his mid-thirties at the most, but he was no *bella figura*. He was surrounded by a faint waft of alcohol. '*Si?*'

'Monsieur, my colleague said you didn't feel well. Is there anything I can get you that might help? Charcoal tablets or—'

'*Porca miseria!* I feel like throwing up because I ate that French slop!' he exclaimed in English, while making a very Italian accompanying hand gesture that meant *this wouldn't have happened on Alitalia*. 'And we're delayed,' he added, as though the lateness of the flight was to blame for his illness.

The passengers in his row rolled their eyes, the little boy, bored, was messing with a coloured pen that had a small LED light on it. The Asian man had an oxygen cylinder in front of him; a see-through tube from it went under his shirt and was visible again at his neck. Two thin little bits poked into his nostrils.

Christine leaned down. 'Monsieur, I'm so sorry to hear that. Our captain has done his best to minimise the delay.' Christine looked apologetically at the other passengers in the row, expressing her sympathy for their having to endure this particular passenger. 'On the food issue, my colleagues mentioned that you may have consumed a mixture of a few too many foods. Could I suggest—'

He grimaced. 'Did *you* just say that it's *my* fault that I want to throw up and my insides make me need to go the loo every few minutes?' Seat 81 threw his hands in the air, the little gold chain on his right wrist jingling softly and glinting in the beam from the reading light. Christine couldn't read the Italian words engraved on it. 'I don't have to stand for this! I've paid a lot of money and in return I get poisoned!'

Christine took a deep breath and straightened up. Her smile widened and became more disdainful. 'Monsieur, please calm down. I promise—'

'I want half my money back,' he cried and looked at her aggressively, giving a suppressed belch. 'No, a full refund would be best, or I'll complain to Air France.' His dark eyes flashed as he crossed his arms over his chest. 'If necessary I'll take a sample of my diarrhoea and have it analysed.' Then he leaped to his feet, squeezed past his fellow passenger and the chief flight attendant and hurried to the toilet.

Christine understood why Marlène had asked her for help. This time *she* was the one to get apologetic looks from the passengers. 'I can only apologise for what's happened, *messieurs dames*,' she announced.

'No problem,' replied the Asian man, who was breathing heavily and wearing traditional robes and a thick black beard. Christine remembered him because he'd produced a special permit for his oxygen cylinder at check-in.

'You can see how much travel broadens the mind: my son is learning more Italian swear words than he will ever need,' added the young woman wryly. Her son was oblivious, concentrating on the penlight.

Christine nodded gratefully. 'Thanks for being so understanding, *messieurs dames*. I'll see if I can improve things.' She left it unclear whether she was talking about the state of 81, or whether she wanted to assign the man a different seat in order to spare the patience and nerves of the other passengers. Two hours next to a professional complainer could be very long indeed.

The Italian was already visible at the end of the aisle again, pressing himself against the cabin wall next to the toilet and waving furtively at her.

Christine approached him and noticed that he looked at her slender legs as she did so. 'What can I do for you, Monsieur? Is there no more toilet paper?'

But 81 was behaving calmly. 'Sorry for how I'm acting,' he said softly and yet kept gesticulating as though he was going to work himself up. 'I didn't want the Arab to start suspecting anything.'

'Monsieur? The *Arab*? I don't understand.'

Seat 81 turned so that his face couldn't be seen from the seats. 'He has been reading the Koran the whole time,' he murmured, 'and talking under his breath.'

'It's not against regulations to read religious books on board Air France aircraft, Monsieur,' she countered. A demanding flyer with paranoia. This was all she needed. She knew exactly what he was getting at. 'The woman in seat 53 was reading the Bible earlier, and one of the gentlemen in the *Affaires* section had the Communist Manifesto in front of him. That doesn't mean they must automatically be terrorists.'

'But – the oxygen cylinder!'

'Monsieur, the man is in possession of a special permit from Air France. Although I'm not allowed to say this, for your peace of mind: he has a lung condition and has a—'

'But he hasn't turned it on.'

Christine had to admit that gave her a moment's pause. 'Maybe he doesn't need to be inhaling all the time?'

He gave her a triumphant look. 'He hasn't even used it once since we got on. The display says *off*. I know that model, my dad was on supplemental oxygen. That Arab doesn't have a lung condition, I'd bet my gold jewellery on it.'

Now her suspicions were truly raised, even if she didn't want 81 to be right. '*Bon.* Monsieur, I'll have the permit checked again.'

'It might be too late then!' He grabbed her arm in exactly the same place that the *Affaires* passenger with the cold hand and tired eyes had. 'We have eleven Arabs on board. I counted them and they're well spread out through the cabins. They were standing at the bar earlier, talking quietly. They know each other! So why aren't they sitting together?' he asked urgently. 'What if they all have links to each other and are planning an attack? If it's a bomb or ... poison gas that the man next to me has got?' He looked quickly over his shoulder. 'What are we going to do?'

'*We* are doing nothing, *I'll* do something, Monsieur.' Christine was annoyed that 81 had finally managed to infect her with his persecution mania. It was unlikely that his Italian fantasies would turn out to be anything other than paranoia, but safety came first. With more than five hundred people on board, she couldn't pretend he hadn't said anything.

'You go back to your seat, Monsieur. I'll check the passenger list and the man's permit and I'll arrange some security measures,' she explained rapidly to calm him down. 'If you notice anything, pretend that you're ill and I'll come back.' Christine nodded to him.

He nodded back, seemingly proud with what he'd achieved, and then pressed his hand against his stomach for a moment. 'Oh, I really do not feel good,' he said. 'But you're right: it's my own fault.' Despite the ashen colour of his face, he winked at her in a very Italian way and went back to his seat.

Not thinking him quite as awful as she had before, Christine hurried to the crew area to carry out the checks.

'Remember my coffee,' someone called longingly after her. 'Extra strong, okay? Otherwise I'll go right to sleep.'

'Of course, Monsieur!' she replied as she went past without stopping, which she ordinarily would never have done. But she had more important things to do now. That pseudo-cowboy shouldn't be making such a fuss. As if Air France would serve weak coffee! 'I'll mention it to my colleague *tout de suite*.'

Christine reached the main deck as the last of the breakfasts were being handed out in the A380. Feeling tense, she sat down at the computer, looked up the passenger lists, compared the information there with the seating plan and went over all the data available.

The Asians in question came from different Arab states; there were no records that made them suspicious in any way.

But then her forehead creased as she read the name of the passenger next to 81: Rub al-Chali.

She thought she could recall a desert in Oman of the

same name. She used to travel around that region a lot with a different airline, so she had quite a good knowledge of it.

Was it possible that a man and a desert shared the same name?

Why shouldn't she call in one of the security people? Among the passengers there were four armed members of a special force, two on each deck. Air France employed them for flights to and from New York as a precaution and defence in case of hijackings by extremists. Unremarkable, dressed like normal people.

Rub al-Chali.

She felt hot and cold, rubbing her temples nervously. The Italian's fantasies were becoming less and less far-fetched.

'Why did it have to be on my flight?' murmured Christine. She decided to tell the *capitaine* her suspicions. He would decide what they should do.

Tommaso Luca Francesco Tremante was wriggling about in his seat, not letting his Arab neighbour out of his sight. His life was shaping up so nicely right now and it was not about to end here.

He had made his money in property and continued to do so: he sold rich French people cheap American houses, which there were so many of thanks to the financial crisis in the USA. Business was booming. The last thing Tommaso wanted was for an extremist to blow him up, poison him with gas, or make him one part of a missile-craft headed towards a French building. Hence the stageworthy fuss he'd made.

Twenty minutes later the lovely mother and her bored child were called up because allegedly, according to the announcement, they had entered an on-board lottery and she was now getting a seat with her son in the first-class cabin. They were both pleased.

After another ten minutes, a tall, broad-shouldered man appeared and settled himself next to the Arab because there was too much noise for him on the upper deck. 'So lucky that something was free here,' he said, and laughed as he opened a newspaper and started reading.

The *bella donna* – the chief flight attendant – had let Tommaso know with a subtle gesture that the man was a member of staff. A sky marshal or something similar.

That had calmed Tommaso somewhat, but he was still worried.

The Arab was acting normally, eating a croissant and drinking coffee, reading the Koran; his mysterious oxygen cylinder remained securely closed.

Tommaso hoped the sky marshal would gun the Arab down if he so much as started to act a bit strangely.

He found it funny that the Muslim was eating the croissant with such relish. Of all things. According to legend, the little puff pastry crescent had been invented after the siege of Vienna by the Turks, so it had been invented by Islam in the broadest sense. The Ottomans had been trying to dig a tunnel underneath the city walls and a Viennese baker had noticed and raised the alarm. Since it was traditional to seal victories with a dish that embarrassed the enemy, they'd created a pastry in the shape of a Turkish crescent.

Tommaso wasn't sure if that story was true. His stomach

hadn't been able to get on with the three greasy croissants he'd eaten for breakfast. Or maybe he felt ill because of the fuss about the terrorists? Or because of the extra-strong coffee, which he'd been given without asking for? When he'd asked a flight attendant about it afterwards, she'd admitted it had been intended for another passenger.

He practically soiled himself during the approach to landing, so he loosened his seatbelt as soon as the wheels of the A380 touched the asphalt and the engines slowed down. Tommaso's insides were seething.

'That's not safe, Monsieur,' said the Arab amicably. 'We haven't stopped moving yet. If someone rams into us—'

'Stay in your seat,' the sky marshal ordered, and gave him a warning look. 'The seatbelt signs haven't been turned off yet.'

Tommaso ignored the warnings and pushed his way into the aisle. 'You'd be better off keeping an eye on that *imbecile*,' he snarled at the security man. 'I'm definitely not about to crap my pants when the loo is less than two metres away. These trousers were expensive.'

He started running, leaning on the seats for support, and approached his saviour, the toilet. The airbus was still moving at quite considerable speed. The passengers watched him go, some baffled, some laughing out of *Schadenfreude*. His little interlude earlier hadn't exactly won him friends. But he'd saved them all!

Just a few more steps and he'd reach the toilet bowl. And not a moment too soon. He swore to himself he would never eat croissants again, no matter how good they tasted.

'Monsieur!' That was the voice of the *bella donna*. 'Sit down immediately!'

'*Scusi*, no can do. Anyway, you're running around too,' he replied and disappeared into the cubicle, slammed the door closed and pulled down his trousers.

Relief came immediately and he sighed happily.

Less pleasant was the angry, authoritative knocking.

'Come out, Monsieur! Right now!'

Tommaso laughed. 'Believe me, you do not want *that*, *bella*.' He rubbed his belly. 'No harm done. And I'm holding on tight. Promise.'

The rapping came again, then her voice.

'I'd like to point out, Monsieur, that it is not permitted, and that there are sanctions associated with disregarding the instructions of staff members.'

The plane moved in a slight curve and the centrifugal force made Tommaso hold on tight to the sink and the side panelling.

'I don't mind. I'll pay the fine. It won't be as expensive as a new pair of trousers,' he called through the door. 'Let me take my crap in peace.' He noticed how warm it was in the little cubicle. The air conditioning wasn't working.

'I'm warning you, Monsieur.'

The intercom above him crackled and then a female voice came on and advised that they had landed safely. The announcement was accompanied by muffled clapping from the passengers. 'For your own safety, please leave your seat belt securely fastened until the aircraft has stopped and we have reached the parking position.'

By now there was silence outside his door. No more threatening knocks, no orders from the agitated chief flight attendant.

'You're not getting the man with the gun now, are you?' The rumblings and groans from his stomach had finally stopped, but he still didn't feel great. And the toilet paper wasn't the softest either. His backside was probably glowing like a guinea baboon's.

'We'd like to thank you for travelling with Air France—' came a voice from the ceiling-mounted loudspeaker, but a horrible, high-pitched rustling as if from a scrambling transmitter interrupted the announcement.

Tommaso had to cover his ears; the shrill buzzing was making his eardrums and head ache.

Suddenly there was silence.

'What was that?' Tommaso stood up, pressed the flush, pulled up his trousers and washed his hands.

The noise from the engines hadn't let up; the A380 was still moving swiftly over the landing field and was looking for its parking space. The pilots seemed to be in a hurry.

Tommaso scrutinised himself in the mirror, dabbed at his face and winked at himself. He passed a discerning hand over his podgy chin. 'I've looked better,' he said, unlocking and opening the cubicle. '*Ciao, bella!* If you absolutely must—'

He almost tripped over the body at his feet, but then he recognised the chief flight attendant lying lifelessly in front of him. A collapse? Her eyes were wide open and he couldn't see any wounds. A heart attack? Stroke?

'*Maledetto!*' He crouched down immediately and looked for a pulse in her neck but couldn't find one. 'Help!' he shouted and ran into the aisle. 'Is there a doctor—' Tommaso's words stuck in his throat: the passengers were sitting in their seats, their limbs limp, their heads on their chests or to one side, some hanging over their armrests. What was wrong here? They couldn't all have fallen asleep at once.

Deathly silence.

Panic gripped Tommaso when he remembered the Arab's gas canister and he held his breath straight away. Poison gas! He was right after all!

He quickly went over to a seat and yanked on the ceiling panel until, in an amazing stroke of luck, it came off and the oxygen mask behind it was released.

At least the bearded Arab was in his seat like everybody else; he had his eyes open, one hand on the canister's pressure gauge, which was turned up as far as it would go. The contents were being released into the cabin with a soft hiss.

The airbus was still taxiing forwards fast, oblivious to the attack.

There was a cracking sound and the plane was gripped by vibrations, and then began rocking from side to side.

Tommaso looked out the window and realised that the A380 had knocked down two gangways. In the glare from the headlights the ground staff were frantically running around in packs while vehicles with rotating yellow lights accompanied the airbus. Blue lights appeared in the distance.

Then he had a terrifying thought – the gas might have crept as far as the pilots! That would explain why the A380 wasn't braking.

The terminal's booms appeared in front of him.

He had no doubt that the terrorists were in the cockpit and were trying to launch the airbus at one of the buildings.

'*Porca miseria!*' Tommaso could imagine the inferno now:

halls collapsing, petrol spilling, explosions and flames, death and destruction.

His gaze fell on the body of the sky marshal who had one eye closed and the other open. His left hand lay on the handle of his semi-automatic pistol, never having been able to draw it.

What should he do now? Flee, or attempt a heroic attack on the terrorists in the cockpit? And if he wanted to get out, then how? He could forget about emergency slides or anything of the sort as long as the plane kept moving. But wasn't the door to the cockpit reinforced and impenetrable?

He could feel the sweat running down over his back and soaking his shirt.

Then any decision was taken away from him when the nose of the A380 collided with Terminal 2E, boring into the glass and steel structure without losing any momentum.

One turbine exploded spectacularly, ripping the plastic glass out of the small oval bulls' eye windows at the back of the plane and drawing blazing tongues of flame inside.

Tommaso was catapulted forwards by the impact, crashing into a seat and collapsing unconscious into the aisle. All around him, the inferno he had feared unfurled.

I

The girl:
Pass by! O pass me by!
Mad man of bones, away with thee!
I am young yet, away!
Away and do not touch me.
Death:
Give me your hand, dear, gentle child!
I come in friendship, not to harm.
Take heart! Not mad, I am so mild,
You will sleep gently in my arms!

Der Tod und das Mädchen,
Matthias Claudius (1740my arm

Leipzig, Germany

Konstantin looked at the clock on the wall next to the door
and saw that it was a little after nine.

A day's work awaited him and his colleagues at Ars
Moriendi, his company, which he jokingly liked to refer to
as Rest in Peace Ltd, like the undertaker's in the German
version of the comedy horror film *The Comedy of Terrors* with

Vincent Price, Peter Lorre and Boris Karloff. Although they had nothing in common with their murderous methods.

'I'll be away again from the day after tomorrow, but I'll bew on my mobile. Is anything still unclear?'

Heads shaking in the little office.

'Off you go then, gentlemen and women.'

The eleven men and women barely fit into the room and most of them had to stand. They had just gone through the week's schedule together: a handful of normal burials at local graveyards, two transfers abroad, two burials at sea – one in the Atlantic and one in the Baltic; and then there was being on-call twenty-four hours a day for new deaths.

Around 5,600 people died in Leipzig every year, which meant an average of fifteen dead people a day. A burial cost approximately 5,000 euro. So there was a lot of work and opportunities for making money, which is why there were also a correspondingly high number of undertakers in the area. Which in turn reduced the money to be made.

Ars Moriendi – his funeral business – had a very good reputation. It was thanks to him – a young, well-respected boss with bright ideas and a steady hand – that they did such good business, even outside Leipzig. He won contracts all over Europe, for which he received bonuses and all-expenses-paid trips.

'Excellent. Have a good day then.' Konstantin looked at the two young men who stood up first. 'Maik, Florian, you're going out if we get a job. Is that okay?'

They nodded.

'And check the air conditioning in car four again for the transfer to the Atlantic. It's meant to be warm this whole week and the journey takes two days by van. Otherwise you might get a rather nasty surprise when you take Monsieur Contignac out of the coffin.' Konstantin stood up as his staff vanished one by one and set to work.

I do have good colleagues. He drank the last of his tea standing up and looked out the window towards the fleet of vehicles his colleagues were heading towards. They picked up floral tributes, prepared for funerals in different places, did their paperwork and so much more as part of their routine, and all tasks were completed with the dignity they were due.

In contrast to some of his colleagues, Konstantin did not stand for ripping people off, inflated prices or a lax, inappropriate attitude towards the dead. Strictly speaking, a corpse might only by a soulless shell, but it used to be a beloved parent, a beloved child or friend.

His gaze fell on his reflection in the mirror. *I really need to get to the hairdresser.* His dark brown hair was tickling his neck and refused to stay in the style he wanted despite the wax. Yet, for a man of nearly forty, he still looked surprisingly good. Most people would put him in his late twenties and that was not down to moisturiser or cosmetic surgery. When asked for his secret, he always answered that death kept him young. And that the formalin he mainlined was better than Botox. Undertaker's humour.

The black cars peeled away from the courtyard as Maik and Florian went into the workshop.

Konstantin strolled into the front room where the secretary, Mendy Kawatzki, was sitting and managing everything there was to manage, from meetings to job applications. 'Where has that job applicant got to, gorgeous?'

Mendy, in her mid-thirties and the faithful old soul of the company, looked over the edge of her black glasses. 'Why did you grow that beard? You look like Johnny Depp in that film—'

'I hope you don't mean *Pirates of the Caribbean*?'

'No. You may also live on a boat, but I meant . . . what was it called again?' She noticed one black button had come undone on her white blouse and did it up again. 'With Jolie. In Venice.'

'*The Tourist*.' Konstantin smiled. He had seen the film and thought the actor's beard wasn't too bad. But Konstantin really did not think he looked like Johnny Depp – his face was a bit longer, with less defined cheekbones. 'Doesn't it suit me?'

Mendy smiled. 'Sure. But whenever I've got used to how you look, you change something.' She shrugged and pointed to the screen. 'The applicant for the apprenticeship has sent an email. He's going to be half an hour late because he still needs to pick up a certificate.'

Konstantin muttered, unimpressed. 'He thought of that in good time didn't he?' He went to the door leading to the studio through a sterile corridor. 'Send him straight to me when he comes in. I'm going to go ahead and start.'

She scrutinised him. 'But you're not going to give him a hard time?'

He couldn't help laughing. 'Are you his spokesperson, Mrs Kawatzki?'

'No. But he looks nice.'

'And he's late. He might have earned himself a look at Mr Meininger for that.' Konstantin grinned. 'Thanks to you, I'll spare him that.'

Treating Mr Meininger, or rather what was left of him, was not exactly easy: a man in the prime of his life who'd fallen into a Leipzig canal and drowned after a boozy night out. He had been carried away gently by the current and found by horrified walkers weeks later on the bank of the canal. After being released by the police, Mr Meininger's family had had Ars Moriendi pick up his bloated, waterlogged, pathologist's-scalpel-ravaged corpse.

The sight of, and above all the smells from, Mr Meininger would have been enough to knock out even the most hardened job applicant. Unless they needed to throw up multiple times first, in which case one mishap could lead into the next.

Konstantin pointed to his watch. 'But if he's more than half an hour late, he's done for. Then he'll get a hard time.'

He vanished through the door and went along the tiled corridor that smelled of disinfectant and led to the actual working area. The two worlds of Ars Moriendi.

He hadn't chosen the name for his company at random, or because a Latin phrase sounded more sophisticated than *funeral parlour* or *undertakers*. He'd chosen it because on the one hand it translated as 'the art of dying', and on the other it referred to the Christian books produced in the late Middle Ages which were intended to prepare people for death in the Christian sense. The *Ars Moriendi* also dealt with the preparation of the dead for a decent, dignified burial.

And death was a type of art to Konstantin.

Literature was constantly coming up with different myths about immortals like zombies, vampires, the soulless. There were curses and elixirs that made them immortal, and of course, there was always alchemy, magic, divine intervention, pacts with the devil and many more things that could give you eternal life.

He had his own particular way of dealing with the Grim Reaper.

Konstantin went into the changing room and swapped his black cloth trousers and black polo shirt for a tracksuit in the same colour. It was one hundred per cent polyester, because smells and stains could only be fully washed out of synthetic material. Plus it was cheaper to replace than cotton.

Over the tracksuit there was the long-sleeved white apron, then purple rubber gloves for the hands. The comfy trainers got foil-like covers.

Ready to go. Konstantin went through the swing doors and entered his work space.

First he turned the mp3-player on. The shuffle setting selected a song and soon the mix of solemn heavy double bass and synth elements from the Leipzig band Lambda blasted out of the speakers. The singer's gorgeous voice filled the twenty-five-square-metre room with a love song. Some might have found the music incongruous, but for Konstantin there was no conflict with what he was about to do.

His kingdom, his work space. Two height-adjustable metal tables with a drainage system and hand-held shower stood in the middle of the room, and on the left-hand wall there was a door to the cold room. In one corner there was a large sink with a cupboard on the wall above it containing the most important utensils that Konstantin would need: surgical instruments, scalpels, scissors, wound-sealing powder, special spray-on plasters, moisturiser. And then there were the little tubs of Vaseline, cans of hair spray and a whole range of make-up paraphernalia, hairdryers and brushes. Not forgetting sewing equipment and fixing tape. Anyone who had seen a detective film would think they were in a pathology lab or an operating theatre.

Part of the service provided by Ars Moriendi was to prepare the dead, to wash, moisturise and dress them, even when they wouldn't be lying in repose in an open coffin. The men also got a shave, the woman had make-up applied. Photos handed over by the loved ones were used as guides to work from.

If someone wanted an open coffin for a person lying in repose and there were a few days between the time of death and the funeral, Konstantin's thanatological skills came into play. Thus, the table on the right was equipped with a pump system to remove the deceased's blood from their body and inject special pink liquid into the arteries, which reached right to the very smallest blood vessels. The pink liquid gave the deceased back their natural skin colour. The chemical mixture, which Konstantin made himself, consisted of a certain percentage of formaldehyde, which delayed the decomposition process.

Simply put, he made the bodies durable so that they didn't have to be kept in a refrigerated room and could even survive extreme weather conditions. So relatives and friends could file past the coffin without being disturbed by smells or other symptoms of decomposition.

Konstantin took a look at the list of the dead who were on the agenda for today and glanced over the information relating to the first name on the list. *This will be an easy case. Just right for a Monday morning.*

He went into the cold room and pushed the trolley with Gerd Pamuk, eighty-one years old, into the treatment room.

He assumed the man had died a peaceful death. Maik had collected the body from an old folks' home yesterday. Heart attack, said the death certificate, shortly after his coffee break. The body had been packed into the obligatory plastic bag and kept at an angle, the feet downwards, so that the blood didn't go to the head and make his face blue.

Gerd Pamuk's relatives had expressed a wish to see the old man again. In an open coffin. It was to happen this afternoon in Mourning Room One at Ars Moriendi, so Konstantin was preparing him. With great respect.

'Let's see how much I have to do then.' He opened the bag.

Thin, silvery hair emerged first, and then a high, creased, tanned forehead, bushy eyebrows, and then the rest of a friendly elderly face. With his pale, waxy skin, the dead man really looked like a doll. His eyes were closed, his mouth slightly open. A sweet odour wafted up out of the plastic bag. Decomposition bacteria worked quickly, despite the refrigeration at five degrees.

Gerd Pamuk was almost dainty, and had a wizened body with very little flesh. Konstantin could easily lift him onto the treatment table by himself. With the stiffness of the cold body – *rigor mortis* – it was even easier.

As he did this, Konstantin noticed an old tattoo on the man's left upper arm. It was pale blue and roughly done: a brig sailed across the wrinkled skin with an illegible name underneath. Maybe Gerd Pamuk had once been a sailor with a girl in every port? Always on deck, in all weathers. Two ancient bullet wounds on his left shoulder suggested he had fought in the Second World War. The aged skipper had disembarked from the ship of life.

Had he truly understood Death?

There was a knock at the door.

'Come in,' called Konstantin and looked expectantly at the swing doors. He had heard the steps in the changing room and knew that it wasn't Mendy. 'I hope you've already changed?'

'Yes, Mr Korff,' came the reply. In came a young man with dyed black hair, a nose piercing, four rings in each ear and eyeliner around his eyes. A goth, there were a few of those in Leipzig. He looked slightly older than twenty. 'My name is Jaroslaf Schmolke,' he introduced himself. 'I'm sorry I was late. My old boss had forgotten to send me the certificate.'

Huh, great. Konstantin sighed inwardly. Gerd Pamuk was lying on the table like a barrier between him and his potential apprentice. 'Don't take this question the wrong way, but you're not by any chance a fan of *Six Feet Under* or *NCIS*, are you?' Since the advent of those series, an onslaught of applications for jobs in forensics had begun, and Ars Moriendi had noticed an increasing demand for apprenticeships. But most applicants gave up when they had a hard time of it. 'You mustn't have any false conceptions about this career.'

Jaroslaf remained impassive; the sight of the dead body didn't seem to bother him either. 'No, Mr Korff. I take it you're referring to the forensic scientist in *NCIS* who plays the token goth? I can assure you that my interest in this job career is not a passing fad and that I don't want to fulfil a cliché.'

He can talk the talk. Konstantin had had to deal with the oddest types before, from former butchers to esoterically minded yoga teachers. He gestured for him to come closer.

'Were you working in a different job right after you left school?'

'The ambulance service. I'm familiar with the sight of a human body in different conditions.' Jaroslaf smiled. 'This man is looking pretty good compared to the victim of a motorbike accident.'

Konstantin nodded and his hopes rose that he had finally found a good candidate. 'You can give me a hand and we'll talk while we work.' He sprayed the body with disinfectant and pushed a plastic support underneath the neck. He had Jaroslaf wind some cotton wool around a pair of pincers and dip it in alcohol, and then clean Pamuk's ears with it. Using two more alcohol-soaked balls of cotton wool, he went under the white eyelashes and under the fingernails. Eye sockets, nose and mouth got equally thorough treatment so that every contaminant was removed. Otherwise, germs could build up and cause nasty smells. He noticed that the man's dentures were loose. 'According to what I've read, you broke off an apprenticeship with one of my colleagues?'

'Yes. He wasn't good enough.'

'Ah. And what makes you think that?'

'He was lax and couldn't teach me the thanatological skills that interest me. But you, Mr Korff, are considered to be the best thanatologist in Germany and, as far as I know, in Europe too.'

Konstantin smiled. 'Who says that?'

'It's in the trade magazines. You're always called upon when a case is particularly difficult or when others in the community have refused to do an embalming with reconstruction beforehand.' Jaroslaf spoke quietly, but carefully. A discreet, pleasant voice.

Konstantin turned on the hand-held shower and sprayed cold water over the body. Warm water encouraged bacteria. 'Hand me the picture of Mr Pamuk from the tray please,' he ordered Jaroslaf and gently dabbed at the wrinkled, waxy face with a soft sponge. He cleaned the white hair with a little shampoo, washed it out carefully and kneaded it dry with a towel. 'Stand there and hold the picture.' Konstantin arranged the hair the way it was in the photo, the hairdryer drowning out the next song by Lambda, which, appropriately enough, was called *Charon*. 'This is my kind of song. Why do you want to learn the craft of thanatopraxy? Open coffins aren't very common in Germany. It varies between five and ten per cent, as I'm sure you're aware,' he said as he turned off the hairdryer.

'It's ninety per cent in England,' the young man shot back like a pistol. 'I'm thinking of going abroad after I've worked for a few years. Somewhere warm, where I can be useful.'

He's clever too. Konstantin had a very good feeling about this applicant, who had both ambition and a basic knowledge of anatomy, but had enough of a desire to accumulate knowledge that he would continue his studies. 'What do you know about the origins of thanatology?'

Jaroslaf seemed to have prepared for this question and answered without hesitation. 'Jean Nicolas Gannal, French military officer and chemist, born in Saarlouis in 1791. Apart from a few other inventions, he was famous for his embalming methods.'

'How did they come about?'

'He didn't want to send soldiers' bodies back to their families mutilated or disfigured. It was about preserving the good memories of a loved one and not the memories of a decayed, tattered piece of flesh.'

Konstantin nodded, impressed. He gently massaged the deceased's cheeks from the temples inwards to the centre to loosen the *rigor mortis*. When the jaws could move and the mouth open, he carefully sprinkled some powder into the dead man's mouth and nose. 'Do you know what I just did?' He purposely kept the label on the tin covered.

'That must have been Ardol. An odour and moisture-absorbing powder that hardens into putty as soon as it comes in contact with liquid. It's also usually covered with a little bit of cotton wool to prevent bodily fluids from leaking out. Or modelling wax, that works too.' Jaroslaf was still holding up the photo. 'By the way, my previous boss didn't do that. That's what I meant by lax.'

'You know a great deal already. Well done. Hand me the eye caps and the cream from the small table, please.'

Jaroslaf handed him the smooth, hemispherical half-shells along with a small tube.

'Thanks.' Konstantin applied the adhesive, placed the caps on the dead man's eyes and closed Gerd Pamuk's eyelids so that they wouldn't open while everyone filed past. It was necessary in order to avoid shocking the visitors and loved ones. 'You can go back upstairs and tell Mrs Kawatzki that you have the job on a probationary basis, Mr Schmolke. So long as you're working with me on the bodies you can keep wearing the earrings and the eyeliner, but as soon as it comes to meeting clients, you will unfortunately need to present yourself in a bit more of a mainstream way.'

'Of course, Mr Korff!' Jaroslaf beamed. 'Can I keep watching until you've finished your work?'

With most other candidates, Konstantin would have assumed they were trying to suck up to him. Not with Jaroslaf. He showed true enthusiasm for this career, for the craft, for the last duty to the dead. *That is rare.* 'Yes. Put the photo away and please push the pale coffin in.'

'Are we going to put Ardol in?'

'No. In such a short time, no fluids will leak. So we can give covering the floor a miss.'

Jaroslaf hurried out.

He is really bright. Meanwhile, Konstantin sewed the palate, lips and chin to the oral cavity using a curved needle so that the jaws wouldn't later open as if to scream. This procedure was called the ligature. Not an easy task, because Konstantin used a special technique. He pulled the thread through the septum in the nose, past the upper incisors and around the lower jaw underneath the skin before knotting the ends. The lips themselves weren't stitched up. Since the dentures were loose, he pushed a mouth mould made from curved plastic behind the lips to be on the safe side and put pink-tinted Vaseline on the mouth. *Done.*

In the meantime Jaroslaf had returned and had been watching him silently, absorbing every hand movement and assisting as though he had done nothing else all his life. But when he reached for the scissors, intending to cut open the beautiful grey suit that Pamuk no doubt kept for Sundays, Konstantin stepped in.

'What are you doing?'

'Cutting it open, so that we can put everything on him easily. That's the way my boss did it.' He put the scissors down. 'I did think that wasn't a good idea.'

'If you ask me, no proper undertaker does anything like that! Clothes are put on in the normal way and not cut up,' Konstantin explained his position. 'If clothes happen not to fit, I ask the relatives to bring different ones.' He nodded to Jaroslaf. 'Remember that.'

They dressed the dead man and together they lifted him into the waiting coffin.

Konstantin laid the head on a cushion, covered the legs with a white blanket and massaged the stiff dead fingers to be supple so that he could fold the hands as though for prayer. 'Good work,' he finally dismissed Jaroslaf. 'Apron off, throw the gloves and shoe covers away, disinfect your hands and up you go to Mrs Kawatzki. This is the beginning of the probationary period. From Monday there'll always be a meeting at nine.'

'Thanks, Mr Korff!' The young man did as he was told and disappeared into the changing room. A stifled whoop emerged from the changing room moments later.

Finally, someone worth teaching. You can rely on goths. Konstantin grinned and brushed cosmetic powder over the dead man's face using a large brush, the final task before rolling the coffin out into the corridor. Then he went back into the room, cleaned the instruments and put everything back in its place.

After he had changed, he pushed Gerd Pamuk into Mourning Room One, and using candles and soft classic musical he created an ambience in which the relatives could say goodbye and surrender to their grief. In complete privacy.

He liked the quote that the dead man had selected for his gravestone while he was still alive:

When the leaves fall,
you'll come to the graveyard,
to look for my cross.
In a little corner
you'll find it.
And there
will grow many flowers.

Even though he'd come across many quotes as an undertaker, tasteless and tasteful, this was the first time he had heard these lines by Lorenzo Stecchetti. He liked the combination of farewell and solace.

Konstantin went back to Mendy who was looking very pleased. 'What's the matter with you then?'

'You hired the young man,' she gushed. 'I just think it's fantastic!'

'He's good, regardless of what he wears or what make-up he puts on. I'd be a bad employer if I didn't see that and acknowledge it. And he still has to get through the probationary period.' He asked her for the black jacket hanging in the little wardrobe and threw it on over his polo shirt.

The mourners would be turning up in an hour and Konstantin wanted to stick to what he'd told Jaroslaf: look professional for the client at all times. The jacket hid the tattooed characters on the inside of his right upper arm. He had carried the written warning on his skin for twenty-one years, and those letters had kept him from making a mistake during some difficult times. A mistake that would have cost the lives of innocent people.

A quick look in the mirror confirmed that he could present himself to the bereaved like this. The black jacket didn't emphasise his athletic physique too much. 'The Pamuks are coming soon, the body is ready. Is the paperwork done?'

'Yes, of course.' Mendy still seemed pleased about the new apprentice. 'Oh, before I forget: Ars Moriendi has received a request about an urgent assignment abroad. It came by email.'

'Where?'

'Paris. Immediately would be best, apparently.'

Konstantin thought about it. He had to go to Moscow the day after tomorrow. That left barely enough time for a detour to the French capital. Pity. 'Send—'

Mendy shook her mass of blonde hair. 'You were requested specifically: the best thanatologist in Europe.' She was about to hand him the printout when there were voices from the main door: Gerd Pamuk's relatives.

'Forward me the email,' he said quietly, and walked towards the people stepping gingerly into the foyer of Ars Moriendi in order to greet them and take away their fear. Fear of the death of their beloved grandfather, father, friend, and of the thought of their own mortality.

Lake Cospuden, Leipzig, Germany

Konstantin was sitting on the top deck of the *Vanitas*, his houseboat, enjoying the dying rays of the magnificent day as they glittered on the surface of Lake Cospuden.

He had gone to the Gewandhaus concert hall after work and listened to the public auditions for the concert of Felix Mendelssohn-Bartholdy's Symphony No. 5 in D minor, the so-called 'Reformation Symphony' and admired the smart blonde cellist, as he had done for the past year.

And she had smiled at him. As she had done for the past year.

It was their ritual, which had formed an incredibly strong, unspoken bond between them: they were a couple, for as long as they were sitting in the Gewandhaus. Him down there, her up there.

Nothing more had happened between them, even though Konstantin would have liked it to, and the cellist probably did too. Her name was Iva Ledwon, she was twenty-five, had studied the cello and came from Stralsund. He had read her online CV.

He didn't dare make any closer contact because he had no desire to lie.

Because the danger for her was just too great . . .

Konstantin was an expert in all things unrequited love, and as far as drama went, he'd had enough for one lifetime. So he pretended to be content with thinking about Iva Ledwon and dreaming of a lovely time with her in a different life.

Maybe I should give up the visits to the Gewandhaus. They wouldn't see each other in the coming weeks anyway because he was away a lot and sections of the ensemble were going on a tour of the Baltic states and Russia. His stubborn, unwelcome feelings could cool off or, best of all, be put on ice.

He slouched in his deck chair, took a swig of his adapted Red Russian and leafed through a book. Oscar Wilde, *The*

Importance of Being Earnest. A writer one of Konstantin's best friends was always quoting.

On the bank, a little further along from his mooring spot, there was hustle and bustle. People were having fun in the bars and bistros, children were laughing and shrieking wildly, others were splashing around, taking boats out and snorkelling.

One of the best ideas the city's authorities had ever had, had been to flood the brown coal mines around Leipzig and the surrounding areas. Leipzig's Neuseenland was growing, becoming a little paradise – and the water quality was getting better year after year.

Konstantin had pulled off the feat of bagging himself a permanent spot for his houseboat at the jetty on the east bank at the Zobigker Winkel marina. With his quick, nifty dinghy he could cross the lake and go up the canals to Leipzig's city centre in a matter of minutes. It was virtually impossible to beat.

He liked living on the water. It gave him a certain amount of security, although a sea would have been even better. Just for fun he had once enquired about the cost of decommissioned drilling platforms, but quickly rejected the idea. He couldn't bury enough people to earn the amount of money it required.

He watched the visitors strolling along the marina pier and marvelling at the ships. After another mouthful of Red Russian, refreshing thanks to the three added mint leaves, he turned back to his book.

A soft *feep* meant he had received a text.

Konstantin picked up the handset and saw a message from

Mendy: 'Please don't forget the client from Paris, even though you've already left work. Love MK.'

She knows me too well. He searched his inbox and found the forwarded email from France.

Since he still spoke the language of his past so fluently, he had no difficulty understanding what it said. The writer, he could see from the first few sentences, was someone with good manners.

My dear Monsieur Korff,

Following the tragic death yesterday of my beloved daughter Lilou, it is a matter of enormous concern to me that I be able to present her body to her family, relations, friends and the wider public as part of a farewell ceremony.

This has little to do with me, although the loss of my daughter is tearing my heart and soul to pieces, it is for my wife, who is in a much worse state. Since the devastating news, she has been on the edge of madness and refuses to accept the death of our daughter. She is not eating, not sleeping, talks constantly about Lilou's return and is sinking further and further into a fantasy world.

We are afraid that we might lose her, too.

Our doctor has advised me to make the funeral a big farewell, as this is important for the grieving process, and might show my wife the reality of our situation. The more sudden the death, and the younger the deceased, the more important it is, they say.

My daughter was just seventeen years old, Monsieur Korff, and a stunning beauty. The pride of our large family.

The impression the authorities gave me about her injuries was enough to make me decide to call on your services without hesitation.

I've attached my private secretary's number here for you, a Monsieur Carlos Caràra. He looks after my affairs and will be your point of contact for everything.

To be perfectly frank, money is no object.

I will reimburse your expenses twice over and pay three times your fee.

Or name a figure to Monsieur Caràra and he will transfer it to you in advance, but I beg you:

Come to Paris immediately. Please save my wife from her delusions.

Please, at least keep this sliver of hope alive!

Most respectfully and from the depths of grief,
Erneste Xavier de Girardin

There was a picture of a young woman attached to the email, looking cheerfully into the camera and laughing: Lilou.

Her long brown hair was blowing in the wind, her blue eyes sparkling with joy, as though her heart was overflowing with happiness. She wore a chain around her neck with a marvellous jewel that glittered in the sun. The photo had been taken on a boat; Konstantin could see the white triangles of sails in the background and the kind of blue sky you only get at sea.

Beauty, joie de vivre, elegance. The words flitted across his mind. He swallowed the last of the Red Russian. *Death has picked a pretty victim.*

Konstantin didn't feel any more sympathy than he usually did. He reserved that for dead children, especially ones who died suddenly in accidents. Suicides moved him too because the victims had been in such despair that they jumped willingly into the jaws of death.

Yet Lilou, he could feel it, had something special about her, something very few people had.

And that's where his thanatological skill came into it: he had to give the dead back this special thing. For a few hours, for a church service, until the lid of the coffin closed and decomposition finally prevailed over the chemistry. The money was less important to him than the challenge.

Konstantin poured vodka and kirsch into his glass while dialling Caràra's number. The ice cubes landed with a clink just as his call was answered so that he missed the man saying his name. 'Bonjour, Monsieur Caràra,' he said, lapsing into French. 'This is Korff.'

'Good to hear from you, Monsieur Korff. May I take it that this is a positive response to Monsieur le Marquis?' Caràra spoke with an accent, but he spoke in a polished and very clear way. No comparison to Konstantin's street French.

He was taken aback momentarily. *Marquis? I should have looked up the name Girardin online.* 'You may, Monsieur Caràra. I'll be in Paris tomorrow morning at the latest.'

'I'd recommend you fly to Saarbrücken and take the TGV the rest of the way. Paris-Charles de Gaulle airport has been closed since the accident and the others are desperately overstretched.'

'Thanks for the tip.' Konstantin added a few more mint leaves to the cocktail, shook his glass to mix the kirsch and

vodka together and took a sip. 'Monsieur Caràra, I hope I can
be frank with you, even if it's unpleasant? I need a few more
details about the seriousness of Lilou de Girardin's injuries.
Are there photos?'

'No, Monsieur. The marquis refused to look, I can only
offer you an autopsy report.'

He grimaced. *Autopsy* and *accident* did not bode well for
the reconstruction. He wasn't surprised they'd requested
him. 'Thank you, Monsieur Caràra. I'll send you a list now
of personal things that I need to prepare.'

'What do you mean, Monsieur?'

'I need her favourite dress, perfume, accessories. To emphasise what made her herself. On the outside anyway.'

'Of course, Monsieur Korff. It would be helpful if you
could also send me a list of items you need to perform the
reconstruction. I'll have a room booked for you at the Hôtel
de Vendôme. It's in an excellent location and has wonderful
service. Call me as soon as you arrive. I'll pick you up and
bring you ... to the place.'

Konstantin raised his left eyebrow. 'The place? That's a
little vague, Monsieur Caràra.'

It was clear from his tone that the private secretary felt
uncomfortable speaking about it. 'Monsieur, you probably
can't be aware of this, but the Girardin family is very well
known in France. To avoid the press photographing the mortal
remains of Demoiselle Lilou, I must insist on keeping the
location where she is being kept a secret. A photo of the
untreated body making its way into the public domain?
It doesn't bear thinking about. I certainly don't mean to
insinuate that you would alert the media, but these ladies

and gentlemen are very smart when it comes to this kind of thing. And no less ruthless or graceless.'

Konstantin understood and wasn't offended. 'No problem. Let's do it the way the marquis wants it.' It occurred to him that Caràra had not asked about the fee even once. He looked into his Red Russian and wondered whether there was anything else he still needed to know.

'Monsieur Korff?'

'Yes, I'm still here. I'll ... read out my email address to you so that you can send me the report.' Konstantin gave it.

'Very good, Monsieur. That leaves the fee,' Caràra said. 'As the marquis wrote to you, money is no object. I take it you have an hourly rate for when you're working outside of Ars Moriendi?'

'I do, Monsieur Caràra. It's—'

'Monsieur Girardin will pay you 500 euro an hour, as long as this figure is higher than your ordinary rate,' the private secretary spoke over him, 'and that is irrespective of the results of your efforts. If you manage to live up to your reputation and prepare Demoiselle Lilou so that she looks like she is sleeping rather than dead, you'll receive a bonus of 100,000 euro. The marquis will reward your discretion with a further 150,000 euro, without any German tax authority having to be aware of it, if that's what you want.' Caràra talked about the dizzying figure as nonchalantly as other people talk about fruit or the colour of a wall.

'Very generous.' Konstantin took another sip of his drink. 'But *too* generous. Please thank Monsieur de Girardin for me, but I don't want to profit from his suffering. I'll take my usual hourly rate.'

'As you wish, Monsieur Korff.' Caràra's voice resonated with deep respect. 'You'll call me as soon as you are ready to get started? Don't forget the itemised list. Goodbye.'

'Goodbye, Monsieur Caràra.' Konstantin hung up and polished off his second Red Russian. It felt incredibly good to be able to refuse that much money. Ars Moriendi made enough, as did his freelance work. He didn't need to prey on bereaved or despairing people. It was a question of professionalism.

He'd been respected for that before.

Before working as a thanatologist.

He picked up his book again and faltered: *The Importance of Being Earnest.*

Wilde had been making a play on words, earnest being a word and a name. Fate had arranged for his French employer to be called Erneste.

No, I don't want to be earnest right now.

After just a few pages, Konstantin's sense of unease was too great to keep reading. He couldn't stop thinking about Paris and Lilou.

He put the book aside and busied himself with getting ready for his flying visit to Paris; booking his flights and trains, looking at the hotel and finding to his astonishment how posh it was. Then he sent Caràra the list and, during his third Red Russian, he searched for the name Erneste Xavier de Girardin. The French nobleman was a magnate, the director of a steel empire with corporate interests all over the world. Married for twenty-two years, four children, all as unremarkable as their parents. A picture book life.

Very little was known about the family's private life, they only attended events on rare occasions. Lilou, as the youngest daughter, had caught the attention of the tabloids because she had been carving out a career as a model, and was successful in a way that barely any girls had managed before her.

Until the previous day.

Konstantin clicked on an article about her: according to unconfirmed reports, Lilou de Girardin had died in an accident at Paris-Charles de Gaulle airport. After landing, an A380 had careered into a building, causing immense damage and a fire, with the loss of over 800 lives.

He resisted using any more of his time looking at the article. Konstantin didn't like sensationalism in news.

He took another swig, the vodka and kirsch feeling pleasantly cool as it went down his throat. Time to pack. He stood up and stretched. *Exercising would be the next urgent task. I could use a little exer . . .*

'Hey! Stop those idiots!' a loud voice rang out. It was Fritz Wutschke, whose sailing boat was rocking across the way, on the same pier as the *Vanitas*. 'They've got my lenses!' The older man was standing in his underwear on deck, holding his forehead where a cut was gushing blood and staining his bare chest.

Konstantin looked along the jetty and saw two men running away with the stolen photo bags.

An wicked smile stole across his face.

II

*Death, the only immortal who treats us all alike, whose
pity and whose peace and whose refuge are for all – the
soiled and the pure, the rich and the poor, the loved and
the unloved.*

Mark Twain

Minsk, Belarus

A spurt of blood bubbled up like a geyser. It filled the wound
made by the scalpel and ran down the patient's neck and
around it. The vertebrae that had been clearly visible until
now were engulfed in blood.

Professor Smyrnikov quickly pulled the scalpel away. 'A
bleed,' he barked his diagnosis in English from under his
mask and was handed the clamp he wanted while the nurses
dealt with the red pool using suction tubes and swabs.

Swearing quietly, he monitored the nurses as they tried
to give him a clear view so that he could clamp the final
blood vessel, but the blood was flowing faster than they
were removing it.

Smyrnikov had been trying to prepare for the separation

of the skull from the spine: tendons, muscles, blood vessels, one after the other until the severance of the vertebrae. This complication had put a spanner in the works.

He exchanged a quick glance with his two assistant doctors, McNamara and Lange. He could see from their eyes they were thinking the same thing.

The blood burbled softly like a small waterfall to the ground and made a second small pool.

'Blood pressure is dropping fast,' announced the nurse on monitoring duty as several machines emitted alarm noises.

A blood transfusion would usually have been the next step, to give the doctor operating enough time to find the damaged vein and clamp it so that the patient did not sustain any injuries.

But the patient, whose number was 77, was not in a conventional hospital and had not ended up on Smyrnikov's operating table by choice. So his doctors didn't do what they had been taught to do during their training.

'Change of plan,' said Smyrnikov to all present. 'We're going to do a removal. Prep everything for the nutrient solution and oxygen supply. I want to see Patient 77's brain removed in record time. Professor McNamara, you do it. Doctor Lange, you assist.'

Nobody dared protest. It was clear to every member of the team that Smyrnikov had written off the man on the table and that it was now a matter of McNamara and Lange, who were new to the team, getting some experience.

'Time is running out . . . now!' Smyrnikov withdrew into the background and watched as the young doctors took over the operation. The monitors were turned off, the man was going to die anyway. But his mind, in its purest form, might still be salvageable.

McNamara and Lange moved Patient 77 roughly onto his back and sat him up, his blood spraying the doctors' surgical aprons. Tubes were removed and in a flash the skull was clamped in a bracket so that it couldn't slip. When McNamara hesitated, Lange picked up the electrical circular saw. The machine revved and sliced through skin and bone and the blood that flowed out was cleared up by the assistants.

Considering there were no incision lines marked on the bald scalp, Lange worked with extreme precision. Smyrnikov reckoned the steady hand of the Brazilian would be a definite asset. However, McNamara, the pale-skinned Irishman, was standing indecisively next to 77. Both were skilled surgeons who had spent years working in hospitals before receiving the invitation to Minsk. Apparently McNamara had a problem with the task.

'I'm in,' said Lange, and had the assistants take away the top of the skull.

The cerebrum underneath came into view: a grey-white mass with the texture of an unripe walnut. Pink cerebrospinal fluid ran down the patient's forehead, over his nose and into his open mouth. His eyes were staring unconcernedly, if not blindly. The anaesthetic was keeping him calm, but 77 was still alive.

Lange had set aside the saw and was looking at McNamara. 'What is it? We're doing well for time! Now ...'

McNamara didn't move. 'I ... I can't do it.'

Smyrnikov saw his assumption had been correct: the Irishman was a coward, a theoretical researcher who left it up to others to get their hands dirty. 'What do you mean?'

'The man ... he—' McNamara pointed a bloodstained finger at 77. 'I can't do it!' he repeated simply. 'My God, no! *I can't do it!*'

'There's no pulse, the heart isn't beating any more,' said an assistant in the background who had taken a reading of the muted vital signs. 'CPR?'

Smyrnikov waved him away. 77 was immaterial to him, the Irishman's sudden attack of conscience was the real problem as far as he was concerned. Next he'd be wanting to leave.

But once anyone made their way to Minsk and entered the operating theatre of the Life Institute, they couldn't just drop out. Silence was easily bought in Belarus, but in the West, the voice of a doctor making accusations about the experiments of an international team would be listened to.

Smyrnikov couldn't allow that.

'What is it now?' Lange elbowed his way in, annoyed, and set about removing the brain. He stood behind 77, whose upper body was covered in the blood that had flowed down him in torrents and was now drying. The metallic, sweet smell seeped through the doctors' surgical masks. Right now they looked more like butchers than doctors.

'Enough!' ordered Smyrnikov quietly. 'Tidy and clean up, 77 is taking a trip to the crematorium. Good work, Dr Lange. I respect your dedication.'

Lange nodded, but didn't seem pleased.

Smyrnikov pointed to McNamara before turning towards the exit. 'Please follow me, Professor McNamara.'

They left the operating room in silence, took off their

bloodstained clothes, washed and dressed. They avoided eye contact throughout.

Smyrnikov let McNamara go ahead of him as they left the changing room and gestured towards the meeting room. 'In there please.'

They went inside.

Smyrnikov sat down straight away with his back to the bricked up window and offered McNamara neither a drink nor any of the nuts that were on the table. He had forfeited any hospitality.

McNamara had stuck his hands in the pockets of his white coat, his shoulders slumped, his scrawny, gangly build turning him into a crestfallen schoolboy who was on his way to the headmaster after a prank had been discovered.

The Irishman was going to say something, but Smyrnikov held up his hand. 'You don't have to explain anything. I understand you want to drop out. You're not the first person unable to cope with our research.'

McNamara looked relieved. 'I'm sorry. I was expecting something different. The transplants, the grafts, I definitely think they're exciting, but I thought we were experimenting on animals. On apes,' he babbled. 'That I—'

'Nonsense. You knew what was in store for you, Professor McNamara.' Smyrnikov wouldn't ease his guilt or avoid the accusation of failure. 'You should admit to yourself that you aren't suited to what we need in our institute. Our benefactress wants results, results from people. Nothing else is any use, Professor, especially any financial use. Apes don't have millions in assets to spend keeping themselves alive.' He lifted an arm and pointed towards the door. 'You can go. Pack your bags and report to reception. A driver will take you to the airport. You know that you are bound to silence. Stick to that. Breaking our agreement would have wide-ranging consequences for you and everyone close to you.'

McNamara made as though to protest, but then nodded in exhaustion. He stood up, nodded to Smyrnikov once more and left the room.

A few seconds later, the director of the institute picked up the phone and informed the guards at the entrance where they were to actually take McNamara.

Then he pondered how to explain the sudden loss of Patient 77 to the investor.

There wasn't much that frightened Smyrnikov. But this woman did.

Paris, France

'Yes, Mamma! I'm safe.' Tommaso couldn't stand the hospital and had taken advantage of the offer to stay in a smart four-star hotel at the expense of the French taxpayers for at least two more days. So long as the critical phase of the investigation was ongoing, they didn't want to let him go. The amount of compensation that Air France had offered him wasn't bad either.

When he had seen the first pictures of the Paris-Charles de Gaulle airport on TV, he had felt sick: Terminal 2E didn't exist any more, it had caught fire and much of it was destroyed. The A380 was barely recognisable: the right wing torn off in the turbine engine explosion, the nose completely collapsed, large parts of the fuselage at the front fragmented and ripped to shreds. The fire, which had ravaged the plane as much as the building, had charred some of the dead beyond recognition. Inferno. Everything suggested an attack.

Faced with the pictures, Tommaso couldn't believe that he – apart from a mild concussion and a touch of smoke inhalation – had escaped unharmed. Firemen had found him and dragged him out. At some point he'd woken up in the hospital and investigators had started asking him questions.

His inquisitorial mamma was asking almost the exact same questions. Just more forcefully and unavoidably. As was his habit, he lapsed into soothing gesticulations, but they didn't help at all, she couldn't see the gesticulations after all. She was expecting a report. Of epic proportions.

'No, Mamma. I came out of the toilet and—'

There was a loud knock at the door.

'*Ciao*, Mamma. The police are here again and want to talk to me. I'll call you later. . . . Yes, from the hotel room. . . . Yes, the French are paying for it. . . . Exactly. *Ciao, ciao.*' He hung up quickly and went to open the door.

He was astonished to see just one man in a black suit. He'd been expecting Radont, the short man from the French secret service whom he'd been in touch with constantly since he'd woken up in the hospital. The man in front of him looked, with his white shirt, black tie and Ray Bans, as though he'd stepped out of a spy film. Maybe the stranger was from the FBI?

'*Sì?*' said Tommaso suspiciously. He jerked his bathrobe round him; he was wearing only underpants underneath.

'Hello, Mr Tremante.' The black-haired man took off his sunglasses with a Hollywood-worthy smile and with his right hand held up ID with a name on it. Tommaso only managed to note the surname because it sounded so funny: Darling. 'My name is Darling, I'm a commander in MI6 and charged with investigating the events surrounding flight AF023.' He gestured into the room. 'May I?'

'*Si, claro.*' Tommaso let go of the door and pointed to the suite of furniture where he'd already spent hours with Radont and his little tape recorder. 'MI6. So, why the English secret service?' He got two glasses and a bottle of water from the minibar. 'Where have the yanks got to?'

'Ah, my colleagues in the CIA will still be turning up.' Darling sat down. He couldn't have been more than thirty. His designer stubble gave his pretty face some harder edges. Pop star, model, actor, the man could have dozens of possibilities to earn money from his looks. 'British citizens were killed in the incident and the reports passed to me by my colleague Radont haven't been satisfactory.'

'Really?'

'Yes. I'm lacking detail. With your permission, sir, I would like to clarify a few things that are still incomprehensible to me.'

'*Si, si.*' Tommaso sat down and poured mineral water into their glasses. 'What do you want to know, Commander?'

The British man smiled in a friendly way. 'Very kind of you, thank you. As soon as you feel you'd like to take a break, stop me any time, sir. I can imagine that this is quite a lot to deal with, being the only survivor of AF023.'

Tommaso nodded. 'It seems as though higher powers

protected me from the gas.' He put his hands in the pockets of his bathrobe.

Darling whipped out a black notebook. '*Were* there higher powers? Sir?'

'How ... what else could it have been? If I hadn't gone to the toilet, the gas would have got me like it got everyone else. This Arab wanted me to stay in my seat!' Then Tommaso understood that the Commander had made an insinuation and he did not like this insinuation. Not one bit. 'You think *I* had something to do with it?' he burst out and he felt his double chin wobble.

'Good that you've brought it up yourself.' Darling's smile remained in place as though it were chiselled there. 'What's your explanation? The toilets aren't airtight, so you should have died like everyone else, Mr Tremante.'

'No!' he cried, aghast, staring at the agent.

Darling ran his hand lightly over his hair, as if he wanted to check how his hairdo was sitting; his hair was shiny, a little wet and glinting in the light. 'More than 500 people, according to your statement, die in about ten seconds from a gas that dissolves into nothing immediately afterwards. No traces of this gas have been found, either inside the airbus, or in the lungs of the dead. With respect, that is the most unlikely story I've heard in my entire life.' He pointed at Tommaso with his pen and he sounded friendly, but firm. 'So what did you do to survive? Or is your whole story a fairy story to protect yourself?'

'I—' Tommaso didn't know how to respond. The accusations were ridiculous, outrageous! He wanted to call Radont to get this British scumbag off his back.

But Darling wouldn't let up. 'Assuming you're telling the truth, you still must have noticed something. A smell, a noise, strangled cries or—'

'A rustling sound!'

Darling's eyes narrowed, the dangerous smile was replaced by a sly expression. 'There was nothing in the Frenchman's report about rustling.'

'Well, it's not important anyway.'

'Maybe it is, who knows? Go on, sir.' The commander smiled again, holding his pen and notebook at the ready.

'The flight attendant made an announcement and . . . then there was a rustling. Like static noise. What do you call it, grey noise or something?'

'Let's leave it at rustling.'

'*Si*.' Tommaso drank some water, his hand shaking slightly, because the memory was coming back with full force. The chain around his wrist swung back and forth. The French trauma expert they'd sent to tend to him straight after his first interrogation had warned him that the images might haunt him for a long time, and that he should consider counselling. He hadn't believed it at first, but thanks to the British man he felt fear for the first time. Horror. He was standing in the cubicle again, seeing himself winking at his reflection while hundreds of people lost their lives outside that door. 'There was silence afterwards,' he whispered.

'First the rustling, then the dying?'

'I think so. *Si*.'

Darling's mouth twisted as he wrote. 'How illuminating. It could be that you heard a malfunction coming from the radio signal or remote control, or the trigger for the release of the gases.'

Tommaso was relieved that the agent believed him. He had been imagining himself in British custody, in a small, narrow cell that reminded him of the airplane toilet – and the anti-terror laws on that island were a good deal more stringent than the French ones. 'Just forget that nonsense with the accusations,' he murmured.

'Oh, *that*?' smiled Darling amicably. 'That was an inter-rogation technique, sir. I was making you stressed. That releases adrenalin which jump-starts the body.' He tapped his temple. 'And the mind too. You know, "man is a rational animal who always loses his temper when he is called upon to act in accordance with the dictates of reason". I made you lose your temper in order to jog your memory. Please accept my apologies. But your new clue will help my French colleagues to make progress too. Anyway, there seems to have been a central mechanism that supplied the gas. The air conditioning, I suppose.'

'But the Arab—'

'The man's steel flask contained nothing but pure oxygen. Mr Tremante, you are probably still alive because of a coin-cidence the terrorists hadn't considered.' He took the glass, held it to his lips and finished the water.

'How did the terrorists get into the cockpit? Is that clear yet?'

Darling shrugged his shoulders. 'The cockpit was too badly damaged in the collision to draw conclusions as to the exact sequence of events. It's clear that the door was open and that, contrary to the regulations of Air France, a flight attendant was with the pilot. Perhaps she was blackmailed into opening it, but it's up to the French to find that out. They should have no difficulty once the black box is found. However, I'm on the lookout for the tiny details that might get missed.'

Suddenly Tommaso remembered the stuffy air in the toilet. 'The fresh air supply was broken!'

'Sorry?'

Suddenly it was clear to him why he was sitting in a cosy hotel instead of lying in the morgue – or having been reduced to ashes – with the rest of the passengers. 'In the toilet! The ventilation wasn't working, air wasn't coming in or out!'

'That must have been it, sir.' Darling put his glass on the table. 'Now that we've got your grey cells up and running, do you remember anything else? You're aware, of course, that it's a question of the smallest details.'

Tommaso rubbed at a spot over his left ear, as though it might stimulate his memory. Yet all he could see were the faces of the dead. Darling seemed to have prompted the trauma with his crappy mind games. 'No. I'm sorry.' Tommaso still couldn't believe he owed his life to something as banal as a broken ventilating system. 'To a broken ventilating system and a horrifically strong coffee,' he murmured to himself.

'Coffee, sir?' Darling had stood up unnoticed and placed a card on the table.

'Sì.' He pocketed it, adding it to the set of a dozen investigators' business cards. 'Apparently I accidentally got a coffee that was meant for another passenger. I've never drunk anything as strong as that before. And I'm Italian! It was as though someone had filled a coffee pot with espresso. It was the final straw for my tummy.'

'But you drank it anyway?'

'It was delicious,' Tommaso said quietly. 'I couldn't complain on the taste front. It was only the effect that was grim. But then again it wasn't – it did save my life after all.'

'What a coincidence.' Darling put on his sunglasses again and offered his hand to Tommaso: dry, strong and warm in comparison to Tommaso's own clammy, cool skin. 'All the best then, sir. If any more details occur to you, don't hesitate to call me. On behalf of MI6 I'd like to thank you for your cooperation.'

'Don't mention it.' Tommaso stayed sitting and didn't look up as the agent went out the door, leaving him alone with the images of the dead.

He turned on the television and flicked through the numerous specials about the disaster.

The more destruction he saw and the more details there were, the less he could get his head around it. Families wiped out, young and old. Good people. His own memories were mixing with the photographs shown. The mother with her son, the sky marshal, the Arab, the flight attendant . . . It was becoming harder and harder to bear the pictures.

'Why did I survive?' he whispered and turned off the television. He didn't want to see any more of it. 'Why me?'

He didn't react to the shrill ring of the telephone.

Lake Cospuden, Leipzig, Germany

Konstantin jumped from the upper deck onto the marina and ran after the pair of thieves, who noticed that they were being followed almost immediately and started running faster. The soles of their trainers thudded dully on the wooden planks.

None of the visitors on the marina got in the men's way. Instead, they made room for them to avoid getting mixed up in it all.

Konstantin felt light: the three Red Russians were having an effect. He was better off being careful because overestimating your abilities under the influence was a quick route to disaster.

He jumped over small obstacles, taut ropes and boxes without any trouble. In his free time he did parkour, an extremely unusual and demanding sport, and this chase was like a training session.

The thieves had reached dry land and were running to a parked motorbike.

Time for a shortcut. Konstantin's eyes narrowed briefly and he planned his route, then he jumped unceremoniously from the jetty onto a boat, slid across the deck, from which he leaped onto a pedalo, whose passengers cried out in alarm, fired himself off and dived onto the closest moored sailing boat, pulling himself up by the railings. From there he crossed over onto a smaller boat. There were a few more boats in such a convenient formation that he was able to use them like floating stepping stones, even though he almost fell over several times. Luckily, so many people were out on the water that the boats, although only just about level, were close enough together.

With a tremendous leap he reached land and stood in front of the thieves' motorbike as they looked at him in bewilderment. He had reached it at almost the same time as they had because he had taken the direct route, while the thieves had run along the whole promenade. 'Hand over the lenses.' Konstantin might have been breathing faster, but he hadn't really exerted himself. His right ankle was throbbing just a bit: one of the leaps hadn't been completely clean.

'Piss off!' The stronger of the two flexed his muscles threateningly.

'I'd rather not. I'm waiting until the police come and nick you.'

The men shook their heads with something bordering on sympathy, put down the stolen goods, pulled the expandable batons from their trouser pockets – and charged. The practised way they went about it made it clear to him that this was not their first time doing this. *Probably martial arts experts. Or bouncers.*

Before either of them could even raise an arm, Konstantin did a sidestep, kicked the stronger one in the left knee and used his heel to kick the right one in a follow-up move. There was an audible snap, the joint broke, and the man doubled over screaming.

'I'm going to kill you!' His mate tried to hit Konstantin with the baton, but Konstantin escaped the blows with quick, precisely calculated dodges, until he finally seized and snapped the remaining thief's wrist. Konstantin used the force the man had put into moving to perform *kaiten nage*, a technique from aikido.

What looked to an observer like balletic, easy twirling movements and steps, ended in the opponent being thrown down onto the pavement. The baton rolled away.

The attacker struggled to his feet and hesitated, thinking what to do next: should he make himself scarce or attack again? He already looked pretty battered; blood ran from a scrape on his elbow and from his right cheek.

'Be smart and stay there until the police arrive,' Konstantin advised him quietly, crossing his arms across his chest. Applause broke out on the marina.

Fritz Wutschke, the owner of the stolen lenses, approached with a towel pressed against the gash on his head, having changed into a shirt and shorts. 'Thank you, Herr Korff,' he said with relief. 'What dickheads!' He threw the thieves evil looks. 'The police are coming now. I've called them.'

'Excellent, Herr Wutschke.'

The older man quickly retrieved his photography bag. 'I had no idea you were so fit, Herr Korff.'

'Do you mean *for an undertaker?*' he finished with a grin, keeping an eye on the criminals. One was still lying on the ground holding his injured knee, the other was tense, licking his dry lips, probably waiting for the right time to make a run for it.

Wutschke laughed. 'Busted.'

'It's all down to exercise: parkour.' Konstantin didn't have a problem with his skills being called upon, but under other circumstances – if he had not had three Red Russians on an empty stomach – he would not have made such a big show of the chase. *Bloody alcohol.*

'Parkour? I've never heard of it.'

'You take the shortest route from A to B and hurdle any of the obstacles as you go.'

'Ah.' Wutschke looked impressed. 'And what was the thing

you pulled with that guy? It looked so elegant, *bam*, and then suddenly he was flying through the air!'

'Aikido. A Japanese martial art. Direct the opponent's strength against him,' he explained abruptly. 'And that,' he pointed to the stronger man's injured knee, 'was just a kick.'

Wutschke laughed. 'That guy was asking for it.'

A police car pulled up, the officers got out and took notes on the facts of the case. The thieves were silent, refusing to make a statement. The police officers called an ambulance for the injured men to be on the safe side and then they let Konstantin and Mr Wutschke go.

'There have been frequent break-ins at the marina these last few weeks. It looks like the culprits have been caught thanks to you. Again, thank you so much, Mr Korff,' said Wutschke as they walked along the jetty. 'The lenses are worth around 10,000 euro. Their loss would have been more than a little annoying. If I can do you a favour, just let me know.'

'No, don't mention it. I'll chalk it up to neighbourliness.' Konstantin was heading back to the *Vanitas*. 'You'd better go and get yourself checked out by a paramedic. Your head wound might need to be stapled together so that it doesn't tear open.'

'Do you have experience of that too?'

'Anyone who does parkour falls from time to time. I know the inside of quite a few hospitals and doctor's surgeries, Mr Wutschke.' Konstantin waved as he walked away. 'Good night.'

Konstantin briefly considered mixing himself a fourth Red Russian. *To celebrate*. But he left it and went below deck because he still needed to pack.

As he was flying directly from Paris to Moscow, he took out

a suitcase big enough for several days' worth of clothes. He would pick up his special instruments for the reconstruction of Lilou de Girardin from Ars Moriendi the next morning. The private secretary, Caràra, had promised to source everything he needed, but there were a few tools Konstantin had made himself: an unsurpassable advantage and the reason for his reputation.

He took off his clothes in the houseboat's small bathroom and checked his skull under the harsh neon lighting. It wasn't a good idea to do parkour without warming up, but because the thieves would have got away otherwise, he hadn't had much of a choice.

Konstantin probed his head. *Not hot, not swollen. Good!*

Feeling relieved, he went down the narrow corridor and opened the door to a tiny little room: two metres long, one metre wide, and there was nothing in it except his bed.

Konstantin climbed in, pulled the door shut and shot the thick bolt across. Only then did he open the little porthole a crack to listen to the waves lapping against the hull of the *Vanitas.*

Having the window ajar was a luxury he could never allow himself onshore.

Paris, France

Konstantin was sitting in the pristine lobby of the Hôtel de Vendôme, surrounded by stucco and splendour and waiting for the marquis' private secretary. He was reading *Le Monde.* He looked up every so often.

Next to the comfortable bench where he had sat down stood his harmless-looking aluminium suitcase, whose contents had already caused a fuss at Saarbrücken Airport. Less because anyone thought Konstantin might be an assassin, and more because the tools were so unusual they invited questions. He had had to show the staff his special permit and explain what he did for a living and what he needed the pliers, cannulas, clamps and other tools like that for. Whereupon the airport employees went pale and lost their initial curiosity. His aluminium suitcase ended up in the care of a flight attendant, from whom he would get his luggage back only after disembarking the aircraft.

By now it was a little after noon and there was a steady stream of people coming in and going out of the hotel's impressive-looking entrance hall.

Although Konstantin was wearing a black suit with a black polo shirt, neither of which were cheap, he still looked extremely underdressed in this setting. The Vendôme was a very upmarket hotel with attentive staff and guests for whom money was never an object.

The luxury extended throughout the building. You could have a basketball game in his room. Everywhere smelled nice and he couldn't find any dirt or dust anywhere, not even in the furthest corners of the cupboards. However pleased he was with the accommodation, Konstantin found it somewhat obscene that his client was paying so much money for a room. For one night. *But with breakfast included.*

Konstantin quickly skimmed the next page in his newspaper before turning it over so that all the photos of ambulances and paramedics, flames and smoking ruins disappeared.

He hadn't been able to avoid learning further details about the disaster at Paris-Charles de Gaulle airport. *Le Monde* and the other French newspapers published specials on the incident and there was a lot of speculation about it. The authorities cloaked everything in secrecy and referred to the ongoing investigations. But it spoke volumes that the highest terror threat level had been imposed.

An attack. What else could it have been? Konstantin put the newspaper aside and looked towards the entrance, his thoughts circled around the attack.

Most newspapers also covered Lilou and her family: how tragic it all was, how beautiful the young woman had been, how many plans she'd had as a model, how dedicated to charity she had proven herself to be, and how she'd made her cold-hearted father a good person.

Konstantin had seen many shots of her and had to admit the journalists were right: Lilou de Girardin had been a beauty throughout her life.

The time for the funeral was now confirmed, which he had also read in the paper: two weeks from now and actually not in a church, in a cathedral.

The cathedral.

In Notre Dame. In public, with countless photographers who would take photos of the dead girl. *Of the incomparable Lilou.*

The papers were assuming that all five bells in Notre Dame would be rung. Even the bell called Emmanuel, which only rang on the most significant feast days and on special occasions. 10,000 people could fit in the huge cathedral, but it was possible it would be a squeeze.

The weight of the responsibility he bore had become noticeably heavier since he'd known this information. He could even admit to feeling a certain nervousness, which would probably only wear off when he saw the body. *Twenty-four hours, all going to plan. I don't have any longer than that to do a good job.*

A Mediterranean-looking man in a discreet, dark green suit came in and looked around, searching for something. As he turned his head, the end of his short ponytail didn't move, as though his black hair was starched. His gaze fell on Konstantin. He smiled curtly, raised his arm and gave a subtle signal for Konstantin to follow him. Without even looking round again, he left the lobby of the Vendôme.

Was that Monsieur Caràra? Konstantin was astonished by his entrance. He watched through the glass frontage as the man got into the middle taxi in a row of five stationed outside the hotel. Konstantin remembered that the secretary had mentioned huge media interest. Ah. A diversionary tactic.

He stood up, put on his sunglasses, picked up his suitcase and stepped into the street. When he got to Caràra's taxi, he bent down to the open window. He had noticed that there were two men in the backseat of each of the other cars. 'I'm sorry, but are you Monsieur Caràra?' he asked in French.

'Yes. Get in, Monsieur Korff. I'll explain everything on the way.' He opened the door for him.

Konstantin took his place in the back seat. 'I take it this is about evading the gutter press and keeping the location where Lilou is being kept under wraps?'

He had barely sat down before the taxis drove off, one after another, forming a convoy that weaved in and out of traffic, constantly changing positions as they overtook each other.

'That's right, Monsieur.' Caràra held out his hand to him. 'Welcome to Paris.'

Konstantin shook his hand. 'Thanks.' Then he looked out the rear window. If he wasn't mistaken, some taxis were being followed by scooters and other cars. *Us included.*

'The marquis rented five taxis and had them occupied by some drivers and colleagues. The GPS transmitters are switched off,' explained the secretary, as the convoy suddenly forked in different directions on a broad street. 'We're also going to be changing cars soon. Nobody will find out where we're headed.'

Konstantin noticed an orange Vespa doggedly clinging to their tail. A woman was driving while the man behind her held a camera with a huge lens raised in the air like a weapon. 'We're still not alone.'

Caràra smiled. 'Soon though.' He instructed the driver to slow down as they turned onto a four-lane roundabout. Konstantin was now witness to the difference between a Frenchman and a German: he knew no fear for his car.

The driver switched lanes, letting the car drift towards the centre of the colourful tin maelstrom and back out again so that Konstantin lost sight of the Vespa. The car went round and round; inside, middle, outside and back again.

Suddenly, among the melee of gloss paint and car shapes, Konstantin thought he recognised a familiar face behind a windscreen, which stared back at him with as much surprise as he felt. But the other man's car had already disappeared.

What is he doing here? His surprise soon gave way to unease.

Is it because of the job I've been given? Did he follow me? No, then he would also have ... in Leipzig ...

Their driver suddenly stepped on the accelerator, cut up two cars and stormed out off the roundabout, turning right immediately.

The Vespa did not reappear.

'Sorry, Monsieur Korff. But you did—'

'I fully understand.' Konstantin nodded. 'I don't suppose you'll tell me where we're going?'

'No. It's not the best area. Somewhere in the *banlieue*.' Caràra kept looking around. He remained alert. 'The press isn't reckoning on that. As I said before: a photo of the deceased *demoiselle* in her current state would be unbearable.'

The journey flew by and ended in a backstreet where a second car was waiting for them: a powerful black Peugeot limousine.

Caràra got out. 'I'll drive, Monsieur. Please sit in the front.'

Konstantin followed him. *It's like before.* He grinned, put his case behind the seat and swung himself into the car. They set off immediately, only this time it was less fast and reckless.

As Konstantin didn't know Paris well, he didn't have the faintest idea where they were. Occasional signs for tourist attractions were some help, but even these were becoming fewer and further between.

And the surroundings were becoming drearier: grey multi-storeys, oceans of rubbish bins, old cars, scorch marks on the pavement, many young people who looked like the children of immigrants.

The ghetto of Paris. Konstantin pondered the fact that parkour had become popular here as occupational therapy for young people, so that they didn't slip into crime.

'Did you find the report I sent you useful, Monsieur Korff?' Caràra's voice interrupted his thoughts.

'Yes, thank you very much. But I'll only be able to assess the condition of the corpse properly when I see it.'

The report mentioned two harmless breaks in the right-hand ribs, as well as contusions that were probably not lethal, but had been suffered post-mortem.

Lilou had likely been flung from her seat by the impact of the A380. The break to the bridge of the nose as well as the right cheekbone wouldn't be pretty. They meant ugly bruises. As soon as he had removed the blood from the blood vessels, they would need to be concealed with tricks and chemistry.

'There was a lot of talk of fire in the news, but there was nothing about burns in the report.'

To his relief, Caràra confirmed this. 'Demoiselle Lilou was in the front part, where the first-class cabin was. The flames didn't touch her. That would have torn the marquis, and especially his wife, apart.' He drove past a group of youths who threw empty cans at the Peugeot and shouted after them. The smart car didn't provoke admiration in this area at all. 'By now you'll have realised the responsibility we have given you, Monsieur Korff. The family has great faith in you.'

'I know.'

Caràra seemed to be thinking. 'Is it true that saying good-bye is so important?'

'Well ... definitely in the case of Madame Girardin; the mind gets a chance to process the loss, rather than having to deal with it in the abstract.' Konstantin could recall many poignant scenes that he had witnessed as an undertaker. Some people dealt quietly with the pain of loss, others screamed and sobbed by the coffin. Only rarely did he find a reaction over the top or unpleasant. 'It would certainly be better if Madame said goodbye to her child away from the public eye. In a neutral place and not just in the cathedral.'

'Ah, you've acquainted yourself with the situation.' Caràra took a turning and they arrived in a deserted area, with big and small warehouses standing in a row. 'What you can see here is the failed attempt to locate businesses in this neighbourhood to give the young people a chance to get some training.'

Konstantin looked at the abandoned buildings.

'It wasn't the young people's fault. The businesses pocketed the state support and then shut down. Crooks.' Caràra's disappointment and anger were plain to see.

They drove into the yard of a company that had specialised in air conditioning technology. Two guards, concealed in the shadow of the building, stood near the doorway; broadly built men in a mixture of camouflage gear and leather as well as plastic anoraks.

'We're here, Monsieur Korff.' Caràra guided the Peugeot into a part of the yard not visible from the street, then parked and got out.

Konstantin picked up his suitcase and followed the secretary through a door, past two more guards and down into a cellar. A dull whirring betrayed the fact that somewhere in the middle of the building a generator was running.

'The building belongs to the marquis,' explained Caràra on the way. 'He bought the whole complex and is going to set up a school soon. The demoiselle suggested it while she was alive.'

Konstantin remembered what the papers had said about the tycoon's positive transformation because of his daughter. *Hopefully his altruism will last.*

Caràra pushed open a heavy door. Cool air hit them. Approximately five degrees. Just right for storing corpses. He switched on the light.

The darkness was dispelled by blazing neon light and a tiled room materialised in front of them.

A trestle table made from aluminium was built into the wall, with all of the tools and chemicals that Konstantin had asked for lined up on it. There was a table in the centre, and on it there was a plastic bag waiting to be opened.

There was also suction equipment for bodily fluids as well as a surgical lamp, a hand basin, even a shower and a bathtub. And someone had also got a temporary wardrobe ready for him where the usual work clothes of a thanatologist were hanging. On another table someone had laid out the deceased's clothes along with personal effects and jewellery.

The coffin was ready too.

As far as shape went, it was a plain model; varnished in white, embellished with gold leaf and minimalist carvings. The upper third of the lid could be opened to allow the dead girl to be seen.

'Is everything to your satisfaction, Monsieur? The marquis would like you to know that he regrets the conditions under which you have to carry out this important job, but security is unfortunately the priority.' Caràra had stayed by the door while Konstantin had walked across the room.

'Yes.' He took off his black sports jacket and hung it on a hanger. He was mainly hoping that the pathologists had refrained from removing Lilou's brain to examine it, which would result in a bald skull, ugly scars and incisions on the forehead. It hadn't been in the report, but sometimes people forgot to list every task undertaken, especially when there were no results. 'You can wait outside.'

Caràra nodded gratefully. 'If you'd like a coffee, or something to eat, come upstairs. We have everything there.' He went out, pulling the heavy door shut behind him with some force.

The bang resonated softly and then there was silence, even the lamps weren't humming any more.

Konstantin knew this silence. And he liked it: the silence and the peace of his work.

He got changed, put on the purple gloves and set out the utensils he needed to preserve Demoiselle Lilou's beauty. *Or give it back to her.*

He hadn't spent months with a cosmetic surgeon learning to mould the shape of a face for nothing. He was lucky in that he didn't need to consider the patient's potential pain, nerve pathways and the like. All that mattered was the result.

Konstantin placed his aluminium case on the implement table, opened it and put his own instruments next to the others.

Finally he got out the mp3-player, fastened it to the back of his belt and inserted the little buds in his ears. Right away the soothing tones of Lambda rang out, which helped him to focus his thoughts as he approached the table and contemplated the white plastic bag through which Demoiselle Lilou's rough outline was visible.

Konstantin took a deep breath, grasping the zip firmly between thumb and forefinger. 'Bonjour, ma belle.'

He pulled it down.

III

Life is just a moment,
Death is just another.

Friedrich von Schiller

Paris, France

'Another,' said Tommaso gloomily to the barman, and poured the *pastis* down his throat. He hated Darling. The longer the day went on the more his disgust at the British agent grew.

'Of course, Monsieur.'

A moment later he had a fresh glass of cloudy opaque liquid, which gave off a pungent aniseed smell.

Up until MI6 visited, Tommaso hadn't been worried; in fact, he'd been glad to have survived the attack. Even the talk with the French psychologist about potential trauma, phobia of flying, fear of certain smells and sounds or cramped cubicles hadn't had any effect.

But since the British man's little psychological stunt, he couldn't stop thinking about the images of the dead. He also couldn't get the question of why death had spared him out of his head. Why him, of all people, someone who hadn't achieved anything meaningful in his life? What's more, there had certainly been better people on the plane than him.

Tommaso had been sitting in the hotel bar since 4.00 p.m., boozing to relieve the haunting memories and thoughts that tormented him. Although he usually took care of his appearance, it didn't bother him right now that his shirt was hanging out of his trousers and that his hair was tousled.

He lifted the glass and drank, half the liquid gushing down his throat. 'Why me?' he asked himself, his tongue heavy in his mouth.

'Why what, Monsieur?'

The bright voice wasn't coming from the barman and he turned to one side.

An attractive woman had taken a seat next to him, her brown hair in a small ponytail that really suited her. Tommaso didn't usually like this hairstyle, but it looked perfect on her. The fitted, tailored red blouse and black trousers emphasised her athletic figure. Her smile was directed at him and she looked interested.

'Why am I still alive?' he explained, making an effort to speak clearly.

She asked the barman for a vodka on the rocks and raised her glass to him. 'Well, you'd have a reason to be happy then.'

'True. But *why*?'

'Monsieur, you're c-c-confusing me.' Her brown, practically black eyes drew his gaze and wouldn't let go.

Tommaso lifted his shoulders helplessly and let them fall again. 'I just don't understand why I, of all people, survived,' he exclaimed and sighed. '800 people, dead. And I'm the only one with the sodding luck to . . . the attack . . .' His head sank and he placed one hand on the back of his neck. '*Porca miseria.*'

She lowered her glass, horror reflected in her face. 'Y-y-you were on board the airbus that crashed into the terminal?'

'Yes.' Tommaso shuddered. 'But I'll tell you one thing: the people on the plane had already snuffed it.'

'Wow.' She finished the vodka and gave the barman the signal for a top up. 'Why did they n-n-not say that on the news?'

'Classified. I wasn't actually allowed to say that at all, and I presume I'll be reported for it. Or my minders who are tucked away somewhere behind me will beat me up.' Tommaso rolled his eyes. 'I don't give a shit. Now you know.' Everything around him was spinning gently and Tommaso had to hold on tight to the bar. The *pastis* was clouding his senses.

The stranger looked curiously at him. 'Do you know the film *Unbreakable*? The main character survives all kinds of disasters, u-u-until it turns out that he's a type of superhero and he is the counterpart to a villain.' She sipped her new vodka. 'Maybe that's how it is with you t-t-too?'

Tommaso let out a brief, joyless laugh. 'Are you trying to take the piss out of me? Or are you a reporter?' He scrutinised her, but couldn't spot a camera or recording device anywhere. Then he looked round the hotel bar. He couldn't see his minders anywhere. They were probably on a break.

'No,' she shot back quickly. The little ponytail that she wore at the back of her head bounced; a long, carved hairpin stuck into a piece of leather with holes punched in it was keeping her hair up. 'I'm in Paris on business. Honestly, I didn't know that you were on the plane. How would I?' She held out her hand to him. 'Kristen.'

Tommaso sighed. He felt miserable. Mentally and physically drained. The presence of the *bella signora* didn't really reduce the pain, but her slight stutter made her quite likeable.

'Tommaso.' He shook her hand. 'Huh. Here we are then.' He wiped his forehead, which felt greasy because he'd been sweating. He must be glistening like a bacon rind. 'Have you ever survived a catastrophe?' he asked, because nothing better occurred to him.

He was a little surprised that he was being approached today of all days. He wasn't exactly in the best state. Maybe she was a prostitute? She looked good and wasn't old, maybe thirty. He couldn't gauge her accent when she spoke English, but it contained mild Eastern European elements and she spoke noticeably slowly because of the stutter; emphatically, as though she had to think about every word. He dismissed the idea that she might be a hooker. The stutter would not be an advantage in her line of work.

Kristen shook her head. 'No, but I survive – a-a-as well as I can.'

'Are you ill?' Tommaso looked at her closely. 'You look perfectly healthy. And very pretty, if you don't mind my saying. Aids?' He didn't know why he'd decided to say that. Probably because he was thinking about sex.

She smiled weakly and sadly. 'Fatal familial insomnia. The ultimate in shitness, let me tell you. I'd prefer Aids.'

'I've never heard of it. What is it?'

'Well, it's an extremely rare pathological modification in the brain which prevents you sleeping properly and sooner or later results in death. W-w-which of us has the bum deal now, Tommaso?' Leaning against the bar, Kristen crossed one leg over the other. She was speaking more fluently now, less thoughtfully. 'The insomnia is annoying and wears me out. It makes me feel dazed and sleepy during the d-d-day. At some point I'm going to have balance and walking problems too, then muscle twitches; my concentration will be affected, my memory will give up on me. I'm still doing well. I hope my stutter isn't a-a-annoying you too much. It's part of the package after all. I'll d-d-drink one more and then it'll be gone. Alcohol helps.'

Tommaso felt sorry for her and his moaning suddenly seemed childish. She dealt with her suffering in a very detached way, which impressed him all the more. Kristen had come to terms with it and not given up. 'Is there nothing anyone can do?'

'No. So far every patient has died within a few years. If I'm lucky, I'll be one of the ones to die of a heart attack or stroke before my consciousness is severely impaired.'

Tommaso didn't know how to respond to that, and left it at a sympathetic look. He smelled her perfume and thought it was just as exhilarating and attractive as the woman herself.

Kristen finished her vodka, the barman already having placed her third in front of her. 'Have you noticed? I'm not stuttering any more,' she whispered as though *she* was the one sharing a deadly secret this time. 'I'm actually very shy, silent from dawn till dusk.' She reached into her bag and pulled out a notepad. 'I usually write people messages so that I don't make a fool of myself.'

Tommaso grinned. 'Very clever. You're sexy.' That last part had just slipped out. The *pastis*.

When she laid her hand on his back for a few seconds, he

felt a tingling. It had been a while since the last time he'd been with anyone and Kristen was turning him on more and more.

'Thanks very much. Same to you.' The expression on her face changed, as though she'd reached a decision. She threw him a look he found profound and erotic. 'There are two people sitting here who know Death, aren't there?'

Tommaso nodded. He felt hot as he laid a hand on her firm thigh.

She didn't pull her leg away. 'Don't you think that's an unusual situation? The two of us?'

Tommaso thought he could hear a clear signal in her voice. 'It can't be a coincidence,' he babbled. 'Fate knows who it must bring together.'

Kristen took a pen and scribbled something on the notepad, tore off the page and gave it to him, and then kissed him on the mouth. 'Let's find out what else it has in store for us.' She slid down off the stool as she took out her phone. 'I'm just going to call my acquaintances and let them know it'll be a late one.' She swayed slightly as she left the bar.

Tommaso looked at the piece of paper: *Room 34*. Her handwriting was gorgeous, looping and somewhat old-fashioned.

He swallowed, looked at the half-full glass of *pastis* in front of him and then thought about the sexy woman waiting for him in Room 34 – and decided to choose fate.

Tommaso followed Kristen.

'Hey!'

When he heard the voice, Tommaso wanted to open his eyes, but he was too tired.

'Get up!'

His face stung from the force of a powerful slap and his eyes snapped open. Confused and sleepy, he sat up in bed. 'Are you crazy?' he muttered. 'You can't just throw me out of the room.'

He tried to remember what had happened. He could see from his watch that he had only spent an hour with Kristen. She had kissed him, started to get undressed and given him something to drink and . . .

Tommaso became more alert. 'Did I fall asleep? Before the sex?'

Kristen was standing in front of the bed in a white bra and knickers that brought out the colour of her tanned complexion particularly well. Her figure was incredibly toned; she must have done a lot of sport. She was turned on and he was exhausted. Two circumstances that Fate must not have considered properly. Unless it liked irony. Quite apart from that, he still had his clothes on.

'Tell me what happened on board.'

'Huh?' he said dumbly, rubbing his eyes. She had tattoos all over her body, including a cross with a loop at the top in different versions and sizes.

'Weren't we going to shag?'

'*You* wanted to shag.' Kristen suddenly seemed very frosty. '*I* wanted something else.'

Tommaso tried to stop thinking about how tired he was. Something was going on here that he did not like. 'But you can't just tear me out of a deep sleep so that I'll tell you . . .' He faltered when he noticed two pairs of male legs on the floor behind the sofa.

Tommaso leaned to the side a little to get a better look

and recognised the two police officers Radont had assigned to him as minders.

Now Tommaso was awake. His *pastis*-fogged brain was working slowly, but even in this condition it was clear to him that no reporter would bump off two officers for a story.

His throat was raw and dry, he didn't know what to do.

'They're dead,' she said indifferently. 'If you want to continue to be a survivor of the accident, you should start talking.'

He was having difficulty making out the meaning behind her words. 'Dead? Why? What—' Tommaso's eyes grew round.

'Okay, off you go. The whole story.' Kristen made a gesture that indicated her boredom. 'I made you fall asleep to test you. But nothing happened. What's wrong with you? How did you manage it, on the airbus?'

'What are you talking about?' He didn't understand anything at all.

She leaped and landed next to him on the bed. She pulled the hairpin out of her hair and rammed it into his thigh; she stifled his scream with another hard slap to the face. He tried to roll away from her, but a second slap hurled him backwards off the bed. He clattered to the floor.

Kristen sat on his chest immediately and held the bloody pin above his left eye. 'I can reach the other side of your brain with this, Tommaso. One thrust straight through the skull. Now just tell me how you managed it!'

The pain in his thigh made him groan. Millions of thoughts flashed through his head. He tried to make sense of it, of what this madwoman wanted from him. Does she think he's the culprit in the attack? Was she one of the loved ones left behind?

A red drop detached itself from the tip of the hairpin and splashed into his eye, leaving him blinking frantically.

The best thing to do would be to talk to the nutcase and hope that the police would notice their people were missing soon. Had he left the piece of paper with the room number at the bar? Then they would . . .

She jabbed the hairpin through his left cheek; it caught his tongue, drawing blood. She choked off the scream rising in his throat with one hand and directed the tip of the hairpin back at his eye.

'I was shitting,' he squeezed out, panting. 'I don't know what happened.'

She gave him a penetrating look. 'Describe what you did and what happened when the people died.'

Tommaso stammered as he repeated what he had reported to Radont and Darling in detail while Kristen sat on him and surveyed him coldly. He was not a person, but a beetle she could simply wipe out with a flick of the hand.

Finally he had finished his account and didn't dare look at her. He was afraid of provoking her. It was too dangerous to fight back so long as the tip of the hairpin was threatening to gouge out his eye.

'Stay where you are and don't move,' she ordered him after a long silence. Kristen leaned forwards and moved the hairpin aside, placing her forehead on his.

Tommaso felt the point inside his ear now. The whole situation was absurd: a seductive woman was lying on top of him almost naked and wanted to kill him. It might have been exciting in a film, but for him the scene did not have the slightest whiff of eroticism. He just wanted to escape alive.

She closed her eyes – and suddenly he felt a tingling starting on the bridge of his nose. The sensation spread out, as though the skin was going to sleep from this point outwards.

Then the brunette sat up and looked at him in disappointment. The hairpin remained by his ear. 'It wasn't you,' she decided disdainfully.

'No,' he said, relieved. 'I don't have anything to do with it.' He swallowed and hoped she would now leave him in peace, whatever she had just done.

She patted his pierced cheek. 'I'm sorry. I made an assumption because you were the only survivor.' She shrugged her shoulders apologetically, her small breasts moving gently. 'Now I know that there must be another person who survived the A380 disaster. I suppose that person is already miles away. Or the authorities are hiding him. But I'll find out.'

Tommaso silently braced himself. The moment seemed to have arrived: the madwoman was sufficiently distracted for him to risk attempting escape. The moment the tip came away another few millimetres, he would chance it, before . . .

The hairpin was thrust with full force through the eardrum and into the Italian's brain. The room was abruptly bathed in dazzling light, it smelled like chocolate and gorse, somewhere a sea was crashing against cliffs, the air smelled like salt, just as it did when he spent weeks with his grandparents on the coast as a child.

Then the first faces of the dead from the airbus appeared in front of him. His heart beat faster; the beautiful memories were chased away by rising panic. As he died, he looked at Kristen.

She looked down at him. 'So sorry. I've got to go.' Kristen

jumped off him. 'As the media reported: there is *one* survivor. Not two.'

Paris, France

For Konstantin, Lilou de Girardin was nothing more than a dead person whom he was embalming, although it was significantly harder to achieve a perfect result this time than it was normally.

Occasionally, dead bodies were delivered to Ars Moriendi after having been through the hands of forensics because the doctor had ticked 'unexplained cause of death' or 'unnatural death' on the death certificate. These people had autopsies to rule out the possibility of a crime.

This had been Lilou's fate too. Peeling her out of the plastic bag, he laid her on the stainless steel table: there was a Y-shaped incision across the breast and stomach, punctures in the skin, stitches where the pathologists had carelessly taken samples from the body in order to investigate the death. Luckily they had refrained from cracking the skull open. Her prominent background had probably prevented this ordinarily routine procedure. Yet the ruined cardiovascular system made embalming extremely complicated. Her throat organs had also been removed, but at least there were no signs of incisions on the neck itself.

Now I know why they got me in. Konstantin examined the bruises on the face, the fractures he would have to remould.

He unpicked the temporary stitches and took a quick look into the corpse's abdominal cavity.

It had been emptied, the organs placed in a bag after the examination. That did make it much easier for him: it saved him the task of bleeding and suctioning. Konstantin took out the bag. He would leave the contents whole, just as they were, and insert an undiluted formaldehyde solution. With time the solution would diffuse into the cells, so they wouldn't need to be treated separately.

Konstantin set to work. Washing with a disinfectant cleaning fluid, loosening the *rigor mortis* through massage and moving the limbs so that the corpse became flexible – the last little bits of residual blood dispersed.

Konstantin carefully inserted surgical needles into the part of the corpse's cardiovascular system that was still intact and connected them to the tubes from the embalming pump. He fed the embalming fluids in through the femoral arteries. He didn't expect any bigger pools of blood to flow out because it was normally drained away via the jugular vein. Lilou's lifeblood had stayed behind in forensics.

Clack, clack, clack, the mechanical pump kept up its rhythm as Konstantin kneaded and massaged the dead girl's body so that the preserving fluid got into the parts that had the worst blood flow.

He kept checking how the mixture of formaldehyde and other substances was distributed, and whether there was any accidental pooling of blood. He had to move the needles to different places because the veins and arteries had been clipped during the autopsy treatment; an elaborate procedure that required the utmost attention.

The *livor mortis* finally disappeared through his efforts and the bruises gave way to a normal complexion. The process had required more fluid than usual.

When he was sure that the preservative had been as successful as possible, he dried Lilou off and laid her on a second table that he had covered with kitchen roll.

Konstantin felt himself getting tired – his blood sugar level was falling. It was very important to concentrate.

Break time.

It was a little after seven in the evening according to his watch and he was hungry.

He took off the surgical mask, gloves, apron and foot protectors, disinfected his hands and left the room. He marched up the cellar steps. At the top he was greeted with a nod by one of the burly guards who pointed to a door that was open a crack. It was less a tip about where to find food and more an instruction not to go outside.

Konstantin went through the door into a room where Caràra was sitting on a chair reading a book with a Spanish title.

It smelled of coffee, sausage and bread rolls. On a dazzlingly clean table a cellophane-wrapped platter had little open sandwiches laid out on it that had no doubt been prepared by a fancy caterer.

'Hello,' said Konstantin.

Caràra looked up. 'Done, Monsieur?'

'Break time. There's a while to go yet. But I'll get it done.' Konstantin did a few stretches. Then he sat down while the private secretary snapped the book shut and poured him a coffee from a Thermos. 'Thanks.'

'Does embalming always take this long?'

'No. I'm usually done in two hours.'

Konstantin chose a ham sandwich garnished with tomato and egg. Embalming makes you hungry. It did him anyway.

'Ah.' Caràra didn't say any more, pouring himself a coffee too.

Konstantin was silent as he went through the next steps in his head. He would still need to spend several hours in the cellar. 'I should be dressing Demoiselle Lilou fully and placing her in the coffin, shouldn't I?'

'That's what the marquis wants, Monsieur Korff.' He offered him milk and sugar, both of which Konstantin helped himself to plenty of. 'I spoke to him on the phone and he has passed on the message that he wouldn't mind if you dropped in once more just before the funeral and checked on the demoiselle.'

How wonderfully paraphrased. 'I really have a lot to do—'

'You would be paid a supplement for your efforts, Monsieur.'

'Which doesn't change anything about the fact that I still have other clients, Monsieur Caràra,' insisted Konstantin with a smile. 'I'll already be on a flight to Russia tomorrow, and then there are Leipzig's dead bodies which I also need to attend to.' He bit off part of the sandwich and chewed.

Caràra's lips thinned. 'The marquis will not be pleased.'

'There's nothing I can do. Let him know it will be enough if he has a make-up artist take another look at the body.' Konstantin took a slurp of his coffee which tasted hot and sweet. The taste of formaldehyde in his mouth was finally fading. 'My work doesn't need to be checked so long as neither you, nor anyone else moves the demoiselle's remains into the sun before the funeral. I guarantee you that.'

'Fine. I will pass on your message to the marquis.' Caràra

also drank his coffee, managing to look both indignant and offended as he did so.

The rest of the break passed in silence.

Half an hour later, Konstantin went back underground.

He swabbed Lilou off again and inserted stuffing into the abdomen, putting the bag with the internal organs inside, and was generous with the Ardol too. Finally he used fine, invisible thread to stitch up the incisions.

Then he turned his attention to the bodily orifices, closing them up and ensuring any odour was absored. Demoiselle should definitely not exude a strong cloying smell in the cathedral.

The next step required instinct: using targeted injections, Konstantin took care of the places where the bruises had been more stubborn and remained in place. This method was called hypodermic embalming.

Then he straightened the bones in the cheeks and nose as much as he could and reached for a lump of solidifying gel for the deformed parts of Lilou's face, gently squeezing it under the skin with a special syringe and moulding it. Konstantin painstakingly compared the dead girl's features to the reference photograph, pushing and amending by the millimetre, checking, nudging and correcting until he was happy. It was the trickiest task he had to do, but it gave Lilou back her beauty.

He didn't notice time going past. He was completely consumed by his task. He took just as little notice of the fact that his mp3-player was now silent.

Five hours later he straightened up and smiled down at the corpse.

Good. The most difficult part is done.

Then there were some routine tasks again that were second nature to him: padding out the throat with cellulose – he didn't need an extra throat seal – packing the ear canals with soft wax, then adding the ligatures for the mouth and eye caps to prevent collapsing and opening.

He was almost finished now. Konstantin prepared the coffin with Ardol. He carefully dressed the corpse in a high-necked white lace dress and placed it in the coffin where he began the cosmetic treatment.

The marquis had wanted something simple and natural for her hairstyle: hair down and straight. A little light foundation, some understated make-up, and his work was done.

Finally he put rings on her slim fingers and folded her hands over her stomach. He placed a simple, dark silk ribbon around her neck with a blueish gemstone dangling from it. Konstantin supposed it was a jewel of considerable value. *Another reason for the guards.* Lilou also wore the pendant in the photo he was working from.

He took a step backwards and studied the dead body, picked up the photo and compared the two one last time before cleaning up and disinfecting his tools. None of the mourners would know how much time it had taken him to make Lilou look like she was asleep.

'This is the best you'll get,' he said to the corpse. 'You only looked more alive when you were alive,' he added softly and felt sorry. *Death is an egoist. He likes surrounding himself with pretty young people too much.* Lilou de Girardin had been a beauty with a good soul. *And Death is an arsehole.*

Suddenly, the musical box that had been among the personal effects went off.

A shudder went down Konstantin's spine.

Superstitious people would have deemed it Death's reply, but he knew better.

The Grim Reaper couldn't reveal himself to him.

It didn't work.

'She ... she looks like she's asleep. Magnificent, Monsieur Korff.' Caràra was standing next to him, looking at the dead Lilou. He didn't seem to be able to get his head around how perfect the result of more than twelve hours of work had been.

'It was less problematic than I thought.' Konstantin smiled, happy but exhausted. He had taken off his work clothes, showered and put on trousers, a polo shirt and a sports jacket. The room still smelled damp, of disinfectant and other embalming chemicals, but that would soon dissipate.

Lilou de Girardin was resting in the coffin in the beautiful high-necked summer dress that had made it easier for him to hide the discolouration on the neck. The eyes were peacefully closed, the hair framed the gorgeous face of a young woman whom Konstantin had made up tastefully. The facets of the diamond shimmered gently in the neon light.

'Can anything happen now?' asked Caràra cautiously.

'You mean: might the decaying process continue and Demoiselle be bloated by the time of the funeral?' Konstantin didn't like when people spoke too euphemistically about the processes that followed death. 'No. I've taken precautions, Monsieur. As I said before: her mortal remains will stay in this condition until the funeral, provided there is continuous refrigeration. I would install a dehumidifier wherever you choose to place her body until the funeral.' He left it at that. It was written across Caràra's face that he did not want to know any details. 'If it's all the same to you, I'd be grateful if you could drive me back to the hotel.' Konstantin lifted up the aluminium suitcase.

'Of course, Monsieur Korff.' Caràra gave a hint of a bow in the direction of the corpse and left the room. 'I must give you your due,' he said as he walked. 'I knew Demoiselle Lilou for eight years, Monsieur, and I . . . was sceptical. I was afraid you would make her look like a wax doll or give her a look that would not do justice to her personality. Now I must apologise, Monsieur Korff.'

'That is high praise, Monsieur Caràra. I'm glad I was able to preserve what made her her.' He thought about the marquis' wife. 'You should send her mother to her soon. But not necessarily in this cellar.'

'That's obvious, Monsieur. We will have Demoiselle Lilou picked up later and brought to another location where the atmosphere is more private and it's more secure.'

They had reached the ground floor and were leaving the building.

It was the middle of the night by now and the air carried the city smell of dust and exhaust fumes mixed with smoke. Someone was burning rubbish somewhere.

Konstantin and Caràra walked past the guards, got into the Peugeot and began their journey back to the hotel.

They were both silent again because there was nothing to say. Caràra wouldn't want to know the details of how the embalming had gone, and Konstantin felt too tired to ask questions about the de Girardin family. *It's none of my business anyway.*

The secretary finally found his voice again as they pulled up outside the hotel. 'Monsieur Korff, about the payment: cash? Straight away? By transfer?'

'You're telling me you carry a few thousand euro in cash on you?'

Caràra smiled knowingly.

'If that's the case, then I'll take it in cash.' Konstantin had an envelope handed to him. He saved himself the trouble of counting it; it seemed heavy enough. *More than had been agreed.*

'The marquis will decide on the bonus once he has seen his daughter, Monsieur Korff. You'll find out the outcome of his decision from me.' Caràra shook his hand.

'As I said before, it's not necessary. Good night, Monsieur Caràra. All the best.' Konstantin put the envelope into his jacket, got out, took the aluminium suitcase from the back seat and entered the lobby of the Hôtel de Vendôme. It was empty except for the concierge.

The hotel employee nodded to him, handing him his key and a small card. 'A gentleman dropped this off for you, Monsieur Korff.'

'Really?' Konstantin opened it. He recognised the handwriting and the quote put paid to any lingering doubt:

I choose my friends
for their good looks,
my acquaintances
for their good characters,

> *and my enemies*
> *for their intellects.*
> *A man cannot be too careful*
> *in the choice of his enemies.*

The Picture of Dorian Gray, Oscar Wilde

So I wasn't mistaken! I really did see him on the roundabout. How odd that one of his best friends would be staying in Paris right now. *Although, surely it wasn't his choice.*

He laughed and lowered the card. The fact that they had met in the metropolis of Paris on a four-lane roundabout, having not been in touch for more than six months before that, was appropriate for their special relationship.

Konstantin took it as a sign to get in touch with him. *But not today. I need a bath and a glass of wine, then I need to read up on the next case.* The Muscovites had a difficult case, and he was excited to find out if he could contribute.

'Good news, I see, Monsieur Korff,' commented the concierge politely. 'That's excellent.'

'Yes, you could say that.' He went towards the lift. 'Good night.'

At that moment a couple walked in the door and came straight towards him. He heard a furious shout from the concierge, but they pushed into the lift with him. The man was holding a camera and was about to raise it.

Or at least he tried.

They're the ones with the Vespa! Konstantin held his suitcase in front of him like a shield and shoved them back into the entrance hall where the concierge was already coming round the desk in a rage. 'I don't think either of these are hotel guests,' said Konstantin gruffly.

'No, Monsieur Korff,' answered the concierge and grabbed the thin photographer by the collar. 'They're press. They were here once before already and I warned them not to come back.'

The man tried to take shots of Konstantin anyway, but the suitcase blocked the view. After a brief scuffle with the concierge, the camera fell to the floor and the lens shattered.

Konstantin picked up the casing and stepped backwards into the lift. He took the chip out of the device quickly and threw the camera to the woman who had the presence of mind to catch it.

'Monsieur,' she called and held a smartphone in the air, the small lens pointed at him. 'Please, an interview! What did you and Caràra—'

Konstantin turned away and the door closed. His face definitely did not belong on the front page of a tabloid. That might catch the attention of the wrong people. Former employers, when he had still been taking on other jobs.

The lift carried him up towards his luxurious room.

He had inspected where he would be spending the night right after he'd checked in: he would make a bed for himself in the dressing room with the large, comfortable sofa cushions.

Because the dressing room, he had roughly estimated, was the smallest room in the suite and provided the best conditions for an undisturbed, undisturbing sleep. The staff of the Hôtel de Vendôme oughtn't come to any grief if he didn't hear them coming into the suite.

IV

Life is an eternal mystery,
And death remains a secret.

Lieder aus alter und neuer Zeit, Emmanuel Geibel

Minsk, Belarus

Ian McNamara was sitting in the back seat of a 4x4 that was a make he didn't recognise. It was probably a home-grown Belarussian product. His copious luggage was in the boot; his driver and another man had sat in the front and were talking in Russian and smoking like chimneys. From time to time one of them laughed. They were both ignoring McNamara.

He looked out of the car's dirty window and contemplated the Minsk that he'd still never really seen: the price he'd paid for a really high salary and being able to work on a ground-breaking medical project was a curfew and a communication ban. Occasionally messages could be sent via the post or brief telephone calls made in order to tell loved ones back home some lies about a fake job in Africa. McNamara's sister, his only surviving relative, believed he was in Burkina Faso and working in a hospital.

Grey façades dominated the urban landscape as they drove through the inner city.

McNamara would have happily indulged in a beer or wine at a bar before his flight home. But he'd make up for it back home later, in Killarney, and flush the last few weeks out of his head with whiskey and Kilkenny beer. Then he would look for a job in some little hospital. Helping patients, not crippling or killing healthy people.

His ambition was to blame for the whole Minsk thing. He had felt honoured that Smyrnikov wanted to work with him.

But even on his first tour through that nightmarish hospital, a thick lump had formed in McNamara's throat, which didn't go away in the days and weeks that followed. The experiments that were carried out there didn't just trample the Hippocratic oath underfoot, they bludgeoned it with machetes, pickaxes and chainsaws.

McNamara sighed. He should never even have come to Minsk. Everything that happened in the different departments of the hospital was illegal and went against all ethics that he, as a doctor, felt duty-bound to uphold. The doctors and specialists whom Smyrnikov had gathered around himself reminded him of the Nazi doctors who had carried out experiments on prisoners in concentration camps. They were criminals.

The justification for these awful actions – for cutting off heads, removing brains, examining cerebrums while the poor men and women were fully conscious – sounded like mockery.

McNamara knew that he couldn't tell anyone about it, even though his sense of justice demanded it. If he did, he was sure that Smyrnikov would make good on his threat, but he comforted himself with the thought that nobody was interested in what went on in Minsk. Who would intervene against Smyrnikov when the authorities and country's rulers were in his pocket? People laughed at diplomatic threats in Belarus.

The sign for the airport whizzed past – it was pointing in the opposite direction.

McNamara frowned, but his surprise was still relatively mild. He had been expecting it. Men like Smyrnikov did not keep their word. The two giants in the front seats undoubtedly had the task of driving him to an isolated spot and making sure he was never seen again.

He had actually been surprised that they hadn't tried it straight away, in the hospital. Probably because of the other scientists.

McNamara stayed quiet; he was prepared. Two days after arriving in Minsk, he had stolen a gun from the security guard at the entrance, and he knew how to handle it. The man probably hadn't reported it missing. One magazine would be enough to escape.

He took the gun out of his jacket, a Makarov nine millimetre, reloaded it so that the giants knew what was going on and pressed the muzzle into the back of the driver's neck.

'To the airport,' he ordered in English. Once he was there, he should be safe. McNamara assumed that they wouldn't touch him in the presence of so many eyewitnesses, to avoid attention. 'I just want to go home. You drop me off, I get onto the plane and you're rid of me.'

His escorts exchanged a few words that McNamara didn't

understand. To be on the safe side, he increased the pressure of the gun. 'No tricks, no phone calls. Get going, turn round.'

The giant behind the wheel cursed as he put on his indicator and took several turns until they had reached the road to the airport.

His mate looked over his shoulder. 'Do you think you're going to make it onto your plane alive?'

McNamara nodded. There was the proof that they hadn't intended to let him go. 'I have a deal with Smyrnikov. If he doesn't stick to it voluntarily then I'll take care of it myself.' He didn't say any more. Why should he?

They were getting closer to the airport and the traffic was getting worse.

Tension spread through the Irishman. He would have to knock the two giants unconscious as soon as they got there. He would leave the gun and the rest of his things in the car and take the first available flight. The main thing was to get out of Belarus and away from Smyrnikov's control. It needed to happen quickly.

He couldn't come up with any other plan in the rush. Getting to the closest border by car, train or bus seemed too risky to him. It would take too long and he didn't speak any Russian.

'We'll do your sister in if you get out of this car,' the man in the passenger seat said, grinding his teeth.

McNamara's blood ran cold. 'Shut up.'

'We know everything about you,' he went on. 'Forget this rubbish, put the gun down and come with us.'

'We don't mean you any harm,' the driver cut in. 'But if you don't surrender, we or a few mates of ours will drive over there, fuck her good and strangle her at the same time. What do you think?'

'I told you to shut up!' McNamara was starting to feel sick with fear. 'You aren't going to touch my sister.'

'We will. We'll fuck her. And when we kill her, she'll know that it's your fault,' replied the man in the passenger seat.

'Then we'll ring your neighbour's doorbell and fuck her too, drink her beer and kill her,' added the driver, throwing McNamara a look in the rear-view mirror and holding his gaze while he grinned. 'We'll do it with—'

'*Stoi!*' yelled his mate suddenly and braced his hands against the dashboard. '*Stoi, stoi!*'

The driver looked forward again and put on the brake. The traffic was backed up in front of them, the glowing red tail lights and hazard lights formed a flashing sea of light. McNamara was thrown against the seatbelt. A shot flew out of the Makarov in the process, zipped through the headrest and ripped off the driver's right ear. The bullet went through the windscreen. Blood spurted out of the wound and sprayed all over the inside of the car.

The driver shrieked and held a hand to his injury. Yet he somehow managed to bring the 4x4 to a stop before he careered into the back of the queue of traffic.

The man in the passenger seat turned round in a flash, grabbed the Makarov and blocked the trigger with his fingers. He gave McNamara a karate chop to the mouth.

McNamara was flung backwards and saw stars. Tears sprang from his eyes and he could taste blood in his mouth. His lips felt like they had burst open. His plan had just been ruined.

The giant in the passenger seat wrenched the gun from him, directed the barrel at the Irishman's head and grinned as his fingers curled around the trigger.

But before the shot came, there was a deafening beep.

A moment later the 4x4 was jolted by an impact that left the side of the car caved in and mangled. The other door was suddenly next to McNamara, as though the inside had shrunk in the blink of an eye. The windows shattered and showered him with shards of glass. He was whirled around, hit his head on the side strut and crashed into the driver's headrest.

The 4x4 was pushed to the side, whirling as it did so, just like a fat, misshapen spinning top, before skidding into the oncoming traffic – and getting rammed by another car. McNamara bit his tongue and tasted even more blood. The car spun around twice more on the spot and then finally came to a stop.

It was difficult to shake himself out of his daze; the deformed inside of the car was wobbling before his eyes. McNamara fumbled at the seat belt buckle with trembling hands until he finally got it open.

He heard several Russian voices shouting over each other. Hands grabbed him and dragged him out through the window.

Before McNamara knew where he was he found himself lying by the side of the road. Someone threw a thermal blanket over him; a woman held his hand and examined his face at the same time. He didn't understand what she was saying to him.

Sudden nausea made him gag and he assumed it was the result of a concussion. He didn't feel much pain because of the adrenalin. But that was yet to come. The world stopped spinning but his vision was still a little blurred.

He turned his head slowly and saw the junction where a car transporter with a dented front had come to a stop, apparently the one that had hit them. And the car that had rammed them stood close by too. There were several injured people in it. People were running around, trying to open the battered doors of the cars, others were on their phones.

McNamara sat up, despite the protests of the woman helping him, and pushed her aside. He had to get away while the adrenalin was still effective. To the airport.

Moving uncertainly he got up and staggered away down the street. He had money and his passport, nothing else was important. He had to get to the airport.

Occasionally passers-by spoke to him, but he strode right past them towards where the terminals were already towering up in the distance. First he needed to call his sister. She had to disappear, get out of Killarney, before the giants' threats could be carried out.

The rattle of an engine was approaching: a motorbike driving along between the lines of cars that were stuck, unable to move forward or backwards, until it had come level with him. The police officer on it signalled to him to stop walking.

McNamara didn't consider it. 'Plane,' he said incoherently and spat out a clump of clotted blood.

The police officer shook his helmeted head and again ordered to him to stop. His tone became sharp and unfriendly.

McNamara wondered momentarily whether the police officer had been sent by Smyrnikov to intercept him. But he couldn't have found out what had happened that quickly.

The man in the passenger seat had to be dead; could the other one have survived and informed Smyrnikov? Whatever the case, any hesitation was an advantage to the other side.

Now the policeman parked the vehicle, got off, ran after McNamara and grabbed his arm.

'No, no!' the Irishman shouted at him. 'I haven't done anything. I have to get to my plane! I want to get away! Don't you understand? I want to get away! I—'

There was a quiet pop behind them.

The police officer groaned and grasped his shoulder. Blood spilled between his fingers as he swayed on his feet.

McNamara's pulse slowed, he wanted to run for cover, but he could only fall forwards. He cried out in pain as he hit the ground. The dulling effect of adrenalin had reached its limit. Bruises, contusions and cuts didn't spare him any more.

The pops came again: the shots were getting closer. People were screaming, car doors slammed shut as engines started and drivers attempted to get away, but only managed to get snarled up with other cars. The injured police officer had crouched down behind a van.

McNamara crawled, groaning, along the pavement for half a metre before he collapsed, unconscious.

He didn't feel the shot from the stolen Makarov hitting him. The gun was now in the hand of the injured driver whose ear had been ripped off. The man fired twice more. Hit by three bullets, Ian McNamara died.

Moscow, Russia

Konstantin was sitting outside the Bosco Café enjoying the magnificent Muscovite weather.

Couples strolled across Red Square, and children were running around playing tag. Tourists mixed with locals in the lively hubbub, creating colourful chaos.

The holidaymakers' cameras reminded him of the memory card he had taken from the reporter. Luckily the photos on it had been harmless: he and Caràra in the car, deep in conversation, then a few blurred ones; out-of-focus shots of him in the lobby. And it had cost the photographer his lens and probably the main body of the camera too.

It was important to Konstantin that his face didn't get into the public eye too much. That's why he had cut up the card with scissors and flushed the pieces down the toilet.

Opposite the café, on the other side of Red Square, stood the house of a client he had just visited.

'House' was not necessarily the right word, given the size of the building. He had been led in secretly through the side entrance, deep into the cube-shaped building made from black labradorite and red granite. Konstantin counted the steps as they descended and had reached thirty when he and his three escorts found themselves standing in front of the crystal casket.

The job was done quickly – a lot quicker than in Demoiselle Lilou's case. The majority of Russians had been pleading for a burial for this prominent corpse for years, but Wladimir

Iljitsch Uljanow was still lying in his mausoleum, receiving guests. At the moment it was four times a week, always in the mornings. *Lenin liked to surround himself with people.*

Konstantin drank some tea from the samovar sitting in front of him and nibbled Russian biscuits with the lovely name *blyo wkusno*, which meant something like *it was delicious.* He merrily dunked and dipped, even when the waiter tried to get him to go for something Italian.

The Muscovites and tourists passed by as he enjoyed the day and pondered the corpse of the revolutionary. *Small, pale and surreal.* If he'd done a job like that on Lilou, the marquis would probably have had him torn limb from limb.

Konstantin didn't want to be unfair because he knew how long the corpse had been lying there and how badly it had been treated over the decades by people who didn't know any better. It was nothing more than a gruesome tourist attraction now.

Even a wax doll would look better. Maybe that was the trick to the whole thing: Lenin needed to look awful in order to satisfy visitors and their morbid thirst for thrills.

Konstantin had been brought to Moscow to examine the mummy that lay underneath its glass case. It lay in state in chemically treated clothes that were exchanged every few years and cost an unbelievable amount of money, which it was only possible to pay thanks to a charitable foundation. And every eighteen months Lenin had to be embalmed again and submerged in a herbal bath, the formula for which the people in charge had discussed with Konstantin.

I would never have dreamed it . . . He watched as a group of Asian tourists tried to get into the mausoleum but were scuppered by the closed door. *That I would one day be asked for advice by the Russians.*

With his help and a correction to the formula for the embalming fluid, Lenin would bear up for a hundred years to come, maybe even a hundred and fifty. After that the repercussions from the past would be too great. Upon his death, Lenin had been given formalin injections with zinc chloride in haste; the embalmers hadn't envisaged an extended preservation period. That was where the problem lay.

'I know you.' A woman had stopped in front of his table, wrenching him away from his thoughts. She had long blonde hair and was wearing a floaty printed summer dress that swirled around her body and went somewhat transparent in the light. Her eyes were shaded by red sunglasses. 'Yes, I'm sure of it! You're the lovely man who watches nearly all of our rehearsals and concerts. Don't tell me you travelled here because of our performance!'

It took Konstantin a few seconds to banish Lenin and his mysteries from his mind. Then he recognised her. *Iva!* The cellist from the Gewandhaus orchestra.

He had expected her to be in Red Square about as much as he had been expecting the Queen of England. Which was why he was now so taken aback that he couldn't speak.

Finally he smiled and managed a 'hello'.

As he did so, he noticed, through a narrow gap in the throng of people, an older man with sunglasses holding a camera with a large telephoto lens and taking photos. What made him stand out among the melee was that he looked, with his hairstyle, like an aged rocker who had been forced to wear conservative, country tweeds.

The wide-angle lens was pointed at the café. Konstantin had a nasty feeling that, more specifically, it was pointed at him.

Iva took off her sunglasses. 'Oh, I surprised you. I'm sorry. I hope I'm not too forward and that I'm not getting you into any trouble with your companion.' She looked at the table, set for one. 'Alone. Like at the rehearsals and recitals. Do you like being on your own?'

Seeing her beautiful smile without also seeing the stage, the cello, the Gewandhaus, confused him. 'It's because of my job,' he said hastily. Konstantin felt trapped and self-conscious.

The wind blew and carried Iva's perfume to him, a strange but exciting mix, feminine and at the same time bitter, nothing like what Demoiselle Lilou would ever have worn. He noticed traces of bergamot, jasmine, roses and patchouli. *It suits her.*

Iva held her handbag in her right hand. 'May I?' She pointed at the empty chair.

Konstantin's childish instinct was to say no or jump up and run away.

He knew it wouldn't end at a harmless conversation. She was just his type, and it was clear she felt the same way, judging by her glances during the rehearsals as well as the seductive smile on her face right now. Sympathy, attraction, curiosity. Here, in Red Square, something that he had been trying to avoid might begin. However attracted he was to the young cellist ... it was too dangerous.

Or I risk everything and tell her the truth about myself straight away. For a moment Konstantin turned back to the square, keeping an eye out for the stranger with the telephoto lens, but he had vanished.

Iva sat down without waiting for a reply. 'So, what do you do for a living?'

Konstantin looked at her and got lost in her lively, brown eyes. 'Sorry?'

She turned to the waiter for a moment to order the same as he was drinking and then spoke again. 'You said your job made you solitary. So I take it you're either a creative type or the arsehole type where it doesn't matter what your job is.' She grinned to show she was joking.

Konstantin leaned backwards very slowly. Iva was a bit too assertive, his own thoughts were whirling around so fast that he could barely grasp them. 'Well, I'm not a musician who gets to play in the Gewandhaus orchestra, like you.'

The waiter brought a samovar of tea and Russian biscuits before immediately disappearing again.

She lowered her head a little, strands of blonde hair almost slipping into her face before she pushed them back with an elegant hand gesture. 'My God, I'm ridiculous, aren't I?' she said in a subdued voice. 'I'm always like this when I . . . am nervous. I always put my foot in it.' Iva smiled. 'I put my calf, knee and thigh in it.'

And Konstantin understood then that she was just as uncertain as he was, she just tried to cover it up with more babbling and bluster. *She is nervous. Because of me!* He felt warm and it wasn't because of the tea. The day he'd feared and longed for was taking its course. 'I didn't know that the orchestra was performing here.'

She was relieved that he didn't comment on her confession and took up the theme gratefully. 'Yes, a wonderful opportunity to get out and about without paying a cent. We got an invitation from the Russian government. A partnership thing: Moscow, St Petersburg and four other cities that I've just forgotten. The links probably go right back to the GDR, I've no idea. It was before my time.' Iva became noticeably quieter, then she laughed. 'This really is incredible, isn't it? We see each other so often and every time I think that I should finally talk to you and suggest a coffee.' She raised her cup. 'And now it's happening in Moscow. In Red Square.' She shook her head and grinned.

'I've had more lucky coincidences than usual recently.' Konstantin's heart was beating fast. The longer he looked at Iva there in front of him, heard her laughing and listened to her voice, the happier he felt. And it was exactly *this* that he'd always wanted to avoid. *Not a good sign.*

They ate biscuits, drank tea and chatted away.

Iva became uninhibited, as he did, and kept trying to make eye contact. They hung on each other's every word, listening carefully to everything. He could almost have placed his hand on hers.

Konstantin soon knew that she liked Ludovico Einaudi, had studied cello and piano, sang in a band, did yoga and liked dancing. She was collecting all the Batman comics and could quote all of the newer films with Christian Bale. She also described herself as a terrible cook, but she could bake, so at least she could make puddings. Her father had been dead for a long time, her mother was called Gabriele and still lived in Stralsund, her five sisters were called Eva, Carmen, Magdalena, Evita and Selma. And yes, Iva liked her Spanish roots, which she had to thank for her brown eyes.

It seemed as though she had been waiting for this day as much as he had so that she could tell him all of this. It bubbled up now, as though to make up for the time they had wasted.

At some point Iva looked at her empty teacup. 'Great. I'm talking and talking. What were you saying about your job and how it made you solitary?'

I could listen to you for hours. Days. But instead of saying these words out loud, Konstantin pointed to the mausoleum. 'That's what I do.'

'Ah. Bricklayers are solitary.'

'Undertaker and thanatologist.'

Iva's forehead creased. 'Well, what is—'

Of course she doesn't know. Who knows that word?

'Embalming. I make the corpse preservable if it is going to be laid out or be transported long distances without constant refrigeration.' He watched her reaction carefully. The first hurdle – although there was a much bigger one in store. A deadly one.

'Oh,' She twirled a golden strand of hair around her little finger. 'And you preserved a rich Russian?'

'No. Not a rich one. A famous one: Lenin.' When he saw that her dark eyes lit up with genuine interest, he continued to explain. 'I was at the corpse inspection to support my Russian colleagues. Around a hundred and fifty pathologists, biochemists and other specialists have cared for the corpse for sixty years. The survival of his ideas has supposedly been coupled with preserving his body, which is of course nonsense. The best thing to do now would be to bury him, but the political machine moves slowly.'

Iva looked at the mausoleum. 'It's closed today. Pity. It would definitely have been exciting with your explanations.'

'You're not missing anything.'

'And how did you preserve him?'

'That's a secret.' Konstantin made an apologetic face that made Iva laugh. He was pleased by her reaction – and by her interest. 'But I can describe it to you: the embalming fluid fills the cells instead of drying them out like in ancient mummies, replacing water as well as bacteria. So the tissues don't decay. With the correct conditions and a little make-up he'll last a really long time. But it's not pretty.' *You are pretty.* He smiled.

'That's probably true.' Then she looked at him in surprise. 'You haven't told me anything about yourself. Apart from your job, which I think is really cool by the way. Even though it wouldn't be my kind of thing.'

Konstantin gave her a cheeky look. 'I didn't want to interrupt your storytelling earlier.'

She looked at her watch and got a fright. 'Oh my goodness. I have to go! The rehearsals!' Iva sprang up, snatched his cup and drank his tea with a wink. 'Thanks. Will you give me your number?'

'We'll see each other in Leipzig. At the next rehearsal.'

She narrowed her eyes. 'Promise?'

'Promise. Undertaker's honour.'

Before he could dodge her touch, she leaned over and brushed his right and left cheeks with a kiss; as she did so his gaze fell unavoidably on her cleavage and he saw her dove-grey underwear, a mixture of sophistication and banality. Her soft skin felt like silk on his. *She smells unbelievably good!*

Then the young woman was on her way. 'The next tea is on me,' she called from a distance.

'The biscuits too?'

'Them too!' Iva waved, laughing, put on her sunglasses and walked away.

Konstantin stayed in his seat and watched her go with a wide grin until she had disappeared into the throng. He was still thinking about Iva as he settled the bill and got on the metro. He thought about her as he paid for a ticket on the train, as he got off and went into his hotel, and as he walked into his room and looked out the window. In fact, she was all Konstantin could think about and he knew it was more than infatuation. The feeling in his stomach lasted: the tingling, the warmth, the place where Iva had kissed him on the cheek – until he noticed the man with the rock 'n' roll hairstyle and country clothes standing on the other side of the street, in front of the hotel. *Him again?*

His smartphone vibrated.

Konstantin pulled it out of his pocket. He had been sent a new email. It opened with a quote again:

It is a very sad thing
that nowadays there is
so little useless information.

Underneath that, a brief report from a French newspaper had been copied and pasted in.

Paris (afp). The bodies of three men have been found in a hotel room in Paris' inner city.

According to initial, unconfirmed reports, they may be two agents in the French secret service and one Italian citizen.

The Italian is believed to have been on board the A380 when it crashed into the terminal at Paris-Charles de Gaulle airport. If so, the man would have been the only survivor of the as yet baffling incident in which 842 people lost their lives, including the musician Fred Dizier and actor Franco Camerone along with model Lilou de Girardin, daughter of the French steel magnate Erneste Xavier Marquis de Girardin.

It has not yet been established whether there is a link between the murders and the incident at the airport.

The authorities have not yet released a statement, citing ongoing investigations.

Further reports to follow.

Underneath were the words:

I hope that wasn't you?
We have to meet up.
Call me as soon as you get back from Moscow.

Konstantin knew who had sent the message from a silly generic email account that would already have ceased to exist.

First Lilou, who was on board the airbus, then the message about the murder of the survivor of the flight. Coincidence?

He didn't believe in them.

It seemed his past had just caught up with him, and it looked as though he had brought it on himself without meaning to. Without asking for it. Just by accepting a job.

Konstantin looked out the window again, but the older man with the rock 'n' roll hairstyle was no longer standing in front of the hotel. *No, that was not a coincidence either.*

Even letting his thoughts turn to Iva again couldn't improve his mood for long. In fact, the contrary was true, because he doubted whether he could resist seeing the cellist again in Leipzig. Which, strictly speaking, he shouldn't do.

Under *any* circumstances.

He reflected. The fact that his friend suspected him of a triple murder was hurtful. But it actually wasn't surprising that he knew where Konstantin was. The man with the zoom lens might have something to do with it.

Or he was in the Russian secret service and wanted a new photo of me for their files. After all, I know one of the biggest state secrets: Lenin's bathwater.

Suddenly Konstantin felt unwell. Too many people were interested in him. People he knew, and people he did not.

Minsk, Belarus

'Did you see that shot, Mum?' cried Eugen excitedly, his young voice blending with thousands of other equally enthusiastic voices. The HK Dinamo Minsk men's game against a Russian all-star team from the national ice-hockey squad was thrilling, quick and hard. 'Whoa, at *that* distance and *almost* in!'

Kristen smiled and ran her hand through her eight-year-old

son's short brown hair, something he had inherited from her. Hopefully that was the only thing that genetics had passed on to him from her side. 'That was impressive,' she admitted.

They were sitting in one of the VIP boxes, above the heads of the players and the almost 15,000 spectators who had come to the Minsk Arena to watch the match. They drank tea, ate snacks from the buffet laid out along the back wall and had fun while the players raced after the puck, fouled each other – mostly harmlessly – scored goals and put on a great show.

'What do you think? Are we going to win?' Kristen didn't expect it to get too rough. They kept themselves in check during friendlies, especially as it wasn't against a team from the West. Dinamo Minsk wanted to prove that they could win against the sport's heavy hitters, even if they had done cat-astrophically badly in the continental hockey league season. At the moment Minsk was two points behind and it was clear that the Russians were holding back.

Eugen shook his head. 'Nah. The Russians are too strong.' He slurped his fruit tea and stuffed a chocolate bar in his mouth.

'Don't eat so fast, young man,' scolded Kristen immediately, but stroked the back of his narrow, childish neck as she did so. It seemed fragile even under her own slim fingers; one of the ankh tattoos on her wrist revealed itself as she stroked his neck. She was enjoying the few hours she spent with him and trying to forget the four men in the room who were not VIP guests like the others.

As usual she didn't manage it. The ubiquitous quartet was a team of minders who worked for her ex-husband: pros, former agents in the FSB, Russia's domestic secret service. They were unremarkable yet unmissable.

To this day Kristen was not sure whether the bodyguards were meant to protect Eugen from her or from outside threats. The boy was worth quite a sum of money to his father. As a mother, she would murder any kidnapper anyway.

Kristen celebrated with Eugen as Dinamo got a goal back and then quickly sent the Russian goalkeeper crashing to the ice. Spectacular, but nothing serious. The ensuing tussle was cut short by the referees. The atmosphere in the stadium didn't really bubble over until the equaliser was scored. An excellent match to make up to the fans for a terrible season.

The minutes by her son's side went by far too quickly. As soon as the final buzzer went, Kristen would have preferred to send the bodyguards back to the airport without Eugen.

But that would not have been a good idea.

Her ex-husband had many colleagues, and money was not an issue. He would have traced her in a matter of days and then she would never see Eugen again. That's what he told her after they divorced. Quietly and matter-of-factly: *one* infringement of the agreement and all she would be entitled to was one photo of her son per year. On his birthday.

Kristen could never have coped with that, so she kept silent. Besides, she needed her ex-husband's money for her research. For research for Eugen.

One of the men looked at his expensive watch and approached Kristen. 'We've got to go, your ladyship. The plane is ready.'

'Of course.' Kristen hated the archaic title. Although she insisted every time that the men not use it, they did anyway.

Her ex probably encouraged them. He had always liked to make fun of her background.

'Take care, pal.' She leaned down to Eugen and gave him a kiss on the cheek, then on the forehead, and clasped him in her arms for a long time.

Her son mutely reciprocated the tenderness, fighting back tears as he did at every goodbye. They wouldn't see each other for a month. 'Bye, Mum. I'll write to you! And we can talk online.'

'Let's.' She smiled and stood up straight. 'I'll think of something fun for next time we see each other. How about the museum and some ice cream afterwards?'

'Oh, yes!' Eugen waved as the four bodyguards surrounded him like pillars brought to life and led him towards the door. 'I love you! Bye!'

Kristen swallowed her tears. 'I love you too,' she whispered and slowly left the VIP lounge.

A single corridor led her and the other well-heeled visitors to a separate exit so that they could leave the large stadium unimpeded by the masses.

Lost in thought, she went to her car, an M-class Mercedes Edition 10. It was dirty, as though it had been in the countryside.

Kristen got in and drove off eastwards into the city, shedding tears behind the wheel she hadn't wanted to shed in front of Eugen. It was hard enough for him as it was.

To distract herself, she turned on the radio. News.

Even in Belarus people were following the accident at the airport in Paris. There were new details that were not new to Kristen: the Italian real-estate agent Tommaso Luca

Francesco Tremante had indeed been on board flight AF023 and had been murdered in a Paris hotel, together with the two policemen who were meant to be guarding him. The excited presenter gushed about the most diverse theories, for example, he suspected Tremante of being a defecting terrorist or informant who had been bumped off by his accomplices.

'He was the wrong one anyway,' grumbled Kristen angrily, fishing a little vial of pills out of the inside pocket of her jacket. She noticed a dizzy sensation rapidly spreading over her. There was something she could take for that. She opened the lid with one hand, let two pills slide into her mouth and swallowed them dry. She put the little vial on the passenger seat.

With Tremante, Kristen had been sure that she had caught one of them. The only survivor. She'd had no time left to gather more detailed information about Tremante or observe him as she usually did. Into the hotel, have a look, take him away with her, that was the plan. His behaviour alone should have made her suspicious. Even so, there was still every possibility that he had unwittingly used his abilities for the first time that day. Yet that hope had turned out to be wrong and so she had had to neutralise him, useless as he clearly was.

She usually acted more subtly, started a fire or another little disaster, but since she'd also had to kill the two French policemen it had to be quick. And unfortunately that meant causing a fuss.

To her relief there didn't seem to be any suspicion of her involvement. They were looking for a male murderer or murderers. She had definitely been noticed, the barman might remember her. But since she had left no other traces behind . . .

Now the fact remained that she still hadn't been able to carry out any further investigation into the real culprits behind the airbus accident. The meeting with Eugen was more important to her. Besides she would soon get her hands on *another* one. There were still plenty of contenders for a visit from her.

It was a while before she left the leafy streets of Minsk and entered the network of small, dirty, potholed streets that led to her destination: a building in the middle of the city which had once belonged to the medical institute. It was old but in working order, so the University of Minsk still held lectures on the ground floor because there was no space for them in the main building.

The floors above and below the ground floor belonged to Kristen.

Or rather they belonged to the Life Institute, a private hospital for severely neurologically ill people who were examined with cutting-edge equipment, from MRI machines to CT scanners. There was an agreement with the government that the state would one day be allowed to take possession of the technical equipment worth millions of dollars. So nobody asked any questions about what was going on. Or the exact procedures.

Kristen parked the titanium-coloured Mercedes in her space, picked up the little vial from the passenger seat and locked the car before getting out and going inside the building.

The guard looked up from his newspaper and nodded to her without checking her ID. Everyone knew who she was.

Kristen caught a glimpse of the headlines, full of talk about the mugging of a foreigner. She wouldn't have been interested if it weren't for the fact that the employee had tried to obscure the words with his arm.

She stopped, went over to the nervous guard and had him give her the newspaper. She skimmed the brief article: an unknown tourist had been shot, his valuables stolen. The pixelated image of the victim, taken by an eyewitness with a poor-quality camera phone, was enough to spoil Kristen's already mediocre mood. Someone had better have a good explanation of how Ian McNamara's body had ended up on the front page.

She threw the newspaper back to the guard and got into the lift. Inserting a smart card into the appropriate slot, she typed out a code on the panel. Only then did the lift move, taking the petite brown-haired woman to the fourth floor.

The hidden camera had long since detected her and matched her face and retina with the security data bank. Nobody could get into the institute if they didn't have any business there.

The pills were working, the dizziness was receding. But exhaustion was setting in due to long-term sleep deprivation and her hands trembled gently.

Kristen took the caffeine-guarana tablets that had been specially formulated for her out the pocket of her jacket and swallowed two of them. The caffeine worked immediately while the guarana ensured a long-lasting effect. The dosage would have made a healthy person erupt into wild hyperactivity and could have caused a heart attack. But she was used to it. If the exhaustion turned out to be too overwhelming and debilitating to be controlled using caffeine and guarana, she resorted to amphetamine powder.

She hadn't lied to Tremante: she really did suffer from fatal familial insomnia, a prion disease related to CJD. But hers was hereditary and contagious.

Kristen existed on a vicious cycle of stimulants and sleeping pills. The insomnia wouldn't let her into the land of nod without strong sleeping pills, her body was not allowed any recovery. She had to compensate for this serious deprivation during her waking phases using pills.

At the same time, the sodding illness had given her an incredible gift!

The last check-up had revealed that the changes in her cerebral cortex, thalamus and cerebellum were increasing: the beginning of the end. Because insomnia was incurable.

For now.

This was one of the reasons the Life Institute existed.

The lift stopped and the doors opened.

Kristen stepped into the antechamber beyond, which was intended to prevent all contaminants caused by germs. She put on a white coat, gloves and shoe covers, hid her hair under the cap and put the surgical mask in place. Beyond the transparent cabin there was an older man already waiting, wearing the same outfit.

He opened the door for her. 'Welcome, Mrs von Windau.' He handed her a tablet computer straight away, with all of the latest reports on recent surgeries on it. He was treating her like everything was normal. Was he trying to keep McNamara's death a secret from her?

'Good afternoon, Professor Smyrnikov.' She scanned the

results quickly and read almost nothing but disappointments. 'Perhaps *good* is not the right word,' she added.

'I'm so sorry, the new recruits you brought us didn't make it through the second and third procedures the way we thought they would.'

Kristen noticed the same causes in all of the failed cases. 'Sepsis?' Several of the patients' organs had become infected and had had to be removed.

'Unfortunately so.'

She remained silent and sombre, scrolling through the data, browsing and examining the pictures. 'Is there sloppiness in maintaining hygiene, Professor?' she asked quietly, furtively. 'What other reason could there be for patients dying without any complications arising during the procedure?'

'There could be many reasons, Mrs von Windau.'

'You've looked into where the germs came from?'

Smyrnikov looked solemnly at her. 'The source couldn't be established beyond all doubt.'

Kristen leaned down to him. 'Pay attention to your staff, Professor, and urge them to be better in terms of cleanliness. It's clear to *you* that we have entered an unknown area of surgery and neurology, and *everyone* in your team must come to understand this. The results of our research will be worth millions in the free market so long as they actually save lives.' She gave the tablet back to him. '*Successes*, Professor. The next person to cause sepsis in one of the subjects will automatically become their replacement.'

Smyrnikov didn't reply.

They were walking along a corridor with many doors and small teams of doctors walking in the opposite direction. They were debating in all kinds of accents of English. Specialists from all four corners of the globe came together here. Eleven men and women. Well. Ten now that they had lost McNamara.

Kristen had hired them from their universities and hospitals on the professor's advice. Quite a few of them had already gained a bad reputation due to their opinions or deeds. That's exactly what distinguished them from others: they were in the tradition of Demikhov and White, their predecessors, but equipped with better resources.

Kristen's programme in Minsk had been up and running for four years in total. Away from the public eye. The medics had been lured by money and the prospect of even more money kept them in Minsk. To be on the safe side Kristen had them all under surveillance. No component of her secret could go missing or become public knowledge. She saw the blunder with the Irishman as a serious error, which made her angry. In contrast Smyrnikov remained a picture of calm. He really didn't want to talk about it.

'What happened with Professor McNamara?' she asked. 'I know it wasn't a mugging. Why do I have to find out about his death from a newspaper? It's your duty to keep me informed.'

Smyrnikov clicked his tongue. 'I thought you'd find out before I could explain.'

'You did, did you?'

He sighed. 'I'm sorry for the lapse on my part.'

'And?'

'He wanted to drop out on moral grounds. There was an accident that ruled out the usual approach: McNamara fled, Dranko just managed to catch him before he got to the airport. The police are holding off, but every idiot's got a camera phone these days. The image got into the hands of a young editor.' Smyrnikov cleared his throat. 'The newspaper printed the report before I could put our man in the government onto him. It was too late to stop it.'

Kristen shook her head. 'It's not good, Professor. This article had better not get out of Minsk.' She didn't believe he had actually wanted to inform her. Smyrnikov was afraid of her.

'It won't be online,' he assured her. 'I was able to sort out everything else. The authorities are helping us to hush up the accident. McNamara's identity will remain a secret. His body will vanish.'

'And his sister?' Kristen recalled her interview with the Irishman. Smyrnikov had been especially keen to have him on the team, and she had hired him on his advice.

'She will receive an urn with his ashes and a letter from Burkina Faso. An infection got him. The telephone number she'll find in the letter leads to one of our staff who will tell her a moving tale.'

'Nice. Let's wait and see if she falls for it. If not, she'll have to find herself in an accident as well.' Kristen was not satisfied. Smyrnikov was toying with her trust. She wouldn't let him forget it for a long time. 'I'd like to see Patient 34,' she said, drawing a line under the topic. 'I have a few more questions for him.'

'As you wish,' replied Smyrnikov. He sounded moody because of his mistake. Or because she'd caught him.

They took a second lift at the end of the corridor and went up to the top, the eighth floor, which differed from the floors below in that it had just four, very spacious rooms for patients.

After a brief knock they went through the first door on the left hand side of the corridor.

The room was full of electronic equipment, automated injection machines and various monitoring stations, with screens displaying readings of biotelemetric patterns. Cameras on the ceiling monitored Patient 34 visually too, while the microphone in front of his lips recorded the smallest sound from his mouth.

Countless IV lines and cables from the measuring instruments ran via a storage system to a Plexiglas cell in the middle of the room and from there to a bed. The naked man inside was restrained by numerous straps and had cables and tubes stuck all over him, pumping a variety of chemical concoctions into his blood. Electrodes fastened to his bald head and clamped into a metal frame produced an EEG for neurofeedback. Everything in and around him was subject to constant scrutiny, from blood levels to brainwaves. He could barely move a millimetre, the straps and skull clamp made sure of that.

The scene suggested a team of concerned doctors had saved the life of someone severely injured in an accident and had immobilised him so that the recovery would be quicker.

The truth was very different.

Kristen noticed the man's open green eyes staring unseeingly into space. 'How long has he been awake?'

'We brought him out of the coma yesterday,' answered Smyrnikov. 'Doctor Willers will be here any moment. She knows the details.'

'You don't?' Kristen noted tartly.

'No, Mrs von Windau. I look after the serious cases.' He pointed at the man with his index finger. 'Patient 34 is not suffering from any physical complaint, he just isn't allowed to move.'

The door behind them opened and Willers came in.

It was hard to tell how old she was, although she must have been at least seventy. She had studied under Dr White and had been refining his methods ever since. Even more importantly, she carried on his spirit, his thinking, his attitude, and conveyed her own interpretation of them to the young doctors and scientists in Minsk.

Kristen smiled at her. She liked this woman – who looked like a lovely grandma with her backcombed, thinning, silver hair – more than she liked Smyrnikov. The McNamara mistake would not have happened with her. 'Ah, the expert.'

'For 34 at any rate.' Willers held out her hand to her. 'How was the Dinamos game?'

She looked at the doctor in confusion. 'How did you make that one out?'

Willers sniffed. 'You smell of a mixture of smoke and fast food and with that jumper that I can see underneath your coat, you're too well wrapped up for this time of year. Which leads me to the conclusion that you were in the ice-hockey stadium.' She grinned.

Kristen returned the smile. 'The Dinamos did well, you have to hand it to them.' She respected the doctor's keen intellect, which was one of the reasons that Patient 34 had already lived so long. Longer than anyone else had. 'How many days is he at now?'

'Seventy-three, of which sixty-one were in a coma. He's

been awake yesterday and today. Or at least that's what the EEG results say. The neurofeedback is clear.'

'Attempts at communication?'

'None so far.' Willers smiled cautiously. 'That might change when 34 sees you, Mrs von Windau.'

'Do you think?'

'Most people would react at the sight of their murderer, given the chance,' replied Willers smugly.

Smyrnikov confined himself to silently keeping an eye on the man's data.

Kristen looked at the Plexiglas cell. 'Can we risk going in? Not that we'd be taking any germs in with us that might kill him.'

The professor laughed quietly to himself. When Kristen threw him a withering look he fell silent.

'No. His immune system has stabilised; the chemotherapy was completed a long time ago. We are clean enough for him, as long as we don't get too close to him. We're going to tackle his memory next. The first dose of propranolol is already in his system to counter the effect of any trauma.' Beckoning, Willers pulled up her surgical mask and led the way. 'The recalibration of his memory is going to work. I studied Elizabeth Loftus' methods and hired one of her junior doctors. Soon Patient 34 will see us as his best friends. Even you, Baroness.'

Kristen followed her. Smyrnikov stayed outside, watching the screens.

Seconds later they were standing by the man's bed as he stared into the distance.

'We moisten his eyes three times a day,' explained Willers,

pleased with herself. 'Do you see? No inflammation at the stitches and no rejection. The air on the eighth floor is healthier than it is on Smyrnikov's ward. They don't die as quickly here.' She took Kristen by the elbow and pushed her forwards. 'Please go closer, so that he can see you. The microphone is on the most sensitive setting. I'm excited to see what will happen,' she said and clasped her hands together over her navel.

Kristen looked at Patient 34. The dark skin of his head – clamped in place with four screws – and the neck was markedly different from the pale colouring of the rest of the body.

She could make out healed scars, some small, some large, the largest of them all encircling the neck. Four tubes ran beneath the skin under his Adam's apple, four more into the back of his neck, and there was a central venous catheter on his collarbone. Discharge and supply. On the darker folds of flesh the remnants of a dissected tattoo were visible: Sanskrit phrases and symbols.

'We have removed the external stitches, as Mr Singh's skin has adhered successfully to Mr Estevez's,' explained Willers from behind her, the mask muffling her voice. 'Leaving them in would only have been a risk.'

'I see.' Kristen waved her hand back and forth in front of the restrained man's eyes to get his attention. 'Hallo, Ranjeet Singh,' she said loudly and clearly. 'Do you remember me?'

'Heart rate is increasing, so is brain activity,' reported Smyrnikov from outside the cell. 'Patient 34 recognises you, Mrs von Windau.'

Then the man's lips moved, twitching. The whispered

words were recorded by the microphone, amplified, cleaned up and reproduced by the loudspeaker. 'What did you do?'

'Me? I tracked you down, overpowered you and brought you to Minsk. She,' Kristen pointed at Willers, 'did the rest. On my orders.'

'Pulse one-forty and rising, blood pressure one-forty over one-ten, be careful,' warned Smyrnikov. 'Not that we're damaging the newly formed synapses with this little game.' He hit a button. He was probably instructing the machines to administer sedatives to the patient.

The Indian man's dark eyes flicked to and fro before fixing on Kristen. 'This is not my body,' said Singh with his creaky, otherworldly voice, which the loudspeaker made even creepier.

'That's not entirely true.' Kristen waved the doctor over. 'Would you explain to Mr Singh how his head found its way onto Mr Estevez's body?' Then she turned to Singh. 'Dr Willers was a student of one of the greatest physicians of the last century.'

Singh gasped, nothing more. A sound of horror.

'Mr Singh, I used to work with Dr White, who, in 1962, succeeded in removing an animal brain from a skull and keeping it alive. Two years later, I was there when he grafted a dog's brain onto the neck of another dog and kept it alive by connecting it to the circulatory system of the recipient dog. There were a few setbacks, but then there was the ape experiment.' Kristen observed Willers' eyes betray the smile underneath her mask. 'We transplanted its entire head onto another body. Like with you, Mr Singh. Back then the head and face could wobble a bit and react to stimuli, but the ape remained paralysed. Sadly.'

'Lunatics!' moaned the man.

'Blood pressure and pulse are rising,' said Smyrnikov, a note of warning in his voice. 'I would stop.'

'Go on,' demanded Kristen, fascinated. 'Explain to him how valuable he is.'

'My mentor was consumed by the thought that people who were stuck in a body damaged beyond repair or whose lives were at risk after an accident could get their lives back by being transplanted into another body,' Willers expounded with enthusiasm. 'A brain in a donor body; seeing your children grow up, family, career, friends ... it would be an incredible gift!'

'You can imagine that Dr White didn't make many friends with his experiments,' added Kristen.

'Officially. Unofficially there were plenty of patrons,' Willers chipped in. 'The US government asked me to continue his research, especially in developing the discoveries made in different areas of research since his time. Let's take, for example, joining the head to a new spine: a mechanical fusion and the stiffening aren't a problem, but how do I prevent the recipient from remaining paralysed? In this case, the patient is you, Mr Singh.'

'No,' he groaned and opened his eyes wider.

'Heart rate and blood pressure returning to stability,' came the report from outside.

Willers pointed at the cables and equipment in the room. 'I found a solution: stem cells. The Department of Physical Medicine and Rehabilitation at the University of California managed to restore a damaged spinal cord using them. The paralysed patients could walk again after treatment! And that's exactly what we're attempting with you.'

'The *patients* Dr Willers is talking about were mice,' Kristen clarified. 'But it works. If you ignore the ethical concerns—'

'The best thing about it is that, not too long ago, the researchers at Berkeley used stem cells to repair and restore old muscle tissue. They changed the biological pathway that nature usually takes in the healing process.' Willers had that light in her eyes that Kristen found so admirable. 'Do you understand what we're doing here, Mr Singh? How important you are? With our treatment we could outwit Death. For all time. By combining different techniques.'

If they were successful, it would save Kristen . . . and Eugen. But any kind of knowledge was useful. Especially relating to insomnia.

Suddenly Willer's bleeper went off and Smyrnikov's pager sounded too.

'What is it?' Kristen saw the horror on the older woman's face.

'Patient 22! His brainwaves have altered. The delta waves are decreasing, the REM phase is complete, the deep sleep interrupted. We have the first theta waves! Sedation is failing,' Willers cried. 'He's transitioning into another sleep phase. How could that happen, Professor?'

Smyrnikov ran out without a word. What was he planning? To go and assist the doctors? Or to flee so that at least *he* survived?

'What floor is he on?' Kristen was trying not to let the panic get to her. The sensational transplant success with Patient 34 would be completely meaningless if they didn't get 22 under control. Otherwise they might as well set off a neutron bomb, a catastrophe like that could not be covered up. They were under enormous pressure, the last vestiges of her fatigue had vanished into thin air.

'One floor below us, on seven. We don't have enough time to get everyone to safety in the cellar.' Willers stared at her boss, placing all responsibility on her.

Kristen set off, rushing to the stairs to the seventh floor.

She knew what had to be done and if she didn't succeed, a huge number of people would die.

In the building and within a radius of three kilometres.

V

A person's life consists of them,
made foolish by hope,
dancing into the arms of Death.

The World as Will and Representation,
Arthur Schopenhauer

Leipzig, Germany

Do not fall asleep until . . .

Konstantin lay on his back in a strange, fragrant bed, absentmindedly tracing the letters on his right forearm that glinted as darkly and freshly as they had on the day he had emerged from the tattoo parlour. He had the fragment of a sentence retouched regularly. This had less to do with the look of the tattoo and more to do with the ritual, with the reminder and the warning to himself.

He turned his head to the right and his gaze fell on Iva.

The young woman was sleeping, breathing deeply and slowly. Full of trust.

Her long blonde hair played about her face and spread out on the pillow. The sheets had slipped down so that Konstantin could see her bare left breast with its delicate pink areola, which he had kissed and caressed hours before. Iva had wonderful skin, pale and perfect, and delicately perfumed.

Konstantin lifted his hand and couldn't resist gently touching the sleeping woman, her shoulder, her collarbone, her cleavage.

He felt her warmth through his fingertips and a shudder of bliss went through him, sending a warm feeling to his core. His thoughts were dreamlike, infatuated. He didn't recognise this part of himself and his fanciful mood surprised him. His head swam with esoteric thoughts and images. *I'm crazy about her! Just crazy about her!*

Everything had gone very quickly since her return from the Russian tour: a visit to rehearsals, a trip to a café, going home, an indescribable, almost supernatural, sympathy between two souls, a confusing yet instinctive desire to merge. An irresistible wave gripped them, simultaneously, carried them away and washed them up on the bed where they had had sex for the first time. Then on the floor and on the table in the little kitchen. Afterwards, Iva had fallen asleep.

Konstantin did not. He *could* not. He reflected on whether he should tell her the truth about himself. He wanted to so that she would be aware. Today. Preferably now, as soon as she opened her eyes. So that nothing came between them.

He looked at the alarm clock on her bedside table: 5.32. *I wonder if she's an early riser? Better not.* He smiled at Iva and suppressed a yawn.

He wasn't used to getting by without sleep any more. After years of half-sleep, his houseboat now allowed him the incredible luxury of lying down at any time and sleeping long and deeply.

This was different. Konstantin was in Iva's bed, in the small bedroom of her period home in the centre of Leipzig. Without the protection of water or control over his surroundings.

The city was waking up on the other side of the small window. Bicycles trundled along the cobblestones, people exchanged greetings as they rushed past each other, a sanitation truck was doing one last round. Heavy rain had started up a few minutes before and the monotonous rushing sound was soporific, but Konstantin could not give in.

So he got up carefully and dressed quietly. He could be very quiet when he wanted to be.

He used to prefer what he liked to call *intermezzi*, brief flings, after which he would sneak out of the woman's house. There were clear conventions that both sides expected to be followed. Two years before, at the beginning of his new life as an undertaker and thanatologist, Konstantin had stopped all that.

What do I do? Wake her? He stood uncertainly next to Iva and crouched down in front of her. He gave her a light kiss on the forehead and took a deep breath of her nighttime smell, before creeping into the kitchen and opening the window to watch the falling rain.

He would tell her the truth. After hours of startlingly beautiful emotions, of euphoria and ardour, this decision prompted something new and unwelcome – fear. It was spreading through him, pushing everything else carelessly aside and painting it grey like the wall opposite him.

How will she take it? Konstantin should have run far away

from Iva, the woman who fascinated him and touched him; he had planned never to see her again after their meeting in Moscow. *Stay away from the rehearsals*, he had said over and over to himself on the plane. *Go home*, he had shouted at himself on the way to the Gewandhaus. *Turn around*, he had muttered in the foyer as he sat in the chair he always sat in to watch Iva anyway.

This is what had come of it: a night full of honest emotion.

Konstantin never wanted to give up this feeling, this irreplaceable togetherness. He didn't want to give up Iva, despite all his fears.

His gaze fell on his forearm.

Do not fall asleep until . . .

To distract himself, he looked in her kitchen for everything they would need for breakfast for them both. Such a long time since he'd last done that! A short while later the table was laid, the water boiling for tea. He quietly took her key along with an umbrella and left the apartment, returning ten minutes later with fresh rolls.

By then Iva had woken up and was waiting for him in the hallway. She was wearing a long, black nightdress with a loose-knit white cardigan over it, her blonde hair falling around her shoulders and she was holding a cup of tea in her hand. Her light brown eyes looked for Konstantin's. 'For a moment I thought you might not come back,' she said softly and let him past to go into the kitchen. She kissed him as he went by, stroking his chest.

'That would make me seriously stupid.' Konstantin sat down.

Iva sat opposite him and rummaged in the bag of bread

rolls. 'You went to my favourite bakery!' She chose a seeded roll and cut it open. 'Try this one. These are incredibly good.' Before putting anything on her roll she poured him some tea. 'You are my hero. When I think how much time we wasted because neither of us had the confidence to talk to the other person.'

He looked at her, smiled nervously and rubbed at his tattoo. His courage had fled through every single tiny pore. He didn't know how to begin. Or where. Because his secret was of such magnitude, because it radiated fear and smothered any other emotion. Because the entire situation was so surreal. *She's going to think I'm some nutter who's read too much horror fiction.*

The kitchen clock ticked gently, second after second passing.

'Iva, I have to tell you something.'

'Yes?' She put her roll on her plate and looked at him. She didn't pester him, didn't drum her fingers impatiently. Iva simply sat on the chair, her legs drawn up and crossed. Svelte and sexy, a woman he wanted to have in his life.

He couldn't rid himself of the feeling of fear. It was choking his resolve to be honest and open.

Konstantin inhaled, took a mental run-up but faltered. He smiled nervously, breathed out and rubbed his arm. He had hidden what surrounded him his whole life, and now that he had found a special person whom he wanted to open up to . . . *Maybe it is too soon.*

'The tattoo.' Iva indicated it with a nod. '*Do not fall asleep until* . . . Is it something to do with that? And with all those scars?'

'How did you—' Konstantin was shocked that the truth was suddenly within reach.

'Were you in prison?' Iva looked at him fearlessly. 'We've never spoken about you. Thanks to you I know a lot about thanatology, about dealing with corpses, I know about your hobbies. But you haven't told me anything about your family or anything from your childhood. Or about the years before Ars Moriendi. Ex-cons are often afraid of rejection once it emerges that they were in prison.' She gave him an encouraging smile that restored his nerve. 'Is that it?'

If you lie now, everything will be okay, said a quiet little voice in his head. *She will put your behaviour down to a quirk of being inside, and you can keep your secret to yourself. You don't have to tell her it. What would be the point? At best she would run away screaming, because she won't want to be next to a monster . . .*

Konstantin balled his hands into fists to suppress the little voice.

Iva noticed his reaction. 'Did I say anything wrong?'

'No. In fact, it was just the right thing. Now—' He held out the tattoo on his forearm, as if the letters could explain themselves. 'I don't know where to start. You're going to think I'm a lunatic or a killer or—' Konstantin took another deep breath and could feel the sweat collecting under his arms.

'Why were you in prison?'

He could tell that she was really asking cautiously whether he was a murderer or rapist. 'I wasn't in prison. I was . . . a soldier.'

Iva relaxed, but only a little. Soldiers could be murderers and rapists too. 'You've shot people. Is that what you're trying to say? Or are you struggling with a trauma from your tours of duty?'

There's no going back now. Konstantin traced each word of

the tattoo on his skin with his finger. 'You are all alone,' he said quietly.

She tried to figure out what he meant. 'Is that the rest of the sentence?'

He nodded and sighed. 'Do not fall asleep until you are all alone. *Schlafe nicht ein, bis du absolut alleine bist.* It's a command to myself, a rule, a warning, perhaps my life's motto.' Konstantin wanted to leap up and run out because telling the truth was like being in free fall and hurtling towards happiness, getting bigger and faster and heavier. Like a weight towards an anemone.

'Why? What happens if you don't sleep alone?'

'I . . . they . . . they die!' he cried out in despair, his eyes blazing. *Just one more sentence!* 'As soon as I fall asleep, Death arrives.'

'Oh, Death just arrives then, does he?' Iva had knitted her brows and she looked baffled. Baffled and very, very sceptical.

'Yes. And he . . . he can't see me and that makes him angry. And he knows that I'm somewhere and he kills anything around me to give vent to his anger. To . . . hurt me,' he burst out. He was speaking quickly, incoherently. *What is she going to do? What is she going to do?*

Iva was watching him like you might look at a crazy person, waiting to see what he would say or get up to next.

His secret was out in the open. Konstantin knew he now had to give it his all to convince her it was true. 'People like me are called Death Sleepers. I am invisible to Death. You're in no danger so long as I'm awake. But as soon as I go to sleep, he appears because I attract him. No idea how. Some say that Death cuts down everything in the vicinity of a

Death Sleeper in the hope that this will catch his opponent. Others say that Death kills people out of vengeance so that our nearest and dearest are taken from us.' He grasped her hand. 'You must believe me!'

'Aha,' said Iva. 'And how does that work exactly?'

She believes it? My God, yes! She believes it! 'Every Death Sleeper has a different amount of power over their environment. Sometimes the Grim Reaper turns on every visible life form, from human to insect, sometimes plants are included, sometimes not. There are different barriers, for example: a locked room or water. The longer a person is invisible to Death and the more often they fall asleep the worse the repercussions become. Probably because the Reaper gets angrier and angrier. And he does not know what mercy means.'

'And if you hit your head and fall unconscious?' Iva seemed to be practically minded. She was looking carefully at him as she drank more tea.

'No, that doesn't work. During a fainting fit or a lack of consciousness nothing happens to the surrounding area, but it does if someone takes sleeping tablets or a mild anaesthetic.'

She gave him a pensive look. 'So you're immortal and indestructible? Like in *Highlander*?'

He laughed. 'No, I wish. I still get hurt like everybody else. I heal normally, but I can't die of an illness, I just suffer the effects of it. It prolongs my suffering, if you like, if things go badly.' Konstantin finally felt relief rising up inside him. Iva sat opposite him and asked questions. Good questions. Sensible questions. 'Sometimes we are the medical miracles you read about in the news. There's a theory that we heal more quickly when we sleep because other people are paying for our sleep with their lives.'

'And there's no way of tricking Death?'

'Water helps. He doesn't like it; it takes him longer to find me. So I live on a houseboat.'

'That means you're also not immune to the effects of time?'

'Right. We might look somewhat better preserved on the outside, but we just keep getting older and older and get wrinklier and wrinklier with all of our frailties.' *Lying in bed, sitting in a wheelchair, wasting away.*

'And if someone were to rip out your heart, what then?'

Drastic. But logical. Konstantin couldn't help grinning. 'Well, without a donor heart or artificial heart I would probably live a while longer until the cells began to decay. At some point I would keel over and look dead.' He ran a hand through his hair. 'From there on, it's all theoretical. We assume that our consciousness, or what people call a soul, stays with our body as it decomposes.'

'How long for?'

Konstantin couldn't say. 'In theory, I'd say that we stay trapped forever. The Reaper can't take us with him into the great beyond.'

'Ah. So then you're ghosts, like people talk about.'

'Possibly. I don't know.'

Iva chewed at her lower lip, looked at the ceiling and then back at him. 'Have you been like this from birth?'

'I think so. With most people it kicks in during puberty or later. We don't have an explanation for it.'

'With most people? But then a baby would kill their own

mother directly after the birth, as soon as it falls asleep for the first time!' She shuddered.

'Childbed fever. If you look at history, there are many clues about the effects of Death Sleepers.'

'Nonsense!' Iva grinned suddenly. 'Is that why you became an undertaker? You provide your own customers. Do you know the film with Boris Karloff, Vincent Price and—'

She thinks I'm joking! 'I'm being serious,' he said, appalled.

She laughed and stroked his cheek. 'Of course you are. What does Death look like? Does he have a hood and carry a scythe? Like you see in films and books? Or is it more like in *Final Destination*?'

'Iva, I'm not pulling your leg!' *No! Please, she's got to believe me!* Konstantin held out his arm to her in a helpless gesture. 'Death has no form, he comes as ... smell, as a smell, as howling, as—'

'Sure, Konstantin. I know other people who have weird things happen to them as soon as they go to sleep. Some are sucked into their dream world, others experience a return to a different life.' She kissed his hand, leaned backwards and tossed back her blonde mane with a smirk. 'You should be glad you can't scare me that easily, you're actually pretty convincing. As though you really believed it. And I like the idea of immortality without any advantages. What with you being an undertaker and all, you should write a book. It's tragic and romantic and so creepy. Like in a tragic fairy tale.'

Konstantin felt ill. *Why should she have believed me? It's absolutely impossible. Something that only happens in films.*

I told you so, gloated the little voice. *You should have lied so that you could hold on to her.*

'I probably should have.' He stood up quickly and left the kitchen because he couldn't stand it any more. His secret hadn't been believed, Iva thought it was a joke, a funny idea, a made-up story. *What shall I do?* 'I've got to go,' he stammered. 'I still have a few burials to do.' He went out into the little hallway.

'Konstantin?' Chair legs scraped across the floor as Iva stood up. She realised that her reaction was the cause of his hasty retreat. 'Did I do something wrong?'

'Nothing. It was me. I did everything wrong. I thought—' He shook his head helplessly, threw her one last look and ran out of the apartment, down the stairs, through the door and right into the rain. The raindrops wet his face and hair, soaked through his clothes. It ran into his trainers.

He felt hurt, ridiculed and helpless. His courage had vanished, common sense now had the upper hand in his mind. *I should have known. It was too early, far too early for the truth. I can't see her again. Being with her would end in disaster, perhaps even in her death.* Konstantin licked his lips, tasting the rain. *Nobody can understand the curse that surrounds me. It's not possible.*

Footsteps rang out on the stairs. 'Konstantin, please, I—'

He ran off down the street, vaulting bollards and newspaper vending machines, climbing over cars, running and running until he was breathing harder and starting to sweat. Konstantin raced through large construction sites where the first shift workers of the day were milling around, they shouted after him in astonishment. He didn't care, he just ran and ran.

Eventually he stopped, panting, in an old courtyard. The house it belonged to had been given up to dereliction.

A bad stitch made him bend over. The exertion on an empty stomach caused black spots in front of his eyes and he felt sick, his knees were giving way.

With shaking legs he sank down onto a pile of rocks and with his eyes closed he let the rain pelt down on his lowered head.

I should have known, I'm an idiot. I can't be with a woman. I'm not allowed.

The constant pounding of the rain on the ground and on the shards of glass, timber, tin cans, stones and puddle-filled hollows that lay around him created a soothing concerto in the otherwise silent courtyard.

Gradually, Konstantin calmed down.

He folded his hands behind his neck, opened his eyes and squinted up at the grey clouds as though there was inspiration up there that was about to swoop down on him.

Do I really have to give her up?

With what he felt for her, it wouldn't be easy. She had enchanted him from the beginning, from the very first moment he saw her on the cello in the middle of the orchestra and she had returned his gaze. With a smile.

Running away from Iva's apartment seemed, now that he was thinking more calmly about it, childish. It made going back to her harder. What explanation could he give her for his behaviour? He should have laughed and agreed that he was joking. She clearly didn't want the truth. Maybe she would come to terms with it at a later stage?

Provided he thought up a good enough story to explain what had just happened, he might be able to go back to her, though he would need to take precautionary measures.

He still had the old tablets for emergencies somewhere. Hello-Awake to the power of ten. Back in the day he'd taken them after his missions to stay on the ball – and to put the greatest possible distance between himself and the place where he had carried out a mission in the shortest possible time.

Would they be out of date?

Meditation was a harmless way to regain strength and be able to resist sleep. Konstantin scowled. *Not exactly my greatest skill.*

Yet, there was no alternative, apart from his usual solitary nights on the *Vanitas*. But Konstantin wanted to be near Iva. As often as possible, for as long as possible. The egoism of love.

I should start by thinking up a story to go back to her with. Or should I? Konstantin sighed and stood up, stretching his cramping legs and shaking them out.

The little voice was whispering all the while that it would be better to give Iva up. To give up love – to protect the lover, paradoxically. He hated his indecision and the hopelessness of the situation.

Above the ever-present rushing sound of the rain, he caught the sound of a slight click far away that came again quickly.

That sounds like a camera shutter. Konstantin turned his head towards the entrance of the courtyard and saw the man who had caught his eye before in Red Square in Moscow: rock 'n' roll hairstyle and rather well-cut clothes, a mix of the outdoorsy and country squire. Rain dripped from the sunglasses he was wearing, despite the early hour. The fact the camera and lens were getting wet didn't bother him.

In contrast to their first meeting there was no doubt that the man's focus was trained on Konstantin. 'Hey!' He took a few steps towards him. 'Why are you following me?'

An arrogant smile swept across the tanned face. 'For the file, son. Just for the file.' The voice carried the patina of endless numbers of cigarettes, of whisky and bellowing, perhaps to songs by the King. He lowered the camera and blew a large bubble of chewing gum that burst with a pop. A flock of pigeons rose up in fright and flapped around. 'Take it easy, okay? Photos can't hurt.'

Konstantin rushed over to the unruffled stranger and grabbed hold of him. 'Did Jester send you?' he demanded – and stood there as the man reached under his jacket and drew out a bulky revolver and promptly trained the barrel on him. Konstantin released him.

'I know your type, son. I figured you became a good one. So I'm not going to do anything to you,' said the stranger in a creaky, grating, rocker voice. 'I could shoot you in the foot now or some other part of your body. The next few days would be ruined. Hospital, police, interviews, the long-drawn out healing of the wound, which doesn't mean you wouldn't necessarily come out of it with permanent damage,' he listed off casually. The two barrels of the revolver sat one above the other, aimed at Konstantin's middle. 'Just stay there while I leave.' He withdrew slowly.

Konstantin's thoughts were spinning round his head. Was the man one of Jester's men? What did he mean by 'your type'? Was he a threat to Iva? What file?

He wanted answers, but he wouldn't get anywhere with aikido when pitted against a revolver. You couldn't use the power of a bullet against a shot itself. He cautiously followed the stranger.

By this point the man had reached the other side of the bow-shaped entrance to the yard, the revolver still pointed at Konstantin. 'Go back, kiddo.' He shifted the firing pin with a click. 'I have incredible aim by the way. Just a warning, in case you think hopping around or martial arts will be any use to you.'

'Why are you following me?'

'I needed a good photo. That's all. The shots from Moscow were rubbish. You aren't going to see me again any time soon, I promise. And I'm not interested in your girlfriend – you don't need to worry. After all, she isn't one of your kind. I wish her the best of luck in surviving you. Sleep can become overpowering; it's a matter of time.' The stranger looked to the left and right.

Konstantin took his chance: he crouched, leaped towards a palette lying at an angle, fired himself off it and onto the wall, then pounced on the attacker.

The mouth of the gun followed his swift, artistic movements and then there was a bang.

Konstantin felt the impact in his thigh, on the right outer side, and doubled up. Less than half a metre away from the stranger, he fell with a cry of agony into the wet mud. Dizziness gripped him, his vision darkened. Symptoms of shock. 'I told you before, son: I have incredible aim. It's only a flesh wound, nothing serious, but it will hold you up.' The man put away the unusual revolver. 'Now you definitely won't be following me.' He lifted the camera again and took two more shots of him. 'I'll send you these. As a memento of your stupidity.' He grinned broadly, baring the yellowed teeth of a heavy coffee-drinker and smoker. 'One more piece of advice and I mean this well: keep away from that sweet girl, before you cost her her life.' He stepped through the yard's driveway out onto the street and vanished.

Shit! Konstantin pushed himself up, bracing himself against the clammy wall and clenching his jaw hard. His blood ran, warm, out of the wound; the pain was excruciating. He could forget about exercise for the next few days.

Limping and cursing, he followed the man, but there was no trace of him. He took his mobile out of his trouser pocket, but it had packed up – whether it was from the rain or the fall, he wasn't sure.

A passer-by approached Konstantin. 'Do you need help?' he asked uncertainly.

'Would you call an ambulance?' he asked. 'I've hurt my leg.'

'Sure. Come on, let's wait inside.' The young man helped Konstantin across the road and into an Asian supermarket called Halal, where the owner was in the middle of wheeling new stock into the shop.

Konstantin was given tea by the Asian owner straight away, who introduced himself as Jussef and staunched the bleeding with compresses and a tourniquet.

'Thanks.' Konstantin held tight to the little glass that was steaming gently and smelled of apple.

'No problem.' Jussef nodded. 'Horrible. So who shot you?'

The passer-by turned pale, and Konstantin cursed inwardly that the cause of the wound was so obvious. 'No, I got stuck on some steel wire. I do parkour.' He hastily explained what parkour was and what had supposedly happened.

'Ah.' Jussef's facial expression made it clear he didn't believe a word of it. 'I used to be a doctor in Iraq, that's why I thought I had recognised a gunshot wound. But I must have been mistaken. It's a long time since I retired from that and it's also none of my business.'

The ambulance pulled up outside Halal, the paramedics came in and tended to Konstantin, asking him about the accident. From their glances he could tell that, in contrast to Jussef, they didn't doubt his version of events.

It suddenly occurred to him that the word *halal* had another meaning, different to the Islamic one. In Hungarian, and pronounced differently, it meant death. *Of all things.* Fate had a black sense of humour.

'All the best, then!' The friendly passer-by went on his way. Jussef wished him a speedy recovery too and gave Konstantin a jar of hummus to take home with him. To build up his strength.

The paramedics took him to the ambulance to take him to hospital where the wound would be cleaned properly.

Konstantin agreed. He didn't want any little shreds of fabric in the hole to lead to an infection. *No blood poisoning! Not that!*

During the journey he used the paramedic's mobile to call Ars Moriendi and told Mendy that he wouldn't make it in today. Then he made himself comfortable on the stretcher and pondered the heavily armed rocker, who had been on his heels and taking photos of him for a long time – obviously, for the ominous file related to Death Sleepers.

Longer than two years.

Longer than a new life in Leipzig lasted.

Leipzig, Germany

The door to the hospital room swung open with the sound of the knock.

Konstantin looked towards the doorway; he hadn't been expecting any visitors. He had just taken his plastic bag of belongings and was about to get going. The taxi was already booked.

A man in a black suit, white shirt and dark tie swept inside, took off his sunglasses and scrutinised him. 'Hello, sir. Allow me to introduce myself: Darling, British secret service,' he said, the practised smile appearing like clockwork on his handsome face. 'I have some questions for you, Mr Korff.' He closed the door behind him. 'Where were you yesterday—'

'Stop it, Jester.' Konstantin grinned broadly.

'Why should I? An MI6 agent never forgets his manners.' He stretched out his arms like a TV presenter. Commander Timothy Chester Darling, nicknamed Jester, loved a big entrance.

'Because I'm not one of your easily impressed bits of fluff?'

'Ah, right. That was it.' Jester held out his hand to Konstantin and shook it warmly, placing the other hand on top and then clapping him on the shoulder. 'What happened, old boy? Why do I have to visit you in hospital instead of on your beautiful houseboat with a view of the gorgeous women in skimpy swimming costumes?' He pulled up a chair and sat down and Konstantin sat back down on the bed. 'I was looking forward to a Red Russian.'

'You're some friend. Always sending me messages, apparently aware of where I am at all times, but when I get gunned down by a rocker of an old man I end up waiting in vain for your support.'

Jester gaped at him. 'Rocker of an old man? You're not serious!'

'More or less.' Konstantin explained in a nutshell the details of what went on in the backyard and what the stranger had said to him. 'Was the guy one of yours?'

'Are you mad?' Jester gave him the two-finger salute. 'My people are so unremarkably normal that they could rob a bank without being identified.' He reached into the inner pocket of the bag and took out a smartphone. 'Could you describe the gun for me again, please? Sounds like an unusual piece.'

'It had more than six bullets, the cylinder was too thick for half a dozen rounds,' Konstantin stressed. 'And it had a second barrel.'

'Hm. Wait a second. I don't have good reception right now,' said Jester, lifting his head and looking at his friend. 'Barely two years into your new life and you're already being shot at. That never happened to you back in the day.'

'Only because you never ran a hit on me, but if you recall, I was stabbed, blown up, run over and thrown out of a plane.' He remembered Iva's face when she'd seen the plethora of scars that criss-crossed his body. He'd explained them away with parkour. *He couldn't have got a medical student to believe that. She would have seen through the lie straight away.*

'Sounds like you were the secret agent, not me.' Jester burst out laughing, but was soon serious again. 'That's not good, Stan. I'll keep an ear out for who photographed you.' He shook his head, then checked how the side parting in his black hair was sitting with a brusque gesture.

'He said something about *your type*. Which probably means he knows us. Our curse.'

'If he classed you as harmless, and let you live, that must mean that, conversely, he is taking action against other people, to eliminate them, insofar as he can.' Jester looked worried.

The smartphone made a noise.

'Ah, seek and ye shall find.' Jester's eyebrows moved upwards as he read the result. 'Uh oh!' He held the screen so that Konstantin could take a look. 'Was *that* the revolver? Would fit with the man you described, Stan. Very old school.'

The photo showed a LeMat cap-and-ball revolver, originally designed in New Orleans in 1856 by Colonel Jean Alexandre François LeMat and General Pierre Gustave Toutant Beauregard. Nine shots could be stored in the cylinder, and the cylinder axis formed a second barrel, which the shooter could use to fire a round of buckshot at his enemies. *Perfect for close combat.*

Later models had a calibre of eleven millimetres, which explained the large hole in Konstantin's leg and the loud report the revolver had made. At least the unusual size for a handgun wound had protected him from questions; nobody had informed the police, which was policy for gunshot wounds. 'Yes, in terms of the basic design, it fits,' he said, hating it when Chester used the abbreviated version of his name. 'But the revolver the stranger used looked much more modern.'

'Maybe a freak who built his own or had one made.' Jester pointed at the information underneath the photo. 'That kind of thing isn't produced these days. He must have got his hands on the individual pieces somewhere or knows somebody who makes them. For example, there's a gunsmith in Suhl who I'm sure could produce this kind of thing. I'll keep my ear to the ground. We'll get him.' He put away the all-powerful, flashy mobile. 'And I'm very excited about his *file*.'

'But that's not why you wanted to speak to me.'

'No, it's not.' He looked at the watch on his left wrist, an expensive analogue model that must have cost several thousand euro. 'If I didn't need to get back to the Queen, I would definitely wait until they kicked you out, and we'd go to Mephisto for a cocktail.' He cleared his throat.

'What is it then, for God's sake? Don't keep me in such suspense. We saw each other in Paris. Does that have anything to do with it?'

'I ... have a job for you,' he said quickly, as though the words pained him.

Konstantin burst out laughing. 'You're joking!'

'Not like the ones you used to do. You're to help me ... catch someone who is causing me huge problems at the moment, Stan. Me and the whole world.'

'You have the power of the whole of MI6 at your disposal and you want me to look for someone? That must mean you really do have problems,' Konstantin concluded. 'And please don't say *Stan*. That name belongs to the past.'

'MI6 doesn't know anything about *us*. So you're much better suited to the pursuit.' He slid the chair closer to the bed. 'You think how—'

Konstantin's decision had already been made. 'No.'

'Please listen properly to what—'

'Jester, *no!*'

'Paris-Charles de Gaulle, 800,' he cried out, staccato. 'One of them was your Lilou de Girardin.'

Konstantin stopped short. '*That's* why you were there!'

His friend nodded glumly. 'Of course, officially it was because of the Britons on board the airbus. But I guessed there had to be a reason other than the poisonous gas that's meant to have caused the tragedy.' He took the smartphone out again and held it out to Konstantin once more.

An inconspicuous, pale-skinned man wearing Western clothes that looked too big for him appeared on the screen. The photo had been taken at a funfair; the man was standing in front of a mechanical bull and grinning. The hat had been tipped back so that it touched his neck and short blond hair peeked out from underneath; below it said in white letters: *BENT ARCTANDER. Picture #23, 13 March 2011, 15.32, Liverpool.*

The man looked harmless. But Konstantin knew that appearances didn't mean a thing, especially when it came to people like him. 'Why did he kill them all?' He didn't understand. 'And why on a plane? He must have been prepared to be seriously injured.'

Jester sighed. 'It's my fault.'

'How so? Since when are you royal commissioner of mass murder?' Konstantin's voice was sharp. That was the exact reason he had got out: too much death, too much pain. 'MI6 *have* become radical all of a sudden.'

'Arctander was one of mine. I wanted to help him learn control, but it wasn't happening quickly enough for him and so he cleared off. Now he's afraid of me because he knows that I have to stop him. One way or another.'

Konstantin knew the Torpor's Men, which Jester had belonged to for many years and whose leadership he now held: an association for men and women whose goal was to gain control over their curse and to live a normal life. Jester and his group embraced a particular moral standpoint, which was not necessarily to be taken for granted among Death Sleepers, and used their abilities to fight criminals whom the normal judicial process had conceded defeat on: they killed these people in a targeted way.

'800 dead. Why did he—'

'He can't control it.'

Konstantin snorted dismissively. 'There's coffee, guarana, Hello-Awake pills, amphetamines, meditation . . . He couldn't have used any of those to prevent accidents like that?'

'Arctander is . . . narcoleptic.' Jester clapped his hands once and rubbed them together nervously. 'Sometimes he just falls asleep. The more stress he's under the more likely it is.'

Bloody hell. Finally, Konstantin understood the point of the visit. 'If you're hunting him down and he notices, he'll have another attack and cause the next mass killing.' Arctander probably knew the members of the Torpor's Men, was aware of Jester's contacts in MI6 and saw everyone as a potential pursuer.

'Exactly. Since he did a runner, he's been travelling all over, trying to shake us off. It went wrong on the return flight from New York. Seriously wrong.'

'And then he went to the hotel to kill the last survivor

too?' Konstantin considered that unlikely and could see from Jester's face that he did too. 'No?'

'No. No idea who killed the Italian and his guards. I'm betting the mafia. As a ruthless estate agent Tremante didn't have all that many friends. He was stabbed to death with a long, thin object through the ear. His guards died from stab wounds to the back of the neck, likely the same weapon. Sounds very much like a classic vendetta.'

'Maybe Arctander was on Tremante's trail and the murderer completed his mission?'

'Don't think so. Arctander is a reckless idiot, but he's no hitman. He was simply sitting on the plane. Tremante told me during questioning, quite off-hand, that he had been given a viciously strong coffee that was meant for another passenger.' Jester put his fingertips together. 'I imagine Arctander ordered that coffee.'

'He wanted to stop himself falling asleep.' That made him a little more likeable in Konstantin's eyes, even if it was unbelievably stupid to get on a plane as an inexperienced Death Sleeper. The news reports demonstrated how that had finished. *A distraught, pitiful guy who felt like everyone was following him.*

'That's right.'

'He travels under a pseudonym I take it?'

Jester looked more and more miserable. 'Yes. Because he was in the Torpor's Men, he got the usual: fake passports, log-in details for bank accounts, locker numbers for emergencies. That makes it difficult to get him.'

Konstantin found that he understood the misery his friend was in, as well as Arctander: the nightmare in cowboy gear who had been released on the world. He looked at the innocent face of the fugitive beaming so happily from the screen. 'He's disappeared again?'

'Yes. He has. I was able to prevent the authorities finding out about him. Officially speaking, he was never on board.' Jester's look became insistent and pleading. 'You know that his powers increase every time he falls asleep, and he constantly falls asleep. The danger he poses is already incalculable. We have to find him before he becomes so powerful that he has the same effect as an atom bomb.'

'Have you found out what restrictions there are on his powers?' Jester tilted his head to one side and seemed to be steeling himself inwardly before saying anything. That was a good enough answer for Konstantin. 'The same as me!'

'Well, well. You understand why I need to ask you for help, old boy? You played cat and mouse with us way back when. We never caught you, nobody could take you out. Not even the Indians and that's an unbelievable honour. You're gifted like nobody else when it comes to keeping a low profile. None of us can understand better than you how Arctander, as the hunted person, thinks – what he's planning, what hiding places might be possible. We have to find him, Konstantin! Besides, we can approach him without dying, should he have an attack.' Jester grabbed his shoulders with both hands and squeezed. 'If he's hanging around in a big city and falls asleep on a rooftop or . . . with an open window, thousands could die because of him! Thousands!'

Konstantin was silent. They'd known each other a long time; they'd clashed over many assignments and missions until rivalry became friendship. The man from MI6 and the killer for a worthy cause. He thought about Iva and the man trailing him with the camera and the revolver. 'First, I need to make sure that Iva will not be in any danger from this guy who shot me in the leg,' he answered quietly.

'Iva? Your cat?'

'My—' Konstantin didn't know what to call her. There was no appropriate name for their relationship status. 'A woman who means a lot to me. He followed me and knows where she lives.' He swallowed.

'I'm sure the guy won't touch her, Konstantin! Please help me catch Bent Arctander and take him off the streets.'

Konstantin's expression hardened. He waved his friend's hands off. 'She's the love of my life. I can't put her in danger.'

'You're doing that already by meeting up with her,' retorted Jester and threw his arms in the air. 'I do understand, but what if Arctander is in Leipzig right now and drops off to sleep thanks to his narcolepsy? If he's sitting on a tram that doesn't have all its windows closed? It would unleash deaths of biblical proportions, and it's possible that Iva would be one of the victims. Just like that, without you being able to do anything about it.'

Konstantin struggled to find the right words. 'I don't want to any more, Jester,' he whispered. 'I want all of that shit to be behind me. Not to have Death around me any more. That's why I got out. And I just want to lie down, close my eyes and fall asleep. In a meadow in the sunshine, on a lounger at the pool, on the deck of the *Vanitas*. When and where I want. And more than anything, next to the woman I love.'

'That's what most of us want, old boy.' He smiled weakly, knowingly. 'But that's not the way it goes.' Jester put a hand on his shoulder. 'We can't enter into a pact with the Grim Reaper. I've already tried.'

'*You?*' Konstantin couldn't help the incredulity in his voice.

'Well, thanks very much. Now I don't feel like a callous arsehole.' Jester pressed the call bell on the control panel next to the bed and straightened his jacket.

'What are you up to?'

'I'm thirsty. The staff can bring us something to drink.' When the door opened and a young student nurse came in, he nodded at her in a friendly way. 'Hello, Sister Moni,' he said in German. 'Would you be so kind as to arrange two coffees for us?' His smile oozed charm and she soon promised to bring what he wanted. When she was gone, Jester turned back to Konstantin. 'So I will tell you what I've found out about Death from my investigations, but I'm warning you: they're just a few neat theories and nothing much to go on. Afterwards I'll be off and will send you everything on Arctander by email, in case you change your mind. And you *will*. You're a man with a sense of responsibility.' He was becoming serious.

The boyish, clowning mode that could wrap everyone around his little finger was switched off.

Nurse Moni came in with two coffees, having also rustled up biscuits, which she presented on their own plate. She vanished again quickly.

Konstantin could barely control his curiosity. Were Jester's theories worth anything?

VI

Lo! Death has reared himself a throne
In a strange city lying alone
Far down within the dim west,
Where the good and the bad and the worst and the best
Have gone to their eternal rest
[...]
So blend the turrets and shadows there
That all seem pendulous in air,
While from a proud tower in the town
Death looks gigantically down.

'The City in the Sea', Edgar Allan Poe

Minsk, Belarus

The alarm rang out through the Life Institute, ordering the employees to proceed to the shelter below ground level immediately. This was not a drill, this was an emergency.

Kristen noticed the oddity of the situation straight away on the way down: an extraordinary tension hung in the air. Air that was filled with a slightly sweet smell reminiscent of warm maize.

Kristen ran down the stairs, typed the code into the electronic keypad next to the door to the seventh floor and pushed it open.

The ward was in the grip of chaos. People were rushing through the corridors in a panic. White-coated men and women crammed themselves together in front of the lifts, or fled in the direction from which Kristen had come, to escape downstairs via the staircase.

'Out of the way!' Kristen struggled against the current to reach Patient 22 before he ruined this project. She couldn't allow that to happen! Because of her father and above all because of Eugen.

Hardly any of the people escaping even knew why they had to get themselves to safety.

Just a handful of high-ranking specialists knew the real reason for the alarm. Most of the staff presumed it was a leaked bacterium or virus, a fire, or problems with something that wasn't meant for the general public.

The fact that a Death Sleeper was transitioning between an artificial coma into sleep, and was thereby attracting Death to him, was not something they suspected.

As soon as a Death Sleeper switched into the dangerous sleep phase, he started giving off theta waves. It was probably these waves that the Grim Reaper reacted to, as though they were a terrifyingly loud alarm. He immediately looked for the source to silence and exterminate them. Since he couldn't see them clearly, he lashed out wildly. Whatever he struck, died. Without exception. Or at least that's how Kristen had always imagined the process.

'Let me through!' Kristen had almost reached the door

with the sign 22 and gave a nurse who didn't get out of the way quickly enough a punch that flung her sideways into the wall.

The smell of warm maize was getting stronger, becoming pervasive. Nausea-inducing. The signs for the proximity of Death varied from Death Sleeper to Death Sleeper; sometimes it was a rustle, sometimes a smell; as individual as the person who summoned Death.

Kristen pushed the door open and stormed into Patient 22's room.

A bald young man lay there, attached to monitoring equipment cables, to the EEG, linked up to infusion tubes and catheters. His naked, emaciated upper body was covered in scars where failing organs had been removed and replaced with new ones; fresh markings announced new incisions. The skin was dyed dark orange in some places due to the constant use of antiseptic. A continuous horizontal line ran across his forehead and bald skull.

He was a pitiful sight, but that was not the problem. On the floor around him lay three nurses and Doctor Dranski. By his hand, a primed syringe full of the anaesthetic that would force the patient back into harmless deep sleep lay broken. The machine that could change brainwaves using transcranial magnetic stimulation was on the wall, but Kristen didn't know how to work it. It stank of concentrated, cooked maize, and the smell was suffocating. Death was already here and was carrying out his work as he had done for millions of years. No human being could get into this room now. Their heart would stop and they would collapse on the threshold – apart from her.

'Hey! Wake up! Get up!' Kristen shook Patient 22 by the shoulder to wake him.

The young man's eyes remained closed, his breathing slow, harsh and noisy. The delta waves would have almost entirely been replaced by theta waves.

It suddenly got quieter in the corridor outside the room, the sound of screams only coming from far away now. Death was coming for the people room by room, and walls wouldn't save anyone. Ceilings and floors couldn't stop the all-powerful Reaper.

'Get up, you bastard!' Kristen hit the patient in the face over and over again, but the sedatives were still working. Soon there would be no way he was going to wake up.

The EEG indicated with a low beep that the transition to the theta wave zone would be complete in a few seconds. The waves were stabilising in the critical zone, the frequency of the oscillations was around five hertz.

Kristen had to act now, even if it meant losing one of her best experimental subjects. She couldn't afford international scrutiny or headlines. There would be both of these things if she hesitated now. And since 22 couldn't be woken . . .

'Bloody hell!' She leaned over him and laid her forehead against his, then activated her unique talent: the gift of insomnia.

She felt a tingle across the bridge of her nose. The ache spread through her entire skull. Even behind her eyes she could feel the pricking of millions of tiny ants swarming around in her head and nipping at her brain with their pincers.

She didn't know exactly how it worked, but ever since her brain had started to show the first symptoms of illness, she had been able to produce theta waves even while awake. This didn't summon Death – she still only did that when she actually slept – but through some coincidence, she'd found out that if her theta waves were connected to a Death Sleeper's waves, they were transferred and changed. Thus she made herself visible to Death, giving the Grim Reaper a target to attack those detested people who would otherwise slip out of his grasp.

And Death never missed an opportunity like that.

The pricking of a thousand needles in Kristen's head was getting worse. The smell of maize became so repulsively overwhelming that she was in danger of throwing up. It felt as though a thousand needles were pricking on her head. She groaned.

The patient screamed out, spraying her with droplets of saliva. He desperately tried to free himself from her grip, his vital signs abruptly shooting up to unsafe levels. The man sensed his death was imminent. A *real* and irreversible death.

Hot, sweaty and stale, his scream surged over Kristen.

She clasped his bald head and maintained the contact, which was not easy, because in his panic the patient had unbridled strength, despite his wasted muscles, despite his state of mind. His arms flailed and cramp ran through his withered body. Kristen stayed there, forehead to forehead.

And finally came the comforting sound of mechanical whistling. Cardiac arrest. Dead.

Thus the life of the Death Sleeper ended before Death could begin to happen on a large scale. Kristen let Death take the life it had been craving.

Panting, she let go of Patient 22's head and vomited on

the body. Tears ran down her cheeks and she could barely breathe. It was only after the third bout of nausea that she managed to bring herself under control.

Coughing, she staggered into the corridor to check how far Death had managed to rampage among the unsuspecting people.

The bodies lay in the corridor and in tight clumps at the emergency exit, and between lift doors that impassively kept trying to close, opening and coming together, over and over again. People were buried underneath overturned stretchers, surrounded by the debris of scattered files, dropped laptops and smashed bottles of samples and chemicals.

Kristen leaned against the doorframe and spat on the floor to get rid of the horrible taste in her mouth. She didn't have the strength to shout as loudly as Patient 22. So much potential, all just wiped out. Even if the fallen looked like they were sleeping, they and everything that they might yet have achieved here, had been destroyed.

Kristen could tell from a glance into the glassed-in hospital room on the seventh floor that the rest of the Death Sleeper subjects were still alive, while their beds were surrounded by just as many dead bodies as 22's. Invisible to Death and therefore spared.

Damn it! This was the kind of accident she had wanted to avoid at all costs.

But the mistake was not Kristen's. The team who were meant to monitor the EEG, under strict orders not to let the man wake up out of the coma and to keep the brainwaves in the delta zone, had failed. Not her.

Figures came through the emergency exit wearing white

protective suits as though they had to protect themselves from a deadly virus. They probably actually thought that was what was going on.

'Mrs von Windau,' one of them called out to her. 'Everything okay?'

What could she say? 'I'm okay. Just a bit of nausea.' Kristen coughed. 'Seems to have been a gas leak. I was lucky that the air conditioning had already absorbed most of it.' She walked towards the men. 'Where is Professor Smyrnikov?'

'In the basement. He says we're to bring you to him and then come back up here and clean up,' answered the man, taking her supportively by the upper arm.

Kristen shook him off. 'No need. Start here straight away.'

Dazed, and with a pounding headache, she walked down the stairs, tossing back two of her stimulant pills as she did so. She practically missed Doctor Willers' corpse. She was lying, eyes wide open, on the stairs on the seventh floor, one hand to her throat, the other clawing at her left breast, as though she had tried to rip Death out of her heart.

'Shit,' murmured a depressed Kristen. This was much worse than the loss of Patient 22. She urgently needed to speak to Smyrnikov and discuss what was to be done from now on. This kind of thing could not happen again. Money could buy you a lot, not least the hugely expensive fitting out of the institute, but a luminary like Willers was irreplaceable.

Her team's drop-out rate was far too high.

'The responsibility for what happened rests entirely with Willers. 22 was her patient. She assured me she had everything under control.' Smyrnikov was sitting with Kristen in a state-of-the-art conference room in the basement, yet again refusing to accept any of the blame.

'I don't care. It shouldn't have happened.' She held up 22's medical notes, which recorded the course of the catastrophe in minute detail. 'First, somebody administered the wrong drug to him, so that he passed into conventional sleep, and then nobody treated him with the Brainwaver.' She angrily shook her head. 'The incident could easily have been prevented.'

'Not my area.' The professor appeared unfazed.

'Don't act the know-it-all here,' Kristen hissed at him. She put her feet up and looked at the wall, massaging the bridge of her nose to relieve the pain behind it. The nausea had given way to exhaustion. She had already taken amphetamines, but the stimulants' effects left much to be desired. At least the irritating stutter hadn't come back. It would have rather reduced the impact of her tirade.

The room fell silent.

Kristen thought of how promising Patient 22 had been. Strictly speaking, he had been comprised of two main parts.

The body came from a healthy young man, whom she had discovered when passing through a Russian garrison town and whose name she'd forgotten. She'd sedated him, transported him to Minsk and delivered him into Doctor Willers' hands: the usual routine for a body donor. The team of doctors would then examine their heart and kidneys and prepare them for the transplant.

After the Russian, Kristen had captured Mr Georg Dickens, an American who was a member of the Deathslumberers and had a reputation for being very powerful. His abduction had been similar to the recipient's, just with more precautions:

the deepest coma-like sedation, so that there was no way he would sleep and attract the Grim Reaper.

In her experiments with Death Sleepers, Kristen used various methods to achieve her goal – sometimes it was the transplantation of the entire head, which was aesthetically very unappealing, but was much easier to pull off than method number two: transplanting the brain into another recipient.

Smyrnikov, Willers and their teams tested where the biggest problems lay in each of the procedures and how the risks could be reduced.

The goal was of course to develop a safe implementation of method two, so that the procedure became as easy as removing an appendix. But perfecting method number one and using it as a stepping stone to number two was actually more promising. Until D-Day.

Dickens was one of a number of people who had had their cerebrum transplanted. Kristen had watched as Dickens' brain was transferred into the Russian's skull. Patient 22 was born. From the first incision, everything had gone well, from clipping off the veins to attaching them inside the recipient's head. And all of this happened during a procedure that most doctors would dismiss as impossible.

They had kept Patient 22 in an artificial coma afterwards to give the rest of his body time to heal using the targeted introduction of stem cells. And of course, to get used to the new brain. Dickens had felt fine in the Russian, and there had been no issues with infection. Complications had only cropped up while they had been trying to regulate the organ function. They'd had to remove a kidney, and had fitted him with a diaphragmatic pacemaker to ensure independent breathing. After that Patient 22 was on the road to recovery.

And now *this!*

At least the incident had shown that Death Sleepers didn't lose their powers when their brains were transplanted. That it had to happen to Dickens was particularly annoying, however. As today had confirmed, his reputation was well earned. His gift had no underlying restrictions. It had turned into an ugly problem with far-reaching consequences for the institute.

And, after all, the experiments were essentially about the issue of whether it was the soul that really made a person themselves.

Patient 22 had been the first case where they'd started to find real success. After the chemotherapy and the transplant they had treated him with embryonic stem cells, which is where the doctors had first seen signs of success. All previous attempts had had to be abandoned at an earlier stage.

Kristen was frustrated. She wasn't pursuing these schemes for herself. In fact there was a department in the institute dedicated to the therapeutic usage of stem cells in prion diseases. She was thinking about her son's future.

He wouldn't suffer from insomnia, she had already had a genetic test done to make sure of that, but she was certain that he would become a Death Sleeper too, like his grandfather and mother before him. However, he would be able to lead a better and perpetual life in different bodies, without the ordeal of old age and everything that might follow that for a Death Sleeper. Eugen would simply transfer his brain into a younger body every fifty years or sooner, just as he pleased. That's why method two had to become safer.

'We were on the brink of a huge breakthrough,' she muttered and threw two guarana-caffeine tablets into her coffee, stirred it and drank it in rapid little sips. 'We could have learned so much from Dickens.' Kristen was still angry, suddenly banging her fist on the table. 'And now he's dead.'

Smyrnikov was looking through numbers and notes on the tablet computer. 'You saved very good doctors with your intervention, Mrs von Windau. There was no other way.'

Kristen snorted. 'I killed my greatest hope because your incompetents forced me into it. If Death hadn't taken them, I would have.' She cursed the headache that was getting worse again because of the stimulants in her bloodstream. 'Has anything hit the news yet?'

The professor swiped around on his tablet and switched tabs. 'Nothing we need to worry about,' he replied. 'Just a short report about the mysterious deaths of some birds. A swarm of pigeons must have chosen the wrong moment to fly over the building. There are also two women on the other side of the institute who were feeling faint, but they're doing fine now. None of these incidents would oblige the authorities to launch a pseudo-investigation.'

'And the Internet?'

'The usual conspiracy theories, saying it's a poison gas test because the metro isn't far away. Two other theories involve the institute, but even those are harmless.' Smyrnikov appeared relaxed. 'You saved *us* bad publicity and *Minsk* a mass burial, Mrs von Windau.' He slid the tablet across to her with a list on it entitled 'Casualties'. 'It does look bad inside the institute though. I've already taken the liberty of noting down the names of people whom I'd like to approach.'

'Feel free. But this time there should be no delicate creatures like that Irishman. Please dispose of the casualties in our crematorium.'

'Most were single, no families, like we usually keep it. And their bogus jobs overseas can hold up to scrutiny, so that shouldn't be a problem.' Smyrnikov tapped two photographs. 'However, these two had wives. I'll feed the families the usual business about a car crash and get the bodies into suitable shape.'

'Excellent.'

'I should say, Mrs von Windau, that I cannot continue my research until the new staff arrive. Too many patients have lost their medical carers and ward doctors in the incident on ward seven. Of course I'm roughly up to speed, but the details . . .' He gave her an apologetic look.

Kristen forced herself to be silent; she imagined punching Smyrnikov's corpulent face. He didn't understand what was at stake: the time trickling through her fingers, her weakening mind, her fatal insomnia and a well-equipped house for her son. She didn't have a moment to lose and yet Smyrnikov was doing exactly that. 'Certainly, Professor. I understand,' she replied softly and coolly as she stood up. 'I a-a-am going to get going and search for a replacement for P-P-Patient 22 among the Death Sleepers.' The words got tangled up in her mouth.

'There are still two good donor bodies being stored in deep sleep, Mrs von Windau. We just need a brain to insert into them. Always prepared, as we used to say in the boy scouts.'

Kristen concentrated harder on what she was saying out loud to avoid going blank. 'Good. I'll probably be back once you've taught the new staff the ropes.'

They shook hands and Kristen left the conference room.

Her route took her along a sombre corridor and past doors leading to the control rooms for the lifts, to the generators, the air conditioning, the MRI and CT scanners. An electrical, clinical smell hung in the warm air and she was reminded of the overpowering smell of maize again.

She'd never come across that one. All Death Sleepers attracted Death as soon as they fell asleep and produced theta waves. But that's often where the similarities ended. There was barely any pattern to what came after that, apart from the death of the surrounding people.

'Maize,' she said quietly and shook her head, her brown hair whipping into her face, one strand tickling her nose. 'Why maize?' She felt sick at the thought of it. 'What was the Grim Reaper thinking of?'

To distract herself, she pondered how she would go about the search for the next candidate. It would take time because quite a few of the secret Death Sleeper organisations now knew that somebody was on the hunt for them and had therefore become cautious.

There were isolated rumours that she was connected to the disappearances of these men and women, but nobody could prove anything. If *what* she was getting up to with the missing people came out, she would be sunk.

Kristen stopped in front of a door with the word *Cryo* written on it.

She typed a code into the keypad next to the door, placed her right hand on the handle and pushed it down.

There were five tanks of different sizes in the room, all draped in blue plastic. Thick cables connected various sockets on their sides to another small room, where the data and surveillance hub was with its own power supply, triply guarded against power outages.

Kristen went to the closest tank with its different warnings written in English and in a Cyrillic script, not to switch anything off or alter anything. The inscription below said:

Friedrich Wenzeslaf Eugen Karol von Windau
Born: 1922
Died: —

She often came here to check on her father even though her visits were confined to standing in front of him and putting one hand on the tank's insulation. She began with a wordless prayer in which she begged for strength for his deep-frozen soul, which had already had to endure these conditions for ten years. 'Hello, Papa,' she whispered. Her right hand touched the blue plastic.

She could never tell him how much longer he would need to spend in the tank at a hundred degrees below zero, until she had found a cure for insomnia using stem cells. And he had wanted to see his grandson so much.

'Eugen is all grown up,' she reported, as though the stiff man, his brain frozen to its core and severely weakened by illness, could hear anything. 'He looks more like you all the time, especially around the chin. He's becoming a real von Windau. I'm looking forward to when you see him and he can give you a hug.' Her fingers stayed on the insulation. 'There's been a setback, as I'm sure you've realised, but Smyrnikov promised me that things will carry on as soon as he has reinforcements for his team. And I h-h-have to get on the road again.' She tapped the plastic twice, a gesture of farewell. 'See you soon, Papa.'

Kristen looked over at the other four tanks.

The two in the corner right at the back were empty and served as spares.

To the right of her father's tank stood the container with her name on it, which she only intended to use in an absolute emergency.

And to the left of that was the container waiting for Eugen.

She had invested her ex-husband's money wisely; she was prepared for failure – or rather for success that came too late – even if she didn't like thinking about it. There were experts in everything under the sun, in death as well as life. She had hired both kinds of expert for the time after her conscious existence. Smyrnikov would keep researching until he had found a safe procedure for transplanting the brain and a cure for insomnia. And in the meantime the cryo experts would take care of her body – and if necessary her son's too.

Kristen pushed this awful, cruel thought away, because she firmly believed she would be successful. At any cost.

She just needed the grey cells of a Death Sleeper, in the most literal sense.

Leipzig, Germany

Jester sipped his hospital coffee and made a face. 'You can tell this concoction is meant to be as inoffensive as possible,' he commented, and looked at Konstantin. 'What is it?'

'I'm waiting. For the information you promised me.' He was still surprised that his friend had researched Death. Konstantin had thought that Jester enjoyed his life as a Death Sleeper, or at least had accepted it, because he knew his curse and kept it under control. And he made use of it, as Konstantin had done, to get rid of the bad guys. Jester had done it for the government, Konstantin for the money.

'Well.' Jester cleared his throat. 'Love spares nobody, not even harbingers of death. It hurts that much more if that happens. Sometimes I think,' he lowered his gaze and considered the dark brown colour of his coffee, 'that Death's strongest weapon is love.'

Konstantin didn't reply. He realised his friend's cheeriness hadn't disappeared for no reason. *Whoa!*

'As unlikely as it might seem to you,' he said with a sigh, 'I fell in love years ago. With all that that entails, except that I didn't dare to start a life with her. *One* careless night and the Grim Reaper would have pounced on her and killed her while I slept quietly next to her. Never!'

Konstantin nodded. *How well he understood!*

'I hoped there might be an opportunity to do a deal with Death.' He leaned forwards, rested his elbows on his knees and held the cup with both hands. 'Most of us believe that he can't see us, but that he knows there are people who can defy his omnipotence. We only draw him towards us in our sleep, leaving a trail for him to follow and annihilate all living things around us. Out of revenge and hatred, to hurt us. Something like that.'

Konstantin nodded. He had spent many a night with his friend, philosophising about what the curse was all about, and what caused it, on different continents, in different races. As always, they never got beyond theories and opinions.

'I began to look for written information on death. In archives no normal citizen would ever have access to.' Jester's voice had deepened, becoming more mysterious. 'In the end I found a clue in art.'

'Please, no conspiracy theories à la *The Da Vinci Code* or anything like that,' said Konstantin under his breath.

'No. No conspiracy. But clues, old boy.' Jester attempted a weak smile. 'You're sitting on it. Now. In the broadest sense.'

'Me?'

'Not right now, but you will be as soon as you're out of hospital.' He finished his coffee, but kept the cup in his hands.

Konstantin reflected and figured out that he meant his boat. 'What does the *Vanitas* have to do with it?'

'The *motif* of Vanitas, not your boat. The symbol of transience, of the pointlessness of human life, and vanity,' Jester lectured. 'The masters of the Baroque immortalised certain symbols of decay in their paintings over and over again. When I looked at it more closely, I stumbled across a legend. The legend of the Grim Reaper's Stones.'

Grim Reaper's Stones. Images conjured themselves up in Konstantin's mind's eye almost immediately: a heavy millstone that could bury someone beneath it, rocks by the wayside that warned people about dangerous places where Death particularly liked to lurk. He was fascinated by Jester's story. *How long has he known about this?*

The British man ran his hands over his side parting again. 'I hardly knew what to search for and then I found lots of clues, mainly in wills and testaments. Because I soon understood *what* I had to keep an eye out for, I found it easy to follow the trail of these stones into the present day.'

Konstantin hung on every word that sprang from the lips of the man opposite him. *Had he not emphasised that he had not been successful?*

'These items are also called the Grim Reaper's Rings, Deathgems, Mortality Amulets or Vanitas Lockets, and one known as a *Gevatterstein* in German or a *Gemme Mortelle* in French. These terms refer to pieces of jewellery that supposedly attract Death. They usually have a particular precious stone and a Vanitas symbol.' Jester put his cup down on the small table next to Konstantin's bed. 'You also find these in old paintings and illustrations, and if you have an eye for symbolism you'll start seeing them almost everywhere.'

'You got your hands on some of these pieces of jewellery!'

'Well deduced. Congratulations.' Jester made a show of saluting Konstantin. 'I put together a whole collection to check the truth of the legends that grew up around the individual pieces of jewellery.'

'What did you want with rings that attract Death? You only need to fall asleep to do that.'

'I suspected they would work differently for a Death Sleeper.'

'I don't get it.'

Jester took the jug of mineral water, poured some into his cup and drank. 'I met an old Death Sleeper, an Indian man. He told me a fairy tale about Kali giving jewellery as gifts, to make our kind visible to her. The stones, or the piece of jewellery as such, act as beacons for the goddess. It's how she sees us and is soothed because she can take us any time. Like a normal person. Mortal.'

'And we could fall asleep without worrying!' To Konstantin, Kali was just another term for Death. One of his many personifications, although the Grim Reaper never appeared in one fixed form, especially not as a hooded man with a scythe; he and Jester had confirmed that in a few experiments. For Death Sleepers, he manifested himself in sounds and smells. 'Fall asleep, what bliss! Wherever, whenever.' He looked gleefully at Jester. *Beside Iva!* But the seriousness on his friend's face dampened his euphoria. 'Please don't tell me it's just a fairy tale.'

'The Indian man also told me that the goddess gets furious if you ever take the amulet off again. Breaking the pact with her like this is apparently the worst thing you can do, and just makes her rampage all the more furiously. Who knows if that's true?' He looked out the window. 'I liked that approach. I formulated a theory that some Death Sleepers didn't even know what they were or what kind of jewellery they were wearing until they were taken by Death. Imagine how funny Death must find it, if you inadvertently make yourself visible to him and proudly wear your new brilliant gem on a ring.'

'Or else you know what the jewellery does and give it to your enemies on purpose.' Konstantin grinned.

Jester laughed quietly. 'I wore them *all*, to see what would happen. Whether he would . . . materialise or I would notice a smell. A noise. Some kind of sign.' He sighed again. 'I looked like an out and out queen: a million rings and medallions and brooches. But nothing happened. He didn't come looking for me.'

'How long did you wear them for?'

'A few weeks. After everything I've got up to and the

number of times I've teased him by deliberately falling asleep all the time, he should have come swooping down to slash me to pieces with his scythe, to use a cliché.' He shrugged. 'As you can see, old boy, I'm sitting here. Alive.'

It gradually dawned on Konstantin that his friend had just admitted to attempting suicide. *Out of despair? Love? Because of the hopelessness of their situation?*

'I myself haven't believed in the fairy tale since then.' Jester stood up. 'It's just a story I pinned my hopes on, the way small children believe in star money. Or Cockayne.' He picked an imaginary hair off his suit. 'Storytime is over. It was nothing more than a ridiculous hope.' Releasing his thumb and forefinger, he dropped the imaginary hair. 'It's gone now. And since then I've been making the most of what I am. By annihilating arseholes that are getting on everyone's tits, or hunting Death Sleepers causing harm with their gift.' He tapped his forehead and pointed at Konstantin. 'Think about Bent Arctander. Don't let me hunt alone. You are the only person who can truly help me. The man who persistently made a fool of the Torpor's Men.'

Konstantin couldn't shake off Jester's story. 'Did that happen a long time ago? Your research and experiments I mean?'

'Oh, a very long time ago.'

'Do you still have everything? The documents and—'

'The jewellery? No. I sold them at Tiffany's. Got myself a tidy sum out of it. More than I'd had to pay.' Jester threw him a warning look. 'You don't want to chase after the same ghost I did, do you? There's no point, pal. I told you all that to scare you off, not to spur you on.'

Konstantin's thoughts were still revolving round the legend of Kali and her gifts. He barely listened to Jester's words. *It would be wonderful if there were a tiny little grain of truth in it. Maybe I'll find something he missed?* 'Do me a favour and send me what you've found out.' He raised one hand. 'Make sure to send me everything, I'll read through at my leisure and do some research myself. In return I'll help you in the search for Arctander.'

Jester's expression brightened and they shook on it. 'Good suggestion! Absolutely marvellous suggestion! You'll get every single letter of the nonsense. But don't waste too much time on it. Better to think about Arctander and all that he could be getting up to.' He shook his friend's hand again. 'I have to get back to London. The Queen has the tea waiting.' Jester looked over to the coffee cup, where a weak brownish residue had formed on the porcelain and shook himself. 'I never, ever, *ever* want to have to drink that again. And get well soon. As soon as I've found out anything about the revolver I'll send you that too.' He left the room.

Konstantin lay down on the bed and looked out the window at the birds bobbing in the air. Their twittering came through the glass softly.

And I christen my boat Vanitas. *As if I'd known.*

He could barely wait to read Jester's research about the pieces of jewellery and to draw his own conclusions. He had spent long nights concocting his own theories on how you could do a deal with the Grim Reaper so that the madness ended without him biting the dust himself. He hadn't had any luck.

He wanted to look for things that Jester might have missed, despite all his MI6 training.

He considered himself superior to his friend in all things intuition, and he wanted to exploit that, as he had done to escape him and his men way back when.

What if he just needed to think along different lines? If there were stones that attracted Death, maybe there were also some that repelled him. A kind of protective stone, that guarded against Death's clutches? *It would be enough to have Iva protected at least*, he reflected. *Or perhaps a stone or symbol that makes it possible to speak to Death and make a pact.* His excitement grew with every heartbeat. He wanted to begin a normal life with Iva. *That* was his future!

Yet, gradually the logical part of his mind weighed in. Konstantin realised that he was acting irrationally. He was in danger of accepting fairy tales as fact. In theory, he could also set about searching for the Grail. Jester had warned him against that exact thing.

He breathed heavily, in, then out. *Calm down. I've got to approach this thing sensibly. I should take the fairy tales as a basis for a hypothesis and I have to think about how to prove or disprove this hypothesis.*

Besides, Bent Arctander was more important for starters, the narcoleptic and highly volatile Death Sleeper. Jester was right. *He couldn't just be left to walk around unchecked.*

Konstantin swung himself out of bed in the scrubs he'd borrowed from a nurse, groaning as a sharp pain reminded him of the injury to his leg, and hobbled to the cupboard where his bloodied trousers lay in a plastic bag. Konstantin discharged himself to go back to his houseboat where his computer was waiting: the starting point for his investigations into death, the stones and Arctander.

As he got into the lift, defying Sister Moni's protests, Jester's downcast face and words came into his mind: 'Death's strongest weapon is love.'

Konstantin had forgotten to ask what had happened with Jester's relationship.

VII

The taste of death
is on my tongue.
I sense something
that is not of this world.

Final words attributed to Wolfgang Amadeus
Mozart, who died on 5 December 1791

Leipzig, Germany

Konstantin was sitting on the Number 1 tram travelling around Leipzig's city centre in the evening light, dressed in white scrub trousers and his black polo shirt; his right trainer was stiff with dried blood.

His mobile was working again; he'd dried it in the hospital under a hand dryer. Yet he did not call Iva. He still couldn't think of anything that would help him live down his fleeing her house and his bizarre story. Konstantin looked down at where the gunshot wounds were hidden underneath trouser material and dressing, and at the filthy trainer. *I would have been better off staying with her and keeping my mouth shut.*

His stop, Clara-Zetkin-Park, was approaching and he got

up from the disabled seat, hobbled to the exit and swung himself out rather nimbly. The wound in his leg had been treated, but it still hurt, throbbed, pulsed and did its best to remind him of his injury. Not being visible to Death did not mean never getting ill or healing magically. Being a Death Sleeper didn't really have any advantages, Konstantin felt.

Even the immortality was a disadvantage.

He remembered an assignment where, under orders from a widow, he was to take out a wealthy British politician. Jester's people had taken over the man's security at the time. Konstantin and the personal security team had clashed and MI6 had made use of its entire arsenal of weapons, from automatic pistols to explosives, to save the corrupt politician from Konstantin. In the middle of all this, Stella, a member of the Torpor's Men, got caught in a petrol flash fire: sixty per cent burns on her skin, eyes scorched and blind, her right leg had been nothing more than a charred piece of flesh – and yet Stella's heart was still pumping relentlessly and keeping her alive, despite the pain, despite the fact that her body could not possibly recover. Jester had taken her to a remote spot and freed her from her bodily pain. Her soul was probably still waiting for deliverance.

I'll be spared that. He limped along Käthe Kolwitz Street. He had placed the plastic bag with his things in it over his shoulder, so that it didn't accidentally knock against his wounds. With his lopsided walk, he felt like an old sea dog on shore leave.

Despite the lateness of the hour, there was a summery warmth to the weather. People were sitting in the outdoor areas of the cafés nearby, enjoying good food, talking over a dark beer or absinthe.

Konstantin was not in the mood for that.

He had to have a serious, difficult conversation with the woman he loved, with all his body and soul. The thought of it going wrong, of not winning her back, gave him cold hands and an ache in his stomach area. He felt unparalleled fear.

Konstantin walked to the rowing club's jetty in the branch of the Elster mill canal where he had moored his speedboat. He untied the ropes and thought about how he would get up and over the upright metal poles with his injured leg. *Maybe I could get the tram to the lake for once?*

'I-i-it's really not very easy to find you,' said a woman's voice behind him. 'But I thought to myself, *I'll find h-h-him at his boat sooner or later.*'

Konstantin turned around slowly, the bag still over one shoulder. *Too many people were taking an interest in him recently.*

He was facing a good-looking woman in her early thirties wearing a flowing designer summer dress. The effect was stunning; the light grey emphasised her burnished brown hair, which was cut short but was still long enough for a clip at the back. Konstantin liked the handle end of the hairpin, which was stuck through a leather loop and held a small brown plait in place: it was a grinning skull, so skilfully crafted that the motif only became clear on a third glance. 'So, who let slip that I have a boat and a mooring spot?'

'Your s-s-secretary. After I'd been to the hospital and they told me that you'd gone, I expected you to be here. Or on your houseboat.' She smiled and held out her hand to him. 'I'm Sophie Kronau and I have a mission for you, Mr Korff. Please f-f-forgive my stutter. It's the e-e-excitement.'

Konstantin found it strange that the woman had been waiting for him so late by the pier rather than just waiting until he was back in the office. Either the issue was pressing – or there was some other reason behind it entirely.

So he remained cautious as he took her hand and shook it; he could see ankhs, Egyptian crosses, tattooed on the inside of her wrist and on the inside of her upper arm. The symbol of immortality. 'Please do come in to Ars Moriendi tomorrow. My business hours are over for today.' He wanted to get onto the *Vanitas* quickly, change his clothes and start investigating.

Sophie made no move to leave. 'That's what your secretary s-s-said too, but it is very u-u-urgent. You ought to come with me today.' She looked down at him, from the dirty polo shirt to the scrubs trousers and the crusted shoe. 'But maybe you'll pack a few things first so that you can g-g-get changed . . . and get through s-s-security at the airport.'

He couldn't quite place her accent with its gently rolled Rs, it reminded him of the Banat dialect of German. 'If I understand correctly, I'm to come with you right now? To do *what?*'

'I hear y-y-you are the best thanatologist in Europe.' Sophie seemed to be irritated by her own stutter and was avoiding his eye. She rummaged in her little handbag and took out a little vial of tablets, opened it, shook two tablets out onto her hand and tossed them into her mouth with a practised gesture. 'Sorry. I-I-I'll feel better in a second.'

Konstantin had never heard of a pill for stuttering before. The tablets were probably a psychological trick from therapy to help tackle the speech impediment. 'I'm sorry, but Mrs Kawatzki should have told you straight away that I'm booked up for the next few days. And with an injured leg I can hardly travel anyway. Ask my colleague, Mr Kuckelkorn in Cologne. He's in the telephone book. Please excuse me.' He reached out to the handrail to climb down the first rungs and onto his boat.

'Please! It will just be a day's work for you. My brother was hit by a tram and my family want to say goodbye. I'm positive that nobody else but you can make it so that my brother looks like my brother again.' She looked imploringly at him, yet something in her expression was a little bit off. There was a lack of emotion in her eyes. An amateur actress.

Konstantin became wary. *Get out of here.* 'I'm sorry, Ms Kronau. I have things to do.'

'50,000 euro, Mr Korff. First-class return flights, five-star hotel inclusive.'

'No hard feelings, but good night.' Konstantin climbed slowly down, gritting his teeth because his leg hurt like hell.

Sophie crouched down so that they were at eye level. 'I know you can't frighten a man who deals with dead bodies, Mr Korff, but if you don't come with me there will be far-reaching consequences,' she said with a friendly smile, which strangely made it more threatening.

Suspicion flooded through him. Konstantin paused and looked into her dark brown eyes. *Is she connected to the rocker?* 'You don't have a dead brother. What do you really want from me?'

The smile vanished, her expression hardened. 'For you to come with me.'

'Where and why?'

In answer, she drew a Taser out of her handbag. The

electricity crackled shrilly as it flashed blue between the electrodes.

Konstantin let go of the handrail and jumped backwards onto his dinghy. He landed hard, cried out because he thought his shot-up thigh would explode, and fell backwards onto the planks.

He lay lengthways in the bobbing boat, looking up at the pier.

Sophie jumped at him. In the air she pulled the pin elegantly out of her hair and was already stabbing out at him as she landed, boring through the heel of Konstantin's right hand; the sharpened end came out the other side.

He didn't have a chance of escaping the attack, especially not while lying on his back. The pain in his hand added to, and even eclipsed, the pain in his leg.

The boat rocked underneath the vigorous movements.

The electric-shocker was already flickering.

Konstantin fended off her attack, using his healthy leg to give Sophie a kick that sent her backwards. He hastily took hold of the outboard motor, turned it on and accelerated. The motor sped up with a roar, the propeller churning up the water at the stern.

The powerful movement caught Sophie by surprise and she lost her balance. The boat shot out from under her. She toppled into the water.

'Is Leipzig full of nutcases all of a sudden?' muttered Konstantin. He heaved himself up and throttled back the engine.

He chugged along the branch of the canal, looking to the banks right and left to see if she would reappear.

Yet Sophie, if that was her real name, had vanished.

He pressed his injured hand firmly between his knees to staunch the bleeding. *Great. Another hole.* Konstantin hoped she didn't use any hair dye and that no dirt had been stuck to the needle that could lead to an infection. *I'm not about to go back to hospital again. Vodka will have to do as a disinfectant.*

He cranked up the motor and the dinghy shot into the canal in the direction of Lake Cospuden. The balmy summer wind wafted about the front of the boat. The bright headlight on the prow gave him advance warning about driftwood on the water which he then avoided without reducing his speed.

He negotiated the lock, reached Lake Cospuden and sped right across it to get to his floating home.

What did she want from me? Her attack with the Taser made it clear to him that she wanted to stun him and take him with her. On the orders of the guy with the LeMat? *Damn it.* He'd led a peaceful life for two years, built up a livelihood, and now he was suddenly attracting dangerous idiots. *Maybe Jester can tell me something about her?*

As he climbed awkwardly on board the *Vanitas*, Konstantin felt just how bone-tired he was. He belonged in bed really, nursing his wounds. But the investigations were waiting for him.

He quickly poured vodka over his hand, cleaning the puncture and giving a stifled groan as the pain flared up. Then he drank two sugar-free energy drinks, took two guarana tablets and made a quick, lethal espresso so that he stayed awake and clear-headed.

After changing his clothes, he sat down at his laptop.

An email flagged as high importance lit up in his inbox. Konstantin was being summoned to Paris.

Leipzig, Germany

The wrist tattoo is new. You're running out of space, why else would you have it done in such a conspicuous place? Using the powerful telephoto lens, Martin Thielke took several shots of the dark-haired woman in the airport terminal who had introduced herself to Korff as Sophie Kronau the day before. They were separated by 200 metres and the glass façade of the airport entrance. *I ought to get you naked in front of the lens again to balance out my file.*

He was hiding in the car park between two mini-vans and was taking photos surreptitiously. It would not be good if von Windau caught sight of him. She still didn't know anything about him. But he knew her. That's what you call a tactical advantage.

Thielke spat out his old cola-flavoured gum and rummaged around in his bag until he fumbled a new one out of the packet. He smoked a filterless fag too, an imported one, with nicotine levels that were not allowed in Germany, but he needed the thing just as much as he needed his insulin. Thielke was well acquainted with addictions.

'What did you want from Korff?' he muttered to von Windau. The cigarette see-sawed between his lips, as ash fluttered to the black-grey tarmac. The casing of the Nikon was yellowed in places and stank of stale smoke, as if he used it as an ashtray. 'Or rather, what did you want with Korff?'

The woman was a mystery to him. She travelled an unbelievable amount, and to countries that meant he needed to apply for a visa weeks in advance to be permitted entry.

Which meant that she often shook him off her trail and then turned up in places he never expected. Like in Leipzig.

Thielke hadn't felt bad about shooting at the thanatologist; after all, the guy had been asking for it when he tried to attack him. His curiosity had been piqued and he wanted to see what Korff would do next, so he had stayed on the man. And then, just like that, von Windau appeared, talked some nonsense and, as the finale of her little show, tried to give Korff an electric shock.

It was clear she didn't want to kill him. *She still has plans for him.* Thielke saw a man approaching the baroness whom she beamed at and greeted warmly. *No comparison to the meeting with Korff.*

He zoomed in on the man's gaunt face and took photos of him: front, side, right, left, eye colour.

He would upload the shots that evening, boot up a little programme and have it browse through all the databases available: Facebook, Google and the rest of the Internet. It was capable of excellent results. Research before the digital era and the Internet must have been so tedious.

Because of his LeMat revolver he didn't dare go into the terminal building, even if security checks in Leipzig couldn't exactly be described as strict. Thielke didn't want any surprises. If his weapon was discovered, he could count on being arrested and if ballistics experts examined it, he would be done for.

So he couldn't get close enough to the two people to follow

their conversation and had to rely on lip-reading. And because people were constantly rushing across his line of sight, the English sentences and words were incomplete.

The word *mint* was mentioned a few times, whatever that might mean. But he understood that the man was looking forward to his assignment, that he had been waiting for this opportunity his whole life. Von Windau replied with something about good payment, outstanding results and cutting-edge research.

Thielke couldn't quite make his mind up about what he was really seeing through his lens. *Either he's a Death Sleeper and she's luring him into the trap meant for Korff, or she needs him for real research.* He took a few more photos. For the file.

The man had a trolley behind him with half a dozen suitcases stacked on top. A name tag was dangling from one of them. Thielke could read it and take a photograph: Tillman, G., Tank Street 3723, Wisconsin, USA.

Tillman and von Windau turned to the board where the flights were lit up, then shook hands and the woman left again. She disappeared into the throng of people.

Thielke lowered the Nikon and went back to his van, an old Bedford Blitz in a faded yellow, bearing traces of various advertising slogans touting ice cream, vegetables and baked goods. He was the eighth owner; a second engine had been installed under the bonnet and it had done just under 139,000 kilometres. In the same way that Korff lived on his houseboat, Thielke spent the majority of his time and life in this Bedford.

He opened the hinged side door and got in.

By this point, he barely noticed the smell of stale smoke

that engulfed him – his fag would freshen up the smell again anyway.

Inside there were little wall-mounted cupboards attached to the struts. A sleeping bag and a roll mat lay balled up in the corner, having had to make room for the table with his laptop.

Now, tell me who you are and why you think the baroness is so great. Thielke sat down on the folding stool and took the memory card out of the camera to copy the photos onto the computer. He set the search request in motion: once for the man's name and once for his image.

In the meantime he typed up his latest report and sent it to a server encrypted, along with the photographs, using a dongle. He never left anything on his laptop except for the most recent information. He stored the knowledge he gathered on the huge web of unlimited possibility. Securely.

Thielke pulled out the drawer with the grey label, took out an injection pen with fast-acting insulin and rammed the thin, short needle unceremoniously into the side of his thigh to inject himself with a dose of his medication. Finally, he got a chocolate bar out of a different drawer and polished it off with relish before opening the little fridge and taking out a Coke. *Screw the sugar.*

He pondered the baroness as he did so. Since leaving the Deathslumberers, she had been a busy maverick. He didn't fully understand what she did or why. She acted too skilfully for that. But he knew one thing: Death Sleepers who had anything to do with her ended up disappearing.

Korff, however, after a wild life as a contract killer, had turned into a good little lamb. *From Saul to Paul.* So Thielke had decided to stop keeping tabs on the thanatologist – up to a point. If there were ever signs that Korff wanted to go back to his old life ... *I won't let you get away with it again.*

Thielke got himself a second chocolate bar, trusting that the insulin had everything under control. At first he had ignored his ill health, and thanks to diabetes he had lost his right lower leg and the sight in his left eye. He had become more sensible since then – or marginally so.

He had already taken the next cigarette out of the packet and lit up. The tobacco crackled as it burned and he inhaled deeply. 'So,' he murmured as he looked at the results of the first, superficial research. 'Ah, social networks. Excellent invention,' he said, laughing.

A comparison with the pictures he had taken confirmed the search results. The man was Gainsborough Tillman from Wisconsin, an American citizen with numerous doctorates who disappeared to South America after a scandal in a hospital. He had been accused of carrying out organ transplants unnecessarily and without patients' permission, or that of their authorised representatives. Where the transplanted organs had come from was still unclear. There was speculation about Mexico and a drug gang.

'My colleague Tillman has experimented a little. Nice one, sir.' Thielke drank a mouthful from his bottle. So the baroness had snared this brilliant but morally reprehensible doctor. Bag and baggage, judging by all those suitcases.

Thielke investigated further, looking for clues that would reveal the man to be a Death Sleeper, even though Thielke would have bet anything he was a normal person. But just in case.

What does she want with you? Thielke stared at the picture of von Windau and Tillman talking. *Does it have something to do with the missing Death Sleepers?*

He knew a lot about the men and women who unintentionally defied Death. And he knew about their secret organisations from first-hand experience. By now he knew many of the mavericks and drop-outs too. Yet the baroness remained a mystery to him.

Thielke thought about what she could be using the corrupt doctor for. *Does she need a new organ and only wants a Death Sleeper's?*

He pulled the LeMat out of his pocket and placed it on the table, then disposed of everything else that could get him arrested. Taking his sunglasses and a camera containing a formatted chip, he got out of the Bedford and made straight for the airport entrance. He wanted to put Dr Tillman to the test.

Just before reaching the automatic doors he flicked away his fag, then entered the hall and looked around.

He found the doctor in the queue for the check-in desk. He was standing patiently in the queue, reading a trade journal while keeping one eye on his trolley with the six suitcases.

Thielke looked at the sign above the desk. The flight went via Warsaw to . . .

Shit, she said Minsk, not mint!

Thielke lifted up the Nikon and openly took photographs, deliberately drawing attention to himself with the frenzied clicking of the shutter. Up close, the man reminded him of a vulture or the caricature of an undertaker.

Tillman turned away but otherwise ignored him. When

Thielke came closer and took more photographs however, he held the magazine in front of his face. 'What is going on?'

'Just a few photos for the Deutsche Presse Agentur, Doctor!' he said brazenly. 'After all, you're Dr Tillman from the USA, the celebrity cosmetic surgeon!'

'No, I'm not,' hissed the doctor. 'Stop this immediately! You have no right to take photographs of me.'

Thielke played innocent and lowered the camera. 'But on your name tag it says G. Tillman. Aren't you George Tillman? Michael Jackson went under your knife.'

'No.' He took a step towards him and stretched out his arm. 'Hand over the memory card.'

Thielke saw that he was carrying his travel documents in the inside pocket of his sports jacket. That might mean more information for him to get. 'Sure.' He opened the cover, took out the memory card, walked towards the doctor and pretended to stumble. Suddenly lying in Tillman's long arms, he snatched the papers before being roughly pushed away by the doctor. 'Sorry.' He gave him the data chip, keeping his stolen goods hidden underneath his jacket. 'Have a good day.'

Thielke limped to the exit and quickly read the pieces of paper before Tillman noticed they were gone and could cause a fuss.

The travel documents didn't tell him anything new, but a printed street map, with thick handwriting noting the words *Life Institute* underneath, was a good deal more interesting.

I see. Thielke dropped the papers inconspicuously next to a bench. If airport security stopped him at the exit, he didn't want to be caught with them.

Thielke left the building without being arrested, swiftly

vanished inside his Bedford and started a new search on Minsk and the Life Institute, cigarette and Coke in hand.

He put his investigations into Bent Arctander and Timothy Chester Darling on ice for now.

VIII

I am Death,
I fear no man.
I arrest all
And pardon none.

Everyman, Hugo von Hofmannsthal

Paris, France

Another ill-fated jewel.

Konstantin was sitting in his suite at the Hôtel de Vendôme. The remains of the breakfast he'd had brought to his room were strewn around him. He wanted to be left in peace so he could read without interruption. *Exciting*. He had been immersed in Jester's information for days. He was also researching Vanitas, with all its facets, symbols, interpretations and crosscurrents. Endless possibilities opened up; he could barely keep up with everything.

Jester had also sent him some information about Bent Arctander, but the files with the research on Death were too tempting. Too exciting.

Of course, he knew what he was really doing: running

away. From Iva, from thoughts about her beautiful face and his overwhelming feelings for her.

He hadn't answered any of the messages Iva had sent him, nor the letter that had arrived for him at Ars Moriendi, nor the handwritten note that he'd found on the deck of the *Vanitas* just before he left. He didn't have the guts to put her in danger, and he still didn't have a credible explanation for his disappearance either.

Caràra's request was therefore just what he needed. By going to Paris, he avoided the Gewandhaus, the concerts and Iva's flat. Konstantin had never wanted to be rid of his curse more. Until he could return to Iva he would keep away from her; otherwise it would be too easy to give in, he knew that. His weakness, his love, was capable of provoking terrible things.

Is there a bit more time left? Konstantin glanced at the time displayed on his monitor: 10.21 a.m.

Caràra was going to collect him at 11.00 a.m. so that he could take one last look at Lilou de Girardin. The private secretary had already assured him that the body was in immaculate condition, but the marquis had insisted on it.

Since Konstantin couldn't have cared less about a lot of things right then, and because he was grateful for any distraction outside Leipzig, he had said yes to the wealthy Frenchman. Mendy had been running the show for him for so long, Jaroslaf had proved himself to be a lucky find as an apprentice, and he could rely on the rest of his team completely.

So let's get on with this. Jester's research on the Reaper's Stones was comprehensive; it dealt with the symbolism of transience, the unusual features of precious stones and much more. Konstantin had decided to get to grips with the effects and properties of precious stones by supplementing his friend's notes with further research.

Up until now, he had never been aware how great a role jewels played in the history of mankind. Particular gems were even mentioned in the Bible, for example in Exodus 28: 17–21.

And thou shalt set in it settings of stones, even four rows of stones: the first row shall be a sardius, a topaz and a carbuncle: this shall be the first row.

And the second row shall be an emerald, a sapphire and a diamond.

And the third row a ligure, an agate and an amethyst.

And the fourth row a beryl and an onyx and a jasper: they shall be set in gold in their inclosings.

And the stones shall be with the names of the children of Israel, twelve, according to their names, like the engravings of a signet; every one with his name shall they be according to the twelve tribes.

And the Revelation of St John, the Apocalypse, also mentioned jewels that Jerusalem's foundations were to be built with:

And the foundations of the wall of the city were garnished with all manner of precious stones: the first foundation was jasper; the second, sapphire; the third, a chalcedony; the fourth, an emerald; the fifth, sardonyx; the sixth, sardius; the seventh,

*chrysolite; the eighth, a beryl; the ninth, topaz; the tenth, a
chrysoprase; the eleventh, a jacinth; the twelfth, an amethyst.*

There was no doubt that humankind had attributed
influences on their own lives to precious stones since time
immemorial.

Christians had assigned the apostles and two guardian
angels a precious stone each, and since the eighteenth century, precious stones had been linked to the twelve months
of the year. It had become fashionable to own different gems
for each month, and later to wear the precious stone from
one's own birth month. *That's still the case today.*

The various early civilisations had produced jewellery too.
On the basis of excavated artefacts, researchers believed the
oldest stones used for decorative purposes were rock crystal,
amber and jade.

So, anything that was easy to find and easy to work with.

Because of this, Konstantin initially suspected one of these
types of stones of attracting the Grim Reaper, but he soon
realised that he could essentially rule out any common gemstone almost automatically, so long as it wasn't part of a
unique piece of jewellery with a special history.

He found it interesting how deeply people used to believe,
and sometimes still did today, in the supernatural power of
gemstones. They were surrounded by secrets and magic, they
promised protection from evil beings, they could supposedly
even make God and the angels feel positive. Detoxifiers,
plague talismans, lucky charms, remedies. Hildegard of
Bingen, the nun and healer, swore by them.

It was fascinating to read about, but only got him so far.

Konstantin saw his research as a puzzle, a mosaic of wrong and right pieces that he could only tell apart when he saw the bigger picture.

Apart from the reports about precious stones, Jester's research was brimming with references to immortals, mostly saints or particularly terrible people. They were supported by either faith or evilness against the power of the Grim Reaper. These kinds of stories appeared in all mythologies.

Maybe they were just cursed like me?

Konstantin drank some of his now cooled coffee.

He had noticed from the different dates of the records and scans that Jester had begun this search more than twenty years ago – probably soon after he found out about the curse – and that he'd given up five years later.

'The diamond, set into a ring, helps the warrior to victory and invulnerability, repels demons and illnesses, protects against poison, jinxes, the evil eye, somnambulance and possession,' he read and made a brief note. That sounded too positive for a Reaper's Stone. So diamonds were out.

Strictly speaking.

Because there were a few exceptions, above all the Blue Hope. This diamond was an incredible 112 carats and, according to ancient Indian tradition, it had once been the eye of a statue of the Goddess Sita. It attracted deaths and catastrophes. And then there was a yellow diamond called the Florentine Diamond, which was at the centre of similar mysterious troubles. But these diamonds were among the most valuable in the world and that might be the reason why they aroused jealousy and kept provoking tragedies. The diamond as such was regarded as *good* in the relevant literature.

Konstantin would also have loved to know which precious stones had been part of the Nibelung treasure. They had given Death plenty of work to do, if he recalled the myth correctly.

That left, as the stone most likely to attract Death, the opal. The fact that it didn't appear in any of the biblical sources cemented his theory.

Konstantin looked for the passages about opals again. They had been associated with famines, droughts and the downfall of monarchies since the eighteenth century.

Opals were considered the stone for artists and musicians, but at the same time it had been forbidden to wear them in the English and Swedish courts. Yet Konstantin found them in the crowns of various rulers.

Apparently the deaths of Alfonso XII, his wife, grandmother and also his sister could be traced back to the effects of an opal ring. Konstantin had found out, however, that cholera was rife at the time.

Or else a Death Sleeper had a hand in it . . . Whatever. One more piece of the puzzle.

The key words for this stone were therefore: conflict, illnesses, decay and division. *Yes, the opal is well in the lead.*

Modern attempts to explain the opal's bad reputation argued that it was difficult to work with, often shattered and not infrequently developed cracks after being worked, which obviously often infuriated the wearer.

But Konstantin thought it remarkable that it was referred to as *the opium of precious stones.* There were astrological doctrines that recommended only a select group of people wear opals. These were the only people who would come to no harm.

This clue was the clincher for Konstantin. He would focus his research on opals – it was the most likely Reaper's Stone candidate so far.

When he looked at the clock again, he realised how quickly the time had gone.

Caràra is about to arrive.

He stood up quickly, picked up his professional suitcase and put his jacket on, then he went to the lobby to wait.

He expected the private secretary would choose the same procedure as last time to outwit the reporters. The lying in repose was happening tomorrow, so they would be flitting around the marquis' estate like flies to get a shot of grieving family members.

He took the lift down and the doors opened.

Konstantin was almost expecting to see the two photographers from last time again, but the lobby contained just one person, sitting on the banquette by the fireplace and reading *Le Monde*: Timothy Chester Darling in his black designer suit with a shirt and dark tie. He looked over at Konstantin and stood up, throwing the newspaper aside.

Konstantin stepped out of the lift in surprise. 'Jester, what are you doing here?'

'Saving your arse, old boy.' He took a photo out of his bag and held it out to him. 'Call me as soon as you see her.'

Konstantin took a look at it: a woman with a short, brown ponytail, nut-coloured eyes and an attractive face. *How could I ever forget her?* 'That crazy woman has already been to see me.'

Jester, who was just about to fix his tie, stared at him.

Santo Domingo de Guzmán, Dominican Republic

Kristen waved at the built-in camera on her laptop and said goodbye to her son, Eugen, blowing a kiss to the lens before ending the connection. She shut the lid, tucked the laptop away in her bag and picked up the bottle of mineral water, which she drank from with a straw.

The Caribbean sea was lapping at the mooring on the boardwalk in front of her. It thronged with people strolling along and enjoying the breath-taking sunset.

Temperatures in the Dominican Republic were bearable in the evenings, and the wind made sure the heat didn't build up during the day.

A group of musicians walked up and down in front of the bars and pubs with their instruments strapped to them, spreading a typical Caribbean atmosphere with tunes on marimbas, steel pans and other drums.

Kristen was sitting in a secluded spot in the bar's outdoor area, watching the people around her. Almost unconsciously, she took the pill bottle out of her bag, shook two tablets out and placed them under her tongue. The stimulants crumbled, dissolved and released their chemicals into her bloodstream. Kristen needed maximum concentration.

Where other people were on holiday, she had some tricky work ahead of her: the hunt. And she was pursuing very special prey.

The Esparcimento was a club and bar for people with deep pockets – the cheapest drink cost the equivalent of twenty euro, which scared off package holidaymakers and hard-up locals. There were lots of little rooms for private parties, while in the main room there was a stylish boozing session on offer every evening, with food, drink and entertainment in an exclusive atmosphere. Glamorous tourists and residents flocked to the Esparcimento.

Kristen's unsuspecting victim was still in the main room, but he would soon disappear into a side room to celebrate his promotion with some friends.

She looked at the clock. In exactly ten minutes she would get into position at the bar and pounce.

A blond man got up from the next table, leaving the protection of his group and heading for her table. Her red-and-white dress had caught his attention; her partly visible ankh tattoos and the mirrored sunglasses obviously weren't intimidating enough.

A moment later, the man was standing in front of her. 'Good evening,' he said in Spanish. She could hear that he was American straight away. Southern states. Probably in the oil industry or a cattle breeder. 'I'm Edward. My friends call me Ed. The guys and I have been wondering whether you might like to sit with us, darling?'

Kristen sucked the last of the mineral water out of the bottle and cast him a glance over the top of her sunglasses. 'Why should I, Edward?' she replied, also in Spanish. She found it astonishing that she mainly tended to stutter in German. Spanish came out of her mouth fluently, as did English and Russian. Could there be psychological reasons for that?

'We would really enjoy your company, babe.'

Kristen smiled her unsettlingly arrogant smile. 'Because?'

'*Because . . .*' The blond man thought about it and eventually understood that she was not interested, so he tipped an imaginary hat brim and went back to his pals.

Kristen grinned after him, stood up and moved to the bar in the room inside. She posted herself near the door leading to the side room, ordered a non-alcoholic Mata Hari and waited patiently. The other preparations were complete.

He turned up ten minutes later, laughing, surrounded by friends. He seemed a little drunk, the laughter sounded rowdy. His brown skin couldn't hide the red blotches that always appeared on his face after he'd had alcohol. Which he seldom did, because he couldn't afford to with the career he had. But the Caribbean was less dangerous for a man like him than Miami or El Paso, where Mexican hitmen lurked around every corner.

He was handed a rum by the barman and then he glanced at Kristen.

Without hesitating, he ushered the group into the little private room as he walked around the bar and came over to her.

She acted as though she hadn't noticed him, pretending to take cover behind the cocktail menu.

'Kristen!' he said, putting an arm around her waist and giving her the suggestion of a kiss on her cheek. 'How lovely to see you!' His delight was real but it didn't stop the suspicion showing in his pale green eyes. 'Holiday?'

'Hey, Clarence! Wow!' She laughed and gave him a quick hug. His body was muscular, he'd been working out a lot. 'Yes, of course, a holiday! Didn't fancy the pretty grim summer at home and figured I would go where the rum flowed.'

'That would be Cuba then,' he replied with a wink.

'As if it doesn't make it to Santo Domingo. You let the smugglers through, and put in an extra crate, don't you?'

Clarence couldn't stop grinning, the mistrust gradually fading from his eyes. An attractive man. 'What are you insinuating? I am the chief special agent in the Caribbean Division! I may not be responsible for preventing alcohol smuggling, but I wouldn't even dream of what you are so casually insinuating. My boss in the DEA would fire me on the spot if I didn't prevent illegal goings-on like that!'

'Really? Would he? But then he would stop getting rum from you.' Kristen cuffed his upper arm teasingly. 'What are you planning? An Iron Man race?'

Clarence tensed his biceps, his shirt sleeve stretched alarmingly, the material twisting. 'Fitness is important. I take on the arseholes myself. We busted a lab just the day before yesterday. The cartels used to use the Dominican Republic as a transfer point, but these days every second idiot is building a little speed or crack kitchen in the backyard. But I catch them.'

Kristen nodded and clinked her glass with his. 'To your successes then. I hope they continue.'

'Thanks very much.' He finished off his rum and ordered two more. 'To the old days, am I right?'

She nodded. 'To the old days forever, Clarence.'

He leaned against the bar, looking at her and seeming deep in thought. She could tell it was the alcohol that gave him the courage he needed for the next sentence. 'Do you want to come back to us?'

By *us* he meant the Deathslumberers, an association for Death Sleepers operating in the US and Canada. They were an offshoot of the British Torpor's Men and had ensured that justice was exported during the settling of the New World. Justice as demanded by fairness, not bizarre laws.

Kristen had once been a member ...

She took her glass in her left hand and swirled the rum around. She breathed in the sweet yet sharp aroma of the alcohol and she was prepared to bet that it came from Cuba. Illegally, the way the barman was scowling. 'To be honest, I have considered it,' she lied.

Clarence gently placed his large hand on her shoulder. 'I've never understood why you left. You were unbeatable in Washington. You had the senators in the palm of your hand and you were able to steer them to act in the interests of our issues. Lots of people took it badly that you left.'

'I know.' Kristen could have told him about the fatal familial insomnia now, about divorcing the husband whom she still loved, about her son whom she seldom saw, and about everything else that was on her mind that he and the Sleepers had no idea about. But she didn't. That's not why she was here. 'But you didn't, Clarence.'

'No. I just thought it was a shame.' He left his hand on her shoulder and squeezed gently, as if he wanted to show her more than friendship. 'What are you up to, now that you have some freedom?

She smiled. 'What are people saying I'm doing?'

Clarence burst out laughing and raised his glass to her, again drinking the rum off in one go. 'That you're dangerous and that some of us have disappeared after meeting up with you.' The suspicion returned to his eyes. 'I know that you travel a lot. With your air miles, you could jet around the globe all year. But as soon as you touch the ground you turn into a ghost. That scares some people, Kristen.'

'But not you, I see.'

'No. Not me.' He looked at her seriously now. 'For that reason alone, it would be better if you joined us again. You could prove that any misgivings about you are unfair.'

She spun the full glass in her hand, letting it tilt, and watched the rum as it sloshed over the rims and ran down the glass in oily streaks. Illegal, good stuff. 'I'm certainly not a ghost, but . . . I can't come back, Clarence.'

'Why not?'

'I was having problems,' she murmured.

'Pardon?'

'I said,' she coughed slightly, 'I was having problems in Washington because Jefferson from New York was meddling in my jurisdiction. It went on for a few years. I didn't want to deal with that shit any more. I didn't want to spread any uneasiness in the ranks of the Sleepers.' Then she knocked back the alcohol. The next lie had been told.

'Jefferson? I knew you couldn't stand each other, but—' Clarence straightened. He positioned himself by her side. A protector through and through. 'What was wrong?'

'A power struggle. That idiot, he thought that authority over New York was more important than authority over Washington. He executed several of my informants in New York city, to keep his cards close to his chest. To me, that was just beyond stupid.' She refused a third rum and sucked the straw in the Mata Hari. 'So who's doing my job now, who gets to do battle with him?'

'Jefferson,' said Clarence and made a face, as though he had a chilli sprinkled with lemon in his mouth.

'What? He controls Washington *and* New York?' Kristen whistled appreciatively through her teeth.

As with the Torpor's Men, the Sleepers sought to control state bodies and influence the government so that the fight against crime could be managed better and, in particular, become more efficient. Death Sleepers were good manipulators and executioners. An abuse of this power became tempting of course, and so the Sleepers kept an eye on each other. Or at least they were supposed to.

'So Jefferson is the next power player in the Sleepers? Has he applied for the chairmanship? How else could he be allowed to consolidate his power like that?'

Clarence took his hand away from her shoulder. 'Shit,' he said absently. 'That little motherfucker! He's arranged that pretty neatly, the dickhead!' The muscles on his chest twitched. 'I knew he was an arsehole, but I'm not going to let him get away with this. He is definitely not becoming our chief.' He took his mobile out of his pocket and dialled a number. 'Excuse me a second.' He turned away and spoke quietly into the phone in Spanish.

Kristen smiled coldly and ordered him another rum. She drew a small foil sachet inconspicuously from her pocket, unfolded it and shook the white powder into the rum. It dissolved immediately.

Two minutes later, Clarence turned back to her. 'Jefferson

always gets on my tits. I thought he had something to do with you leaving.'

'Who did you call?'

Clarence leaned forward and gave her a kiss on the cheek. 'Chang from the NSA. He's going to have a word with Jefferson and look into everything he's been up to in the last few weeks.'

'Chang is at the NSA now? Wasn't he at Homeland Security?'

'They headhunted him last year and we were happy with that. He has access to the best secret service resources there are.' Clarence looked at her. 'You should have told me long ago, Kristen.'

She looked at him in mock surprise. 'I . . . just had the impression that you would believe Jefferson, not me.' Her gaze darted to the other end of the bar, where two friends of Clarence had appeared and were beckoning to him. 'You're missed.'

'Yes, I should get back to them.' He took the rum. 'What's this for?'

'For your faith, Clarence.' Kristen heaved herself up off her stool and hugged him. 'Thank you. Thank you for believing in me.'

He returned the hug, the fingers of his free hand slid down her back and stroked her tenderly. It was not the touch of a friend, but that of a man who wanted to be more than a friend. He hadn't lost his weakness for her, which made him easier prey. 'Come back to us. If I can prove anything against Jefferson, two jobs will be freed up. Then you choose one for yourself, I promise you. New York or Washington?' He let go of her and looked her in the eye. His suspicion was gone.

'New York. Jefferson had great apartments,' she replied and stroked his cheek.

'Done.' He finished his rum without taking his eyes off her.

She shoved him away from her playfully. 'Now, go off with your friends. I need to get going anyway, my flight leaves early tomorrow morning. But I'll call you next week, I promise.'

'Really?'

'Yes. Now go.'

'Talk to you next week then.' Clarence visibly pulled himself together and turned around. He walked through the door to the private room.

Kristen checked her watch and waited exactly ten minutes. Then she stood up and went to the toilets to lock herself into a cubicle in the men's without being seen. She took the electric Taser out of her bag and placed it on the toilet lid, even though she didn't think she would need it. Clarence would hardly be in a position to put up any resistance.

Half an hour and many unwanted visitors later, including a couple who treated themselves to a quickie in the cubicle next door, she heard the door being pushed open and someone suppressing a retch.

Kristen looked through the gap below the door.

She recognised Clarence's legs. Wasted from the alcohol and the drug she'd administered, he staggered towards one of the cubicles. Then there was a loud retching sound followed by splashes.

Kristen left her hiding place, looked around quickly and was pleased to note that they were alone. So she took the 'Cleaning – shut briefly' sign from the hook next to the mirror and hung it on the main door. She locked it from the inside with a skeleton key. Thus she had the few minutes to herself that she needed.

While Clarence threw up and groaned, she opened the large windows with the grille meshing. She'd parked her rented 4x4 in front of the windows, an old green Wrangler with an open truck bed. Two quick whacks against the thin iron struts that she had sawn notches into last night, and the metal mesh could be tossed aside. It landed with a clatter on the street.

She needed to be quick now.

Kristen got into position in front of Clarence's cubicle and waited until there were more retching sounds. At that moment, she rammed the door open, hitting him in the back and sending him crashing headfirst into the cistern.

Snorting, he made to turn around.

'No, Clarence.' She pulled his legs out from under him and gave him a sharp karate chop to the back of the neck. He collapsed next to the toilet bowl, right over the loo brush.

Now began the most laborious part, quite literally: she pulled the muscular man out of the cubicle by his feet, dragged him to the window and expertly heaved him through the opening. He fell onto a soft bed of jute sacks on the floor of the truck. Dust flew up as he sank down into the heap.

Kristen leaned out and spread a few sacks made from the rough material over the unconscious man and grabbed her things.

There was the sound of voices outside the door, somebody was fiddling with the lock. A customer with a small bladder had probably gone and fetched a member of Esparcimento staff.

Kristen hesitated and considered her options. She could escape through the window, but the open window – it couldn't be closed from the outside unfortunately – and the missing mesh would immediately draw attention, which she could do without. She needed a little head start to get Clarence out of the Dominican Republic.

Kristen ran to the window and shut it, dashed into Clarence's puke-strewn cubicle and locked it. A moment later there was a click and the main door opened.

There were voices, followed by a laugh. But it was just one man who strode over to the urinal by himself. A zip opened, there was splashing, followed by a loud fart and a sigh of 'Yee-haw!'

The man had a large bladder. It was a while before he was done.

Kirstin was getting impatient. She didn't know how Clarence was. She needed to give him the antidote to the vomiting powder and put him into an unnatural, deep sleep with a sedative. His curse could not be allowed to flare up now.

The man hummed a tune and went to the sink, and there was more splashing. At least he washed his hands. The hand dryer came on. He was obviously in no hurry. 'What is that stink? Did someone throw up all over the place?'

As his steps rang out over the dull tones of the hot air ventilator, Kristen felt cold. The man moved to the window. He wanted to air the place.

There was a cracking sound and the window was opened.

Kristen silently left the cubicle and saw it was the man who had approached her earlier standing with his back to her. Edward was looking at the sawn-off meshing, his eyes fixed on the jeep right at that moment. She took the Taser out of her bag and placed it, turned on, on the back of the man's neck.

Edward went 'gnnnhhhh' and collapsed like a rag doll.

Kristen gave him three kicks – for the *yee-haw* while he was peeing and for the fart – then jumped out the window.

She climbed out of the flatbed and into the driver's seat of the Wrangler, started the engine and drove down several streets before stopping and injecting Clarence with the antidote and a sedative.

Feeling calmer, she turned into the road leading to the small airport, San Juan de la Maguana. An aircraft was waiting there for her and Clarence. Next stop: Mexico. Getting to Belarus from Mexico was absolutely no problem with her contacts in the drug cartels.

On the journey, Kristen pondered what could still go wrong. The remaining DEA agents might act more quickly following the disappearance of their boss than she had anticipated.

It would have been so much easier if she could have lured Korff into the trap or overpowered him. But he had caught her off-guard, which was beyond frustrating for her. The last time she'd fallen overboard had been as a child.

Korff would know to be on his guard from now on. But she didn't need the German man for the time being. She would soon turn Clarence over to Tillman as a replacement for Patient 22.

If she did need Korff, she would ambush him and stun him, without letting herself be too conspicuous about it. She was damned good at it.

IX

*It is a curious thing
that whoever longs for death
will die only when frail
and whoever tries to escape it
has it granted to him very quickly.*

Partonopier und Meliur, Konrad von Würzberg

Paris, France

Konstantin tapped the picture. 'Sophie Kronau.'

Jester looked at the photo in surprise. 'She introduced herself with *that* name?'

He nodded. 'Yes. She stuttered slightly and said she wanted me to take on the thanatological treatment of her brother. It wasn't hard to see through the lie.' He briefly summarised his meeting with her and showed Jester the healed stab wound; it was now just a red spot. The gunshot wound wasn't bothering him any more either. When he had finished his account, he looked enquiringly at his friend. 'What's your connection to her?' Then he understood. *She's one of us!*

Jester pulled him into the corner of the lobby where they

could talk without being disturbed and picked out a second picture, this time of a man, around fifty, who was very strong and tanned. The stranger was standing in front of a desk and in the background there was a billowing American flag that had been edited in on Photoshop. The emblem of the DEA, the American drug-fighting authority, was plastered across the photo. 'She has something to do with this man's disappearance. That's what the Sleepers think anyway.'

Konstantin glanced at the entrance because he was expecting Caràra to arrive. 'Who is that?'

'Clarence Hicks, head of the DEA's Caribbean division. He vanished without trace during a party. Went to the toilet and never came back. But he was chatting to her beforehand. There are witnesses to that.' Jester held up the woman's picture.

'Kronau.'

'Baroness Kristen Sophia von Windau. That's her real name. She was a member of the Deathslumberers and was responsible for crime-fighting and networking in Washington DC until she left the group unexpectedly.' Jester put the photos away again. 'There's a rumour going around that she has something to do with the disappearances of several Death Sleepers around the world. But nobody has been able to prove anything against her yet.'

I was lucky. 'She tried to stun me. Do you need any more proof?'

Konstantin remembered the ankhs on her arms.

Jester pointed at his chest with his thumbs. 'MI6 is dealing with it from now on. I've already sent my people off looking for her. Please explain to me again, in detail, everything that she actually said.' He took his mobile out of his jacket pocket and turned on the record function.

Konstantin repeated his story. Then he asked: 'What's the deal with the old man in the country clothes?'

'Ah, the gunman with the LeMat replica.' Jester stopped recording. 'No, nothing I'm afraid. The next time he turns up, take a photograph of him. I can run it through our database and do a facial comparison. MI6 has good programmes for identifying people, believe me. If he has ever been in England, especially in London, he'll have been captured on CCTV. Then we'll soon know more.'

'I believe you.' Konstantin saw a commotion in front of the Hôtel de Vendôme. Instead of a line of taxis, a single car came to a stop outside, a black Jaguar S-type. Caràra opened the rear door and waved to him both as greeting and summons. He seemed to have made less of an effort on the diversionary tactics this time. 'Jester, I've got to go.' He gestured towards his aluminium suitcase.

'I know. Lilou.' He put out his hand. 'Be careful. The baroness has her eye on you. We don't know what she's up to with the Death Sleepers who have disappeared. They're not turning up as corpses anyway.'

'I'll keep my eyes open and I'll call you immediately if I meet her.' Konstantin nodded to his friend as he walked towards and got into the chauffer-driven Jaguar.

The car purred away down the streets of Paris.

'Bonjour, Monsieur Korff.' Caràra was wearing a dark green suit again with a black waistcoat underneath and a white lily in his buttonhole. 'The marquis would like me to inform you that he is very pleased to know you are in Paris.'

He and Konstantin shook hands. 'It was possible to arrange it,' he remained vague. 'And I'm pleased too. But as I've already said, I don't anticipate there being anything to do.'

'Neither do I, Monsieur. But it serves to calm a soul in turmoil, as tomorrow will be the most painful day of Monsieur le Marquis' life.' Caràra smiled gently. 'It's difficult to see your boss, whom you know as a tough businessman and loving family man, in that kind of state. The marquis is hardly himself any more.'

'I know how it is.' Konstantin had seen relatives standing in front of him who, in the course of a few days, abruptly lost weight, went grey and got wrinkles like an elderly person, as though Death was sapping their will to live. 'How did Madame take it?'

Caràra was silent a moment. 'Not well,' he replied slowly. 'But she has understood that she has lost her daughter and that she will not come back. No matter if Madame cries, curses, screams or damns God to Hell.'

Konstantin was glad not to have witnessed the mother standing by the open coffin of her youngest daughter and falling apart. *That's the drawback to life: it ends some time. For most people.*

He noticed that the Jaguar didn't turn onto the motorway going away from the city, but was moving into a different district. According to the signs, they were getting closer and closer to Notre Dame. 'The demoiselle is already lying in repose,' he concluded.

'Yes, Monsieur Korff. The marquis wanted to do all of the preparations in complete calm and has already had the coffin transported to the cathedral.' Caràra gave the driver instructions on which route to take.

Konstantin was again struck by how powerful the de Girardin family must be, to have a Parisian landmark close to thousands upon thousands of tourists at their behest without any fuss. 'Has the press pack gathered yet?' Konstantin was afraid the car would drop them off in front of the ranks of cameramen and photographers. If that was the case, he would hardly be able to stop his face showing up in the paper.

'Of course, Monsieur Korff, but there's no need to worry. Nobody will bother us. The police have cordoned off a large area around the entrance to the cathedral.' Caràra pointed to the left where broadcasting vans were parked. Cameramen were wandering around and chatting, reporters were doing interviews with passers-by because they didn't know what else to do.

Their car passed the press at a safe distance and drove in through a temporary double door system next to Notre Dame that had been built with fabric-covered sections of construction hoarding. Caràra and Konstantin got out of the car without being seen and entered the cathedral by a side entrance.

It was cooler than he'd expected inside. The muted light penetrating through the window bathed the nave in a soft, multi-coloured glow.

Through his work, Konstantin had seen quite a few churches, even cathedrals, but it was the atmosphere in Notre Dame that impressed him most.

He and Caràra strode down the central aisle together. The secretary's hard soles clacked almost blasphemously, the sound echoed under his soles and spread out in all directions.

Konstantin could see the coffin even at a distance. Large

candles flickered on either side of it, illuminating Lilou de Girardin. Two empty chairs stood a few metres away.

The closer they got the more observant he became. He checked the air as he inhaled deeply. There was no odour of decomposition, he had done a good job. *But nothing was impossible.* Incense wasn't just burned to glorify God in the olden days, but also because people stank. Especially dead people.

'Monsieur le Marquis is carrying out a vigil and I will stay with him,' Caràra said, explaining the two seats. He sat on a chair. 'If you would like to begin, Monsieur Korff?'

Konstantin nodded and put the aluminium suitcase down on the marble floor. Despite the rubber stoppers, the soft noises became a racket in the quiet of Notre Dame. He made an effort to be even quieter as he undid the clasp and flipped open the lid to get at the make-up brushes.

Then he went up to the dead body in its final, white bed and looked critically at it, as a thanatologist and undertaker checking his work.

Everything was perfect, right down to the tiny details, hardly anything had to be fixed. *Hair, complexion, lip colour,* he went through the checklist in his head.

The beautiful girl's mouth and eyes were closed. To be on the safe side he checked her eyelids again, touched up the make-up around the edges, examined the dress for potential stains that could form due to condensation. But his embalming fluid had worked, there were no signs of unpleasant marks anywhere.

Good. Just as I thought: all clean.

Konstantin straightened up. It seemed as though Death

hadn't dared to rob her of her mesmerising radiance and beauty.

He looked at her rings and the diamond necklace that she had been wearing in the photo that had served as the guide for him to work from. On that lovely day, on the deck of a boat, at sea, surrounded by water, wind and joie de vivre.

Konstantin looked at Caràra. 'We can go. As I said, there's nothing to worry about.'

'Excellent, Monsieur Korff. I'll take you back to the hotel then. The marquis says you're welcome to come to the funeral, if you would like.'

It didn't take Konstantin more than a second to make up his mind. 'It would be an honour for me.'

The diamond flashed as he took one last look at Lilou, as though it was glinting just for him.

Paris, France

Konstantin sat in his suite, staring at the screen without taking in the words.

Caràra would soon be collecting him and taking him to Notre Dame, where around ten thousand guests and bystanders were expected to attend. People had been allowed to file past the young dead girl and say goodbye since ten o'clock that morning – or see her for the first time and have a gawp.

He could see Lilou de Girardin in his mind's eye: perfect, wonderful.

His gaze fell on the letter poking out of his suitcase with Iva's handwriting on it. It was the message he'd found on the deck of the *Vanitas*. He carried it around with him everywhere, unopened. His talisman, his motivation not to give up until he'd found a solution and could stand in front of Iva, free. Free from the curse, from the bond with the Reaper that he didn't want. And free from the truths as well as the lies that stood between them.

It hurt to remember their last meeting that began so well and ended so catastrophically badly. The scene at the kitchen table they'd made love on.

Death Sleepers – '*a joke, no*', she'd said '*like in a fairy tale*'. Jester had talked about a cure for the curse in the same breath as Cockayne and the Star Money.

Konstantin didn't think it was a bad comparison. Their stories were in books and were read to children as entertainment and education. You could go into raptures about the Star Money, or wish for a holiday in Cockayne. Neither of them existed.

I'm the hero of a tragic fairy story, unaware of how it ends. Iva's nonchalant words resonated in his thoughts, refusing to be suppressed. They reminded him of something that he had read in Jester's documents.

Fairy tales!

Konstantin checked Jester's notes. There was the story of Kali but apart from that, had he delved much down this path? It would seem his friend had discounted this aspect. It didn't even appear on the To Do list, one of the last documents that Jester had drawn up back then. Because it was too fantastical, or crazy? Could you even use the word *unrealistic* in relation to *Death Sleepers*?

Konstantin did a quick Internet search for fairy tales

involving Death. He downloaded them without reading them, saved the links and copied them into a table he quickly set up. Another irrational hope: first the legendary Reaper's Stones, now fairy tales, sagas and legends. He must really be desperate to be looking for clues from children's stories. *But whatever. So long as something might come of it, I'll try anything.*

After the demoiselle's funeral mass he would concentrate on it in more detail. But now he needed to get changed.

He slipped into a black shirt for the Mass, put on a tie and threw the sports jacket on over it. Combined with the sunglasses and the hat, nobody would ever recognise him. He didn't want any smart photographer finding out who he was.

He left his suite and took the lift to the ground floor. He knew the lobby like the back of his hand by now. He kept an eye out for paparazzi prowling around the cathedral en masse to ply their repulsive trade and to 'shoot' as many famous people as possible.

With the concierge's permission, Konstantin got himself one of the umbrellas out of the umbrella stand near the exit, to use as cover from prying eyes if it came to that. He called Caràra to let him know that he didn't need a chauffeur. He fancied a walk. There was still an hour and a half to go before the Mass.

Enough time to stretch my legs.

He strolled down Rue de Rivoli, past the Tuileries and the glass pyramid of the Louvre, and followed signs until he knew he was more or less on his way to Notre Dame. The Centre Pompidou appeared at a junction up ahead and to the left, then Notre Dame loomed up on the right. It was swarming with police and private security forces.

That was quick. The walk had only taken a little over half an hour and Konstantin had no desire to plunge into the melee just yet.

He looked around, indecisive, and his gaze fell on a small island in the Seine that was referred to as Île Saint-Louis. Although it was directly opposite the cathedral, it was an oasis of calm. Along its edge there were ancient-looking buildings packed together all in a row. His new destination.

In just a few minutes he had reached the bridge to the island and discovered a little *brasserie* on a street called Quai de Bourbon.

Konstantin sat down outside, surrounded by smokers, tourists and a handful of French people.

From here he could see the huge building on the other side of the bank where Demoiselle Lilou lay and where friends and strangers were taking their leave of her. Speechless, tearful, suffering, moved, apathetic, screaming loudly – Konstantin was familiar with every form of grief and how to deal with it.

He ordered himself coffee and a croissant from a lovely French waitress and, contrary to his habits, a *pastis*. He simply felt like having a shot of alcohol in his bloodstream. It loosened things up and might give him new thoughts that could help him in his research.

He couldn't get the link between the Grim Reaper and fairy tales out of his head. *Wasn't there a fairy tale about a dead girl and a pot full of tears that her mother had shed?* His laptop with the stories was waiting for him. *But first the farewell to Lilou.*

'"The good ended happily, and the bad unhappily".' Jester took a seat next to him so naturally it was as if they had arranged to meet. '"That is what fiction means".'

'You could at least quote Wilde in French, now that we're in Paris.'

'As long as I live, I will quote Wilde exclusively in English.' Jester picked up the menu and looked over at Notre Dame. 'Such a beautiful girl.'

'Death was gracious to her. There were victims on the plane and in the terminal so badly burned that even DNA tests didn't work.' Konstantin wasn't surprised his friend had turned up. After their brief conversation in the lobby yesterday he'd expected to see him again. Plus he'd just observed him creeping up to his table out of the corner of his eye. 'As though the flames spared the demoiselle at the Reaper's request.'

'Well, well, well. Very romantic and morbid.' Jester ordered himself a coffee when the waitress came with Konstantin's order, and glanced at the *pastis* that she placed in front of Konstantin. 'You're already drinking, old boy?'

'Just the one. I reckon today is going to be tough.'

'The drinking?'

'The church service.' Konstantin looked at the cathedral.

'I was in Notre Dame briefly earlier. Kudos. Lilou looks good, practically too perfect.'

Konstantin clicked his tongue and drank some of his *pastis*, which he didn't dilute with water the way the French usually did. 'How are the investigations coming along?' He slowly turned his head away from the imposing cathedral and looked at the MI6 agent.

'I'm mainly here on your account. We were interrupted yesterday. It's not just about the baroness.' Jester smiled at the waitress who served him his coffee and waited until she was some distance away. 'I know you were going to get in touch with me as soon as anything about our target occurred to you. But this is urgent. Bent Arctander has struck again. He has no control over his narcolepsy.' He held out his smartphone to Konstantin and opened a website from *La Repubblica*:

Roccastrada/Grosseto (ed). In the Tuscan province of Grosseto, a number of mysterious deaths have occurred in the Roccastrada area.

The bodies of thirteen of the village's inhabitants were found in the vicinity of a sanatorium, including the head of the sanatorium, Professor Massimo Auro.

The dead lay in the street, outside their front doors and in their homes. They appear to have died from heart attacks, according to initial examinations. Unconfirmed reports state that the time of death for all victims was identical.

The dead, ranging from eleven to sixty-one years of age, did not show any signs of pre-existing illnesses or the use of external force.

The investigating authorities have a mystery on their hands.

Further reports to follow.

For anyone in the know, this is easy to recognise. 'Are you sure that it—?'

'We know what Arctander looks like, old boy. There are surveillance photos that indicate he was in the area.' Jester put his phone away again. 'He's looking for hiding places from us, in nice, isolated villages. But with numbers like that he's attracting more attention there than in a city. Although with the choice of the sanatorium he was halfway clever.'

'Do you think?'

'Yes. In old folks' homes or similar institutions people die so regularly that questions very often aren't asked. Stupidly, Arctander was half a kilometre away from the sanatorium when he had the attack.'

'Well, when a disproportionate number of people all die suddenly at the same time, it attracts attention one way or another.' Konstantin observed Jester carefully. His friend was getting very angry. That was of course understandable, but . . . *There's something else.* 'Let's forget that he's dangerous for a moment – what *else* is it about him?'

'You know me too well.' Jester took Konstantin's *pastis* without asking and drank the whole glassful in one gulp, then shook himself. 'What great stuff! No wonder we were at war with the French so often before the Germans became our preferred opponents.'

'What's worrying you so much that you're touching alcohol voluntarily?' Jester drank just as seldom as Konstantin did, like the majority of Death Sleepers. Alcohol made you sleepy too easily.

Jester rubbed his hands together and clapped once quietly, as though cheering himself on. Finally he whispered, '*Phansigar.*'

Konstantin hadn't heard this word in a long time and his heart automatically started beating faster. He leaned back in silence as the bells of Notre Dame began to toll. One after the other they rang, first the small ones and then the big ones joined in. Their cast-iron knell boomed full and majestic across the Seine, calling people to Lilou's mass. 'How do they know about him?'

'They'll be following the news and they still have a few informants.' Jester tilted his head back. 'If *they* lay their hands on him, we'll have very different problems from a few hundred random victims on an A380.'

A shiver went down Konstantin's spine. *Bent Arctander would do very well in their human arsenal.*

The Phansigar, also known as Thuggee Nidra which could be translated as Sleep Murderers, were a group of Indian Death Sleepers whose roots went back as far as the thirteenth century and who used to be called Thuggee.

Their mindset towards the curse of the Death Sleeper made them unpleasant for a start: just as the Torpor's Men ensured justice and order, the Phansigar earned their money with contract killings. Murderers for any occasion, without scruples or limits.

They worked for every political side, from secret services to terrorists.

Secondly, they had trained sleepwalkers in their ranks who could operate with incredible accuracy even while asleep. These murderers approached their victims as Death rampaged around them. Thus their lethal nature increased many times over.

And thirdly, they considered themselves little gods, not people. Most of them had more than 500 people's lives on their conscience.

The Phansigar operated in three-man teams to provide each other with backup, just like their predecessors in the past. The Indian Thuggees emerged for the first time in the thirteenth century; there was speculation that they had been Death Sleepers from the very beginning and that this was the reason why the number of victims attributed to them was so high. Some researchers estimated there had been 50,000 victims over the centuries – in the *Guinness Book of Records* it said 2,000,000.

Konstantin knew that Jester wanted to keep the Phansigar from setting foot on European soil. He had declared war on them in the tradition of the British colonial power that the Thuggee had already tried to destroy in the nineteenth century – which it had, officially speaking, succeeded in doing.

Konstantin launched into a reply. 'I can—'

'No, listen to me! I have officially tasked the Torpor's Men with killing Arctander. No matter where, whether it's at Piccadilly Circus or in front of Buckingham Palace or in the middle of the Tube. For the Phansigar, Arctander is the perfect weapon for big missions.'

'That's cynical.'

'But, unfortunately, not exaggeration, old boy.' Jester looked at him. 'When are you going to start looking for him properly?'

'The Indians might want to kill him too if they think he's too dangerous.'

'Sure. And Hitler was misunderstood, and only wanted to conquer everyone so that peace reigned on earth.' There was an incoming email alert. He picked up his phone again. He quickly skimmed the message. 'Ah, I need to get going yet again. Things are pretty dicey at the moment.' He stood up and took a twenty out of his trouser pocket, placing it on the table. 'Here, this one's on me. I'll call you later. We have to find the narco.' He smiled a less convincing showman smile than usual, and left the *brasserie*.

Holy shit. Konstantin watched as Jester crossed the street, strode over to a parked black Bentley and got in. The vehicle didn't move. He could see Jester having a conversation with another man inside it.

Konstantin took his own phone out of his jacket pocket and briefly considered what prefix he needed. 0091? He decided to try it, and after the four digits he dialled a number that he had not called in a long time.

There was a click and a hum on the line, the pips followed by a dial tone that sounded steady and loud.

Jester should have let me finish speaking. Konstantin drank a mouthful of his coffee and bit off a piece of the croissant.

Apparently there was nobody there.

After the thirtieth *tooooot* Konstantin hung up and looked back over at Notre Dame. All the bells were going, as if a new pope had been elected or the French Prime Minister had died. Lilou was being granted the greatest honour that the cathedral could bestow.

The black Bentley started moving, did a U-turn, ignoring the protests from oncoming traffic, and shot right past the *brasserie*. Jester waved at Konstantin again and pointed to his smartphone.

You're enjoying yourself, Mr Bond. He took a second bite of the croissant. Konstantin adjusted his sunglasses and quickly grabbed at Jester's twenty to stop it being carried off by a breeze.

He weighed the note down with the sugar dispenser – and in its metal surface he caught sight of a familiar figure behind him, hidden behind a pillar. The photographer who'd shot him in the leg!

The stranger had his camera with him, and he was holding it just in front of his bearded face ready to unleash it.

I led him to Jester. Or did Jester lead him to me? Frantic, Konstantin considered what to do.

Konstantin reckoned that the man would have his LeMat revolver on him. So an open confrontation would probably end in another painful shot to the leg. *For now I'll wait and see what he wants. He has up-to-date photographs of me for his file already. It can't be that.* Konstantin acted as though he hadn't seen him and watched his distorted image in the sugar dispenser.

When the stranger left a while later, Konstantin stayed in his seat for a few seconds and followed him at a sufficient distance.

Unfortunately, his route didn't take him towards Notre Dame, but through the streets of Île Saint-Louis. Lilou de Girardin would probably have to receive the last rites without her thanatologist.

X

Here lie
my bones,
I wish,
they were
your ones.

Epitaph, Unknown author

Ciudad Mier, Mexico

Kristen was sitting in a worm-eaten rocking chair on a deserted veranda attached to a house that lay at the end of a street called Colón, on the southern outskirts of the small town of Mier.

Apparently there had been 5000 inhabitants living there at one point, but since her arrival, she had not set eyes on two people together.

She suppressed a yawn, teetering on the thin line between waking and sleeping. Deliberately.

Her car was right next to the veranda: a battered dark green Dodge Ramcharger that didn't really attract any attention in the town – provided there was someone who could pay attention to it. The residents had already fled once before, after the drug cartel called *Los Zetas* had announced they were going to kill everyone in the village. Some returned, but Mier was on its knees. Banks, shops, petrol stations, public institutions – all closed: a ghost town.

It basically looked like a Tarantino film after the final showdown, featuring the shot up, burned houses, the tattered car wrecks, and a handful of dead bodies in the street. It seemed the tape hadn't finished, going on to show the sad, unheroic remains of the earlier fights. A cleaning crew certainly did not appear.

The advantage of watching films of course, was that you didn't get the smell.

No matter where Kristen went, there was a sweetish smell, the stink of rotting flesh. Criminals, police officers, innocent residents – Death had certainly had a good haul here. And yet there were actually very few corpses visible on the streets. They were somewhere though. And they stank. Upwind and downwind.

Kristen took a drink of Coke and washed down the tablets that she had placed under her tongue. She had a headache, was seeing double and nausea was washing over her in waves. The insomnia was trying to make her life hell.

Clarence, the head of the DEA's Caribbean division, lay in the 4x4's massive boot. Tucked into a metal box with air holes, he was sleeping very, very deeply, thanks to a potent sedative. It was necessary in order to make sure he didn't fall into a normal sleep. Like Patient 22.

She looked at her watch.

Her contact, Trejo, would be arriving any minute and

bringing her to the landing strip southwest of Mier, which had once been a broad motorway called Carretera Federal 54. Now it ended three miles from the town at a pile of concrete blocks stacked into a tower that looked like a breakwater. Although there was no sea in this part of Mexico.

The *Zetas* had a base for their helicopters and light aircraft right next to the USA. No wonder Mier was considered one of the hottest drug dealing spots. Kristen figured that was why the *Zetas* had delivered the death threats to the residents of the town: no witnesses to their business. She had already counted four lorries heading away from the little border town and they certainly weren't carrying anything innocent judging by the escort of armoured, highly equipped Humvees. One would think gold was being transported. It was in fact white gold, the kind that goes up through the nose.

In the distance, a black Humvee 4x4 with showy chrome accessories and a detailed painting of a cartridge on the bonnet swerved into the street and roared up to the veranda. The sunroof was open and a man in a bulletproof vest and headset stood behind a military machine gun in a rotating gun carriage. Another gunman was sitting in the back with a short-barrelled grenade-launcher. Their look, with mirrored sunglasses, beards, and neck and face tattoos was straight out of a Tarantino, too.

Kristen stifled a yawn and stood up, then leaned against the pillar riddled with bullet holes that was holding up the roof.

The Humvee stopped, the broad, deep-tread tyres slipping on the gravel and sending brownish billows of dust wafting over to her.

Four armed men got out of the car, barely distinguishable

from the man at the large machine gun. They wore Kevlar vests, high-tech headsets, modern automatic rifles and hand grenades. The *Zetas* were paramilitaries with good equipment and good training. It hadn't surprised Kristen to learn that they ruled large sections of the Mexican countryside and even held off the Mexican military.

'Hello,' she greeted them in Spanish, smiling slightly.

'Hello, beautiful,' said the man closest to her. A spider tattoo splayed across his face. The bilious green arachnid began in the upper left corner of his forehead at his black hairline. He would have difficulty finding employment in a reputable business with it, but that probably wasn't something he was planning. He was thickset but muscular. 'You're the Russian bride?'

Seeing no reason to correct him, she nodded. She was aware that she stuck out like a sore thumb in her fancy clothes, but it didn't bother her. 'I'm Sophia.'

'Aye, aye. I'm Trejo.' He grinned, revealing two gold incisors. 'You ordered a Learjet to Toronto?'

'Indeed. Direct.'

'Do you have the money?'

'Do you have the jet, Trejo?' Kristen slowly put on her sunglasses and looked up at the blue sky as though she was sunbathing.

He tapped the headset. 'I can summon the plane as soon as you've shown me your cash. It won't land until then.'

Kristen used her heel to lift up a loose plank in the veranda, exposing a suitcase underneath. If they'd already stumbled into a Tarantino routine, she might as well exude a little dramatic flair.

Trejo dispatched one of his team with a nod, who fetched the suitcase, put it down in front of his boss and opened it. Inside there were stacks of violet 500 euro notes: 100,000 euro for a trip to Canada.

The *Zetas* didn't know her actual destination. 'So, where is the plane?'

Trejo grinned broadly and switched on a channel to the pilot, gave him orders to land at Mier Airport and finally got ready to move off again. 'I'll take you to the terminal,' he said, laughing, and made a gesture to usher his team back into the Humvee.

Kristen left the veranda, got into the Ramcharger and sped after the gang, who hurtled through the streets as though racing to an unknown finishing line.

Very quickly, a very clear picture emerged of the terror that the *Zetas* invoked: as soon as the man with the machine gun saw a possible target, be it an animal or a car in their path, he opened fire. Empty casings flew in a high arc, raining down on the Ramcharger like metal hail. He was encouraged by the man at the grenade-launcher, who kept trying to destroy the machine-gunner's targets before he could hit them.

The heavy-calibre artillery left a trail of devastation in their wake. Buildings, wooden huts, fleeing trucks and bystanders disappeared with a flash, leaving behind piles of rubble, crumbled auto parts and dismembered limbs.

Kristen switched on the windscreen wipers to get the machine gun shells and dirt off the windscreen. Disgust rose up within her, but she couldn't do anything. The *Zetas*, like all other cartels, were unscrupulous thugs, but she needed them. With their help she had already abducted two Death Sleepers. Mr Estevez was one of them.

By the time Carretera Federal 54 was in sight, the destruction by Trejo's troops tallied one person dead, nine blown up dogs and cats and fresh bullet holes in practically every façade they passed.

Above them, the chartered plane was moving into its approach with screeching engines: a Learjet 40 that would take her to Toronto in just three hours.

She felt good. Very soon she would be enjoying the comforts of an air-conditioned cabin and relaxing with a bit of TV, if while urgently tossing back some essential Hello-Awake tablets.

To sleep properly – insofar as it was possible with insomnia – she'd have to wait until Minsk, and use anaesthetic if needs be. But first she needed to get through the interview in Paris that she was due to hold with an applicant for the position of doctor. She wondered if she should ask the woman to come to her.

The Humvee braked to a halt suddenly before leaving the shelter of the intersecting road that was called Palacios something. The bullet-riddled signs on the walls were barely readable.

The guy with the machine gun changed his ammunition belt and the gunman with the grenade-launcher started frantically reloading his machine as well.

'What the—? Hey!' cried Kristen and stopped too. She opened the door to ask Trejo what he was playing at. She wasn't in fear of her life. She knew she was worth more to the *Zetas* alive. What was this? A potential renegotiation? A second helping? 'Hey, Trejo! What's going on?'

Then she noticed a man in desert fatigues and a helmet emerge at the turning a little to their right, carrying an M16; Kristen saw the Mexican emblem on his sleeve. Unbeknownst to the *Zetas*, he knelt down under the cover of a wall and spoke into a two-way radio.

'Shit!' Kristen knew what that meant: the military was making an attempt to clear Ciudad Mier of drug barons. A million-dollar jet was a lucrative target for an army that otherwise had few successes against the cartels.

The soldier stood up again and slowly moved backwards.

Kristen leaned out of the window and shouted at the machine-gun shooter. 'Hey, you, to the right, military!' The man shouted something to her that she didn't understand. But clearly neither his weapon nor the grenade launcher were ready for action. The sadistic shoot-'em-up had used up the ammunition.

The Humvee in front of them suddenly reversed and rammed the Dodge.

Kristen was flung against the seatbelt, then cursed as she put the car into reverse and swerved around the armoured 4x4. Trejo seemed to have lost interest in his client.

Then she realised why the *Zetas* were in a hurry: an armoured reconnaissance tank was coming down the street towards them, the artillery directed straight at the Humvee.

Trejo's driver reacted as quick as a flash and took off. The salvo fired from the tank ripped up the ancient asphalt. Seconds later, two armoured military jeeps tore around the corner and took up the pursuit.

Kristen turned off her engine, lay down across the gear stick and passenger seat and didn't move. With any luck the inconspicuous Ramcharger wouldn't be linked to Trejo's troops in the initial confusion.

She listened carefully to the noises, ready to leap out of the driver's cabin should the volleys get nearer.

One car and then another rolled past, then came the muffled rumble of the armoured reconnaissance tank and shots from far away. The impact of far-off explosions made the windows of the Dodge shudder.

When she judged it safe, she sprang up in her seat and saw to her relief that she was alone. She immediately started the car, put her foot down and drove towards the Carretera Federal – smack into the middle of a group of advancing infantrymen. *Damn.*

Kristen didn't slow down. Soldiers collided with the Ramcharger, she could see the men's shocked faces. They bounced off the car and were flung away. A large backpack radio smashed to pieces on the radiator grille, blood sprayed across the scratched paintwork and windscreen, a helmet careened into the side door. She had crashed her way right through the crowd.

The Mexican troops behind her opened fire. There was a strange clinking as the bullets pierced the bodywork and whirred through the interior like angry insects.

Kristen took a turning, leaving the soldiers behind her. She headed for the wide national road, where she could make out the jet about two hundred metres away. It was already surrounded by a military unit and two pilots were coming out of the narrow door with their hands up.

An olive-coloured, angular helicopter swept over her head, and she recognised the two fully automatic Gatling machine guns on the fuselage boom, with legs that had been set to rotate. But to her relief the helicopter joined in the search for Trejo. The Ramcharger had been deemed a secondary target.

The jet was getting closer; the military unit there noticed her. Four men knelt down and raised their guns, the muzzles swivelling towards the Dodge.

'No! I'm an American!' she shouted out the window. Kristen took her foot off the accelerator as she put the headlights on full, still beeping, and waved out the window. She shrank down behind the wheel to give them a difficult target until she was deemed harmless, and took a small tin with a blue label out of her jacket. She quickly swallowed two pills from it and washed them down with piss-warm Coke. 'American! Do not shoot!'

She released the clutch and stopped the battered, blood-splattered Ramcharger twenty metres away from the army unit.

She opened the door carefully, and got out with knees shaking, her hands in the air. She was glad now to be wearing the designer clothes that were so unusual for the area and which distinguished her from the *Zetas*. 'Don't shoot! I've been abducted!' she cried in Spanish with an American accent. Covered in red stains and streaks, she staggered from the car towards the baffled men, then stumbled and fell. But this was no longer an act. Her body was barely obeying her any more; the contents of the tablets were having their effect. Just a few more seconds.

Two men broke away from their formation and walked

over at the double, the guns still pointed at her. 'Stay down, stay down!' they shouted. 'Down, down!'

Kristen felt the warmth of the asphalt underneath her cheek and smelled the dust.

Trejo's black Humvee appeared some distance away. The attack helicopter cut off its path as the Gatlings fired incessant rounds into it; the shell casings hailed down in black streaks.

The armour-plating of the 4x4 was no match for the projectiles. It exploded as the grenade ammunition detonated. The helicopter crashed through the blackish-red oily fireball that had launched itself at the sky, the Gatlings still shooting. Apparently the *Zetas* also had ground troops.

Kristen's sight blurred, sounds became muted. Small black dots wavered on the roofs of houses in the distance, thin lines with flames flickered out of them. Everything was swimming.

Hands grabbed her, frisked her roughly and turned her over onto her back. Two indistinct faces looked enquiringly at her from underneath a helmet and balaclava.

'Can you hear me?' she heard from very, very far away.

The sleeping tablets finally had an effect and Kristen closed her eyelids with an evil smile.

. . . only to open them again immediately.

At least, that's how it seemed in the first seconds of being awake.

But the heavy darkness around her – darkness and silence – betrayed how much time had gone by. Hours certainly. She looked at her watch. She had slept for two hours.

Groaning, she stood up and took a deep breath of the Mexican night air, then cast a look around. It smelled of chemical fire, of death mingled with a strange whiff of chlorine.

That was her personal trademark, just as the smell of maize had been for Patient 22.

Beside her lay the two dead soldiers who had frisked her.

The rest of the troops were lying around the jet along with the pilot of the civil aircraft; from their positions it was clear that the people had dropped where they were standing.

The military helicopter had ploughed into the first row of houses in Ciudad Mier and started a fire that had extinguished by itself due to lack of fuel. The explosions that had blown up the houses must have been spectacular.

The armoured reconnaissance tank lay on its side in the middle of the Carretera Federal, a 4x4 snarled up in it. A second jeep was parked safely five metres away, the passengers in their seats as though asleep.

Kristen spat. She didn't like the taste the sleeping tablets left in her mouth.

The smell of chlorine gradually evaporated, the smoke from the fires in the city remained.

With uncertain steps, she walked to the Ramcharger and opened the bullet-riddled tailgate. Without the protective metal box that had held off all of the bullets, the American's body would no longer have been any use. Kristen opened the crate, heaved Clarence over her shoulders and trudged forwards.

Puffing and panting, she carried him past the dead bodies and up the narrow steps of the jet into the cabin, and arranging him on one of the seats, she strapped him in.

Bathed in sweat, Kristen closed the hatch, her thigh muscles shaking from the exertion.

She swallowed three of her Hello-Awake tablets, followed

by a pill for her headache. That should be enough for now. If the effects wore off she would take amphetamines. She found an energy drink in the minibar, rinsed out her mouth and spat.

Then she continued on to the cockpit and sat down in the pilot's seat, pulling on the headphones and activating the radio.

Messages were coming through the ether thick and fast: agitated warnings to avoid the Ciudad Mier area due to the release of poison gas by the *Zetas*, which had killed off one of the military's special units. A second special commando unit was apparently already on its way.

'I'll be gone by then,' murmured Kristen, and booted up the plane's flight control system. One of the advantages of being the wife of a multi-millionaire for many years was that she had learned many things. Like flying.

The military wouldn't find poison gas. The death she brought left no traces. Her stay in Mier would have been the only clue, but nobody was left to say anything about her.

Kristen brought the jet into the starting position, called up the navigational information and changed the route. For the time being she would fly under the radar inland and then backtrack to be certain that the Mexican military weren't on her tail. The tanks of the Learjet were full and despite the detour they would last until Toronto.

The engines purred as Kristen accelerated.

The airplane gathered speed, shooting across the Carretera Federal 54. At around 300 kilometres an hour she raised the nose up and the Learjet lifted into the evening sky as she kept the propulsion steady to rise quickly. At 800 kilometres an hour, she swept towards the Mexican interior, only to loop back after fifteen minutes and swing towards Canada.

She was sorry she'd had to kill the soldiers, but she had been forced into it. No other way. She didn't fancy hours of interrogations by the Mexican authorities or having the DEA intervene to get their hands on her. The head of the DEA's Caribbean division in the boot of the Ramcharger would have raised some questions that she didn't want to answer. Especially since Clarence and the Deathslumberers seemed to know that she was responsible for the disappeared Death Sleepers. She couldn't have had that.

Kristen just hoped that it hadn't caught too many residents in Ciudad Mier.

The extraction of Clarence had obviously got out of hand, but it was still what you'd call a success. That was all that mattered.

Paris, France

Konstantin followed the still unidentified man as he walked away with a slight limp. He'd plenty of opportunity to take photos on his phone, although he doubted whether any of them would be usable for identification, given the man's beard and sunglasses.

They didn't leave Île Saint-Louis. The LeMat owner was heading towards an old delivery van parked opposite a church on the rue Poulletier. Traces of now meaningless advertising slogans and paintings were still visible on the faded paintwork. The man took the key out of his pocket, opened the side door and disappeared inside.

A Bedford Blitz. God! An ice-cream seller used to drive around the streets where we lived in a van like that: A box-shaped mini-van with a short nose and probably no more than eight horsepower. The stranger seemed to be a fan of old cars and not one to set much store by speed, which suited his unique sense of style. Or else his financial means didn't allow for anything more.

Huh. Konstantin was thinking about what to do next when the door swung open again.

The stranger had put on a simple denim jacket and slung another photography bag around himself. The rocker haircut had vanished underneath a worn-out dark blue peaked cap. He waved down a taxi, got in and disappeared.

Konstantin's gaze drifted over to the Bedford Blitz.

He took his time looking around, then went over to the mini-van, smashed in the window with one elbow and opened the door.

He jumped in and immediately began coughing. The atmosphere inside the van was like a smokers' pub that hadn't been aired in ten years. The windows were coated with a yellowish film. He tore the casing off the cable harness and looked for the right wires to hot-wire the car.

The Bedford came to life with a sputter on the third attempt.

Like riding a bicycle.

With a powerful wrench he broke the steering wheel lock and drove away, leaving the street and island behind. He parked the Blitz in a car park on boulevard Morland and then slid between the seats into the back.

The smell of stale smoke clung to everything, but it was

quite tidy, which surprised Konstantin. He had anticipated more mess. The built-in cupboards showed a great desire for organisation.

A laptop had slipped off a small table while Konstantin was driving the unfamiliar car and landed on a roll mat without getting damaged. He pocketed the memory cards lying around on the floor.

He scoured the cupboards quickly but carefully and found camera equipment, directional microphones, night-vision goggles, recording devices, hand-held video cameras and miniature lenses, tracking devices and other gadgets you needed if you were going to try to spy on someone unnoticed.

A small electronic box no bigger than an old-fashioned mobile phone remained a mystery. It was powered by a battery that weighed a kilo and looked hand-made, and had an on-off switch and a short, thick antennae. Konstantin suspected it was a scrambling transmitter.

Amid everything else, Konstantin also found fags by the packet in a brand he didn't know, nicotine plasters, sweet treats and insulin in injection pens and small glass vials with disposable needles.

He obviously has trouble with his blood sugar levels. And nicotine. Konstantin started up the laptop, but ran into difficulty at the first request for a password.

He packed the machine away to hand over to Jester later. His MI6 experts would definitely have the electronic security barriers cracked in seconds. And then the man's secrets would undoubtedly be laid bare – or at least be much easier to ferret out.

No identity documents, no personal belongings, he didn't

even find a name. But he did make a note of the number plate. He'd have Jester check that too. *It will have been stolen.*

Konstantin kept looking.

A notepad with one last blank page caught his attention. He found a pencil in the cupboard and shaded over the paper very carefully.

Gradually, letters emerged but the words overlapped and clashed. A puzzle that he would rather begin at home or in his hotel rather than inside the Blitz.

Konstantin took an empty plastic bag out of a small cupboard and put the computer and notepad inside. It was time to clear off.

His mobile vibrated.

The number was withheld but he had an idea of who it might be. He took the call without introducing himself.

The sound of soft breathing issued from the loudspeaker, 'Durga,' said a woman's voice.

Konstantin smiled. *Just as I thought.* 'Hello. This is Oneiros.'

'The fact that you're getting in touch is a stroke of luck that I absolutely welcome,' said the woman in Indian-accented English. '*Namaste.*'

'*Namaste,*' he returned the greeting and caught himself bowing slightly and almost wanting to put his hands together out of old habit. 'How is the weather in Chennai, Durga?'

'I don't know. I'm not in Chennai, Oneiros.' She laughed. 'I was thinking about you just last week.'

'Really?'

'Yes. They were talking about how you escaped back then.'

'Without your help, Yama and his troops would have caught me.' Konstantin got out of the Blitz and left the door open so that tramps and Parisian youths could let off some steam in it. It would wipe out any traces he'd left and make the theft look like a coincidence. 'You're travelling on business, I assume.'

'You assume correctly. I'm getting ready.' Her voice sounded pleasantly soft, like warm milk. What a contrast to her career and to what she was about to do. 'It must be something important if you're calling. You haven't called in a long time.'

Konstantin saw her in his mind's eye, the small-boned, light-footed Indian woman with the striking face who looked just as good in a business suit as she did in a traditional sari. Or with nothing on at all.

Vivid memories of their encounters conjured the scent of her perfume as he walked along a road taking him back to Notre Dame. But they came from a life that he had believed was over. Until events had started to escalate.

'I'm sorry to disturb your preparations.' He knew that in the next few hours a person would die at the hands of her gift. He couldn't change that, no matter what, and he didn't criticise Durga. It wasn't his place. Not with his history. 'There are storms in Europe right now. The Torpor's Men are looking for a man called Bent Arctander who used to be one of their members. He's a narcoleptic who is extremely dangerous because he cannot control the curse. And one of my friends—'

'You mean Commander Darling,' she interrupted him, amused. Her voice resonated with unmistakeable disgust. 'The man who thinks he's a new and improved James Bond.'

'Yeah. Darling has found out that the Phansigar are after Arctander.' Konstantin hoped he wasn't making a mistake with this phone call. But he trusted Durga. 'Can you tell me what you're planning to do with him?'

The Indian woman was silent for a few beats. 'I'm sorry, but I don't know this Bent Arctander.'

Now Konstantin was baffled. *Would she lie to me?* 'Do you have a record of him under a different name?'

'I would know if we were looking for a narcoleptic, Oneiros. An unusual issue.' She giggled. 'You don't believe me. I can just see your sceptical face.' There was a rustling, it sounded like she was transferring the receiver into the other hand. 'By the goddess whose name I bear, I swear to you that, until you called me, the name Arctander meant nothing to me, and therefore we, the Thuggee Nidra, aren't hunting him.' After taking a breath she added, 'To me, the question that now arises is: why is Darling claiming this?'

Konstantin was asking himself the same thing. *Is Jester so desperate that he's actually ready to lie to me?* 'I'll find out. Thank you so much, Durga. Take care.'

'That's what I should be saying to you. I can't save you again, Oneiros.'

'I'm leading a different life—'

'— that still links you to MI6, and so you're still living practically the same life.' There were quiet clangs in the background, she was handling something metallic. 'Beware of us, Oneiros. Every day, Yama hates you more.' She hung up.

Konstantin was standing in front of a shop window and could see himself in it; with the plastic bag, fancy suit, tie, hat and sunglasses he thought he looked like a stranger.

She's right. I should watch what I do, or soon I'll be leading that life again, the one I'd had enough of.

He put his mobile away and strolled to the cathedral.

The bells weren't ringing any more, and the Mass had definitely begun; a latecomer would stand out immediately.

Konstantin decided to look in on Lilou later. He couldn't get Durga's image out of his head. Rising up out of his memories, it got stuck like an old picture wedged into a mirror frame.

He didn't know her real name. Death Sleepers who worked as assassins generally used codenames. His had been Oneiros, the demon of dreams. Durga was the angry manifestation of the goddess Kali, which essentially translated as 'difficult to grasp'. *She couldn't have put it any better.*

Similar to how he had come across Jester while on a mission, his first meeting with the Phansigar had been unintentional and had gone violently.

Where the MI6 man certainly showed some humour, the Indians had less of a sense of friendly collegiate rivalry. Apart from Durga, with whom he'd had a passionate affair. A kind of cat-and-mouse game – sometimes they slept together, sometimes they tried to beat each other at their job, only to end up in bed together again later.

During his fourth operation in New Delhi, the Phansigar, under the leadership of Yama, suddenly turned up and tried to kill him. They had almost caught him. Durga had saved him from her own people.

If they ever find out about that, they would punish her without hesitation.

When he'd quit two years ago he'd broken off contact with her. To protect her, to protect himself. He was never sure what the reason was.

Sometimes Konstantin regretted not staying with Durga

and persuading her to quit with him. It was something special, having a relationship with somebody who understood what it meant to be a Death Sleeper. It didn't make their curse any less dangerous for the surrounding area; on the contrary in fact, two people with the same deadly gift staying in the same place were even more dangerous. But you could look out for each other more.

Don't kid yourself. If we had got out of it together, the Phansigar would have hunted us both down and destroyed our bodies.

Durga was . . . so very different from Iva. The thought of Iva pushed aside all memories of the Indian woman, as though his emotions were trying to tell him who had the upper hand over his heart and soul.

He pulled himself together and made an effort to divert his thoughts to the issues at hand. He knew Durga too well. She wasn't lying to him. And so a simple but important question remained unanswered: *Why would Jester be claiming that the Phansigar are after Arctander?*

His friend probably wanted to build up even more pressure to get him to change his mind and join the hunt for Arctander. *I understand it, but it's not nice.*

Konstantin felt the weight of the laptop in the bag and decided not to hand the computer and memory cards over to Jester just yet. He had promised him he would do some investigating. *And that's what I'm doing right now.* He would find someone who could crack the password. His apprentice Jaroslaf was sure to have a friend studying IT who would like to earn a few euro on the side. *Jester will be astonished if I can give him something MI6 couldn't find out.*

As he passed a pharmacy, he had an idea.

Konstantin went inside and looked for the digital photo stand. He found the machine and had an extra stroke of luck: the ungainly piece of machinery offered ten prints for an exorbitant price, as well as the option to order them. From CD, memory card or USB. *Perfect.*

Konstantin put down the bag and fed the stolen memory cards into the photo stand one by one to display the photos the stranger had taken.

In the first few photos he saw himself and von Windau in Leipzig. After that came pictures of the brown-haired woman from different angles taken with a powerful telephoto lens, then pictures of her and a tall, scrawny man at Leipzig airport; and finally a photo of the flight announcement to Minsk.

Was von Windau planning to go there or was it the bag of bones? Konstantin printed out a picture of the woman and the man and made a note of the flight number.

Awaiting him on the second chip were photos that had been taken with an infrared night-vision device. The faces in the photos were unrecognisable and the high ISO number distorted their features. The next photos showed a blurry building that looked a bit like a train station, shops and a recurring figure, always from behind. Another train station, a platform with a handful of people.

Finally there were two photos that were so clear that Konstantin could recognise who the bearded stranger had been following: *Arctander!*

The Scandinavian had been caught from the side, holding a train ticket in his hand. In the other hand he had a half-eaten pretzel; he was carrying his things in a small suitcase that would go through as hand luggage. He looked unbelievably tired.

The next picture showed the zoomed in ticket. It had been issued from Munich Main Station to Venezia Santa Lucia. According to the date he had set out the day before yesterday.

The lagoon city. He was hardly going there for romance.

Should he get on the next flight and fly to Venice to look for Bent Arctander? The small city was easy to search, he didn't stand too bad a chance of finding him. But Konstantin dismissed the idea. *He was there two days ago. He could be somewhere else entirely now.*

What he found more remarkable was that the unknown photographer, who had a weakness for files, nicotine and sweet things despite his blood sugar issues, was able to find the narcoleptic, photograph him and not intervene while Jester was run off his feet and pulling out all the stops at MI6 without even coming near him.

What is this man's game? There's no doubt he knows how much of a danger Arctander is to the general public.

Konstantin printed out two copies, paid by credit card and left the pharmacy.

He would look for Arctander, but without the help of the Torpor's Men and MI6. It was all too messy. To begin with, Konstantin wanted to do some investigations of his own and draw his conclusions from that before he discussed it with Jester. *Jaroslaf will help me to crack the laptop. With the information on it I'll be a bit more in the know.*

Plus, he figured, he would have more of a chance if he looked for the narcoleptic on his own. Arctander knew the face of every one of the Torpor's Men and would panic if he saw them. The panic would cause a narcoleptic fit – and thence the next catastrophe. *Jester will understand my reasoning.*

Konstantin crossed a bridge, sat down on a bench in the square in front of Notre Dame and waited. He placed the plastic bag with the laptop next to him.

As soon as the people had left the cathedral, he would go inside. One last visit to Lilou de Girardin.

Without his make-up and thanatological case.

Leipzig, Germany

'And he cracked it?' Konstantin looked at the laptop that he'd nicked from the Bedford Blitz and given to Jaroslaf after he'd got back. His trainee didn't ask any questions when he heard his boss' flimsy explanation. He brought the computer back the very next day. 'This quickly?'

Jaroslaf nodded. Underneath the open coat he'd put on, a black T-shirt with the words Undertaker Squadron printed on it showed through. Goth humour. As long as Jaroslaf only wore it in the backrooms, Konstantin had no objection to it. 'Yes, Mr Korff. Wasn't easy, but he ... let's say he's got certain programmes. He buys used computers and wipes the hard drives before handing it over to the customer. Otherwise Nana Müller's porn pictures end up somewhere else. So he's really good at it.'

'Thank you.' Konstantin was about to give him a hundred euro for his friend.

Jaroslaf waved it away. 'No need, Mr Korff. He did it for free.' He went to the door, opened it and vanished.

Konstantin flipped up the laptop screen and turned it on.

Seconds later the start-up tune sounded on cue and a basic user interface appeared with a password request.

Who are you, you diabetic nicotine junkie? His fingers settled on the touchpad and began to search.

More quickly than he'd have liked, Konstantin realised that there was very little information that he could make use of. Jaroslaf's colleague may have removed the first hurdle, but many areas remained locked beyond his reach. Every attempt to open a programme faltered at a password request. Underneath *properties* and *user*, Joe Bloggs had been entered.

'Shit.' Konstantin snorted.

After thinking it over quickly, he opened up the Internet browser and connected to the Internet using the Wi-Fi connection in the office.

This time he was not disappointed. Using the browser history he visited the pages the stranger had surfed: airlines, travel agents and train operators all over the world.

On top of that there were two data storage servers, password-protected, of course, as well as articles from different newspaper websites, including various reports on the plane crash, the survivor killed later, the baffling deaths in Roccastrada, a brief article on the death of a swarm of birds in Minsk and a few other pieces that made sense in relation to Arctander or the photos of the baroness, some more than others.

It was up to Konstantin to assemble the information. He connected the printer and printed out the browser history so that he could make notes on the pages.

He still couldn't understand what the stranger was trying

to achieve by what he was doing. He shadowed, documented, kept himself in the background, but didn't necessarily shy away from any confrontation if spotted, as had happened with Konstantin. What's more, the chain-smoker had an accurate idea of what it meant to be a Death Sleeper.

Suddenly a pop-up window opened with a chat protocol in it.

NoOne has logged in.

A message appeared in the little box.

NoOne: Whoever stole my computer, I'm going to find you, you arsehole!

He logged in on another computer and waited. At first Konstantin wanted to break off the connection, but then he typed – and he couldn't believe his eyes. A name flashed up in front of his words: *Thielke*. The stranger had used a name in this programme.

Thielke: How is your Bedford?

NoOne: I WILL FIND YOU. And then you'll get what's coming to you.

Konstantin thought of the LeMat revolver and the wound in his leg.

Thielke: You'll be searching a long time then.

NoOne: Going online was a mistake, you arsehole!

The little green light next to the webcam in the monitor frame lit up.

NoOne: Aha? The gentleman thanatologist? Well then, I can skip the IP search. Judging by the looks of your background, you're sitting in Ars Moriendi.

Konstantin cursed. 'I take it you can hear me, Mr Thielke?'

NoOne: Yes.

'Don't you want to speak to me?'

NoOne: No. I'll write.

'Fine.'

Konstantin assumed he was in a public place, probably in an Internet café.

'Did you find your van again?'

NoOne: Yes I did.

'And?'

NoOne: Everything was still there. Suspected someone else, but now I know who I have to thank for it. I was careless. I'll hijack your houseboat in return – how would you like that?

'Not funny, Mr Thielke. Would you answer a few questions for me?'

Konstantin leaned forward so that he could look directly into the camera.

'For instance, how come you know about Death Sleepers and why are you following Arctander?'

NoOne: No.

'Then perhaps a hint about von Windau?'

NoOne: Ask your MI6 friend. I'm just an observer. Mostly. Well, let's put it this way: I'm capable of shooting body parts other than legs, if I think it's appropriate.

'A threat?'

NoOne: No. Just a statement.

'But you didn't do anything to Arctander, even though, on an A380, he—'

NoOne: I didn't get close enough. Limited range. But you don't understand.

Konstantin looked pensively at the screen. *He wants to take the narcoleptic out of action too.*

NoOne: You robbed me, Korff. I take that personally.

Konstantin burst out laughing.

'You shot me in the leg. How should I take that? Not personally?'

NoOne: To be fair, I had warned you. You would have taken out a cripple like me with your aikido moves.

Why cripple? 'Don't you think it would be easier to meet and we can dis—'

NoOne: I've already met you. :o)

Hilarious! Konstantin started again.

'— we would meet without injuring each other and then we could talk?'

NoOne: So that your MI6 friend can do me in? Not a chance, Korff. Besides, I prefer to work alone. You can keep the laptop. I deleted my data during our conversation and have installed various viruses. So now the thing is junk. Have a great day.

NoOne has logged off.

The little green operating light next to the camera switched off. At the same moment, the screen went black and the laptop turned itself off.

Konstantin decided against trying to restart the computer. He believed what Thielke had said.

The hum of the printer stopped too and it said ERROR on the display. There hadn't been enough time to get all of the browser history onto paper. There were eleven pages.

Konstantin picked up the piece of paper from the notepad in the Bedford. Under the light from the reading lamp, he tried to decipher the handwritten notes and wrote them down on a page of his own.

Soon it said:

Roccastrada, Via Balzina
Venice, farmacia al lupo coronato
—eMorocco, Daoudiate? Avenue Palestine?
Reloub E./ EDbl-O, 23.8
—eMadrid, Almudena
Minsk, Life Inst.?

Konstantin tried to work out what this was. *A kind of travel itinerary of Arctander's?* Had Thielke used his technical wizardry to find out where the fugitive was headed?

Since Venice was already crossed out, he supposed that Arctander had already left there. So Morocco? The 23.8 must refer to a date. It was in three days' time. Enough time to find out where in Morocco this street was located. Konstantin's Arabic was admittedly not the best, but it was good enough to find a place and ask a few questions.

Although this was difficult for him, Ars Moriendi would have to get by without him for the next while. He left his office and informed Mendy that he had to go away on urgent business matters. She made no comment.

'You have post.' Mendy pushed an envelope over to him. 'Yet again.'

Iva's handwriting was emblazoned across the envelope.

He took it and put it in his pocket. 'Hold the fort for me, Mrs Kawatzki. Give Jaroslaf plenty to do.' He ignored the letter to discourage Mendy from asking questions about it. Which she was dying to do, he could tell by looking at her.

'Of course.'

'If anything goes wrong, you can call me any time.'

Mendy shook her head and looked over the rim of her

black glasses. 'Just standard burials, nothing special. There'll be no need to worry while you're away, Mr Korff.'

Konstantin nodded to her and went outside to the fleet of cars where he'd left his bicycle.

He cycled to the pier so that he could take the speedboat to the *Vanitas*. He didn't think that Thielke would do anything to him. *He had long since had the opportunity.*

His mobile rang on the way: Jester. 'Yes?'

'"The true mystery of the world is the visible, not the invisible",' came the immaculate British English. 'So, old boy, do you want to chase the visible by the name of Bent Arctander with me?' Jester sounded confident.

'I don't think so.' Konstantin thought his own voice sounded different to usual. Cool and wary. 'I'm looking for him, but I have a few leads that I want to chase up by myself for now. Incidentally, I had a lovely chat with a man called Thielke.'

'Thielke? Who on earth is that?'

'The owner of the LeMat.'

Jester took a deep breath. He didn't seem pleased that Konstantin was going it alone. 'Well, well. You are the lone fighter yet again. But please keep me in the loop.'

'Any news on the baroness?'

'No,' he croaked.

'And on the Indians?' He couldn't resist throwing out the hook.

And Jester took the bait. 'Yes, I found out that the Thuggee Nidra are putting a team together. So of course that makes it even more difficult for us. If Arctander realises how many people are hunting for him, he will have one fit after another and you know what that means, old boy.'

You liar! Drop your secret service bullshit! I'm going to give him a piece of my mind soon, but only when I can enjoy presenting him with new information about Arctander. 'Well, good luck with your search then.'

'You too.'

Click.

Sulking. Typical. Konstantin sent him the pictures he'd taken of Thielke without any explanation. Then he steered the boat through the canals and headed for the lock. With the motor turned off, he let the boat float into the lock, which had to be worked by hand. Silence fell around him.

The silence reminded him of Notre Dame, of his visit to Lilou's coffin as its last guest. Around her neck, the beautiful young woman wore the blue diamond, enticing with its sparkle. It reminded him about the Reaper's Stones again. *I can't lose sight of that.*

He felt Iva's letter in his jacket pocket and could hear it rustling softly. A gentle reminder.

Konstantin thought about her, her words. He was on the trail of the fairy tales because of her and Jester's offhand words. He still didn't want to believe they could be right, but he couldn't just write off the lead without checking it.

How does one examine ancient stories for their factual content? It's totally mad. He sighed. Once he had sorted out his flight to Morocco, he would search the cupboard for his old book of Brothers Grimm tales. *Whatever. This is just crazy. Let's see what – if – the Reaper left any traces behind there.*

Godfather Death

There once was a poor man with twelve children who had to work day and night just to give them bread to eat.

When the thirteenth child came into the world, he was at his wits' end so he ran out onto the large country road and planned to ask the first person he met to be the godfather.

Then scrawny-legged Death walked up to him and spoke: 'Have me as the godfather.'

The man asked: 'Who are you?'

'I am Death, who makes everyone equal.'

Then the man spoke: 'You are the right one, you summon the rich and the poor alike, you will be the child's godfather.'

Death answered: 'I will make your child wealthy and famous; because whoever has me as a friend can want for nothing.'

The man spoke: 'Next Sunday is the baptism, be there on time.' Death appeared, as he had promised, and stood as godfather very respectably.

When the boy grew up, the godfather came one day and asked him to come with him.

He led him out into the forest, showed him a herb that grew there and said: 'Now you're to receive your present from your godfather. I am going to make you a famous doctor. When you are called to an ill person, I will appear to you every time. If I am standing at the head of the ill person, you may say boldly that you will cure him and then give him some of this herb and he will recover. But if I am at the feet of the ill person, then he is mine and you must say that he is beyond help. But beware that you do not use the herb against my will or you may fare badly.'

It wasn't long before the youth was the most famous doctor in the whole world.

'He just needs to look at the sick person and he knows how things stand, whether the person will get better again or die,' people said of him, and from far and wide people summoned him to see sick people and gave him so much money that he was soon a rich man.

Now, it happened that the king fell ill.

The doctor was called and he was to say whether recovery was possible or not. But as he approached the bed, Death stood at the feet of the ill man, so there was no cure for him.

'If I could indeed outwit Death once,' thought the doctor, 'he would certainly resent it, but since I am his godchild, he will probably turn a blind eye, I'll bet.'

So he seized the sick man and laid him the other way so that Death came to be standing at the man's head. Then he fed him some of the herb and the king recovered and was well again.

But Death came to the doctor, his face wicked and sinister, wagged his finger and said: 'You pulled the wool over my eyes, I will overlook it this time because you are my godchild but if you dare do that again, your time will be up and I'll take you away with me immediately.'

Soon afterwards the king's daughter lapsed into a severe illness. She was his only child, he cried day and night so that he began to go blind and he let it be known that whoever could save her from death would become her husband and inherit the crown.

The doctor, as he came to the sick girl's bed, saw Death at her feet. He should have remembered his godfather's warning but the great beauty of the king's daughter and the fortune of becoming her husband beguiled him so, that he cast all thought to the wind. He did not see that Death was giving him furious looks, raising his hand in the air and threatening him with his withered fist; he lifted the sick girl up and placed her head where her feet had lain. Then he fed her the herb and right away life stirred in her once more.

When he saw himself cheated of his property for the second time, Death strode over to the doctor and said: 'It's over for you, now it's your turn.' He grabbed him with his ice-cold hand so powerfully that he couldn't resist and led him into an underground cave.

There he saw thousands and thousands of lights burning in rows as far as the eye could see, some large, some medium-sized, some small. Every moment, some extinguished and others lit again, so that the little flames seemed to be in constant flux. 'Do you see,' said Death, 'those are humans' lifelights. The large ones belong to children, the medium-sized to married couples in the prime of their lives, the smallest to the elderly. But children and young people often also have just a little light.'

'Show me my lifelight,' said the doctor, thinking it would still be very big.

Death pointed to a small stub, which was just threatening to go out and said: 'Look, there it is.'

'Oh, dear godfather,' said the shocked doctor, 'light me a

new one, do it for my sake, so that I become king and husband to the beautiful daughter of the king.'

'I cannot,' answered Death, 'one must go out before a new one is lit.'

'So set the old one to a new one, so that it immediately goes on burning when that one comes to an end,' the doctor begged.

Death made as though to fulfil his wishes, handing a fresh, large light to him, but because he wanted to avenge himself, he deliberately made a mistake during the relighting and the little stick fell and went out.

Immediately the doctor sank to the ground and now he himself stumbled into the hands of Death.

Brothers Grimm, *Children's and Home Fairy Tales*, 1812 edition

XI

I often think of death so bleak,
The end I know I'll surely make?!
I'd like to die in sleep so meek
And hence be dead when I awake!

Carl Spitzweg

Marrakech, Morocco

Konstantin was practically sweating to death underneath the sunshade of the tea stall.

He was drinking boiling hot mint tea along with bottle after bottle of mineral water. The fluid seemed to seep straight out of his pores the moment he took a sip.

The 'Godfather Death' fairy tale had given him hope. You could talk to Death in it. You could outwit him – but also be outwitted by him.

But because it was in a fairy tale, it was still far from being fact. Konstantin was absolutely aware of that and he still felt strange analysing the story.

It was a thorough investigation, but he hoped to be able to discover clues and maybe patterns that would shed more

light on how to get in touch with Death. *If that's even possible.*
He can't see me of course. Ultimately, I need someone who will speak
to him for me.

Most of all, he needed time to sift through all of the
material. However, he had barely any free time to devote
to his investigations because he had to find Bent Arctander
first – in Marrakech, as he had found out from the Internet
and Thielke's notes. Yet, however helpful the notes were
in finding Bent Arctander, the photographer remained an
enigma. Jester had written to Konstantin saying that the
photographer's face didn't mean anything to him, but that
he was running the photo through the available databases.
Nothing had come of it yet.

Avenue Palestine had been relatively easy to find, particularly as Daoudiate, another word from Thielke's page of
notes, turned out to be the district of Marrakech where the
street was located. But when he asked after *Reluob, E, EDbI-0*
he didn't get anywhere. Konstantin could already see himself
making a pilgrimage from house to house reading the Arabic
nameplates next to the doorbells.

He had arrived in Marrakech one day before 23.8, the date
on the scrap of paper. So he was able to have a good look
around Avenue Palestine and find little hints that would work
to his advantage tomorrow.

He'd already done one expedition and realised that the local
temperatures were not designed for Western Europeans. As
a thanatologist, he would have had to work miracles to stop
the decomposition of a body in this climate – and poison the
flesh for the blowflies who were all too happy to lay their
eggs in it.

He avoided the medieval city centre with its hordes of tourists, despite the recommendation from the guidebook he'd read on the plane and its status as a UNESCO World Heritage Site.

He'd laughed especially when he'd read this passage:

... Come.

We particularly commend our main attraction in the old town to you, esteemed visitor: the Djemaa el Fna, which translates most accurately as 'Gathering of the Dead'. It is a world-famous medieval square where executions used to take place along with market activities.

Do not worry, today you will not ...

The Gathering of the Dead. Konstantin mopped the sweat from his forehead with a handkerchief. He had already walked up and down Avenue Palestine without finding anything particularly remarkable. This part of the city, the new town, fell outside the usual tourist attractions, if you ignored the nearby Jardin Majorelle.

No colonial glamour, no traces of the early days of Marrakech and there was certainly no modern bling.

Daoudiate contained a handful of small guesthouses, but was otherwise set aside for locals. It was especially populated by those families that Konstantin supposed had worked their way up from the working classes and were glad to have a little house in Marrakech. Judging by the style of architecture, which was loosely based on Europe's, he assumed they'd been built in the eighties. This area was also inhabited by traditional craftspeople who didn't produce tat and trinkets for gullible tourists, but instead, relatively low-priced items that were everything one needed for daily life.

The Avenue Palestine itself boasted several shops in which there were, among other things, baked goods, woodwork and metalware. In between these shops there were little tea shops serving the traditional brew of strong mint and sugar. The posters on the walls advertised a music festival and there was also an exhibition of contemporary art somewhere.

The sweet delicacies that Konstantin saw in the windows of the tea shops were tempting, but he didn't trust the glossy exterior. He didn't want to upset his stomach, even if the colourful confectionery cried out to be tasted.

The air was redolent with the scent of freshly baked bread and ground spices. It belonged to life in the new town; it wasn't part of a show put on for foreigners so that they could rejoice in the exotic and sensual Orient.

Konstantin rarely saw tourists, which was unfortunately a disadvantage. A light-skinned man like him stood out straight away, especially as he was wearing black, which wasn't exactly common in Marrakech. *No wonder, in this heat. I should have packed something white.*

As he sipped his tea, he considered whether he should put off exploring the street further until the cool of the evening time. *I'd better go for one last stroll around, I'm all sweaty anyway.*

Konstantin paid, stood up and felt his clothes stick to his clammy skin. *Maybe I'll buy something traditional to wear. Those flowing white robes don't seem too bad in these temperatures.* The Moroccan-Arab garment for men was called a *foqia* and because of his height, it would only reach his shins. *Plain linen trousers underneath and I would be suffering less.*

Walking in the shade, he strolled along Avenue Palestine, keeping an eye on the doorbells and the names next to them. He passed stands with dried fruit, fresh dates and figs, spiced meat that the locals bought and ate without thinking twice. Konstantin didn't dare. Travellers' diarrhoea would not come in handy for what he was planning.

He preferred looking at the woodwork on offer, the tables fitted with little iron tiles and enamel mosaics that were sturdier than they looked. He played the harmless tourist extremely well, he thought.

From behind his sunglasses he observed his surroundings, keeping an eye out for Thielke in particular. But he found neither the German, nor the nameplate he was after. He carried on looking for the needle in the haystack.

He went past a shop for *hammam* accessories and decided he would definitely visit one of the baths before he set out for his third patrol that evening. The facility was available where he was staying: a palatial hotel with rooms in a comfortable, converted Riyadh layout with a wonderful enclosed courtyard. *It will do me good!*

Konstantin thought about what he would do if Arctander really did turn up here. Killing him, as Jester planned to do, was not quite fair. *After all, Arctander hadn't been falling over himself to become a mass-murderer with a curse.* There were alternatives. An island for example. *Where there is nothing and nobody that he could harm.*

Konstantin thought his idea was better than what Jester had planned. Unless, of course, Arctander proved to be a psychopath who killed people randomly. *But Arctander has at*

*least earned the opportunity to speak to me. If he agrees to become
a hermit, I'll convince Jester.*

If Jester remained stubborn, he could also get the narcoleptic into exile without the knowledge of the MI6 commander and keep the place a secret. Jester would not find that funny.

In the reflection of the shop window he could see the entrance to a small shop behind him that was already closed.

His gaze fell on the owner's yellowed nameplate in the window and he couldn't tear his gaze away. E. Bouler.

It was quite a while before Konstantin realised why it had caught his attention. The letters gradually settled in a new order by themselves: *Reluob E. Is that the name that was on the piece of paper? Did Thielke get it wrong?*

He slowly turned around, crossed the street and positioned himself in front of the window.

The display was expensive but not very impressive: typical Moroccan jewellery, old watches, portraits of Moroccan rulers from different eras, everything at unaffordable prices and nothing for tourists who wanted to spend a few dirhams on a souvenir. Not even the residents of Daoudiate seemed to be the main customers. The pieces were too special, too old and too expensive for that.

The shop probably belonged to an antiques dealer or a pawnbroker. Konstantin placed a cupped hand on the glass and leaned forward to get a better look at the interior behind the reflective window. He was looking for clues as to why Thielke and Arctander wanted to come here.

The shop window gave no clues to *EDbI-O*, the abbreviation linked to Bouler.

In the reflection of the glass, he could see a figure in a

pinstriped black *foqia* emerge from the *hammam* accessories shop and make his way purposefully towards him. 'Mister,' came a voice behind him.

Konstantin turned around. 'Yes?' he said in Arabic.

The man, probably a Moroccan, smiled when he heard his mother tongue. 'Hello, sir. Are you interested in one of the pieces?' He put one hand in his pocket and looked around quickly.

Expecting an attack, Konstantin got ready to put his aikido into action. 'I collect unusual things,' he replied, the sunglasses hiding the mistrust in his dark brown eyes.

'Oh, well, in *that* case, you've come to just the right place: to Monsieur Bouler's.' He pulled out a key.

'You're Monsieur Bouler?'

'No, I'm his neighbour and occasional partner. My name is Rabih. Monsieur Bouler won't be back until tomorrow, but it would be criminal to turn a customer away because of that.' He smiled mischievously and opened the door for Konstantin. He was hit by the smell of stale incense, dried wood, leather, paper and spices. 'Here we are, sir. Come closer.'

Konstantin still wasn't convinced that this wasn't a trap, and remained on his guard. He took a step over the threshold.

Monsieur Bouler's shop seemed small, part corner shop, part thieves' lair, somewhat rundown with a pinch of opulence. The beams were old, the walls littered with cracks and sparsely furnished with ancient paintings.

'Impressive,' murmured Konstantin before turning to Rabih and taking off his sunglasses. 'I thought Daoudiate was a new town?'

'Oh, there are just so many treasures in Marrakech, you

know,' the Arab replied and grinned as though he were the brother of the sphinx. 'Where do you come from?'

'France.' He reached out his hand to the man. 'My name is Laurent. I was a bit surprised to discover the name of one of my countrymen on a shop.'

'That surprises you? The French were here quite a long time.'

Konstantin cursed inwardly. Correct, the French had been the colonial power. His knowledge of French history had never been the best. *How did it go again, with Casablanca and the period after that?* 'Yeah, but not in a district where there are supposedly only Moroccans around,' he tried to salvage his remark. 'How long has Monsieur Bouler been living in Morocco?' He gestured vaguely towards the room. 'Judging by this, he seems to have been living here a very, very long time.'

Rabih roared with laughter and clapped his hands. 'I'll tell him that. He is around seventy years old and has had this shop as long as I can remember. But I don't know exactly.' He went to the counter and pulled open some drawers. 'So, what can I do for you? Jewellery? Antiques? Old books by Arabic scholars?' He looked at Konstantin, waiting for an answer.

Is Bouler a Death Sleeper? Or is it something else about him that Arctander is interested in? He peered into the drawers and saw necklaces, medallions and rings that all bore the patina of age. 'Rings wouldn't be bad,' he said to occupy Rabih and give himself a chance to think. 'Preferably unusual ones.'

'Unusual, sir?' He pushed the drawers shut and took two steps to the side, bent forward and used his body to hide the movements of his hand. There was a squeak and a click, the hum of cogs.

A hidden safe. Good to know. Konstantin waited patiently, thinking.

First the dead people in Roccastrada, then the trip to Venice, now Marrakech. Why did Arctander want to meet Bouler? The narcoleptic broke off his escape from the Torpor's Men rather than keep moving. If he settled in a place he could be caught then the risk that he was taking was not insignificant.

Since Thielke had already traced Arctander to Venice, Konstantin assumed that the information about Marrakech was correct too. That in turn meant that Arctander must have shared his plans with someone, by phone, fax, email, text or some other way. In theory, MI6 could also have found out the time and place of Arctander's meeting with Bouler. That made this meeting very dangerous indeed. *He's probably also under more stress than usual. I have to read up about narcolepsy in the hotel straight after this.*

Rabih came back, balancing two strongboxes connected to a steel ring by a chain; just what this safeguard led to could not be seen. He put the boxes down on the counter, scurried to the door and closed up the shop. 'You will like this, Monsieur Laurent!'

He turned on a reading lamp and directed its pool of light at the chests, then turned the little wheel for the combination code so that the heavy locks snapped open. 'Voilà, Monsieur!'

The lids were lifted one by one.

The room was instantly bathed in sparkle and lustre. Innumerable facets refracted the light from the lamp and it danced colourfully around them, on the counter, on the men's faces, on the roof, into every last nook and cranny. Ali Baba's treasure trove couldn't have shone more.

Konstantin looked in awe at the emeralds, rubies and diamonds. He was certainly not an expert when it came to precious stones, but he knew a little bit about it through dealing with the jewellery of deceased people. If the stones weren't fakes, then the value of the two chests was in the hundreds of thousands. *Just like that. In the safe.*

'Is there anything here that takes your fancy?'

'Am I allowed to know where they come from?'

Rabih's laugh boomed out again and he slapped his chest. 'I swear to you, sir, that they were acquired legally. Monsieur Bouler and I will provide you with the certificates.'

'Hmm. Excellent. How much?'

The Moroccan smiled again in a very oriental-mysterious way. 'Which ring do you like, sir?'

'This one,' he said and pointed randomly at a ruby. He had been hoping to find an opal, but coincidence hadn't done him this favour.

'40,000. Non-negotiable.'

Konstantin had four hundred dirhams and two hundred euro in his bag. He thought it unlikely that Rabih accepted debit or Visa cards, not that his bank would ever let him transfer that kind of money. *And quite apart from that, what would I do with a 40,000-euro ring?*

'Ah, I see, you don't think the ring is so pretty any more. That can happen to anyone.' Rabih had mastered the art of allowing a customer with a small budget to save face. He packed away the chests with the precious stones and they vanished into the safe with the sound of rattling and chains jangling. Then he placed a small wooden box in front of Konstantin and opened it without any fanfare.

A selection of rings materialised in front of him, fixed in place on a black cushion, some more carefully than others. They had been expertly crafted, but the embedded jewels were little more than chips, hardly as big as an ant's eye.

'You said you were looking for something unusual and I think that this could be something for you.' Rabih held up a silver ring with a semi-precious stone in it, probably jade, as though rubies, diamonds and emeralds weren't worth anything anyway.

'Hmm,' said Konstantin, rubbing the stone and then the tarnished silver. *It's certainly old. Old and uncared for.* He put the ring down again and saw that a piece of the black material from the cushion had been tucked over. When he tried to fix it, another piece of jewellery appeared to his surprise, and it was out of the ordinary: a white ring for men in aged ivory covered with decorative carvings .

The broad upper part was modelled on a signet ring, with four carnations made from silver arranged in a cross shape, with the buds pointing outwards. A jewel the size of a fingernail sat in the centre of them, covered by a thick layer of grime.

'Oh my goodness. That old thing,' Rabih let slip. 'A real shelf-hugger. I think we've sold it three times already, but it came back to us every time.'

Konstantin was suddenly gripped by excitement. He recalled his investigations into the subject of Vanitas. Ivory stood for perpetual life, for purity. And the carnations ... what did they mean again? A coffin! No, *nails*. They stand for the suffering that Jesus bore on the cross. 'Can I take it out?'

'Of course, sir.'

Konstantin took the ivory ring out of the little box, turned it over and on the inside he spotted a barely visible engraving that with a lot of imagination could be interpreted as a skull. *Could that really be?* 'Why was it given back?'

'The buyers claimed they felt uneasy while wearing it. Which is clearly nonsense. We only sell rings without curses.' Rabih grinned.

'Is there a certificate for this one too?' He rubbed his thumb over the stone to get rid of the dirt. The base colour was a pale, watery blue with dark veins meandering and branching off through it. *Not an opal.* The surface was curved slightly, the carnations held the gem in a vice setting.

'Not against curses. You'd have to take my word for it on that.' He pointed to the ring. 'I don't know where we got it from. But Monsieur Bouler would know.' His body language clearly implied that he would prefer Konstantin to put the ring down and choose a different one.

Konstantin wouldn't even dream of it. 'What kind of stone is this?'

'This?' Rabih looked openly disappointed that he was so interested in the ring. In other words: the ring was too cheap for the salesperson's tastes. 'It's a harlequin opal, sir. I don't think this is quite the thing, if you're looking for something unusual.'

Two Vanitas motifs, an opal, the sign of the skull. This could be a Reaper's Ring! Konstantin had to have this ring, no matter how much it cost. He swallowed, wishing he could have a glass of sweet mint tea for his dry throat. 'How much?'

'I'm practically inconsolable to have to name this figure to you, which will certainly be an insult to you, because it doesn't do justice to you and your style.' Rabih made a grim face. 'Just 10,000 sir. Euro.' He flashed a smile. Konstantin understood: Rabih was an extremely cunning businessman who had skilfully lured the potential buyer and now held him tightly in a stranglehold of greed. *And I fell for it.*

Minsk, Belarus

Kristen watched the slumbering Clarence as he lay in the room where Patient 22 had been kept before the incident.

Professor Smyrnikov stood next to her, looking at the initial results of the tests on a tablet computer. He nodded approvingly. 'A very good test subject, Mrs von Windau. Blood and urine results are excellent, the cerebrospinal fluid is clean, no hidden meningeal infections. The CT and MRI have revealed that the man—'

'Patient 23.'

'— that Patient 23 is perfectly healthy. He has a flawless brain and is ready for the procedure.' He wedged the thin computer under one arm and looked expectantly at her. He wanted her to tell him what to organise now.

'Do you think Dr Tillman is capable of carrying on Willers' work?'

'He has settled in well, but you can tell that he is still a bit unsure.' Smyrnikov pointed to Clarence. 'Procedures where people like him undergo a serious change, without suffering from illness, is not on the agenda during medical training. But he claims to have already carried out research on people before, although he still needs to get used to our kind of experiments. Theory and practice.'

'And *will* he get used to it?' Kristen had met Tillman several times before she'd brought him to Minsk. He had given an impression of being steadfast and ambitious, someone who put scientific success before the good of the individual. But McNamara had been a promising candidate too, and she didn't want a repeat of that kind of fiasco.

Smyrnikov rubbed his chin. 'I'm keeping him under careful observation. We should wait half a year and see how he behaves during the operations. While we're on the subject, I'll deal with your new applicant's documents soon.' He pointed at Clarence. 'Prep for brain transplant, Mrs von Windau?'

Kristen looked at the sleeping man whom she had put into an artificial coma. He was linked up to an EEG to monitor his brain activity and to a brainwave stimulator to keep him in the delta zone using electrical impulses, no matter what happened.

A disaster like the one with Patient 22 could in no way be allowed to happen again. It had been hard enough finding replacements for the staff who had died. Besides, every approach was delicate. It would only take one slip to draw the attention of the Western media to the Life Institute.

'Send me a list of the potential recipients for Patient 23's brain. I'll select one. Meanwhile you can begin the first round of chemo on him,' she said and turned to leave the room. Smyrnikov followed her. She wanted to make sure that Clarence found a good new home. A body he felt comfortable in as soon as she took him out of the artificial coma. 'How long will the stem-cell treatment take to fix the severed connections?' She thought the ongoing results of this therapy boded very well. The complete fusion of recipient and brain was getting closer.

'We estimate sixteen weeks to achieve a rehabilitation of seventy-six per cent. Patient 22 took three months to reach sixty-six per cent. It will be safer to extend the immobilisation period to four months, to allow the stem cells to do their work. It's a shame that we also lost Patient 34 in the incident.' Smyrnikov looked truly upset, although Kristen knew this was mainly due to the loss of the results of his work.

'Yes. Very unfortunate.' The hybrid of Singh and Estevez had been coming on so well. The researchers were making incredible progress, however, and were putting into action the ideas that Mary Shelley had raised with *Frankenstein* nearly two hundred years before. 'I have to go to a meeting, Professor. Please keep the appraisal of the Parisian applicant in mind. Any other urgent issues?'

'Yes,' he answered hesitatingly and pointed to the door of his office just as they were passing by. 'Please come in.'

'Will this take long?' Kristen wanted to go and see her son. Eugen was waiting for her at the airport in St Petersburg. She had promised to come in her own plane. Thanks to a donation to the Belarusian air traffic authority, the Mexican Learjet had a new official identification and a fresh transponder with a harmless code. *Los Zetas* would never get the plane back.

'No. But I don't want to talk about it in the corridor.' He opened the door for her and Kristen went into his office with her arms crossed.

Smyrnikov went round the desk, sat down and looked up at her. 'It's about the results of your last routine test.'

When she didn't sit, he started to explain. 'We have found that the medication we are giving you for the insomnia is losing its effect more quickly than we had predicted. It's not responding to the stem-cell treatment either. More areas of your brain have already been affected. The symptoms of the condition will get worse.'

Kristen felt her stomach heave. 'How much time do I have left? Are you talking years, months, weeks?' she whispered. Her voice became husky in spite of herself. Meeting with Eugen was now all the more important to her and he was holding her up with bad news.

'I couldn't tell you. We will increase the stem-cell supply and try to be more aggressive in inhibiting the prions that are causing your brain to deteriorate. In my opinion, the treatment needs to be more direct than before. Administering it via lumbar puncture isn't enough. I would advocate a direct attack on the epicentres that we have identified in you.'

'Or?'

'You are already suffering from an extreme sleep disorder and cannot get into the important deep sleep phases under your own steam, Mrs von Windau. It cannot be long until oneiroid states occur. You will no longer be able to distinguish between dream and reality. Hallucinations, attention problems, muscular spasms and memory lapses will follow. You know that.' Smyrnikov looked at her, full of sympathy, and this time it might actually have been considered genuine. 'With all that we've achieved with you, we should already be guaranteed a Nobel prize.'

'An injection directly into my brain,' Kristen voiced what he had expressed in such a roundabout way. So she was going to become one of his test subjects. She thought about the risks, about the possible damage caused by the treatment. The needle administering the cells would need to go through sensitive regions of her brain. What would she do if she lost her speech, her sight or more? She still had too much to do to let herself be restricted to that extent. 'It's out of the question.'

'Mrs von Windau, if the insomnia in the—'

'How long?' she snapped at him, slamming her hands down on the desk. There was a tingling in her skull, electric shocks were racing through her brain. The colours in the small room were suddenly lurid, like in an overexposed film.

'I don't know,' he replied defensively. 'You know as well as I do that you're not a normal case.'

Kristen had had enough of his deflection. 'Tell me, Professor,' she murmured menacingly. Her brown eyes flashed. The taste of sulphur was on her tongue, her stomach was rebelling.

'You won't have more than a year without the invasive procedure that I recommended to you,' he countered with resignation. 'I can only estimate – you're aware of that. With stem cells we could, all going well, put off the transmutation of the protein as well as the symptoms for another year.'

Kristen was still seeing everything through a lurid filter, the room was bathed in white-tinged discolourations, at once very violet and pale grey. 'I'll stick with my no.'

She left the office and hurried down the corridor, got into the lift and went to the ground floor. A moment later she was standing on the street and rushing to her Mercedes.

A year.

Her lapses would get worse. How long could she wait before

climbing into the cryogen tank? And who would she entrust with looking after her and her father? Eugen was too young and too far away.

Kristen unlocked the car and jumped in. She stared at the dials on the dashboard as she took a little vial of tablets out of her jacket and swallowed two of them. One for the headache, one for the distorted vision.

There was no other way: she needed to speak to her ex-husband and ask him for a big favour. This undertaking would be more difficult than abducting Clarence, that was for sure. Not because it was more dangerous, but because the chances of achieving anything were much lower.

Her sight gradually returned to normal.

Kristen started the Mercedes and drove away. She made good progress, even though the volume of traffic seemed higher than usual. Almost like in Paris.

At least the stopover in Paris hadn't been a waste of time. The conversation with the applicant – a young professor called Rambois recommended to them by a doctor from the institute – proved very promising. The hints she dropped about the type of research they conducted hadn't been met with dismissal, and they had arranged to meet in Paris again. Privately, Kristen was surprised there were so many women interested in this area of research. She would have thought that the mothering instinct would have won out over unscrupulousness.

The phone rang, Smyrnikov's name appeared on the display.

Kristen switched on the hands-free mode. 'Yes, Professor? I'm listening.'

'Hello, Mrs von Windau,' she heard the doctor's voice. 'I'm going over the information on the French doctor, as promised. This Professor Rambois.'

'And?' Kristen turned onto the slip road to the airport. People made space for the impressive titanium-coloured Mercedes. 'Can we use her?'

'Her references are excellent, no doubt about that. The marks in pathology and surgery indicate a pendant, which is what we need,' he said thoughtfully. 'But there is an inconsistency that you should look into at your next meeting.'

'What kind?'

'It's less about the medical side of things. Rambois has stated that she has worked with Professor Wischner in Homburg, at Saarland University Medical Centre in Experimental Surgery. And this over a period of' – he leafed through some pages – 'a year and a half; and that she was in experimental neurosurgery. Also for a year and a half.'

Kristen had read the CV, but she didn't recall the details. 'What made you suspicious?'

'I know Wischner. He was in America for a year during that period as a guest lecturer at the University of Philadelphia.' Smyrnikov snapped the files shut. 'He could not have supplied that reference. At least, not in Homburg.'

Kristen asked herself how unworldly the professor was. 'Post? Email?'

'Mrs von Windau, don't you think I would have considered that? But unlike you, I am aware that Wischner *always* hands his references over in person and also addresses some celebratory words to his colleague. Always and without exception.' Smyrnikov was audibly pleased to be right. 'Either Rambois flew to America for her reference or Wischner happened to be in the country, which I doubt significantly. Which leads me to the conclusion that the reference is highly likely to have been forged. I'm not interested in having a fraud in my ranks.'

'Neither am I, Professor. Thank you. Ask Dr Dancer why he recommended her to us. I'll take care of Rambois.' Kristen hung up.

The French woman probably just wanted to embellish her CV. Another reason for the possible deception formed in her mind. A secret service had noticed the institute and had sent one of their spies there. It would be possible to find out whether Dancer, who had been doing research in Minsk for two years, was caught up in the deception. Perhaps he had been blackmailed to smuggle Rambois in.

Kristen reflected on whether she should drive straight to Paris and meet Rambois.

But Eugen was waiting for her in St Petersburg ...

In light of what Smyrnikov had revealed to her about the progression of her illness, she desperately needed to see her son and speak to him. He was the main reason she was doing all of this.

There seemed to be no end to the complications. First the thing with Patient 22, then Clarence and the *Los Zetas*, now a fraudster whose real motives Kristen would need to investigate.

She decided to find even more Death Sleepers in the coming days and bring them to Minsk. As reserves. In case her condition worsened quickly and she had to get into the freeze tank, Smyrnikov needed quite a few more of her kind.

for experiments. And because she didn't think the doctors would be capable of taking on the Death Sleepers who were well trained, armed and organised, she would have to do this preparatory work herself. She didn't need to be careful about keeping her identity a secret any more – as far as the Death Sleepers were concerned anyway. Since the thing with Clarence, the Deathslumberers would be sure of who to blame for the disappearance of the DEA agent.

Once she had reached the airport, she forced herself to stop brooding. More pleasant things awaited her: Eugen. The hours with him. His love, the radiance of his eyes, his sense of humour and his cheerful presence that gave her the strength to bear her insomnia and do her job. For him and for a shared future.

She parked the Mercedes, got out and walked across the car park and into the building where she headed for the transit area for private jets.

Out of habit, she came to an abrupt stop and turned around. It was an old test to see whether she was being followed.

A woman who had been about ten metres behind her turned around immediately, walked towards a magazine stand and considered the magazines on display with a very careful show of interest. She didn't look at Kristen once, but her behaviour was conspicuous enough.

On closer inspection of the airport concourse, she reckoned she had spotted two more people: a man and woman, behaving as though they had been busted. Nervous glances, fake laughter, agitated movements.

From this Kristen came to three conclusions. Firstly, the

agents were novices, secondly none of the three were Death Sleepers and thirdly a secret service operating in Belarus had recently taken an interest in her.

She changed her plan on the spur of the moment.

Take-off would be delayed for a few minutes.

The Messengers of Death

In the olden days there once was a giant who was trudging along a large country road. Suddenly a strange man jumped out at him and cried, 'Stop! Not one step further!'

'What?' said the giant. 'You midget, I could crush you between my fingers! You want to stop me in my path? Who are you, that you speak so boldly?'

'I am Death,' replied the other man, 'nobody can resist me, and even you must obey my commands.'

But the giant refused and started to wrestle with Death. It was a long, fierce struggle and finally the giant had the upper hand and struck Death down with his fist so that he crumpled next to a stone.

The giant went on his way and Death lay there defeated and was so weak that he could not get up again.

'What would come of it,' he said, 'if I were to stay here, lying in the corner? Nobody else in the world would die and it would become so full of people that they would no longer have space to stand next to each other.'

Meanwhile a young man came along the path, pink-cheeked and healthy, singing a song and casting his eyes here and there. When he caught sight of the half-unconscious man, he approached in sympathy, sat him up, poured a reviving drink from his bottle down his throat and waited until he regained his strength.

'Do you even know,' asked the stranger, as he sat up, 'who I am and whom you've helped get back on his feet?'

'No,' answered the youth, 'I don't know you.'

'I am Death,' he said, 'I spare no one and I can make no exception for you either. But so that you can see that I am grateful, I promise you that I will not pounce on you unawares, but rather I will send you my messengers before coming for you.'

'All right then,' said the youth, 'it will be an advantage to know when you're coming anyway and to be safe until then at least.'

Then he went on, was jolly and in good spirits and lived for the moment.

Only youth and health didn't last long, soon came sickness and pain that plagued him by day and robbed him of peace by night.

'I'm not going to die,' he said to himself, 'because Death will send his messengers first, I only wish the terrible days of illness were over.'

As soon as he felt well, he began to live a life of pleasure again. Then one day there came a tap on his shoulder; he looked around and Death was standing behind him and saying: 'Follow me, the hour of your departure from this world has come.'

'What,' answered the man, 'are you going to break your word? Did you not promise me that you would send me your messengers before you came yourself? I did not see any.'

'Silence,' replied Death, 'did I not send you one messenger after another? Did the fever not come, knock you, shake you and crush you? Did the dizziness not stun you? Did the gout not pinch your every limb? Did the toothache not gnaw at your jaws? Did your vision not go dark? Above all, did my blood brother, Sleep, not remind you of me every evening? Did you not lie in the night as though you were already dead?'

Not knowing what to say in response, the man yielded to his fate and went away with Death.

Brothers Grimm, *Children's and Home Fairy Tales*, 1857 edition

XII

I do not fear the death
that comes to take me away;
But fear so much that death
shall take my loved ones some day

Epigrams, Friedrich von Logau

Marrakech, Morocco

Konstantin held the ivory ring in his finger and watched the harlequin opal flash in the light and the silver carnations glint.

10,000 euro. The sum echoed like the chime of a bell in his head. *Is that too much or is it appropriate?* How was he meant to be able to check this quickly whether the fee was excessive? After all, he could be paying for nothing; even if the stories were true, there was no certainty that this piece of jewellery was one of the legendary Reaper's Rings. 'What misfortune did it bring?'

Rabih hadn't moved, but his dealer's smile made it clear that just this once there was very little room for negotiation. Not even with the stories of curses that had grown up around the piece of jewellery. 'I don't know, sir. Monsieur Bouler could help you there.' He took the ring out of Konstantin's hands carefully but firmly. 'You're best off coming back tomorrow.'

Konstantin hesitated, but he had little choice. He couldn't pay for the ring without looking for a bank first anyway. 'Good idea. I would like to know what misery I'm inviting to dog my footsteps before I invest 10,000 euro in a ring.' Putting a brave face on it, he watched as the wooden strongbox disappeared into the safe somewhere underneath the counter.

He'd have time to get the money by tomorrow. It would definitely make more sense to pay the stipulated amount to Bouler himself. And Konstantin wanted to find out why the ring had been returned so many times. Had it been blamed for deaths? It seemed like fate that his search for Arctander had become intertwined with his investigation into the Reaper's Stones. *Retreat.* 'Thank you for your time and effort.' He pulled all of the dirhams out of his pocket and pressed them into Rabih's hand. 'Oh yeah, do you happen to have a *foqia* I could have? It would be more pleasant than my clothes.'

'Certainly, sir. Follow me.'

Together they left the shop and returned to Rabih's own shop, from which Konstantin re-emerged fifteen minutes later in a white *foqia* with silver edging, having bought two others, in grey and black. He was carrying both of them, along with his old clothes, in an old plastic bag. Plastic bags seemed to be his favourite accessory these days.

Once back at the hotel, he treated himself to a trip to the on-site *hammam*, letting the fatigue and sweat wash away. He got a foam massage and then threw on the black *foqia* to go to a restaurant nearby. He had the Grimm fairy tale collection with him to read.

It doesn't really get any cosier than this. Over tea and an orange salad, he turned his attention to 'The Messengers of Death'.

Death was real in this one too, a character you could speak to and even knock down. But fairy tales weren't facts, even if he wished he could treat the Grim Reaper exactly like that. He could only take suggestions and inspiration from the Grimms' stories.

What would happen if Death died? Konstantin tried to find out more about the giant who had succeeded in knocking down the Reaper, but didn't find anything.

He was interested by the detail that Sleep was the brother of Death.

That's where the connection to me is. To the Death Sleeper. He looked down pensively at his steaming tea, then grinned suddenly. *I should write my own fairy tale. About how I fought Sleep and Death and about how Sleep invented us to annoy his brother. A family quarrel.*

Konstantin developed the theory that Sleep had a personified form, just like Death.

Sleep was a joker anyway, a sadist and source of joy, who gave people good and bad dreams as he wished. Konstantin thought such a volatile character would be capable of creating Death Sleepers for his own enjoyment, to gloat at his brother's rages.

He dismissed the idea. Since he didn't expect to meet a giant in the real world whom he could get to knock the Grim Reaper down and keep him there, he turned to another idea.

He used a pen to jot down his thoughts on the restaurant napkin.

After reading the Godfather Death fairy tale, he supposed it might be possible that some doctors could perceive Death intuitively. He didn't believe that there were people who actually saw Death as an embodied figure like in the fairy tales.

Konstantin sighed. *It would make everything a lot easier, though. I could ask the doctor to talk to the Grim Reaper on my behalf and propose a deal with him. Quid pro quo. He could take everything I have in return for me being allowed to live a normal life.*

First he needed to find a doctor who had a link to Death. The number of doctors in the world was incalculable, but if there were among them some of the people he was looking for, then they were surely the most effective doctors in the world. Doctors who saved terminal patients when the experts were unable to find an explanation, without there being a verifiable reason. Religious people or self-proclaimed healers who saved the severely ill from death.

He stirred his tea thoughtfully and looked at his scrawled notes. *It's an unbelievable amount of work. Searching and eliminating, searching and eliminating.*

Konstantin worked out a plan: he would start with the most successful doctors and medics, those who were written up in serious newspapers. That simplified things. At the same time he would have to read the gossip rags and trawl through Internet forums for obscure cases of spontaneous remission and healing. He was aware that his plan was flimsy, but unfortunately he didn't have a better one.

He had just as little clue how he should present himself and his concerns to these doctors. He could see himself going into a doctor's surgery: 'Hello, I'm Korff, and I'd like to know whether you see the Grim Reaper at a patient's bedside. Yes? Really? Wonderful! Well, I just have a few questions for him. Would you be so good as to translate?'

What am I doing? He looked despondently at his notes and the book of fairy tales. *Anyone with half a brain will laugh at me, they'll think it's a joke. Like Iva did.*

Thinking about her was painful. He had been carrying her message with him, unread and unanswered, for the last few days.

Konstantin was too afraid to read her letter. His fear was that there could be something in it that destroyed his hopes irrevocably. Pithy sentences like 'It's over' or 'It was nice' or 'Piss off, you lunatic!'

Maybe she's sent me a psychiatrist's address? Konstantin laughed out loud. It wasn't clear what she thought of him after his strange departure. All the more reason for him not to give up hope of a happy ending.

I'd rather worry about Bouler and Arctander. At least they're real. He cleaned his plate, the sourness of the oranges tingling slightly in his mouth. Fresh, they tasted absolutely marvellous.

To finish, Konstantin treated himself to two mochas and tossed back an extra guarana pill to keep himself drugged up, so he wasn't in the best mood on his way back to the hotel where he dropped off the documents.

Then he walked back to Avenue Palestine to find a good vantage point and survey the shop from there.

Konstantin wanted to build a better picture of Bouler before going to see him. What kind of antiques dealer stored jewellery to the tune of 100,000 euro in a safe? *Was there even an alarm system installed in the place?*

It couldn't be a secret in Daoudiate, the stuff that Bouler had squirrelled away. The businessman seemed respected, otherwise the shop would get robbed on a regular basis. *Is he left in peace out of awe or fear?*

Konstantin walked back along the street, which was pretty quiet now. Unlike in the tourist areas, the locals disappeared to their beds so that they could pursue their craft the next day before the sun was too high and it was too hot. It was only in the tea shops and in two small cafés that a small number of men sat together over tea and shisha, playing chess or backgammon, watching football on old television sets and celebrating the players' goals.

Only a few of them noticed Konstantin and they seemed not to care. TV and board games were more important than a stranger who had strayed into Daoudiate in disguise.

A little after midnight he walked back to Bouler's shop. The closer he got, the warier he became, keeping an eye on the shadows. It was possible that the ominous Thielke had hit upon the same idea he had. *In his shoes, I'd already be here.*

The windows of the houses around the shop were lit up and open, and there were conversations spilling out: loud laughter and chatting. Music rang out and it sounded live. While stillness descended over the rest of the district, this was where people of Daoudiate really partied.

I would have preferred some privacy. He had chosen the rooftop diagonally opposite Bouler's shop as his lookout point. Konstantin effortlessly scaled the façade of a house and noticed that the *foqia* allowed for enough legroom to move around easily.

With one movement, he swung himself over the edge of the roof and ended up on a terrace where white bed sheets were hung out to dry on short washing lines. They smelled of soap and fluttered gently in the warm night breeze, brushing the back of Konstantin's neck as he got down behind a little wall and watched the door of the shop over the ledge.

Konstantin felt alert and relaxed, the coffee and guarana were working. The night would pass quickly and he hoped the owner would turn up over the course of the morning. *Otherwise I'll be fried on this terrace.* Apart from the thin washing lines, there would be no protection from the African sun.

The minutes ticked by. It was 12.30 a.m., then 1.00 a.m.

The local residents were settling in for a party. The sounds of a tourist extravaganza echoed across to him from the old town. Spotlights shone in the sky, a laser show painted pictures in red and green amid rising dry ice.

A little after 1.30 a.m. there came the hum of engines. Old, black Mercedes limos appeared in the street below. They were seventies models and the suspension was very low.

Armoured?

They stopped in front of Bouler's shop.

Now Konstantin stood up without abandoning his cover. *Ah, is that the boss?*

The car doors opened and no fewer than eight bodyguards slid out while the drivers stayed put. The men were wearing *foqias* with sports jackets over them. So that their guns could be concealed better, Konstantin assumed.

He didn't have a gun on him, he never would have got it

through customs. But even in his assassin days, he had carried a knife because he was a terrible shot.

One of the bodyguards knocked on the roof of the middle limousine. An old man hauled himself out and Konstantin would have put him around the sixty mark. *Is that Bouler?*

There was Rabih coming out of the house, wearing a dressing gown and with tousled, long black-silver hair that made him look like an intrepid explorer. 'Monsieur Bouler!' he cried out in agitation and waved. 'You're here already? What's wrong? How come you didn't say anything, I would have—'

'You betrayed me. Robbed me. After so many years.' Bouler snapped his fingers and pointed at his partner. One of the bodyguards reached under his jacket and withdrew a micro-Uzi with a silencer, the thickened barrel directed at the sleepy salesman of *hammam* accessories.

Rabih's mouth fell open. 'But Monsieur! Monsieur, I—'

Zvipp, zvipp, zvipp, zvipp it went. And another *zvipp*. There was no tell-tale flash visible from the muzzle, but the soft rattle of the cartridges on the asphalt echoed through the stillness of the night.

Red spatters appeared underneath Rabih's chin. He looked down at himself, at the holes in his dressing gown and the bloodstains that were growing rapidly, and staggered forwards, his right arm twitching briefly as though to stop himself, and then fell into the street.

Konstantin was following what was happening, mesmerised. What was going on?

'Take him into the house and eliminate his family. Hurry. We don't have much time,' Bouler ordered his men. 'Interpol is right on our heels.'

Two bodyguards dragged the body back into the *hammam* accessories shop and disappeared, three others following behind.

Interpol? It was clear that things were about to get unpleasant for Rabih's family. More than that. *Shit, and I can't do anything.* Konstantin wondered why Bouler was murdering the whole family immediately. *Is he afraid that his secrets will be revealed?*

Meanwhile, Bouler went to his shop and disappeared inside. Two of his people stayed outside by the door and guarded him; the last one went inside with him.

The light in the shop went on. Glass and porcelain smashed and there were loud crashes, followed by clattering and rattling. Konstantin could see Bouler through the open door. He had taken the strongboxes out of the safe and flipped them open, examining them carefully.

Not the little wooden box! Not the little wooden box! Konstantin pressed his hands together. *Leave it there, whatever else you're planning. Please, I need it!*

But the wooden chest disappeared into his bag too. Then Bouler stood in the doorway and shouted directions through the shop.

Seconds later, a warm glow flared up. The bodyguards had started a fire, art treasures and collector's pieces were ruthlessly exposed to the flames.

In front of the door, the bodyguard on the right suddenly turned his head, drawing out a gun with a silencer as he did so, and shot without warning into the shadows. His companion spoken into his headset and wrenched his micro-Uzi into a shooting position too.

The *zvipp* from the bodyguard's barrel was followed almost immediately by cracking sounds, *BAMM, BAMM, BAMM, BAMM*.

Long lines of fire became visible at the opposite corner of the shop, throwing an orange-yellow glow on the faces of the people struck. Thielke pressed himself against a brick wall, the arm with the LeMat revolver outstretched.

Both bodyguards' *foqias* and sports jackets bulged out at the back and completely exploded. Blood and scraps of flesh splashed all over the building and the street, splattering the limousines and spraying the shop window. The men were flung backwards by the impact of the twelve-millimetre projectiles before falling. Red pools spread out around the dead bodies.

I'm glad he only shot me in the leg! Konstantin stayed in position. He couldn't and didn't want to step in – not unless the opportunity presented itself to get to the strongbox with the potential Reaper's Ring. *As far as I'm concerned, Thielke can get rid of the bodyguards. I hope Bouler isn't on the receiving end. I need him.*

Bouler appeared again at the threshold, looked over to where Thielke was still hiding and yelled orders. The fire in his shop made an escape through the back exit impossible. He stayed crouched in the doorway and sent his bodyguard ahead, who fired blindly in the direction of the assailant to give his boss cover on his way to the car.

A precise shot to the head, between the eyes, blew open the back part of his skull and sent the man flying into the middle limousine where he came to rest, lying across on the bonnet. Blood from his gaping wounds cascaded over the expensive paintwork in torrents.

The remaining bodyguards must have heard the thunderous shots from the LeMat, but they seemed to prefer to stay in the safety of Rabih's house. The drivers cowered in the cars, not daring to get out or drive away.

Bouler was still shouting, but didn't leave his shop. Only when swathes of smoke were floating out of the door, engulfing the man and the street in front of him, was he ready to venture out himself.

Clever. That will protect him from Thielke's bullets better than his bodyguards could. Konstantin considered whether he should step in now. Bouler had the Grim Reaper's Ring and could not be allowed to escape.

Then, Bent Arctander appeared. He stepped out of a side street on the left, looking confused but alert.

The Frenchman called something to him and raised one finger threateningly at him.

The narcoleptic immediately disappeared back into the lane he'd emerged from. *Zvipp, zvipp, zvipp* – stone exploded on the corner of the building the narcoleptic had just disappeared behind. The bodyguards from the *hammam* accessories shop were shooting at Arctander. Unlike Thielke, he was directly in their line of fire.

Konstantin ducked as he ran along the roof. *They are going to hound him into a fit, these idiots! And the terrible consequences that could come of a fit had been documented in the papers often enough.*

On the street below, Bouler hurried out of his shop and dived into a limousine that moved off immediately. It turned at high speed into the little street that Arctander had run into.

Konstantin straightened up as he jumped from house to house at a run, following the laneway where the Mercedes was hurtling along with its headlights on. It drove around rubbish bins, smashed through old fruit and vegetables and collided head-on with two late-night pedestrians; they bounded off the bumper and flew screaming through the air, until they lay motionless where they landed.

Just a moment later the Mercedes reached Arctander and slowed down. He was racing down the lane in a white *foqia*, not five metres ahead of the blood-stained bonnet, trying to escape. In vain.

Konstantin watched as the Mercedes drove into the narcoleptic's calves, bringing him down. The driver braked immediately so as not to run him over.

Arctander somersaulted, grazing the right side of his face against the wall.

Bouler, holding a micro-Uzi in his hand, got out like a scalded cat and grabbed the unconscious Death Sleeper so that he could drag him to the car by the collar.

No. He's mine. Konstantin didn't think too much before jumping down over the edge. He landed right on the roof of the Mercedes, the thin metal taking the brunt of the impact and sagging. There was a cry of surprise from inside.

Bouler reacted with a certain detachment, pointing the micro-Uzi at Konstantin and pulling the trigger.

With a somersault backwards, he got himself out of the line of fire, landing on the driver's side. He ducked his head and waited for the high-pitched *zvipp*ing and the hail of bullets to come to an end.

There had hardly been the sound of the click before he shot into the air – and found himself staring into the muzzle of an automatic pistol. *Shit.* Konstantin froze.

The Frenchman hadn't reloaded, he'd simply swapped the Uzi for a different weapon.

Bouler looked at him over the sight. 'So who are you then?' he rasped. Judging by the accent he was from somewhere in the Languedoc region. 'Where's your buddy?'

'MI6,' said Konstantin. *If it worked for Jester, why shouldn't it work for me?* 'I'm an agent in the British secret service and am under orders to get you and Monsieur Arctander safely out of Marrakech.'

Bouler screwed up his face, his scepticism was obvious. 'What?' He ordered his driver to heave the unconscious man into the car.

'Monsieur Arctander is the carrier of a rare virus which he caught in the course of an experiment,' Konstantin continued, listening carefully. *No sirens, no other pursuers?* 'Because of him, a huge number of people could lose their lives, Monsieur Bouler. I've—'

'If you'd said Interpol or diamond-smuggling I'd have believed you. And I'd have killed you anyway!' The Frenchman fired a number of times in quick succession. The shots discharged with loud cracks, there was no silencer.

Konstantin dived behind the car before Bouler had even finished the sentence. The bullets missed him by a hair's breadth.

The Mercedes sped off, leaving him in the street.

Konstantin stood up angrily. 'What a—' He kicked at the remains of a shattered fruit crate in frustration. Arctander gone, Bouler gone, ring gone. *Well, this trip to Marrakech has really been worth it.*

He wiped the dust off his *foqia*, which had fared very badly.

Around him people were daring to come to their windows, to balconies and roofs to look for the source of the trouble.

He didn't know where exactly he was in Marrakech, but he thought it would be safer to get far away from Avenue Palestine so as not to be picked up and questioned by the police or Interpol. Bouler was involved in international crime, probably to do with the jewellery he sold. Konstantin hoped he hadn't caught the attention of the investigators, otherwise he would have troubles that not even Jester could get him out of.

Signs helpfully explained that he was near the old town: mosques, museums, various tourist attractions were shown. *All right then. I can find my way back to the hotel from here.* Konstantin was just going to turn right when he saw a figure lying stretched out on the ground in an archway. A local. He was holding a broom made of twigs in his right hand and in front of him was a rubbish bin with a rubbish brush dangling from it.

A road sweeper. Konstantin approached him and knelt down next to him, checking his pulse.

Nothing.

The soft crackle of fire pierced his ear. Music, perhaps from a cassette tape that had been recorded over a hundred times, droned nearby. It smelled of cooking meat, of spices and a city at night, the air was full of dust and exhaust fumes, the odour of warm stone and tarmac. A gentle wind was blowing, whistling slightly and playing with the fabric banners and flags, making them flutter and rustle.

Otherwise everything was inexplicably quiet. No voices or laughter or any other noise that came from a human.

The rich glow of a flame fell across him and he lifted his head. The road sweeper was lying under an archway that led to a large square. Konstantin went on a few steps – and was seized by horror. He felt sick, his scalp tingled.

People of all ages were lying around the square. Shop-owners were draped over the displays in their stalls, a cook had fallen forwards onto his grill and was now burning up along with the meat he'd been roasting. The flames danced over his body, roasting his skin, his hair, his clothes.

Konstantin stared at the awful scene as if under a spell. He realised that the dead had all fallen in the same direction, like trees felled by a powerful storm. The soles of their feet pointed towards an old, black Mercedes limousine. The centre of the death. The sight was reminiscent of the stalks of ominous crop circles in fields of grain.

Bouler's car! Konstantin walked slowly towards it, his legs shaking. *The work of the angry Reaper.* He could not even estimate how many victims there were.

2,000?

3,000?

The silence in the square horrified him – it was so absolute. There were neither whimpers from the wounded nor cries for help from the survivors. Death, in its purest, more natural form, had cut life short. Extinguished the light of their lives. Stopped their hearts.

This is . . . Konstantin couldn't find the words to describe his horror. Bent Arctander must have awoken from his faint and suffered an epileptic fit. And this was the result. He truly was standing in the middle of the *Djemaa el Fna*: the Gathering of the Dead.

He reached the limousine and noticed that the right rear door on the other side was open. The driver was sitting dead in the seat, Bouler next to him, his eyes open wide. A small strand of saliva leaked from the corner of his mouth as though a spider was going to abseil from it. Bent Arctander had disappeared.

Why does that idiot not stay away from cities? Konstantin told himself to calm down and looked through Bouler's bag, pocketing the wallet as well as the expensive smartphone and two envelopes. With any luck it would contain information linking the Frenchman, Thielke and the Death Sleeper.

Suddenly a long-drawn-out cry rang out through the Marrakech night. The massacre had been discovered.

He hurriedly looked for the little wooden box and found it: a shot from Bouler's silenced gun destroyed the lock.

The screams became more frequent. Any minute now the place would be swarming with special forces and emergency teams.

Konstantin opened the lid and rummaged around in the rings any old way until he saw the ivory shimmering. He grabbed the ring and left the square taking the quickest route back to his hotel.

Feeling shattered, he flopped down in the dark red leather armchair in his room. *Fuck!* With jittery movements he poured himself a whisky from the minibar and knocked it back. *Fucking hell!*

He switched on the television and flipped to a news channel. It couldn't be long before there would be reports on the incident in Marrakech.

Then he placed the suspected Reaper's Ring on the table

in front of him, leaned back in the armchair and stared at the opal.

He was too shaken to be able to form clear thoughts, faces of the dead in Djemaa el Fna thronged in his mind's eye. The faces of the locals, the tourists. Guilt bubbled up inside him.

This isn't your fault. Bouler is to blame. He put Arctander under pressure, he said to himself. *I should disappear before they shut Morocco down for fear of biological weapons.*

Konstantin stood up, packed what little he had brought with him and left his accommodation, thankful he'd paid in advance.

He carried the stolen ring in his trouser pocket, close to his body. It was too dangerous for Konstantin to put the ring on his finger before he had got to the bottom of its secrets. He thought the events in Marrakech tragic and unremittingly terrible.

In the taxi to the airport he closed his eyes and leaned back. He wondered how long the images of the dead would keep dogging him. *If Iva had been around . . .* It didn't even bear thinking about.

His humane idea of island exile for the narcoleptic unravelled in the face of those images. Jester was right about one thing.

Bent Arctander must be stopped. Immediately. It no longer matters how.

Marrakech, Morocco

Thielke stood surrounded by curious bystanders on the north side of Djemaa el Fna, a cigarette in his mouth and the Nikon at the ready. 'Holy shit,' he murmured as he snapped pictures of the corpses.

The square was cordoned off with crime-scene tape and policemen in gas masks marched around between the bodies. The Marrakechites seemed to be of the opinion that a gas mask in the sealed off area was sufficient, although nobody could say whether it had been a gas, bacteria or a virus. But beyond the thin plastic tape there was barely any anxiety. The curious clustered round, while camera crews and photographers documented the massacre.

Thielke zoomed right in on the old Mercedes and photographed Bouler, the ruined little box and the rings lying around it.

Not the work of local looters. They would have taken all of it. The narco had been looking for something, a particular piece of jewellery from the Frenchman's collection. He just couldn't figure out why. *Could also have been Korff, of course.*

He lowered his camera and took in everything around him with his healthy right eye. The fact that he had been spotted in front of the shop had been the trigger for this catastrophe. He was complicit in this massacre.

'This wasn't how it was all meant to work out,' he murmured in dismay. He had wanted to inhibit Arctander's curse with the help of his little invention and reason with him: there was a sleeping technique that did *not* attract Death and that you could learn. Thielke had mastered it and he was pleased if anyone else tried to learn it, with his support. He only offered the opportunity to select people.

For Arctander, this option was out. He might still have been able to view the plane episode as an unfortunate, isolated incident, but Arctander was pushing his luck too far by visiting densely populated areas. And the results were once more on view in Djemaa el Fna. The narco's sleep condition was out of control.

The first vans trundled across the square, reversing into a narrow pathway between the bodies that the rescue workers had made for them. They drove by, right up close to the shoes, the fingertips, the limbs of the dead. Soldiers marched out of a side street dressed in NBC suits and set about dragging the dead to the vans. Hauling, dumping.

Thielke could imagine how overwhelmed the world's secret services were right now. Exhausted and in shock, the staff would be yelling, jumbling up pointless names – al-Qaida, Nazis, anarchists – and looking for gas residues and viruses without any luck.

Meanwhile, the solution was as simple as it was unbelievable: Death had lashed out blindly all around him whilst trying to hit Arctander.

Thielke's hand clutched the Nikon's battery grip more tightly. He had been too slow. He *should* have been able to prevent it without shooting the narco in the head with the machine that was in his tote bag. Invented and built by himself, he could use it to block a Death Sleeper's devastating brainwaves, but it was only effective at short-range.

A neurologist acquaintance of his, whom he had been chatting to about the latest findings in sleep research, put him on the right track: altered brainwave patterns. According to Thielke's theory, Death was attracted by particular waves, so all you had to do was to change this pattern.

After extensive research on the brain and its possibilities

for manipulation, he had come across transcranial magnetic stimulation. Neurologists used a device to check the neural pathways: electrical impulses were fired at the brain from outside and stimulated specific areas. The response time gave an indication of the state of the nerves.

Thielke had then had a portable TMS machine built; it emitted a continuous pulse for several seconds. It was enough to alter the Death Sleeper's brainwaves. As a result, there was no signal for the Grim Reaper to follow.

Only this time I was too slow.

He withdrew without attracting any attention when he saw that other European men were turning up, guided by an officer from the Moroccan military.

The Western secret services were closing in. He guessed they believed that the same attackers had been at work in Paris and they weren't wrong. It was equally certain that the media would soon be speculating about a new, as yet unknown terrorist group who had it in for both Christians and Muslims, perhaps a strange, fanatical doomsday cult. There would probably be claims of responsibility from copycats soon. Absolute chaos.

Thielke vanished into a teashop, sat down in the window and smoked another cigarette. He could feel the weight of the TMS machine that hadn't been used yet in his bag.

I was too slow. He stretched out his leg, which only went to the knee, the rest being prosthesic. The stump tingled and pulsed: a change in weather was in the offing.

Thielke ordered a mint tea with plenty of sugar, counteracting it immediately by injecting two units of insulin into his pinpricked belly. Then he looked for the piece of paper where he had noted a handful of names and terms that he had found out while running surveillance on Arctander.

Thielke kept tabs on all the Death Sleepers he had located so that he knew what they were up to. He had first seen Arctander in Britain. He had crossed paths with him by chance a few weeks ago and stayed on his trail, but he'd kept losing the narcoleptic and only a few names and addresses, which he'd caught by lip-reading Arctander's telephone calls and through glimpses of ticket purchases, had put him back on the right track.

The attempt to decipher Arctander's intentions from them failed. He looked down at his handwritten notes.

Roccastrada, Via Balzina
Venice, farmacia al lupo coronato
—eMorocco, Daoudiate? Avenue Palestine?
Bouler E., EDbl-O, 23.8
—oMadrid, Almudena
Minsk, Life Inst.?

He could cross Morocco off the list. *Which means I'm flying to Madrid.*

Thielke had already had a lot to do with Death Sleepers in his life, with smart ones as well as stubborn ones.

The stubborn ones, who didn't care about the repercussions of what they did or specifically used it for gain and advantage, he put out of action with three shots from the LeMat so that they didn't harm normal people. The smart Death Sleepers, who were considerate about their surroundings, like Korff, he observed and bided his time.

Through his observations, he was able to better evaluate them. If they proved themselves to be responsible and disciplined, he offered them the chance to learn a special sleeping technique, which kept the Reaper quiet.

Thielke had smoked his cigarette down to the butt and lit up a new one.

He found it frustrating that he'd only managed to pass on his own, environmentally friendly sleeping technique successfully in three cases. It was too difficult, too complicated, and there were too many side-effects.

Death Sleepers active in the organisations such as Torpor's Men couldn't expect any mercy. They abused their power and their dominance, played at being judges and executioners, served as contract killers. He couldn't let them get away with it.

Thielke sipped his tea, letting his thoughts as well as his gaze wander.

Something was going on in the great Death Sleeper family and it had nothing to do with the narco. Since the baroness had resigned from the Deathslumberers, the structure within the community was changing. Von Windau wasn't just concocting her own soup, she was cooking a whole secret menu and was crafting something that needed special ingredients: her own kind. In Paris a short time ago, a new, surprising ally had joined her ranks, someone whose ambitions Thielke could not gauge. The next time they met, he would eliminate the man. As a precaution.

But before I worry about von Windau, I have to catch the narco. As far as I'm concerned, she can kill as many Death Sleepers as she wants in the meantime. He inhaled the tobacco smoke and flicked away the cigarette stub.

Thielke looked back at his list.

Originally the narco had wanted to go to Madrid after Morocco, to meet an Almudena or something. Thielke couldn't guess whether he was still going to do that after the events in Morocco. Neither could he guess the reason behind the visit to Bouler and the diamond thing.

Thielke swallowed the last mouthful of hot tea, took a nicotine patch out of his bag and stuck it to the inside of his right upper arm. Next he lit up a cigarillo. He had to suppress a cough after the first puff.

There was nothing for it: his next stop would be Madrid. If he didn't find Arctander there, he would just follow the tracks that led, among other places, to Minsk.

XIII

So swiftly striding, Death comes towards man,
It gives no grace, no time, no stay;
It fells him there, right on his way.
It plucks man from wherever it can.

William Tell, Friedrich von Schiller

Minsk, Belarus

Kristen looked over at the woman at the newspaper stand who was struggling to feign interest in the display, and made a beeline for her. 'Hello. Are you following me?'

'Eh ... what?' replied the stranger. But before the woman could stop her, Kristen brushed the stranger's hair back. There was a pale plastic plug in her right ear with a thin, transparent cable running out of it and underneath her collar. 'What are you playing at?' said the woman.

'Blowing your cover. What company are you and your friends from?' Kristen pretended to be fixing the stranger's jacket to avoid drawing any attention. In doing so she noticed the gun hidden in a holster under the left armpit. A Walther

P6. 'Nothing Eastern European. You've got the wrong make for that.'

Kristen thought about the meeting in Paris with the applicant who had a fake reference in her documents. Was this surveillance part of a big plan to smuggle a mole into the Life Institute, or were there different teams on her tail?

Damn it! What had happened was *exactly* what she had wanted to prevent: she was drawing too much attention to herself.

Kristen ran through different relocating scenarios in her head: leaving Minsk, finding a new location and starting all over again – but she didn't have time for that. Every interruption meant an unforgivable delay. Her illness was progressing relentlessly, so Kristen needed to be just as relentless.

Relentless like in Ciudad Mier.

The agents had to take responsibility for the consequences, not her. She never killed for fun.

The stranger was looking around furtively for help. Her colleagues were already approaching, their faces pure menace.

'I propose we go outside.' Kristen nodded in the direction of the exit. 'We can clarify what you want from me there. Or start spraying bullets all over the place here. Then you'd better think up a story now for the local secret service. Belarussian interrogation techniques are not the most pleasant. They practice waterboarding with turpentine, or so I've heard.'

Meanwhile, she had been surrounded by the woman's backup. One actually showed her the outline of his gun, a Beretta 93R, to intimidate her, which prompted an abrupt laugh from Kristen. 'Are we all here now? Can we go outside?'

'No, Mrs von Windau. There is nothing to discuss. Just

continue on your way immediately, we will come with you,' the man shot back angrily.

'Ah, I get it. You're not meant to let me out of your sight or intervene. The classic surveillance. Normally the target isn't meant to notice.' Kristen grinned at the agent who had had her cover blown first. 'I can't take you with me unfortunately. It's a private flight.'

'Then we've got a problem,' replied the man.

'You could give me a tracking device to take with me. I'll be very good and even wear it, promise.' She was really enjoying teasing the agents.

Kristen considered how long the trio had been following her. No cars had caught her eye on the trip to the airport. They had probably lain in wait in the terminal because it was known that she travelled a lot.

Kristen wasn't interested in which secret service they belonged to. The rookie team were annoying her and restricting her freedom of movement. She should just eradicate them. For her, there were no serious consequences to ending up on the hit list of a secret service because she would be dead soon anyway, or disappearing into a cryotank. She classed the resultant risk to her son as low. As long as he was protected by his father Eugen was safe from strangers and enemies. And they didn't seem to have discovered the institute yet.

Kristen looked at the three agents, one after the other. She had made her decision. 'That's decided then? I'll get a tracking device? I also promise not to tell anyone that I spotted you.' She lifted her arm slowly and rubbed the back of her neck to get her hand closer to her hairpin. The attack had to happen very quickly so that she could she make it through the private check-in before commotion broke out at the airport. Due to Arctander and his fits, even Minsk was on the highest state of alert because nobody could work out what the unpredictable terror attacks were all about.

'Very funny,' said the female agent from the newspaper stand. Her black-haired female colleague was inconspicuously securing the area.

'*You* had better not say anything. After all, it's your fault that we're all standing around here like absolute idiots because you keep making rookie errors. A dilemma: you can't complete your mission and I have to think through how we are going to do business together,' Kristen snapped at her – and pulled the hairpin out of the leather loop. She stabbed the man through the eye and he collapsed as though struck by lightning. He never got to his Beretta.

Kristen struck the black-haired woman in the throat with her elbow, so that she stumbled backwards, gasping, and fell against the newspaper stand. At the same time she stabbed the needle into the stomach of the other agent. The stab wound wasn't deep enough to kill her, but that wasn't the point anyway. It was to distract her while Kristen reached into her holster, released the safety catch on the gun and pulled the trigger twice without drawing the weapon.

The bullets penetrated the woman's upper body at an angle.

Then, walking backwards and threading the needle into the material lining of her coat as she did so, Kristen cried shrilly for help and pointed at the trio. 'Terrorists! Terrorists!'

People were already fleeing, the reports from the gun had startled them.

Kristen plunged into the throng, made her way to check-in unnoticed and hurried out to the runway, heading straight for her jet. She didn't care what happened in the airport in the meantime. Or who the agents were working for. They were obstacles to be eliminated.

Once on board the plane, she closed the hatch and went into the cockpit.

She skipped the routine checks and requested immediate clearance for take-off from the control tower, which she promptly received. St Petersburg was waiting. Eugen was waiting, excited to see the jet his mother owned. Then there was Kristen's priority list, which contained several names of various Death Sleepers whom she needed to collect so that Smyrnikov would have enough material for testing and experimenting in the future. She still needed to have a conversation with her ex-husband too.

Lots to do for someone whose time is running out, she thought and started the turbines.

Frankfurt am Main, Germany

Konstantin had withdrawn to a bistro in a quiet corner of Frankfurt Airport to look through Bouler's information. It had been an inspired decision not to travel home straight away. Since he was in the largest airport in Germany, he could – depending on the results – immediately depart to virtually anywhere in the world. His laptop stood open on the table. The Internet was the greatest information vortex of the present era and he intended to use it.

Luckily Bouler hadn't put a lock on his smartphone. Over a water and espresso, Konstantin rooted around in the shady antique dealer's texts, emails and contacts.

He recalled the brief exchange he'd had with the man. *Perhaps Interpol were hot on his heels because of diamonds. The ones in the rings? Or did he handle stolen goods? Did he smuggle African blood diamonds?*

Most of the messages were trivial, some funny, for example the instruction to a Lady Rousseau to wear men's clothes that evening and paint on a moustache.

Bouler had exotic tastes, by the looks of it.

Konstantin didn't find any reference to diamonds. However, the initials, SH, appeared regularly in messages cryptic enough to make them interesting: combinations of numbers, separated by commas and slashes.

Konstantin suspected there was a code behind it, linked to a specific key such as a book. Without the key it was no use him even trying to solve it.

Since SH was using a secret code, he looked for the letters in the phone's address book and found them: SH, first a mobile number and then a landline number with the prefix 06781.

The Internet didn't return any hits on the mobile, but it did for the prefix. *Idar-Oberstein.*

Konstantin looked at the shaded-in piece of paper with the clues he'd obtained from Thielke's notebook. *I-O! That could be what it meant.* He was glad to have his first breakthrough, although he had never heard anything about the town before and couldn't guess where this lead might take him.

But after just a brief investigation, he felt electrified. The town was known as Germany's centre for gemstones and diamonds.

Just a few seconds later, he thought he'd deciphered the whole abbreviation EDbI-O: *Edelstein und Diamantbörse Idar-Oberstein*: Gemstone and Diamond Bourse Idar-Oberstein. From this he concluded that Bouler had done a brisk trade with the bourse there.

Illegally, probably. Hence Interpol. Can I quickly find out anything else? Who is SH? He checked the first few digits after the prefix.

The Internet told him that it was the number for an office in the bourse area. Unfortunately it couldn't give him the relevant office name.

Konstantin thought about what to do.

If he called the number from Bouler's smartphone and SH already knew about the Frenchman's death, then he or she would be forewarned. Calling and hoping for the best, giving the excuse 'Oh sorry, I've got the wrong number,' seemed little use. SH might answer with 'Hello?' and besides, then the person would know his voice. Turning up as a fake customer could similarly backfire. Konstantin knew too little about gemstones and diamonds for that.

The most effective thing would simply be to burst into SH's office, seize them and question them himself. Idar-Oberstein wasn't far from Frankfurt by rental car.

'Oh shit,' somebody said loudly at a neighbouring table. 'Look, Silke! What have these sick terrorist pigs done now? Those poor people.'

Not only did Silke look up from her plate of schnitzel, Konstantin did too.

A large flatscreen was hanging over the tables with the

news on. The Breaking News banner along the bottom of the screen was reporting 3,711 dead in Marrakech, all having lost their lives in the famous medieval square, Djemaa el Fna.

The special programme about it began and the waiter turned up the volume at the customers' requests.

'. . . them baffled. The Moroccan authorities are assuming a terrorist attack. So far no claims of responsibility have been made,' said the newsreader in a voice that was sonorous and calm, but with a very grave face that said: *it's bloody dangerous out there.* 'Initial investigations have not given any indication of the reason for the large-scale loss of life. Following testing, viruses and poison gases have been ruled out. We understand from reliable sources that scientists from the CIA are currently working on the assumption that the event signals further development of the gas that was used at the end of a hostage situation in a Moscow cinema in 2002, in which the perpetrators and hostages lost their lives. The Russian authorities have refused to tolerate speculation with regard to this, but have nevertheless sent their own specialists to Marrakech.' Now pictures of the destroyed Paris-Charles de Gaulle airport were faded in, along with shots of body bags that Konstantin still had vivid memories of: Lilou had lain in one of them. 'The incident is strikingly reminiscent of the incidents in Paris when an A380 . . .'

He stopped listening after that. There was no new information, the authorities were not searching for either him or Arctander. Officially speaking.

Konstantin didn't think that he had got caught in the crosshairs of the secret services. *Jester would have called me ages ago to warn me.*

He opened a document on his laptop that he'd downloaded from the Internet. It was an academic article about narcolepsy. He didn't want to make any mistakes and provoke Arctander into a fit when they finally met. That would have a catastrophic effect on the surrounding area.

Narcolepsy was described as a neurological disorder that was recognised in very few cases. Sleepiness, tiredness, dozing off, everybody was familiar with these. It happened to an estimated 20,000 people in Germany in everyday situations, and not in the innocuous armchair in front of the TV, but without them wanting it, or being able to control it.

Konstantin swore quietly as he read on: narcolepsy was incurable. Treatable, but not curable. A list of the medications was appended. *And every time he involuntarily fell asleep, Arctander became more and more deadly.* He had to admit now that Jester was right to conclude that the Death Sleeper had to be eliminated. *He is too dangerous.*

The reason for the illness was a disturbance in the regulation of the sleep-wake-rhythm, the article said. This led to a deficit of the neurotransmitter hypocretin, usually produced in the interbrain, the hypothalmus. As so often with the brain, the scientists were wracking their brains over what lay behind the abrupt sleep attacks. Little progress had been achieved in recent years.

Makes sense. The number of people affected is so small that there is no monetary incentive for the pharmaceutical companies to develop a drug.

No chance for Arctander.

It wasn't just that narcoleptics suffered from sudden sleep attacks. Besides muscles going limp, there were reports of total paralysis and hallucinations. On the other hand it was also possible that an affected person could, during an attack, continue doing what they had begun *before* falling asleep, without being aware of their behaviour, causing harmless or catastrophic consequences for a person, depending on the situation. Cutting vegetables could cost you your finger, crossing the street your life.

No matter whether it was on the tram, in a lecture or while ironing, there was no protection. The muscles went limp, the narcoleptic crumpled and they had to give in to the irresistible urge to go to sleep.

Oh my God! As he read, Konstantin became conscious for the first time of the scale of this illness. Most narcoleptics fell asleep several times a day, the length varying from seconds to minutes to hours. In Arctander's case, that was sufficient for Death to strike immediately.

People dreaded cataplexy in particular, where all the muscles went limp and weak, as in sleep. The triggers were usually strong emotions.

Konstantin skimmed over the lines: *laughing, worrying, banter, stress, excitement, surprise. Or even during sex.* If it wasn't so unfortunate, he would have laughed. During cataplexy, which lasted between a few seconds and several minutes, the person affected remained fully conscious.

Perversely, the people with this illness almost always slept badly, were restless and couldn't get to sleep at night, which made them more vulnerable to attacks during the day.

Nobody wants to have to carry a burden like this. Konstantin rubbed his hand over his forehead and drank some of his water. He felt incredible sympathy for the man. Hunted by the Torpor's Men, by him, by Thielke. Arctander probably just wanted to be left in peace, yet was fleeing around the world in search of refuge. Nonetheless, it would be irresponsible not to stop him. *He was putting innocent people in danger without even thinking.* Just as Konstantin's morals were trying to make themselves known again – asking him whether the narcoleptic's death was justified or whether exile in a deserted place was enough – they began showing close-ups of the dead in Marrakech as they were being loaded onto trucks by soldiers in NBC suits. *Inexcusable.*

Konstantin decided to drive to Idar-Oberstein straight away to suss out SH. He turned off the laptop, gathered up his things, packed them into his little suitcase, paid and left.

He went to the rental car companies' little booths to get himself a car. It ought to be unremarkable and reliable, and able take him to the Pfalz region quickly, to the town he'd never heard of before, despite it being Germany's centre for gemstones and diamonds.

On the webpage of the international trade magazine *Jeweler's Circular Keystone*, Idar-Oberstein was described as 'the world centre of coloured stones'. The bourse dealt in rough stones among other things and had very secure safes at its disposal where stock could be placed in case there were periods of unrest in the countries of origin and the prices shot up. There was also talk of direct deals and mining investment. Foreign rough stone dealers also had offices in the town.

Hopefully in a few hours he would find out why a French-Moroccan antique dealer had been staying in regular contact with SH.

Konstantin patted the pocket with the Grim Reaper's Ring

as he walked. Maybe he could tackle this puzzle in Idar-Oberstein too.

He thought about the price that he should have actually paid for the ring. Which gave him an idea. *I'll save myself the cost of the car.* Before he reached the counter with the pleasantly smiling woman from the rental company, he pulled his mobile out of his pocket and called Jester. 'It's me,' he said.

'Ah, what a pleasure,' answered his friend enthusiastically. 'An enormous pleasure indeed. Marvellous! Where are you?'

'In Frankfurt. Shall we meet here tomorrow? There's quite a lot to tell.'

'Of course, old boy.' Jester named a hotel and a time to Konstantin.

'All right. By the way I need a rental car for my search for Arctander. Can that be charged to MI6, Mr Bond?'

Jester laughed. 'I'll transfer £10,000 into your account. That should be enough to be going on with, to cover incidental expenses. Everything else can wait till tomorrow. I'm intrigued as to whether you've found out anything that we don't know yet.'

'You may well find that I have.' *But I don't know whether you'll like what I find.* Konstantin hung up and went up to the counter where the woman in uniform was still beaming her pleasant smile that suggested she either wanted to get him into bed or wanted to palm a super expensive Porsche Cayenne or a BMW X6 off on him.

Konstantin chose a more modest model.

He reached Idar-Oberstein in the early afternoon.

It was appropriate for a diamond and gemstone town that

it had been built in a hollow on a mountainside. The access road ran through a long tunnel before revealing the view of the valley. A rough-hewn church stood enthroned over the old town, a classic and modest sacred building that seemed to have grown out of the mountain face.

The navigation device in the Audi A1 guided Konstantin confidently through the streets towards the bourse building.

Under normal circumstances he would have thoroughly investigated the town and the bourse, which must have been around since the Middle Ages, prior to his arrival and learned something of the history of the gemstone and diamond trade. But as he couldn't surf the Internet while driving – and hadn't wanted to wait – he had very little grounding in these. The prospect of being able to find out something about his Reaper's Ring or Grim Reaper's Stones in general, given that Idar-Oberstein dealt in jewellery, gave him hope.

He approached the bourse, an unattractive multi-storey building from the seventies or later, he estimated.

He parked a little way off, got out and retrieved an envelope from underneath the driver's seat in which he'd placed a small box with the Reaper's Ring inside. He would turn up very officially as the dealer's messenger. So it didn't make a difference if SH already knew of Bouler's death. *I might have already been sent on my trip before his death.*

He walked briskly up to the high-rise, the padded envelope clamped under his arm and sunglasses balanced on his nose. He looked serious, even a little dangerous, in his suit. *Like in the old days.*

Konstantin marched through the automatic doors and

found his way through a double door system with countless surveillance cameras on the ceiling.

He went over to the porter who sat behind very thick, bulletproof glass. Conversations were only possible using a microphone and speaker. A second, armed employee in a bullet-proof vest kept him company. 'Hello,' said Konstantin in a French accent. 'My name is Mané. I am a private security messenger under orders from Monsieur Bouler and I have a delivery for SH.' He named the extension number he had found on the dead man's phone.

The slim porter blinked. 'Excuse me?'

'I said, I'm a private security messenger, my name is Mané and I have a delivery for someone with the initials SH and the extension 246,' he repeated stubbornly and made an aloof face. 'That's as much as I know.'

'The initials and the extension. Hm.' The porter scrutinised him. 'Can I just see what's in that envelope?'

'The contents are confidential. You should know all about discretion in this industry.'

The porter exchanged glances with his colleague then typed something into his computer. 'According to the extension, you mean Ms Herbst.'

'Please inform her that I am here.' Konstantin retained his obliging smile, even though he was getting impatient. *I have to speed this up.* 'If you give me your phone, I can call her on the mobile number that was given to me. That ought to set your mind at ease?'

The porter nodded and manoeuvred the cordless receiver through the sliding mechanism in the window. Konstantin took it and dialled the mobile number. It was only a few seconds before a woman's voice said, 'Yes?'

'Hello, Madame Herbst.' He turned away so that the microphones didn't broadcast what he was saying. 'Monsieur Bouler has sent me with a delivery.'

'And you are?' Noticeable suspicion, but there were also notes of surprise and curiosity from Herbst.

'Hercule Mané. A private security courier and a friend of Monsieur Bouler. It's a little dicey in Morocco at the moment, as you've been following. I'm glad I left Marrakech in time.' Konstantin was praying she would fall for the story.

'Yes, I heard about that. Wait, I'll come down.'

Oh no, not that! He had wanted to prevent that. Out here, she would be sure to send him away within minutes. 'Madame Herbst, I don't think it would be sensible for me to display my delivery in the double door system and in front of the cameras.'

Herbst took time over her answer. 'I don't mind,' she relented.

'Would you tell the porter to go ahead and—'

'Will do. Seventh floor, room 711. Give the phone back to the porter, I'll let him know.'

He turned to the porter and placed the phone in the sliding mechanism. He spoke to Herbst briefly, then opened the inner door with a nod to Konstantin. In the narrow corridor beyond, there were two lifts. Konstantin took the one on the left up to the seventh floor and looked for Herbst's office. When a woman came out of an office at the end of the corridor and looked expectantly at him, he seemed to have struck lucky.

Sandra Herbst – as the nameplate next to the door said

– was short, a little plump, and in her mid-fifties. Her pale yellow trouser suit did not go with the red shoes or her badly dyed black hair at all. 'You're Mané,' she noted more than asked.

'*Oui*, Madame Herbst.' He slipped past her into the soberly decorated office. There were neither gems hanging from the ceiling nor posters of jewellery on the walls or any other personal belongings anywhere. Filing cabinets and shelves, clocks with various times on them, a computer and a large telephone system. Efficient work happened at the bourse, without any nonsense or frippery.

She followed him, her small green eyes still looking accusing. 'I hope for Bouler's sake that he has a good reason to send *you*, instead of sticking with the usual method.'

I'm really in now. Konstantin didn't dare ask how a deal usually came about. 'Sorry, Madame.' He handed her the envelope. 'For inspection. Monsieur Bouler requests your expertise.'

She took it. 'For inspection?'

Konstantin showed his smile again. 'Monsieur Bouler requested it.'

'Bouler is getting stranger and stranger.' Herbst sat down, opened the package and shook the box out. She picked up the Vanitas ring, held the piece of jewellery under the lamp and examined it thoroughly with the help of a magnifying glass. Her eye looked cyclopean through the smooth glass.

Say something already! Konstantin could barely stand it any longer. 'Do you want to let me know what you think of it and whether you could use the ring, Ms Herbst? Monsieur Bouler thinks it's something special.'

Herbst turned the ring, moved her face closer to it, then further away again, held it at an angle, looked at the inner side with the skull, then turned up the brightness of the lamp. She put the magnifying glass away and pulled a small pen with a cable out of an open drawer, which turned out to be a high-definition USB camera, and took photos.

'What can I tell Monsieur Bouler?' Konstantin asked again.

She ignored him and continued her examination. Finally she fixed her gaze on him, opened her mouth as though to speak and turned away again. She wrote something on the computer, took a cursory look at the screen and with an exaggerated gesture hit ENTER.

Was that good for me? 'Madame?'

She kept her eyes fixed on Konstantin. 'Would you like something to drink?' she asked, as sweet as pie.

The change in her tone, from brisk to pleasant, was unmistakeable. 'I would prefer if you gave your opinion on the ring first.'

'Monsieur Mané, I'd like to apologise for my cold manner,' she replied. 'It's been a long day and things weren't going well for me. Have you heard about the unrest in Côte d'Ivoire? It is of course making our customers anxious. And *whom* do they call?'

'No doubt they call you, Madame.' Konstantin cleared his throat. 'I don't want to be rude, but—'

Herbst raised one hand. 'My colleague will be here any moment.'

'Your colleague, Madame?' A feeling of unease crept up his spine. 'I don't understand.'

'That makes two of us then.' She turned the screen of the

computer around so that he could see an image of the ring that was lying in front of her.

It was not one of the photos that had just been taken, in any case.

The screen showed the scanned in pages of a brochure or exhibition catalogue, which, judging by the style, seemed to date from the nineteenth century.

Konstantin suspected that, by turning up in the gemstone and diamond bourse, he had set something unexpected in motion. *Herbst wasn't expecting this ring at all.*

There was a brief knock and the door opened.

In came Herbst's opposite: she was tall and well built, dressed in an elegant white business suit and had long chestnut-coloured hair. She looked considerably younger than mid-fifties and her smile could stop a firing squad from pulling the trigger. If Iva weren't anchored in his heart and in his soul, Konstantin would have fallen in love on the spot.

'Hello, Monsieur Mané,' she greeted him and offered him a faintly scented hand, her perfume was light, bright and fresh but with a mild dark note which made the blend a little unusual.

'Bonjour, Madame—?'

'Herbst,' she answered in a friendly way. The gaze from the grey eyes tinged with red, as though the colours couldn't make up their minds, was free from suspicion; the light grey glasses heightened the unusual effect. 'Marna Herbst. I'm afraid it's me you really wanted to see.'

Sisters? Sisters-in-law? For a moment, Konstantin didn't know what to say. 'That—' He looked to the other Herbst. 'I'm confused,' he said outright.

Marna laughed good-naturedly. 'Monsieur Bouler neglected to brief you properly. My sister is responsible for the—'

Sandra made a gesture that meant: that's enough. 'The internal workings have nothing to do with him. He is a courier.' It was clear who was in charge. 'My sister will decide whether we will accept the delivery or not.' She looked at Marna and pointed at the ring with the small pen camera. 'That's your area.'

Konstantin considered how much further he could get with the role of the messenger. They would find it odd if he asked too many questions and certainly wouldn't answer him. *Sit tight. Let's see what happens.*

He tried to read the scan of the old catalogue on the computer screen surreptitiously.

The Fraktur calligraphic lettering was blurred, the paper hadn't absorbed the ink correctly. But Konstantin could make out some things. It was indeed about an exhibition. The organiser was advertising the fact that he was displaying the most important Indian and Australian diamonds and precious stones – and those with spooky stories surrounding them.

Just as Konstantin was about to read what the deal with his ring was, Sandra turned the screen back round to face her.

Marna walked past him, stepped behind her sister and read the brochure. Then she placed her hand on the mouse and clicked several times. Her gaze was alert, her reddish-grey eyes narrowed in concentration.

Konstantin saw the reflection of what she was looking at in the lenses of her glasses. It seemed to be contemporary photos of the ring, then magazine articles that were older, small announcements and larger reports.

Konstantin was starting to get worried. Since there were reports about the piece, he assumed that it was a case of stolen goods – which he had coolly smuggled through Moroccan and German customs in his pocket. *Surely the ring is being hunted.* He began to feel warm.

It took Marna a few minutes to finish reading. Then she picked up the ring, weighed it in her hand and repeated the process that her sister had already gone through with it. She took a cloth out of her pocket, gave the jewel a thorough wipe, took out another cloth that gave off a faint chemical smell and polished the silver. Finally she opened her mouth and bit into the ivory.

Marna put the ring back on the table top very carefully. 'Send Monsieur Bouler my thanks and congratulations on this specimen.'

Enough of the act. I'm about to get busted anyway. 'Unfortunately, I can't do that.' Konstantin watched the two sisters, then his gaze fell on the letter opener and he reached for it. He didn't intend to threaten the Herbsts with the blade, but instead was moving a potential weapon out of their reach. Under no circumstances did he want to hurt Marna with aikido techniques, and Sandra . . . well. A little. At most. 'Monsieur Bouler is dead.' He eagerly waited for a reaction.

The shorter, chubbier woman didn't seem particularly surprised by the news. Even her younger sister made a face as if to say she thought it was high time.

'What happened?' asked Marna after a moment's silence.

'A shoot-out in front of a shop in Marrakech. His body-guards died, he was able to escape. As far as I know, he is one of the dead in Djemaa el Fna Square. I'm not a courier.

I'm the owner of the ring.' He reached out his hand and took the piece of jewellery. 'I'm looking for explanations about my property.'

The women seemed to be coming to an agreement with silent looks. When they looked at him again, Sandra pulled the pale yellow suit jacket up slightly. A shoulder holster with a gun emerged from underneath, the safety strap open.

You shouldn't underestimate diamond traders. Konstantin sat down and put the letter-opener away. He wanted to show by this that he honestly meant it and didn't intend to attack them.

Finally, Marna nodded. 'My sister and I thought that something was off about you,' she replied matter-of-factly, but without the beautiful smile from earlier. 'We were curious to know what your performance was about. You probably won't give away your real name?'

'No. But I won't give you two away either, not to your boss and not to Interpol. It makes no difference to me if you sell stolen jewellery. Whatever you tell me about the ring will remain between us.'

'Impressive. You've got guts.' Marna pulled up a chair and placed a soothing hand on Sandra's shoulder. 'You've gone to a lot of trouble and showed imagination in tracing Bouler's tracks back to us,' she answered. 'Monsieur Bouler is not somebody to mess with. If the news of his death is true, it's not that much of a pity.'

'It's a pity about his contacts,' Sandra quietly chipped in. 'He had access to the best African rough stones.'

Marna ignored her sister, her gaze remaining fixed on Konstantin. 'Why should I explain the ring's significance to you?'

'Because I've asked you to.'

'Oh, if only everything in life were so easy to arrange.' Marna looked across at him over the pale grey rims of her glasses. 'Since you are the owner, you can of course give us the name of the ring?' Her tone was challenging.

Konstantin decided he was better off sticking to the truth. 'No, I can't.'

Marna smiled. 'You stole the ring from Monsieur Bouler. Because if you had bought the ring, and by that I mean *legally* purchased it, you would know, Monsieur.'

Cunning, attractive and dangerous. 'I snatched it when Bouler was already lying dead in his car. He didn't die at my hands, I swear.'

Sandra rolled her eyes and exhaled. Her doubts about his story were obvious.

Marna, on the other hand, was looking curiously at Konstantin. She seemed to like him. 'What would you say to discussing it over something to eat? You're taking me out.'

Konstantin felt ambushed. Marna apparently liked adventure, if she was ready to put herself in the hands of a potential murderer. Or did she have plans Konstantin could not even guess at? 'Fine by me,' he said, not very graciously. 'Just the two of us?'

'Just the two of us.' Her reddish-grey eyes settled furtively on him. She opened her white jacket to show that she wasn't carrying a gun. She had a stunning figure. 'There are good restaurants in Idar-Oberstein.'

Konstantin acquiesced. 'But I'm choosing.' He couldn't shake the feeling of disaster gathering above him like cloud while he sat at the table with Marna and chatted. Sandra could, in the meantime, set all that was needed to bump him off in motion, thus making the ring the sisters' property. 'You won't make calls or do anything during the dinner that might lead me to believe that you're going to betray me?'

She nodded and her gaze was laced with scorn.

The unknown Marna Herbst was undoubtedly dangerous, but he stuck to his guns. Konstantin desperately needed information.

XIV

Youths slumber away, and old men stay
Awake. Death lurks here now, then there now,
If he raises the sickle, hurry, in case he reaps,
he often does not wait for the ears

Der Frohsinn, Friedrich Gottlieb Klopstock

Idar-Oberstein, Germany

They were sitting in the Agate Rooms: a simple restaurant with regional cuisine. There were dark oak beams on the ceiling with matching furniture that had been whitewashed and inlaid with semi-precious stones, there were little bunches of flowers on the table: the decor was appropriate but not exactly imaginative.

Konstantin had chosen the restaurant at random so that the Herbst siblings hadn't had a chance to organise an ambush. They were sitting as far away from the entrance as possible, by the large window, beyond which there was a lovely view of the rough-hewn church and the old town below it with its half-timbered houses and the huge number of shops selling all kinds of semi-precious and precious stones.

Marna had told him most of the tourists didn't know that none of the jewels came from Idar-Oberstein any more. The local agate quarries had been abandoned more than 130 years ago.

There were museums as well as tourist tunnels to convey a sense of how the work had been conducted back then, besides prospecting fields for children who could find the semi-precious stones placed there and proudly take them home. So-called 'precious stone camps' offered young people the opportunity to use instruments to go hunting for over-looked amethysts, rock crystal and agate in the slag heaps that were almost entirely exhausted.

Otherwise, the town made a living from working on raw stones from all over the world, and did a roaring trade in jewels at the bourse, no matter whether they were raw, cut or in the form of jewellery. The complete service available in the local area ranged from the designer to the gemcutter, to the manufacturer of display boxes.

Konstantin chose a salad with smoked trout fillets, Marna chose the Angus steak with fried potatoes. The waiter seemed annoyed by the order because it looked back to front. When he left, Konstantin decided the time for small talk was over. 'Have you and your sister started up a small black market in stones?'

Marna looked at Konstantin and raised her water glass. 'To our meeting, Monsieur Mané.'

'To you, Ms Herbst.' He maintained his French name and accent. Why should he tell the truth anyway? He was sitting at a table with a woman who fenced stolen goods or worse. He still felt tense. He didn't trust the friendly impression that Marna made. 'Go ahead then: what's the story with my ring?'

'Things are going a bit quickly for me. First we should—'

'No. That was the deal: we eat, you tell.' Konstantin looked at his watch. It was a little after six o'clock. He didn't want to linger in Idar-Oberstein too long, and he especially didn't want to give the Herbst siblings a chance to make his life more difficult.

'The ring. Great. It's old. Judging by the ivory, which was examined in the last decade, it could be estimated as seventeenth century. There are legends about it, the events surrounding them are said to have happened in medieval times, but the style of the opal's cut hadn't been mastered in Europe at that time.' Marna swirled her mineral water and looked at him over the rim of the glass. 'The stone is a harlequin opal and it comes from Persia. Does that mean anything to you?'

'No.' Konstantin took out his mobile and turned on the record function.

'It comes from a small mine near the mountain of Ali Mersai that wasn't around for very long. The tunnels collapsed several times and wiped out workers by the dozen. So the myth grew up that Death and the Shaitan personally had a hand in it. *Shaitan* is the Arabic word for devil.'

Konstantin pricked up his ears. 'I know. An Oriental fairy tale?'

'More of a Persian legend.' She pulled a folder of printouts that she had brought with her from the office out of her bag and picked a page to read aloud.

On Death and the Shaitan's Mine

Once upon a time a greedy man, who owned many things and always craved more, entered into a pact with the Shaitan. He called him to him and said: 'I'll sell my soul to you, if you get even more treasure for me.'

And the Shaitan rubbed his hands and said: 'Excellent! I will fill your mine with jewels for you, so that you will never be without income again.'

And soon afterwards the greedy man's poor workers brought back fire-coloured opals from the mountain tunnels, which was an evil miracle. The wealth grew and grew beyond measure. Kings and kaisers became jealous.

But that was not enough for the greedy man.

So he called Death to him and said: 'I will surrender the lives of my sons and daughters if you get me more treasures.'

And Death rubbed his hands and said: 'Excellent! I will fill your mine with jewels for you, so that you will never be without income again.'

And it happened that besides the fire-coloured opals suddenly blue opals were being plucked from the ground too.

The greedy man became so rich that the rulers of the world could borrow money from him, as much as they wanted, and he still had an infinite number of coins.

In return, every child borne by the wife of the greedy man died as soon as they had left the womb.

This grieved the woman so much that she drowned herself after the loss of her fourth child.

The greedy man was glad to have one less mouth to feed and did not marry again. He lived with his treasure in his castles and looked at his riches all day long.

Yet Death appeared to the greedy man. 'You have betrayed me. I gave you treasures upon treasures, but you denied me my due. To punish you, I will smite you with eternal life. You will get older and older, you will suffer infirmities and illness like everyone else. But you will never die.'

The Shaitan heard about this. He felt betrayed because he was no longer to receive the soul of the greedy man.

You have betrayed me,' he said. 'For that, I will put a curse on all treasures that issue from this tunnel: the red opals will spread evil in the world so that nobody will want to have them any more. While if anyone finds the blue opals and wears them, it will cost them their life.'

He disappeared in a cloud of foul-smelling sulphur, dived into the mine and pressed his hoof deep into the wall as a sign of the curse.

The greedy man did not dare tell anyone about this, and let his workers keep toiling away without telling them anything about the curse.

But evil befell every man who found a red opal and death came to everyone who had held a blue opal in their hands.

Soon the men refused to go down into the tunnels.

The greedy man ranted and raved, he lashed out at the poor people and ordered them to dig up new treasures for him.

But the workers had seen the Shaitan as he prowled through the tunnel and touched the walls; and they had seen Death as he swung his scythe at the people reaching for the stones.

They grabbed the greedy man and threw him down the deep shaft, from which he would never be able to escape, and sneered, 'Stay with your stones then and dig yourself out. Eat them if you're hungry. We will never set foot in your mine again. Death and Shaitan will have to find other victims besides us.'

There he was, the greedy man, sitting and wailing. He called for Death, whom he had cheated.

But Death was racing around the world, looking for the people wearing the blue opals in order to kill them, and he rushed to the places where the red opals had ended up. Since it never took long for dire conflicts and fierce wars to develop in these places, it allowed him to gather rich harvests into his charnel house.

The greedy man still sits in the abandoned mine to this today because he did not die.

His howls pierce the marrow and bone of the living and anyone who is desperate enough to set foot in the tunnel, that mine of Death and the Shaitan, must know that their life is forfeit if they touch even one single opal.

'. . . That's as far as legend goes. I found the story in a little booklet from the Lichtenberg Press, based in Hamburg, and I was surprised when I found out that this mine really did exist. My investigations revealed that it was closed in 1632, within two years of opening, on the orders of the Shah Safi I. The man in charge committed suicide, the family died destitute. The blue harlequin opals, like the one in your ring, were attributed to Death, the red fire opals to the Devil.' Marna was visibly enjoying telling the story. Her face was that of an actress wrapped up in her role.

Konstantin could have hugged her. This story alone had made his trip to Idar-Oberstein worth it. He was becoming more and more convinced that he was dealing with a Reaper's Ring. 'Can you lend me the stories?'

'Sure.' She drank from her glass and Konstantin couldn't help his gaze straying to her red lips. 'Since the mine had a short lifespan, hence a limited output, the fairy tale about the Devil and Death did the rest and the opals were very sought after. Soon people were attributing the most outlandish things to them. And yes, I can give you this information too.' Marna smiled. 'You know nothing about the ring of course.'

'No. Just that it's something special.'

'Have I mentioned the name it was given in recent times?' Konstantin shook his head.

'Harlequin's Death.'

Now there's a statement. He wanted to take the ring out of his pocket and look at it, and search for the engraved skull – only he could not put it on. Not yet. He wanted to know the whole story first. *I have to be grateful to Arctander and Thielke for leading me to Bouler.* 'Who had it made? Do you know anything else?'

'But of course, Monsieur Mané, that's my job. Harlequin's Death is made up of various elements that can be attributed to Vanitas symbolism,' explained Marna and confirmed the significance of carnations, ivory and opal that he'd already suspected. However, the next piece of information left him stunned. 'The panel that the opal and silver are mounted on is made of human bone matter. Lord Richard Wenthsworth, who commissioned the ring, also ordered a relic attributed to

Mark the Evangelist to be stolen in February 1699. The ring was finished in the same year. He gave back the evangelist's remains and pretended he had caught the thief and executed him. That's how they were, the nobility.'

'And then the ring vanished?'

'After the death of the lord, who lived in York, the ring initially remained in the family, but they were struck by illness, murder and madness. Eventually the ring was sold and vanished until it turned up again at the World's Fair in London in 1851, whose brochure you've seen. It was meant to wind up in a museum, but a robbery prevented that.' She pointed to his mobile. 'Off.'

'How come?'

'You will have to memorise the details, Monsieur Mané. I'm certainly not going to give you evidence against me.' Marna waited for him to turn off the record function before continuing. 'Ten years ago I discovered the ring in an estate auction in Cologne, but it was stolen before I could pounce. My investigations came to nothing. Monsieur Bouler is, let's say, a specialist in acquiring rare pieces of jewellery, and I asked him for help. Three months ago he wrote to me to say he had found Harlequin's Death and that it was just a question of price. The negotiations with him were . . . tough.'

'How much money are we talking?'

'Around half a million. Euro. That is the collector's value, not the real intrinsic value – that is significantly lower. Bouler was asking too much.'

Konstantin thought about the bargain price the unsuspecting Rabih had almost given him the ring at. *Because of a coincidence.* 'Did you want to buy it for yourself or was there a prospective buyer for Harlequin's Death?' Maybe he would get a name, maybe the buyer was someone who knew much more about Reaper's Rings than Konstantin and would share their knowledge with him. He would have some certainty. *That would be* . . . He hung on Marna's words, waiting for her answer.

The stolen goods fence let him squirm. She poured a little bit of water and ordered herself a black tea. 'I don't think you need to know that, Monsieur Mané,' she replied dismissively.

'What do I do if you tell your client about me after our dinner and he hunts me down because he wants the ring? Would it not be fair for me to know something about him?'

She smiled mischievously. 'I don't even know if you're really called Mané, why should I should tell you the name of my client? Come on, you can't seriously expect that of me.' Marna looked at the waiter approaching with their food. 'Ah, excellent. I'm hungry.'

Her expression changed, her eyes were riveted on the entrance. 'Are you expecting someone else, Monsieur Mané? Perhaps a colleague from Interpol, so that she can search me after the arrest? I would have thought that you'd have had fun doing that yourself.'

Konstantin looked up from his delicious salad and followed Marna's gaze to the door. He had let his watchfulness slip: concentrated too much on the story and the pretty woman. *Was that one of her tricks?*

His appetite vanished abruptly when he recognised the person at the other end of the room.

Madrid, Spain

After a brief nap, Thielke directed his attention to his LeMat revolver. He disassembled it and cleaned the parts thoroughly before putting it back together again. Then he loaded the heavy cartridges into the barrel, placed the shotgun shells in the single chamber and stuck the revolver in the belt holster. The weight pulled the belt downwards, but he was used to that.

He never left the house without the LeMat. To carry it through security control, he took it apart down to the smallest screws and smuggled the ammunition in the heels of his shoes and in the prosthesis which had been appropriately prepared. The LeMat simply belonged with him. The sight of it alone was enough to stifle discussion with a nervous petty criminal about the whereabouts of his wallet.

Thielke was puffing away on a cigar. He had treated himself to a smoking room in a Madrid hotel and was now making full use of that. Two nicotine patches were stuck to his arms, constantly releasing their active ingredients and keeping his neurotoxicity at a permanently high level. The nicotine flowed into his veins day and night, it was vital.

After a bite of a sinfully sweet piece of Spanish pastry, he gave himself a shot of insulin through his shirt into his stomach and stood up. He had to get going for his meeting with Arctander.

As he had found out by now, Almudena was not a person, but rather a place, namely a graveyard and supposedly the most beautiful one in Madrid.

Thielke was in possession of a survey map from the graveyard office. He had a vague idea where he could find Arctander today before he unleashed another episode like in Marrakech. The narcoleptic was probably already the most powerful Death Sleeper in recorded history. The more often the man fell asleep the more his power grew. Death was simply becoming angrier and angrier at the person denying him.

After a brief hesitation, Thielke took eleven more cartridges out of his calf prosthesis, inserted them into a speed-loader and put this in his jacket.

He left the room, limping slightly. The stump was still bothering him because of the weather; pulsing and aching uncomfortably.

Once Thielke was standing on the street, he hailed a taxi and asked to be taken to the graveyard. The inevitable piece of chewing gum found its way into his mouth, without it his breath smelled like a mixture of Coke and cigar smoke.

During the journey he studied the map of the graveyard. Although Bent Arctander came from Sweden, some of his ancestors had come from Spain. From Madrid. That had been more than a hundred years ago though, and there weren't any visible Spanish traits in the narco any more.

What the Death Sleeper now wanted with the grave of his great-grandfather, Thielke could not imagine. A nostalgic reunion while passing through? Or did he want to meet someone again, like in Marrakech? What he had wanted from Bouler was unfortunately still not clear.

There were still two addresses to be checked out, although Thielke knew they may now be irrelevant: Via Balzina in

Roccastrada and the chemist in Venice, numbers one and two on Arctander's little holiday list; places Thielke had looked up in advance. Before now he hadn't really concentrated on them, because he would rather have met the Swedish man at his future travel destinations. 'I will definitely meet him,' he murmured. The LeMat was pressing into his back, waiting to be put to use. 'Even if I have to "meet" him with a bullet from a hundred metres away.'

'*Qué*, Señor?'

'*Nada*,' he replied. That was the only word of Spanish he had mastered: *nothing*.

The Madrid heat assailed him, making Thielke sleepy and gently pushing his eyelids down.

He didn't fight it, sinking calmly into a shallow sleep, without needing to fear that he would kill the taxi-driver. His trick: the way out of the misery of the curse.

Eventually the car came to a shuddering halt.

'Señor. We're there,' said the driver in practically incomprehensible English.

Thielke leaped up with a snoring sound and wiped drool from his cheek. 'How much?'

'Thirty euro, Señor.'

He narrowed his eyes and looked at the meter, which was already turned off. 'Is that an estimate? How about you show me the display again so that I can believe you and the machine?'

'No, no, Señor. It's exactly thirty euro.' The man was bored, apparently this was not the first time he had had this conversation.

Thielke considered whether he should use the LeMat to

find out the real price, which he would actually pay without any problem, but the video camera installed inside the car, which was being broadcast to the taxi's headquarters, held him back.

'This is a scam!' he said clearly into the lens and made a 'fuck you' sign. He spat the chewing gum out of his mouth and into his hand, folded it into the note and made a ball out of it. He stuffed the sticky wad deep into the gap in the cushion. 'Keep the change.'

Thielke left the car without closing the door. He accepted the driver's swearing and cries of *bastardo* with a broad grin.

He limped to the park-like graveyard and consulted the map, then looked for the right grave.

Arctander's relatives had been called Ibanez, and the great-grandfather had had some illustrious Christian names: Jesús Domingo Hérnando. With the aid of the map, he quickly found the position of the grave and found himself a bench nearby, underneath a sprawling olive tree less than fifty metres away, which sheltered him from the hot sun. Sunglasses on, he took the Nikon case out of his bag and screwed on the largest zoom lens.

Thielke hoped that the narco hadn't already turned up and disappeared again, but he doubted Arctander could have left Marrakech more quickly than he did.

Using the zoom, he brought the gravestone right up close to his healthy eye.

'Hmmm, I see,' he murmured as he read the subtle message on it. Barely visible to the average eye, a time had been written in chalk in the bottom right-hand corner: 6 p.m.

Four hours to go. As long as it referred to today.

'Shit.' Thielke licked a salty layer of sweat from his upper lip and made himself comfortable on the bench. He ate a softened chocolate bar that he had stashed in the camera case, and injected two units of insulin.

Two hours later and he found that sitting down was making him too uncomfortable. He set an alarm on his smartphone for 17.30, lay down, closed his eyes and drifted off to sleep. If it were the wrong day, he would at least have had a relaxed siesta in the shade: a luxury that responsible-minded Death Sleepers couldn't indulge in. But he could. Thanks to his tricks.

At the first *beep* Thielke opened his eyes wide and sat up slowly so as not to draw any attention with a sudden movement.

It had grown darker and was not quite so hot any more, but it was enough to make him keep sweating.

Carefully, as though he were a nature photographer who didn't want to frighten off shy game, he lifted the camera and pointed the lens at the area surrounding the grave of Jesús Domingo Hérnando Ibanez.

A woman in a red dress was standing in front of it, looking at her watch. Then she placed a white rose on the grave slab. She held a second one in her hand. She wore a wide-brimmed straw hat, flat shoes and jewellery on her wrists that betrayed the fact that she was not exactly among Madrid's poorest residents. She had plaited her long black hair into a thick braid. He estimated she was in her early fifties, but her figure was like a model's.

'Good genes or sports mad,' he said softly, and lit a cigar. He took a stick of jerky out of his trouser pocket and opened it with one hand. Standard.

Zoom, *click, click, click* – her pretty face was captured on the Nikon's memory chip. *I wonder who she is?* He couldn't detect any similarity between her and Arctander.

She looked around now and again.

This unidentified beauty is definitely waiting for someone. Thielke looked at his watch, feeling terribly thirsty. He hadn't thought of bringing something to drink with him, and was feeling dehydrated, which wasn't exactly good for his diabetes.

A little after 6 p.m. a man appeared. He was wearing a peaked cap and huge sunglasses, and had ducked his head, making an effort to make sure his face couldn't be recognised.

But the Nikon's zoom would not be thwarted: Bent Arctander.

There were countless creases in his white and blue checked shirt and no fewer in his jeans. He was definitely sleeping in his clothes.

At first he wandered near his great-grandfather's grave, apparently aimlessly, then he approached the woman as she lay the second rose on the grave, and spoke to her. In English, as Thielke could see from his lip movements through the lens. Good, he could understand that – so long as he could see their mouths through the viewfinder.

But they kept turning away. They didn't allow him more than a few clues. He thought he had understood *stadium*, *Barcelona*, *match* and *tickets* from Arctander.

'You're not going to go to a football match with a woman like this, are you?' he mumbled and followed Arctander as he shook tablets out of various dispensers from time to time and swallowed them.

Click, click, click.

He thought he saw the word *ring* along with *deal* on the woman's full lips, but it wasn't possible to make out anything else until they shook hands.

Thielke shot a few more photos of the pair, then quickly put his camera away. He had to make up his mind now: should he follow the woman to find out the purpose of the meeting? But then he would lose the narco who was evidently planning to go see a football game. In his condition. *Are you a psychopath after all, killing everyone on purpose because you get a twisted kick out of it? Or are you suffering from unrestrained hubris?*

These hypothetical questions would be settled immediately. As curious as Thielke was, there was only one correct option. Two shots in the head and Arctander wouldn't be causing any more trouble. Ever again.

They set off in opposite directions, just as Thielke had feared they would. With a heavy heart he followed Arctander in order to shoot him. He hobbled after the Swedish man, his right hand resting on the handle of the LeMat.

With the onset of evening, Madrid's bereaved had decided to storm Almudena. There were people walking around everywhere, armed with watering cans, rakes and other equipment for taking care of graves. He couldn't finish off Arctander here without being seen.

Too many witnesses. Thielke stayed on him, waiting for a better opportunity.

The Swedish man went back across the graveyard to the street.

Okay, now I need to risk it, otherwise he's ... As Thielke went to draw the LeMat, and scatter the narco's head over the pavement with two or three shots, a shrill, frantic ringing sound distracted him.

Out of the corner of his eye he saw a flapping pink pennant at eye level, then something dashed between his legs and a hard object banged into his genitals. A child's voice squeaked out in alarm as Thielke fell onto his back, though he had the presence of mind to take his hand away from the trigger of the revolver with its safety catch off.

It was as though someone had thrown a bowling ball at his nuts. His vision went black. He found himself being helped back to his feet by Spanish-speaking people. His rescuers spoke in rapid apologies, while a little girl stood in front of him next to a pink bicycle. She was the one who must have carelessly mown him down. They grabbed the camera bag from his shoulder and dusted the dirt off.

'It's all right, it's all right.' Thielke waved his hands, fending off their well-intentioned patting, before they accidentally saw the LeMat or even let it off. '*Nada, nada.*'

He looked in the direction of the exit and could just see the narco getting into a taxi.

Shit. Thielke limped through the concerned crowd, knocking over the little girl as punishment, and lost vital seconds when he had to wait for a free taxi. One gesture brought the next one to a halt.

Amid complaints from the parents and howls from the child, he leaped into the passenger seat. The car with Arctander had long since disappeared.

'Do you happen to know which stadium has a match happening this evening involving a team from Barcelona?'

'*Sí,* Señor. Estadio Santiago Bernabéu. Barça against Real, a duel between champions,' the driver said proudly, as though he was on the team. There was a little sign on the dashboard with his licence fastened to it. He was called Miguel, the rest of the information having been made illegible by sunlight. He had a short beard and long black hair, like the poster boy for a Spanish tourism campaign.

'Then drive me there.'

'Do you have tickets, Señor?'

'Can you not get them there?'

Miguel roared with laughter. 'The match has been sold out for a long time, Señor. Shall I drive you there anyway?'

'Yes. Put your foot down, mate. I have to go there.' If needs be, Thielke could get himself a ticket using the LeMat. 'Do you happen to know how many people there will be in the stadium?'

Miguel drove swiftly though the evening rush hour traffic, which wasn't all that easy. It required the skills of a matador: reflexes and a good eye. 'Well, since it's sold out, I would say around 80,000 people. It's a great stadium, Señor. But as you don't have any tickets, you unfortunately won't see it from inside.'

'It'll be okay.' Thielke was glad he had his gun with him. Twelve millimetres through the middle of the head would end the narco's life. Or at least insofar as it counted. He'd better pump the whole magazine into him, just to be sure. He had the wave generator in his other bag. He doubted he could get close enough to Arctander for the machine to be effective.

Thielke used the tortuously long journey to look through the photos he'd just taken. He whipped out his smartphone and did an online search for the drugs that Arctander had taken at his great-grandfather's grave.

The pills called Modafinilin and Oxybatan had active ingredients that kept you awake and were meant to aid concentration. They were mentioned in forums in connection with narcolepsy; this fitted with the medicines Clomipramine and Reboxetine, which combatted cataplexy, or at least suppressed muscular paralysis and hallucinations. The other pills with the lovely name WU stood for Wake Up: caffeine, guarana and plant-based active ingredients for boosting circulation.

Thielke couldn't deny that Arctander was doing everything to fight his illness – but was it enough?

In a stadium full of people – 80,000 men, women and children – Thielke could not take risks or hesitate. The fact that they would most likely catch him afterwards and arrest him for murder didn't matter to him. With his poor shape and his prosthetic leg, he lost races against little children. He would simply play the confused, diabetic, nicotine-addicted cripple, demand extradition to Germany and treatment in a mental asylum from where he could easily disappear.

The stadium was now in sight. Crowds of people were building up in front of it. People were moving through the entry points in orderly lines. The fans were waving flags and scarves, there was yelling, battle songs resounded from different directions and came through the windows of the taxi. The atmosphere was upbeat and relaxed, the football fans were expecting a party, in the stands as well as on the pitch.

And in among them, without them knowing it, was imminent death in the form of Bent Arctander.

The hairs on the back of Thielke's neck stood up. He felt cold with fear for all those people. *How do I find the narco in this chaos?*

The idea came to him a moment later: since he was about to shoot a person dead in front of thousands of witnesses, and was ultimately going to be arrested anyway, he could storm the security headquarters immediately and use the surveillance cameras for the search. A little bit of coercion and false imprisonment would make no difference any more and would even be more evidence of his confused behaviour.

'We can't get any closer. Traffic jam.' Miguel grinned at him. 'So, Señor? Still convinced you'll get tickets?'

'Black market. I'm sure someone is standing round some-where flogging tickets at extortionate prices.' He paid and tipped the driver, got out and lit a cigar. One hand on his camera bag, he hobbled off, reaching the boisterous crowd ten minutes later. The air smelled of barbecued meat and beer and once outside the car, the songs rang out even louder than before.

'I can forget about it.' Thielke didn't expect to find Arctander even with the help of the security hub and the camera surveillance. Before him was a sea of faces, incalculable in number.

But giving up and leaving these people in danger was not something he could do.

He needed a new plan.

Thielke spotted a few touts selling tickets for 300 euro and bought one without bothering to haggle. He swiftly made it through the lax checks at the disabled entrance, after he had made it unmistakably clear that he was missing a lower leg.

Thielke pushed his way through the crowds of people, shoving and squeezing. To his silent horror, he came across many children and young people among the fans.

That was another incentive for his thankless undertaking. *80,000 people.*

He didn't even consider going to the designated areas reserved for the disabled. He looked for a way to get to the stadium's commentary box instead. A look at his watch told him there was still half an hour till kick-off. The stands were already more or less completely full.

He limped hastily up the steps to the large glass booth with the commentary box, cursing his stump.

A security man was making sure that no pranksters tried to get inside. His name was Raphael, according to the badge on his chest. He was sipping a can of Coke, smoking and chatting with a cute Spanish woman who had the Real colours painted on her cheeks and an impressive cleavage.

Distracted by the flirtation, the security man only noticed Thielke when he was standing in front of him and pressing the LeMat inconspicuously against his stomach. 'Open up.'

Raphael's eyes widened. He slowly took out his lanyard and opened the booth.

'You go first,' Thielke ordered, throwing the baffled Spanish woman, who couldn't see the revolver, a quick glance. 'He'll be back. Be a good girl and stay here.'

They entered a glass room dominated by camera monitors and a long desk with levers, buttons, microphones, LEDs and several telephones, with five office chairs behind it. Four were occupied: three men and a woman were chatting in Spanish. They didn't even turn around when the two men came in.

Twenty minutes till kick-off.

The warm-up act had started: youth teams were showing how the next generation was being nurtured at Real. Every shot on goal was greeted with an enthusiastic *olé*. A Mexican wave sped around the stadium.

Thielke knocked Raphael unconscious with a blow to the back of the neck. The muscular man collapsed, crashing to the floor with a noise that was impossible to ignore. The quartet turned around.

Enter the confused assassin. 'Hello,' Thielke said in English, pointing the large muzzle of his LeMat at the group. 'You understand me, don't you?' General nodding of heads. 'Okay, I'm Igor, former FSB, Russian secret service, and sent by the great Manitou to redeem humanity from its sins. Those things with the A380 and Marrakech were me. And the same gas cylinders that I stole from the FSB are lying scattered throughout the stadium. Now we're going to play a fun game called "run for your life". Let's see how many people you can save. Manitou says the innocent will be free, the sinners will die.' He reached into his pocket and drew out his insulin pen, holding it like a detonator. 'This is the remote detonator for the opening valves. Understood?'

The quartet nodded as one. They had all gone chalky white.

Thielke pointed to the woman. Distraught women were always good on the phone. 'You call the police and tell them what's wrong. If they want, they can come here and run for their lives too. And you,' he pointed to the dark-haired man, 'call the people who are responsible for security in the stadium. They are not to let anyone else into the stadium. We have enough participants.'

Trembling all over, the woman lifted the receiver and dialled the emergency number.

Ten minutes went by.

The youths clapped happily as they came off the pitch, to the applause of 160,000 hands in return. Then they ran into the tunnel that led to the changing rooms.

'Which of you is the stadium announcer?' The shortest man raised his hand. 'What's your name?'

'Ringo.'

'Ringo, go to the microphone and announce that the game has been cancelled at the last minute due to a stomach virus, which struck the Real team after eating the food provided by catering. Say that the tickets will remain valid and that the match will be played at a later date. Send the people out! Off you go! Make some effort and repeat the lines until the people have understood. I'm releasing the gas very soon.' A crazed attacker wanting to avoid panic among his victims was admittedly not completely logical, but the revolver and the supposed detonator ensured that nobody questioned his instructions.

Ringo did what he was ordered to do and played a jingle first to get people's attention, then followed it up by blaring a cheerful tune and reciting his lines.

Thielke pointed to the third man. 'You call the team dressing room and tell them what's wrong. I don't want to see any players on the field. They are allowed to run away and escape.'

Ringo talked and talked, speaking about the diarrhoea and that it was regrettable and that the match would be played at a later date and so on. He repeated the request to leave the stadium monotonously. Considering he had to wipe drops of sweat off his face and was shaking like a leaf, his voice was surprisingly calm.

Meanwhile, the young woman was howling down the phone to the police, one man was on the phone to the security division and the other to the players in the dressing rooms. It was like stockbroking on Black Friday.

The dramatic tension in the booth seemed out of place, given that in the stadium itself there were Mexican waves happening again and loud laughter was surging through the stands. The fans thought it was a joke and weren't moving. Some were booing and striking up abusive chants against the announcer.

Oh, piss off! How can you be so stubborn? The display showed phone calls coming in on the only free telephone. Thielke suspected they were television crews or reporters who couldn't understand what was going on and why they hadn't been told anything about it before.

Ringo looked anxiously at him. 'They're not leaving! They think it's a joke!'

'Try again, damn it!' screamed Thielke and cocked the trigger of the revolver with a loud click. 'In ten seconds I'm pressing the button for the valves. Do you want everyone to be sinners? Oh, that will really please the great Manitou, so many bad people exterminated.'

Five minutes till kick-off.

Instead of the mascots, the stadium security team walked onto pitch, accompanied by well-equipped police officers who were to ensure an orderly evacuation.

The widespread laughter gradually died away, the events on the field were attracting attention. But still nobody moved.

And then, in a panic, Ringo did something Thielke was not prepared for. Out of desperation, or perhaps the pressure of the situation, he shouted into the microphone: 'Bomb! We have a bomb in the stadium! Everyone out, immediately!'

Shit! You idiot! Before Thielke could do anything, the two other men in the booth called out more confused warnings. The distraught woman sobbed so loudly and convulsively that she could be heard over the loudspeakers. This sound of fear, amplified many times and spewed out of the speakers, ensured that the atmosphere suddenly shifted. The woman's emotion was palpable.

The spectators' eyes were riveted on the commentary box. Finally the first wave of spectators began to flee.

'Shit.' Thielke turned the microphone off. He prayed that Arctander didn't succumb to panic and have a fit. It hadn't been going too badly before Ringo had undone everything with his efforts at heroism. *If there is a God, please . . .*

The laughter in the stadium had disappeared, the whistles and chants ebbed away. They could now hear loud cries coming from the booth.

Another wave broke towards the exits. Policemen tried to maintain order, asking people to leave the arena using hand signals. Indistinct megaphone instructions rang out like distorted voices from a gramophone.

And then, from one second to the next, it was as though someone had unleashed the bull in Pamplona. There was shoving and jostling. The relentless flood of fleeing people swelled and broadened, spilling towards the exit stairs. People got carried off, swept away and separated from their companions. Elsewhere people stumbled, fell and got trampled on.

Thielke was staring at the mass panic. *This was exactly what was not supposed to happen!* Arctander was somewhere down there, the real bomb, ready to go off any time. Thielke could practically hear it ticking.

The door to the booth caved in, splinters flew into his lower back and a moment later he was seized and thrown to the floor. He breathed in the odour of the policeman who had thrown himself on top of him, aftershave mingled with plastic and kevlar.

'I surrender, I surrender!' Thielke cried, as he tried to throw the LeMat away, the policeman yanked at it, to disarm him – and the trigger flipped downwards and let off a shot.

Bam!

The woman shrieked as though she had been hit.

There was a rattle, and glass broke as the bullet whizzed through the window of the enormous booth. Shards rained down on Thielke and the policeman.

A collective scream arose from the other side of the booth, which spurred the frenzy below as spectators fought to escape the cauldron of the stadium.

The concrete floor vibrated under the rolling thunder of thousands of stamping feet, the air reverberated with the squeal of those hemmed in behind the barriers, like so many animals scared to death.

A hot pain shot through Thielke's arm. The policeman had probably dislocated his shoulder. 'It's all right, it's all right,' he cried through gritted teeth. 'I was the n—'

The hissing of a snake, the crackle of a fire, the quiet rasp of the pick-up on dirty records, the snarl of aggressive cats, gas streaming from a pipeline – the noise piercing Thielke's ears sounded like all of these rolled into one.

It wasn't overwhelmingly loud, but it came through above the crashes and screams. It seemed to be getting louder until he understood: the fizzing wasn't increasing, the surroundings were getting quieter.

A heavy weight landed on Thielke's back. The policeman's helmet hit the back of his head, the man's mouth was level with his ear. The last breath, the soft 'hhhhhhh' swirled around him, the stranger's Odic force enveloped him. Warm, with a hint of mint and acid that had risen from his stomach. The man lay limp on top of him and died. Simply and swiftly. Unspectacularly.

Thielke shook the dead man off with a frustrated cry, whose lonely echo rolled across the stadium. There was no longer any other noise.

He took the LeMat and hauled himself up using the desk, reset his shoulder with a bang against the wall and screamed again. High-pitched and long, to give vent to his frustration, his anger.

He limped out, knowing the sight awaiting him – the sight he would never forget. As Thielke stepped out of the booth, his mouth was dry. He felt low blood sugar levels coming on. 'Please,' he groaned in despair, 'some God or other, please, a miracle. Please!' Then he looked around him.

Dead bodies.

Thousands.

Tens of thousands.

It was as if the photographer Spencer Tunick had invited people to a crazy art installation and instructed them to lie down. A whole stadium full of prostrate people: in the stands, on the stairs, on the pitch, in shirts, in police armour, with flags and drums in their hands, colourfully painted, some still with a snack or their beer mug in hand. The Reaper had felled them all, mown them down, not ears of corn, but people. 80,000 of them, and all irrevocably silent.

From the way the corpses were lying in the stands, they looked like they were piled up in mountains: an ancient sacrifice to a cruel god. A few dead pigeons slid off the stadium roof and tumbled down on to the bodies below. The lush green pitch had lost its colour, becoming wilted and stunted. All life was extinguished.

'Arctander!' shouted Thielke with tears in his eyes, kicking the backrest of a seat with his good leg. The plastic shattered, the little pieces flying away and landing on corpses. 'Arctander, wake up, you fucking narco!' He raised the LeMat and held it, ready to open fire. *Show yourself!*

His raw, rough voice resounded through the arena, echoing indistinctly back to him: the only sound that disturbed the silence.

'Arctander! Where are you?'

On the other side of the stadium, almost directly opposite him, a person suddenly moved among the mounds of dead bodies. The person was taking great pains to creep out from between the still warm corpses. Since there were no other survivors in this place apart from Death Sleepers, there was only one person who it could be: Arctander.

Thielke got the man in his crosshairs, took aim and fired. *BAMM!*

The LeMat bucked and the bullet sped towards the narcoleptic. Arctander threw himself to the side, but too late. He yelled out. He had been hit, but not fatally.

Thielke saw him crawling forwards, using the dead bodies

as cover. 'What the hell, narco?' he roared. 'Are you a psycho, putting yourself in the middle of all of these people?'

BAMM!

The corpse in front of Arctander twitched from the impact and another yell rang out.

He is too far away. 'Stand up, you arsehole, so that I can blow your head off!' cried Thielke, the LeMat in his outstretched hand. 'Let's tie up the loose ends.'

'This isn't what I wanted,' Arctander called back plaintively, his voice barely audible. 'I thought the drugs were helping and would prevent it. I've tried so many things and—'

'How long have you thought that?' barked Thielke. 'Since Marrakech? Since your flight on the A380?'

BAMM!

The bullet missed the man's head by mere millimetres because Arctander had slipped. He rolled down over the dead bodies, tumbling down clumsily like a small child and hit the ground behind the corpse of an armoured police officer.

Thielke waited to see which direction the Swedish man would go so as not to waste the next bullet.

'I can do it, honestly!' cried Arctander, begging.

'Have you taken a look around you, you idiotic wanker?' he bellowed back. 'You've killed them!'

'No, not me. Death did. The . . . curse! I can't do anything about it. *They* made me into this! *They* want me to be like this! Stop following me!'

'You should have taken your arse off to an island and stayed there, looked up your friends on the Internet, used messaging and cameras, but pissed off out of the areas where people live.' Thielke was deliberately talking about alternatives to lure him out. It was clear to him that he could not let the narco out of the stadium. He would die here and today, that was Arctander's fate. He deserved it. A thousand times over. 80,000 times over.

Arctander suddenly rolled behind a large advertising hoarding several metres high with a car manufacturer's logo on it. It wouldn't hold off the bullets from the LeMat, but it did conceal Arctander's exact position on the other side.

The free-standing hoarding moved forwards slowly: the Swedish man was behind it, pushing it towards the exit.

Thielke fired rounds from the LeMat in quick succession, the reports from the detonations a persistent, low thundering.

The bullet holes moved from right to left, piercing a gaping hole every half metre.

'I don't want to die. I know the stories: Death Sleepers don't pass on. Their souls never rest in peace,' cried Arctander from his cover.

Thielke got himself into a better shooting position and raised his arm. He saw a few fair hairs jutting out on one side. He had one last shot, the ninth round, before he would need to reload. He trusted his calm, steady hand and the eye he still had left.

Click.

No! Surely he couldn't have miscounted!

Thielke cocked the hammer, aimed again, looked precisely at the fair head and opened fire.

Click.

'I want it to stop too, but I want to live,' Arctander shouted to him and slipped again.

He dropped the hoarding and it tipped forwards. The

Swedish man was kneeling on the ground, looking at Thielke in shock. A clear line of fire. They stared at each other for a few seconds, their eyes met.

Then Arctander realised that the other man's ammunition had run out. He pulled himself together and ran towards the passageway that led to the dressing rooms. 'I promise,' he shouted. 'It will stop! I'll manage it soon! But don't follow me!'

'Stay here! I—' Thielke fired a round of shot from his other gun at Arctander, even though it was completely pointless. It didn't even reach the other side and scattered far too much to be able to do the narcoleptic any damage anyway. But he'd felt he had to do something, one last attempt.

Bent Arctander had vanished into the passageway.

Thielke spared himself the pursuit; he wouldn't catch up with him because he'd have to climb over soft corpses with his prosthesis.

Deeply shaken, he sat on the steps in front of the commentary box, where Raphael had been standing guard earlier, and let his gaze wander.

Nothing less than the impact of a meteorite or a violent explosion in the centre of the arena could have covered up the legacy left by Arctander.

Thielke did not want to forget.

Never. The image burned itself into his memory.

The 80,000 dead in Madrid would keep him motivated to find the Swedish man and kill him. Because nobody could hunt this dangerous man without being struck by his curse.

Nobody, apart from another Death Sleeper.

Sirens started to wail around the stadium. The emergency services had launched into action, but they would be overwhelmed by this disaster. The world would be over-whelmed by it.

Thielke swallowed. Even if every one of the deceased was carrying ID, the identifications would take weeks. *How are they going to transport the bodies away? In dignified hearses or in dumper trucks like the Moroccans did?*

He opened the barrel and let the empty cartridges pour out of the revolver onto the concrete floor, along with the dud. In case the forensics teams got excited about clues and were looking for Igor from the FSB.

In the silence of the stadium, the metallic clink sounded just like a wind chime nudged by a gentle breeze.

Thielke reloaded, clicked the barrel back into place and stuffed the weapon into its holster. Then he stood up to look for the security headquarters and delete the recordings. He didn't want to see his face in the news. Afterwards, he would disguise himself as a corpse and wait until the chance to disappear presented itself.

His gaze drifted down the body-strewn steps.

He was filled with horror at having to climb over the dead. On the dead. But he could not hesitate, so he lifted his foot and took the first step.

XV

Death must be so beautiful. To lie in the soft brown earth, with
*   the grasses waving above one's head, and listen to silence.*
To have no yesterday, and no tomorrow.
To forget time, to forgive life, to be at peace.

                    'The Canterville Ghost', Oscar Wilde

Idar-Oberstein, Germany

Konstantin saw Kristen von Windau coming towards the
table.

What Jester had told him about the baroness flashed across
his mind, the rumours about missing Death Sleepers. *This is*
her second attempt on me.

He didn't intend to wait and politely ask Kristen what she
wanted from him. A swift exit was clearly the better option.
Especially if he didn't want to put Marna in danger.

'No, not a friend of mine. On the contrary actually.' He
stood up abruptly.

'What is it?' asked Marna in alarm. 'Who is this woman?'

'Later,' he replied brusquely. 'We're going, Ms Herbst.'
He pulled her up by the elbow, ignoring her protests and

pushing her towards the exit. As he did so, he shielded her from Kristen with his body.

The waiter watched in bewilderment as the guests whose food he'd just served bolted. 'Excuse me, but—'

Konstantin threw a fifty-euro note at him and just kept going.

Kristen pressed her lips together and moved parallel to the pair to cut off their path.

By now the Agate Rooms was rather full, and around seventy customers were sitting in the restaurant, talking and eating. This precluded Konstantin having a chat with the Death Sleeper. What was going to happen as soon as they were out the door, he did not know. Judging by her facial expression, the baroness was not exactly in a reconciliatory mood.

They had almost reached the door when von Windau slipped in front of it, feet apart. 'If you come with me, Korff, i-i-it will all be okay,' she said softly so that the other customers couldn't hear anything.

'I've found out that people who meet you are disappearing without trace. I'm not interested in that.' He glanced over his shoulder. *The passageway to the kitchen.* 'Get out the back way,' he whispered to Marna. 'Get into your car. Go!'

'And you?'

'I'll follow. Wait for me. There's still more I need to know.'

She ran off, the sound of her steps retreating.

Konstantin noticed the looks that he and Kristen were getting. Nobody liked it when people stood around in restaurants. Their obvious, latent aggression was spreading unease and worry.

The waiter was making his way towards them to restore order.

'Which is it, Korff? Are you going to cause trouble or are you going to come with me?' Kristen was holding her right hand as though something was hidden inside.

Careful! 'The restaurant is full. Would you risk—'

'Korff, I don't have any time to lose. So come here! Right now,' she cut across him. 'I won't harm you or kill you. I just want to take you with me, show you something and tell you about my vision of eternal life for our kind. Without ageing, without decaying.'

Jester's right: she is a lunatic. Konstantin walked slowly backwards towards the kitchen. 'Not if I can help it.'

Kristen followed him – until the anxious waiter slipped in between them. 'Madame, sir, how can I help you?' he asked solicitously, which essentially meant *If you want to fight, then please don't do it in the Agate Rooms.*

Kristen thrust him aside and followed Konstantin to the entrance of the kitchen. When the waiter subtly tried to stop her, she dealt him a lightning-quick blow to the throat with the side of her hand. He fell between two tables, pulling a white tablecloth, the cutlery and food down with him. Plates and food landed on top of him and in the laps of the customers, who immediately leaped to their feet.

Konstantin had reached the kitchen and was getting his bearings. Three chefs were cooking the orders, and it was hot and smelled of fat for deep-frying and fried food. 'Where did the woman go?'

The youngest one, probably a trainee, pointed towards a door next to him. Konstantin had hardly taken two steps when Kristen joined them. Loud voices were coming from the dining room, somebody was shouting for the police.

'What's all this then?' snarled a broad-shouldered man in a stained chef's apron who was holding a meat mallet in his hands. 'Is this an open day, or what?' He pointed to the exit. 'Out, and make it snappy!'

Suddenly, an almost invisible wire was dangling from Kristen's right hand. A blunt metal stick the length of a finger hung from the end.

A kind of garrotte? Konstantin prepared himself to respond to her attack.

'Get out, the pair of you!' barked the kitchen heavyweight, and came towards Konstantin, reaching his arm out to grab him.

He countered the attack, channelling the strength of it into a simple aikido throw, and flung the heavy man over his hips and onto the work surface where he crash-landed on a pile of chopped vegetables with a groan, blinking at the neon lights above him.

'This is how you wanted it, Korff.' Kristen sprang forwards and pounced. The metal stick whirred upwards, to the exact height of Konstantin's temple.

With a leap backwards, he escaped the attack, which was seamlessly followed by more. Kristen masterfully whipped her handled garrotte around, driving him back further and further until he hit the edge of a table.

Out of the corner of his eye, Konstantin saw a soup ladle and snatched it up to block as the metal end came whirring upwards again.

The wire immediately wrapped itself around the ladle and

got tangled. Kristen snatched his improvised defence away from him, but the garrotte had been rendered useless for now.

Two waiters stormed into the kitchen, one armed with a baseball bat with *Power Base* written on it, the other with a poker from the chimney set. 'That's enough,' cried the one in front. 'You two are staying and paying for the damages.'

Four against the baroness.

Kristen whirled to face them; in one smooth motion, she dropped the garrotte and grabbed a frying pan simmering with hot oil as she vaulted over the table with the meat.

They don't stand a chance.

Already on his way to the door, Konstantin turned back with a leap to kick the aluminium table laid with tenderised schnitzel so that the edge smashed into the Death Sleeper's hip. The oil sloshed harmlessly onto the floor, away from the waiter.

Kristen growled, hurled the empty pan at the trainee and attacked the waiters with her bare hands.

They'll have to handle her themselves now. Herbst won't wait for me much longer. Konstantin wanted to clear off, but the still dazed kitchen heavyweight planted himself in front of him. He swung his schnitzel hammer.

The nice thing about aikido, thought Konstantin, *is that it works even in a small space like a kitchen. I just have to improvise a bit.* Konstantin grabbed the cook's powerful wrist with his left hand and let the momentum of his opponent's movement carry the man further, then he turned towards the man and wrenched his own right elbow upwards. This move may not have been aikido, but it was effective.

Konstantin's sharp elbow smacked sideways into the man's

cheek and flung him to the right. The blow knocked him off his feet and made him fall once more against the table with the vegetables. The head chef hit the ground surrounded by chopped carrots and courgettes.

'It didn't have to be like this.' Konstantin looked around for his female opponent.

The two unconscious waiters and the trainee lay scattered around Kristen. She gave the last chef a hard kick: her right leg shot up into the air and hurtled straight towards the forehead of the man storming towards her, who went down, gasping out for air. She sidestepped his fall with a turn, picked up her garrotte, and began to disentangle the wire from the soup ladle.

I hope Herbst is still there! Konstantin sprinted out of the kitchen of the Agate Rooms to the car park.

Marna was indeed waiting behind the wheel of her Audi TT outside the door, the motor purring. She had put her hair up into a ponytail, which made her look very casual, as if she was born for adventure. *Someone who flogs historic jewellery illegally has got to be tough.*

He got in and Marna stepped on it.

Kristen came out the door, saw them fleeing and raced across the car park. Konstantin couldn't see which car she got into because they were taking a bend. *She won't drive anything slow, I'd say.*

'Who was that?' asked Marna again.

The TT sped down the hill to the city centre and from there onto the broad street that ran through Idar-Oberstein.

Konstantin was surprised by how confidently she was driving at this speed. 'It's to do with the ring.' And that wasn't even a lie really, in his book. It was indirectly related to Death Sleepers. 'She would like to have it, but I was quicker.'

'You spent a long time in the kitchen.'

'It got violent.'

She glanced over at him as she let the sports Audi zoom into a bend. 'Are you hurt?'

'No, but the Agate Rooms will have some recruiting to do. We left some people injured unfortunately.'

'Badly?'

'I think they'll survive it.'

Marna shook her head. 'I'll never be able to go for a meal there again, are you aware of that?'

'You can say I had an ex who is crazy or something. That'll put you in the clear again.' Konstantin looked into the wing mirror. A pair of headlights was coming closer.

'Already clocked it,' said Marna. 'Somebody wants the ring, and really desperately.' She accelerated.

'Are you surprised? With that collector's value?'

The lights were getting bigger and behind them the high, angular nose of a car was briefly visible before it ploughed into the back of the TT.

Metal screeched, glass and plastic shattered. The muffled blow shook Konstantin and Marna hard. The car swerved, but she managed to bring the skidding under control by putting her foot on the accelerator and clutching the steering wheel tightly.

Konstantin could see that Marna was scared now, but he didn't know if he could have driven better.

'Are you sure you don't have a gun on you?' she cried anxiously.

'No. I'm not a good shot.' Konstantin looked around. He was looking for something heavy: a car jack or a full spare canister that he could throw at their pursuer. He climbed into the backseat and folded the seat down, groping around in the boot. The impact had badly damaged the rear of the Audi, the window was missing and it smelled of petrol. *Please not the tank.* 'I thought the TT was a sports car?'

'Something's wrong with the engine. If I had known that you would get me involved in a cha— Watch out! She's coming back!'

Konstantin raised his head. He saw the light grey Mercedes 4x4 thundering forwards, its battered front about to drill into them again. Kristen clearly had the upper hand in terms of HP and durable material.

The Mercedes rammed them.

Marna again managed to keep the TT in lane, although it grazed the crash barrier, emitting a fountain of sparks that engulfed the 4x4 in pursuit. 'Shit,' she shouted. 'She doesn't want the ring. She wants to kill you!'

Konstantin refrained from revealing that she probably wanted to kill Marna, because she still needed him alive. Or at least intact. *For whatever it might be.*

Beeping, Marna swerved around slower vehicles, driving slalom and running red lights. Luckily the B41 was quite quiet, otherwise they would definitely have already caused a crash. 'I hope I survive this,' he heard her murmur.

'You will.' *If I've got anything to do with it anyway.* As he was searching he grasped something large and the smell of petrol got stronger. *A spare canister.* He dragged it towards him, drew out his pocket knife and slit open the plastic so that there was a large hole and rips. 'Drive more slowly and, when I say, drive into the crash barrier again.'

'How come?'

'Just do it.' Konstantin saw the Mercedes speeding forwards.

Kristen was behind the wheel and making an angry gesture for them to pull over to the side and stop.

He tossed the pierced canister at her instead.

The tank flew through the air and hit the bonnet of the 4x4 where it unleashed its contents before it rolled up the windscreen and disappeared over the roof.

'Now!' he cried and held on tight.

Marna wrenched the TT to the right, the metalwork emitting a piercing grinding sound.

The sparks sped through the night and hit the Mercedes. The petrol coating caught fire immediately. Bonnet, windows, roof and the wings burst into flames, the airstream pushing the hissing blaze backwards. A comet on four wheels sped through Idar-Oberstein.

Konstantin hoped that the flames would strike as far as the vents and block Kristen's view.

But the 4x4 lurched forwards with a roar and pulled up level with the Audi. The fire had already died out; the speed had put out the flames.

'The Altenberg tunnel is up ahead,' announced Marna. 'If we meet anyone coming the opposite direction in there—'

Konstantin guessed what Kristen was planning. 'Watch out! She's going to crush us into the wall!'

The cars hurtled into the empty tunnel side by side.

The Death Sleeper edged closer in her Mercedes. Marna kept a distance, driving on two wheels in the narrow emergency lane, then braked and drove faster to escape their pursuer.

Konstantin threw the car jack and the spanner at Kristen. The side window of the Mercedes exploded, but she didn't let it bother her.

A loud, low horn boomed, things got bright, dark, bright, dark. Headlight signals from oncoming traffic.

'Lorry!' said Marna anxiously.

Konstantin had run out of missiles so he climbed towards her in the front.

They were just a few metres from the exit of the tunnel, where a fuel tanker and its trailer were moving forward like twin rocks.

Konstantin put on his seatbelt. 'We're on the better side,' he said to Marna and to himself. 'The emergency footpath, just—'

'I know,' she hissed at him and gripped the trembling wheel even more tightly. The tie rod had bent out of shape.

Kristen could also see the lorry and shifted to the left to let it pass between the cars.

But the lorry driver tried, as anyone would have, to swerve into the outer lane. He was in the middle of the manoeuvre when Kristen cut in front of the tanker and attempted to drive along the wall and half on the second emergency footpath.

That won't work. Konstantin looked back while Marna followed the drama in the rear-view mirror.

The lorry driver immediately veered in the other direction to avoid crushing the 4x4 and the heavy trailer started rocking from side to side. The Mercedes was grazed by the back wheel first and then by the bumper.

The Audi TT sped out of the tunnel, but the 4x4 smashed into the wall of the passage through the mountain, rebounded with a growing shudder and flipped as it moved across over the whole roadway and out of the tunnel on the right.

The crash barrier couldn't handle the weight and speed of the Mercedes: the car broke through the barrier, shot upwards and turned like a spinning-top around its own axis, before tumbling into the depths and disappearing out of sight. The headlights shone dully for two seconds from the abyss and went out.

Konstantin was still expecting a movie-worthy fireball, but it didn't happen. 'We've got rid of her.' He took a deep breath and looked straight ahead. He'd experienced dicey moments like this before on his missions. But his heart was beating fast. Pure adrenalin.

'She fell into the Nahe river,' explained Marna and put on her indicator.

'What are you doing?'

'Stopping. I don't feel well.' Marna drove around 400 metres down the street, through a roundabout and into a business park until she reached a car park at a DIY centre where she stopped. She got out and threw up.

Konstantin followed her. 'I'm sorry,' he said guiltily. One look at the TT made it clear that it was worth, at best, scrap value now. He sat on the battered bonnet and looked around.

Blue lights flared in the distance, sirens blared into the night. Fire engines and police drove along the Bundesstraße towards the tunnel, the road would soon be cordoned off.

Marna spat several times, then she came over and sat down beside him. She ran her trembling fingers through her chestnut hair and tossed back the strands that had slipped out of her ponytail. 'Apparently the ring really does summon Death, like the legend says,' she said huskily. 'Have you got a cigarette I can have?'

In his mind, Konstantin saw Kristen lying at the bottom of the Nahe. *Jester will be pleased about that. I've reduced his workload.* 'No. I'm a non-smoker.'

'Sensible, but right now, shit.'

Red lights were shining on the B41, warning the approaching traffic about the accident. Police officers with torches and reflective safety vests stood on the street and directed the traffic. *It was over and done with.*

Marna looked at him. 'What's your actual name? And don't lie to me, Mr I-am-a-Frenchman. Not after all this.'

'Sorry?'

'Your French accent disappeared when you were giving me orders.' She swallowed. 'Sure I've experienced a lot, but *this!*' Marna breathed deeply in and out, wiping her eyes. 'So?'

Konstantin rubbed his right hand on his trouser leg and held it out to her. 'Konstantin. Konstantin Korff. Like you, at first I got into all this by chance. I found the ring next to a dead body and took it, like I said. But I couldn't have known it was so sought after.' It was better if he put what had happened down to the ring. She wouldn't be able to understand anything else. 'The woman, Kristen von Windau, is after the so-called Reaper's Rings, which include Harlequin's Death. That's why I asked you earlier about the customer who had ordered it from you. It may be that he set von Windau on me, because he was having the ring hunted on his own account, without your knowledge, Ms Herbst.'

Marna nodded dumbly, staring over at the B41 where more and more lights were gathering. She ignored his hand.

Does she believe me? That was perhaps a little thin as an explanation. He lowered his arm. 'Who ordered the Harlequin's Death from you, Ms Herbst?' he insisted.

'Ruben Hoya. He has a weakness for stones from the forgotten Ali-Mersai mine. I've already sourced four pieces of jewellery like it for him.' She didn't turn her head, following the proceedings in the road.

He has four of them! 'Where do I find this Hoya?'

'What for?'

'So that I—' Konstantin cast about for a suitable lie. '— can sell the ring. Otherwise, characters like von Windau will be turning up on my doorstep every few weeks. I can't always have a great driver like you with me. Plus I want to get to know him. Anybody who sets a murderer on my trail because of a ring must be pretty special.'

'I can arrange that. Then you'll be free of these worries and potential financial issues too.' Marna rubbed her hand over her face and looked at him. 'What I wouldn't give for a cigarette, Korff. And you're fully aware I'm taking commission, aren't you? It would be my deal, after all.'

'Of course.' He pointed to the street where a coroner's truck was driving up and stopping at the police cordon before being let through. 'It will be better if I get rid of the ring before I share von Windau's fate. Tell Hoya the ring is a family heirloom that I got back from Bouler and want to sell.'

Marna seemed to be thinking. The businesswoman in her was coming through. 'Okay. I'll call Hoya and ask if he'll agree. But I'm coming with you.'

'Oh?'

'Purely precautionary. Because of my commission.' She knocked on the bonnet. 'And because of this. Thanks to you, Korff, I can have my TT used for scrap.'

'But you said it was faulty?'

'I said something was wrong with the engine. Apart from that, my insurance definitely won't cover damage by crazy ring collectors. And we would probably both rather not provide an explanation for this incident, would we? That'll be 5,000 extra from you. Until then I won't leave your side. I'll also need to check your identity beforehand.' She held her hand out. 'ID, please.'

Konstantin gave it to her.

Marna got up, went to the car and took her handbag out from behind the driver's seat. She took a few steps away from Konstantin, dialled and had a quiet conversation.

Meanwhile, Konstantin considered how to tell Jester he was not going to turn up in Frankfurt tomorrow.

He looked at Marna on the phone and couldn't help thinking of Iva.

Of the night with her, her laugh, her cello playing and how much he missed the looks she gave him from up there on the stage. Just for him. He was doing all this for her and a future with her. For a life without the curse.

Konstantin shuddered. He realised how close he had just come to death. To his physical demise, at least – the end of his body. If von Windau had had a touch more luck, he would have become a ghost, trapped for eternity in a non-descript tunnel in Idar-Oberstein.

Or drowned in the Nahe.

Or . . .

Konstantin gulped. He whipped out his phone and looked for Iva's phone number. The string of numbers lit up, the connection was being established.

'The person you are calling is currently . . .'

Damn. Konstantin hung up in disappointment. He didn't want to talk to voicemail, he wanted to hear Iva's voice and tell her that he longed for her. He rubbed his thumb pensively across the flat surface of the screen.

Footsteps were approaching.

'Hoya has agreed to a meeting,' said Marna. 'We can go to his house. I have his address.' Hence she made it clear that she would take him. She gave him back his ID. 'A thanatologist, Mr Korff? The ring really does suit you.'

'You could say that.' Konstantin looked at the battered TT. 'We probably won't be able to go in that.'

'We wouldn't go in that anyway. Señor Hoya lives in Spain. In Madrid. We'll drive to my flat and I'll get rid of this pile of junk and pack a few things. We can fly tomorrow. How are things looking for you?'

'I have a hotel in Frankfurt. My luggage is there too. Can you drive me to the bourse? My rental car is there.'

She nodded. 'Sure, but it would be easier if you stayed the night here.'

'And go to Madrid from here tomorrow? I didn't know Idar-Oberstein had an international airport.'

'All we need is an airfield where we can leave the helicopter. It belongs to the bourse, for fetching international guests from Frankfurt. Diamonds and gemstones are always transported the shortest possible distance.' Marna got in and looked at him as he walked round the disaster that was the TT and took a seat beside her. 'I have a couch that's all right. What do you think? Around ten we'll jet off to Frankfurt in the heli and from there take a flight to Madrid.'

'And what will your gentleman friend say?'

'My gentleman friend? He won't bite.'

Marna started the engine and drove off. Metal grated squeakily against metal, something was grinding somewhere. After two metres she stopped again. 'I'll call us a taxi. You're paying.'

Konstantin grinned.

Idar-Oberstein, Germany

It wasn't until Konstantin opened the door to leave the guest toilet the next morning, fully clothed, that he realised that Marna Herbst had meant *friend* and *bite* literally: in front of him stood a light brown Great Dane who could have effortlessly ripped off his balls. *Where on earth did that come from?*

The dog hadn't made an appearance when they had come into the house the night before. There was probably a room where the four-legged creature was usually kept. *In her bedroom, maybe?*

The Great Dane watched him carefully, but didn't growl.

Hopefully he knows that he shouldn't bite? 'Ms Herbst?' he said loudly, taking a step backwards and bringing the door between himself and the dog so that he could close it if necessary. 'Your *friend* is standing in front of me!'

A laugh came from inside the apartment, followed by an authoritative: 'Zerbo, come here!'

The Great Dane gave him a look that lay somewhere between offended and menacing, then turned around and trotted to his mistress.

Konstantin left the toilet where he had secretly spent the night: a small, isolated room without windows. Perfect for granting his stewardess an undisturbed sleep from which she would wake up again. Less than perfect as far as Konstantin's sleep went.

He had made it as comfortable as possible with towels – if Marna looked in on him during the night and the sofa cushions and blanket were missing, she would have asked questions that he could not have answered properly – but after a night between the toilet and door, with his head under the sink, his back hurt.

He had dreamed about Marna Herbst. That probably wasn't all that surprising, but it still gave him a guilty conscience. He might not recall the details any more, but it had been a blend of spy and erotic thriller. Stupidly, in his little night film, she had the same ankh tattoo as von Windau, but she had it all over her, even on her throat. He found it disconcerting. A psychologist could definitely interpret the dream better than he could.

'Good morning,' he said, and walked into the sitting-cum-dining-room for the first time. A sofa with artfully rumpled cushions was in her library, which also functioned as a guest room.

Marna apparently had an edgy, weird style. Paintings hung on the walls and they went beyond the popular art prints from a typical furniture shop. Modern, sometimes dark, sometimes bright, sometimes abstract, sometimes not.

He liked the Miró best, which an artist had dumped in front of the background of Da Vinci's Mona Lisa – just without the Mona Lisa. On a flat screen that was a metre across the diagonal, there were landscape scenes alternating. A collage showed the Twin Towers in New York with the attackers' planes rebounding off and in bold above it read, in a comedy font, *The Boing-Boeing!*

At the sight of the planes, Konstantin thought of the A380, of Paris and of Arctander whom he should really have been pursuing instead of mythical Reaper's Rings. There was no escaping his sense of responsibility.

'Good morning.' Marna was standing at the stove. She was wearing grey-and-blue check pyjamas under a grey bathrobe, like Jeff Bridges in the film *The Big Lebowski*. The outfit hid her figure. If it weren't for his dream he would hardly have given any thought to what lay hidden beneath the material. 'Breakfast will be ready in a moment. I hope you don't have any allergies?'

'Hazelnut pollen.'

'I rarely use that in cooking. I meant foods. Lactose, gluten or anything like that?'

'Hazelnuts. Appropriately enough, what with the pollen,' he answered, grinning, and came over. Zerbo lay next to his mistress, watching her every step. 'When does our helicopter take off?'

'As soon as we want. I booked us a flight out of Frankfurt at twelve o'clock. That would be in four hours.' Marna nodded to the table that had already been laid. 'Help yourself. The eggs are hard-boiled and I'm having an on-going battle with the espresso maker.'

Konstantin sat down. He immediately felt hungry at the sight of so many delicious things. He reached for a bread roll, cut it open and spread it with butter, placing a slice of cheese and a slice of sausage on top. 'Shouldn't we switch to first names?'

'How come?' she retorted amiably. 'Because of our shared experience?' She took the little espresso pot off the hob with a potholder, its contents seething and hissing. The brew splashed blackly into the little cups already waiting, which she carried to the table straight away. 'I don't need that, Korff.' She sat opposite him and smiled tentatively. 'I resent you for dragging me into something I have nothing to do with. You don't deserve first name terms for that.'

Whatever. Konstantin chewed. 'Well. You illegally buy and sell historic jewellery. In that sense this does have something to do with you.' He tore a little piece of sausage off his slice and threw it to the Great Dane.

Zerbo watched it soar towards him and slap quietly down on the stone floor in front of him. He didn't eat it; he stared at Konstantin again.

'My dog makes friends as slowly as I do,' commented Marna, amused.

Konstantin noticed a photo on the fridge of Marna kissing a cheerful man on the cheek. Handwritten on it in silver, it said *The Kiss of the Omen*, followed by a little heart. 'Tell me a bit about this market.'

'What market do you mean?'

'The one for historic and . . . let's say, mysterious jewellery.'

'Why should I?'

'Because you now know I'm not from Interpol, I'm an undertaker. Besides we could go into business,' he tried to appeal to her businesswoman's soul. 'I see huge numbers of dead people with old jewellery that's meant to be buried with them. Up till now I've always turned them into cash in other ways. I can do illegal too, you know.' Konstantin didn't for a second consider letting this lie become true. The dead were too sacred to him for that. But the story might have helped him with Marna.

'That is not such a dumb idea at all.' Marna opened a natural yoghurt and stirred it. 'No details and no names,' she made it clear from the beginning. 'I've built up a network that benefits many people and institutions. Museums, private collectors, exhibition organisers, historical institutes, and that's all over the world. Humankind's treasures, whether retrieved from the ground or later found in an attic, need a home that appreciates their worth. Let's take your dead bodies, Korff. What do the worms get out of a necklace or a wonderful brooch? The only people who are going to be happy are the archaeologists of the future, who will take our graveyards apart. Or grave robbers.'

'And your bosses at the bourse know about this?'

Marna rolled her eyes, but didn't give an exact answer. *Whatever that means.* 'I presume you work with various suppliers of Monsieur Bouler's calibre?'

'Monsieur Bouler is a special case and in no way comparable with our usual suppliers, as you so beautifully put it, Korff. He is . . . was the Indiana Jones of North Africa.'

Konstantin pictured the old man as he gave the order to kill

Rabih – and his family. 'Well, that's flattering to him. I would have described him as a ruthless gangster. His bodyguards were really trigger-happy with the Uzis.' He roughly outlined the events of that night, presenting Thielke's showing up as an attempted robbery that he had become caught up in.

'Really?' From time to time Marna took spoonfuls of her yoghurt. 'I knew him as a cultured expert in matters of pharaonic jewellery and rings of exquisite quality. What you're telling me is surprising.'

'Hmmm.' Konstantin had finished his first bread roll and was preparing a second: cheese and ham. 'This Spaniard, Hoya, why does he collect the stones? Did he ever speak about it?'

'Because of their value, I think.'

'No esoteric tendencies?' Konstantin took a bite. He had hoped she'd confirm his hunch that the collector had insider knowledge.

Marna put aside the spoon and the empty carton and was reaching for a slice of wholemeal bread when she hesitated. 'You don't really believe in horror stories?'

'No, no.' He brushed it off quickly, probably too quickly to be believable. 'But you have to admit that a lot of deaths are happening in connection with the Harlequin's Death and many people are doing evil things. A curse is plausible.'

'You should discuss that with Señor Hoya. He knows all the stories that surround the jewellery and the Ali-Mersai opals. As far as I know, he is a strict Catholic and very devout.' Marna took the slice of bread and spread a thin layer of butter on it. 'What did you actually want in Marrakech when you stumbled upon Bouler?' she asked casually.

'Work stuff. A thanatological job. I often travel to hot countries because the preservation of bodies is most difficult there. The marketplace of the future.' *Jaroslaf would be proud of me. I have learned something from him after all.* 'And suddenly, in front of his shop, I got dragged into the mess.' He looked around for a newspaper. 'Has anything from yesterday made its way into the press yet? About our car chase and the accident? It practically ought to be on one of the public-service channels.'

Marna shook her head as she chewed, her chestnut-brown ponytail jerked. 'Haven't seen anything,' she answered with her mouth full. She pulled open a drawer in the table, took out a remote control and pushed a button.

The landscape scenes disappeared from the flatscreen and it now showed a news programme.

She switched over to Teletext while the voice-over reported news from all over the world, searched for the regional news and called it up. 'There's something here.'

Konstantin turned in his chair so that he could read better.

Idar-Oberstein (ed.). Last night, two vehicles on the B41 were involved in a car chase in which material damages costing several tens of thousands of euros occurred. A stolen vehicle was involved as well as a rental car. A collision with a tanker took place in the Altenberg tunnel, whereupon one of the cars came off the road, broke through the crash barrier and fell into the Nahe. The body of the suspected driver was recovered by firefighters half a kilometre downstream. The stolen car and its driver are still being sought. The B41 had to be closed off for several hours and there will still be delays today due to repair work.

'You registered your car as stolen yesterday?' Konstantin turned to his third bread roll and took some onion *mettwurst*. Of course, they hadn't asked the taxi to stop at the TT yesterday, ordering it to a street some distance away instead.

'I thought that would make it easier for us. The police will still call me because of the incident in the Agate Rooms, I'm afraid. Even though I already made a formal apology to the manager this morning.' Marna did not look pleased. 'As I said before: I've experienced a lot, but what you're doing tops it all.'

'Tell me all about it! I'm all ears. What things do you go through when you peddle illegal jewellery?'

'It probably works exactly how it does with corrupt undertakers. You have to soothe nervous customers, get certificates, bribe experts, withstand harassment and constantly go for dinner with men who go on about how attractive I am,' she reeled off and drank some espresso. 'With you it must be grieving widows who want to pick you up.'

Konstantin laughed. He liked her wicked sense of humour. 'What is the most dangerous thing you've experienced so far?'

'Two robberies. One during a deal, the other afterwards. That's why bodyguards usually come with me.' Marna looked at her watch. 'I'll get dressed and then we should get to the airfield. The helicopter is taking us to Frankfurt and you should pick up your luggage from the hotel. Señor Hoya values a groomed appearance.' She got up.

As she did so, a small slit in her pyjamas gaped open and

Konstantin saw a flash of her ample breast. A small, dark halo with a pert little raised point. *No tattoos.* He found seeing her breast awkward, he felt like a peeping Tom.

She disappeared into the bathroom.

He took out his mobile and called Jester to let him know about the change of plan.

The MI6 agent answered after the second ring. 'You've heard too?' he asked agitatedly.

Konstantin stopped short. 'I don't know what you mean. Good morning, by the way.'

'To fucking bloody hell with *good morning*! Arctander has been in Madrid and had an attack. Again,' Jester sputtered quickly, beside himself. '80,000 dead.'

Oh my God!

The mobile slid out of his fingers. He snatched up the remote control and flicked through the channels before finding a report. The still unidentified terrorist group had apparently struck again. The attack with the insidious poison gas had surpassed every terror attack in human history. The site had been sealed off, so there were only helicopter photographs from the stadium, but the shots were harrowing: crowds of people in the stands, all lying together, looking peaceful. The curse had struck.

The image of the stadium shrank and shifted to the side. A panel of specialists made up of doctors, military personnel and intelligence officers speculated about the gas that was still believed to be the cause of the attacks and seemed to have had a strikingly similar effect to the incident in Moscow. A high dosage of an anaesthetic like carfentanyl or halothan, the benzilate gas BZ or another banned chemical weapon, laughing gas with valium added, an acetone-derived chemical weapon – the experts were falling over themselves to come up with possibilities.

Yet nobody could explain how this gas could be deployed in a stadium, in the open air, where there was wind, and kill all of the visitors equally quickly without exception – so quickly that barely a text or phone call had been initiated by the victims.

I know. Konstantin wanted to turn it off, but his fingers clenched around the remote control.

'Can you hear me?' Jester's voice came bellowing from the mobile lying on the floor.

Konstantin stooped down, picked up the phone and held it to his ear. 'Yes, I can hear you again. The reception was bad,' Konstantin replied lamely. 'I'm looking at pictures from the stadium right now and I—'

'Where are you?'

'Not in Frankfurt yet, but about to get going.' Konstantin didn't want to let on what he was up to. Could he have prevented this incident if he had used all of his efforts to dog Arctander's footsteps straight away?

'Good. We're changing the plan. I have to rearrange things,' said Jester, sounding stressed. 'I'll call you again tomorrow and I'll tell you where I'll pick you up. By then we will know where Arctander has disappeared off to.'

'How so?'

'I have an international manhunt alert out for him, as the mastermind of the terrorist organisation who are linked to the attacks,' he explained through gritted teeth. 'I can't afford to leave any resource untapped, as Madrid has shown.

All intelligence services are under instructions to call me as soon as they find him. Hopefully nobody will muscle in between us.'

Konstantin wished it would work. The smallest amount of excitement, emotion or panic would plunge Arctander into sleep, which in turn would kill thousands of people. Or tens of thousands.

How on earth did he get so powerful in such a short time?

'Fine. Let's talk tomorrow.'

Jester hung up, even foregoing a quote from his esteemed Oscar Wilde, which was not a good sign.

Marna came back. She had tucked her chestnut brown hair under a black cap and was wearing a red blouse underneath a black business suit. The same perfume as yesterday spread through the apartment. 'We can get going.'

Konstantin pointed towards the report with the remote control.

She quietly gasped in horror. Her eyes frantically followed the info-banner along the border of the screen. 'For heaven's sake!' she stammered. 'That is . . . horrific. Those poor people, so many of them!'

'At least they didn't suffer,' murmured Konstantin and went into the guest bathroom to wash his face with cold water.

'How would you know?' she called after him.

He didn't answer. She wouldn't understand the truth, just like Iva hadn't either.

He wanted to get on with his research into death during the flight. Whether it was any use to rely on sagas, fairy tales and legends was another story.

Death and the Gooseherd

A poor herder was walking along the bank of a large and turbulent stream, herding a flock of white geese.

Death came to him across the water and was asked by the herder where he came from and where he wanted to go.

Death answered that he came from the water and that he wanted to go out of the world.

The poor gooseherd asked further: how could one even get out of the world?

Death said that one had to go across the water to the new world, which lay beyond.

The herder said he was tired of this life and asked Death to take him over there with him.

Death said that it was not yet time and he still had much left to accomplish.

But there was a miser not far away in his warehouse at night, striving to accumulate even more money and possessions. Death led him to the great river and thrust him in. Yet, since he could not swim, he sank to the bottom before he could get to the bank. His dogs and cats, who had run after him, drowned with him too.

Several days afterward Death came also to the gooseherd

and, finding him cheerfully singing, said to him: 'Do you want to come with me now?'

He was willing and went over safely with his white geese, which all turned into white sheep.

The gooseherd regarded the beautiful landscape and heard that the local shepherds were becoming kings, and while he was taking a careful look around, the chief shepherds approached him, Abraham, Isaac and Jacob, and they put a royal crown on him and led him into the shepherds' castle, where he is still to be found.

Brothers Grimm, *Children's and Home Fairy Tales*, 1812 Edition

XVI

Do not despise death,
but make your peace with it,
as a link in the chain of changes
that are in keeping with nature's will.

Meditations, Marcus Aurelius

Madrid, Spain

Damn it! Konstantin couldn't make sense of the clumsily written fairy tale. Death appeared as a real figure, like in the other fairy tales, but apart from that, this story did not get him anywhere. The thing with the water, the Jesus-like figure and the young man weary of life, provided no insight into Reaper's Rings or the possibility of summoning Death.

The good get into paradise, the bad drown along with everything that follows them and belongs to them. What a surprise!

The airbus was bringing them closer to Madrid, kilometre by kilometre, while Konstantin sat over his laptop and worked his way through the masses of fairy tales that he had downloaded or bought as an ebook. While he used to have to spend hours in the library, he could get literature practically anywhere now.

By now he was familiar with Death in fairy tales, even finding him where he was not directly named, but turned up harmlessly, as sleep, Sleeping Beauty and Snow White, for example: women saved by being woken up.

By a stretch of the imagination, different phrases could also be interpreted as evidence that Death had personally appeared to a select group of people. Not only could one be 'snatched' from the jaws of death, but one could stare it in the face, or stave it off, and there were those who bore the stamp of it.

Konstantin had broadened the scope of his research now, setting off on a worldwide fairy tale hunt, and found mentions of death in everything from Asian to Native American folklore, which did not really surprise him. The more he looked the more he found.

The Grim Reaper is just a businessman who operates all over the world. Or as the writer Miguel de Cervantes put it in a quote he had found, *Death is not a reaper who takes a siesta. He reaps at all hours and cuts the arid grass along with the green.*

Among Jester's old files he found one remarkable clue in the Greek sagas. Asklepios, the most famous doctor in the world in his day, was supposed to have freed his patients from their suffering with the help of a healing sleep. According to the story, he was an apprentice to Chiron, that is to say Cheiron. This name was strikingly similar to that of Charon – the ferryman to the dead. *Another connection between death and sleep?*

Another example was Osiris. The ancient Egyptian god and

lord of the dead appeared in contemporary representations in the form of a person. The flail that he usually held in his hand may have been interpreted as a symbol of fertility, but Konstantin saw much more of the connection to death there. *Flail, scythe, same general idea.*

Apart from the many interesting things, he also obviously found absolute rubbish on strange forums and on websites. He particularly loved the well-intentioned advice to visitors to Asia, not to stick chopsticks vertically into a rice bowl because they look like joss sticks: offerings for the dead.

Konstantin closed his eyes and rubbed his eyelids. *If I have to read one more fairy tale I'll start feeling ill.*

He had a number of hypotheses by now, but otherwise nothing. And above all, he still didn't have a proper plan for finding someone who could speak to the Grim Reaper for him – insofar as people like that even existed. His research into miraculous lifesaving doctors and events was barely progressing. He just didn't have time. *First the meeting with Hoya, then I'll look for Arctander. Once he has been taken out, I'll have a clear head for my own things.* He saw Marna looking out the window beside him. 'Are you okay?'

Madrid appeared below them, the plane had already begun its final descent.

'Well, I'm fine. You're working like someone possessed. Have I seen correctly, are you reading fairy tales about death? Is it because of the Reaper's Ring?' She clipped her little table into place. 'Don't you think that you're attaching a little too much significance to the whole thing?'

Konstantin couldn't answer as openly as he wanted to.

'Ah, you never know when it might come in handy,' he replied instead. He thought she seemed unnerved. 'What is it? Afraid of Hoya?'

'No, definitely not. He might be demanding and rich, but he's not dangerous.' Marna looked down at the city. 'I can't get the awful images of the stadium out of my head. The terrorists could strike again.'

'Up till now they've switched cities every time: Paris, Marrakech, Madrid. I don't think we need to worry,' he tried to soothe her fears. 'There are probably some arseholes behind it who want to blackmail the governments out of millions, or maybe billions, to end the deaths.'

'I hope the fee is paid. I don't want to be one of the victims.' She swallowed. 'You have to put away the laptop. The flight attendant is coming.'

'That's enough, anyway.' Konstantin turned off the computer and stowed it in his suitcase.

The airbus leaned into a curve, plunged noticeably downwards, then corrected its course and descended further.

'Is the black suit okay?' he asked Marna, and she nodded. He kept the fact that he had also worn it for Lilou's lying in response to himself. 'What should I know about Hoya?' he asked. 'What does he absolutely detest?'

'Apart from nosy questions about his collection? Hmmm, let me think, Korff.' Marna played with a strand of hair. 'Don't make any jokes about his wife's paintings. He has them hung up on the wall out of love for her.'

'Is she dead?'

'No. Just abominably bad.' She laughed. 'She calls her stuff an 'homage to cubism' and he just hangs the pictures up and says nothing. Don't refuse any drink he offers you, unless you're allergic to it.'

'Why?'

'Well, because it's expensive and he would pour it away otherwise. And that in turn is something he can't stand, in spite of all the money he has.' Marna kept thinking.

The airbus took a sharp turn, the earth was coming closer rapidly. It wouldn't be long before the landing.

'Don't touch him, Korff. A handshake as a greeting is his limit. He sees everything beyond that as awkward and beneath him. That's it for the list of *don'ts*.'

'Thanks.' Konstantin saw the ridges of the runway appear next to the window, their momentum had eased off. *I'd better keep you distracted from the stadium.* 'What happens to Zerbo while you're travelling, Ms Herbst? Do you put down a few cans of dog food for him and he just eats the tin with it?'

She laughed. 'No. My sister looks after him. She's more of a domestic type and carries out *her* business from her office.'

The emphasis made Konstantin wonder. *What does she mean by that?* So as not to complicate the situation however, he didn't ask, but he did stay on personal topics. 'Tell me, why did it say "Kiss of the Omen" on the photo of you and your boyfriend?'

The plane landed, the brakes slammed on and it got noisy in the cabin. The airbus shook as it slowed down. Through the window you could see the airport buildings, the control tower, the terminals.

Marna seemed uncomfortable at his question. 'It's because of my two first names.'

'Were your parents horror film fans?' he joked.

'No. My name is Philomena.' She pulled out her phone. 'I'll call Señor Hoya and tell him we've landed. He wanted to send a car for us.'

Konstantin nodded.

After a short journey across the runway, the airbus stopped in front of a terminal, an airbridge was pushed towards it and the passengers disembarked. As Konstantin and Marna were travelling light, they didn't need to wait at the conveyor belt and simply went straight into the main hall.

It didn't surprise Konstantin that there were long queues of people backed up at the departure terminals. *Fleeing from death.*

The plane to Madrid had been half full: nobody wanted to go to a place where horror and doom had set a historic record. The city was on a list with Paris and Marrakech and it took the top spot.

A chauffeur was waiting for them at the exit in a classic outfit with a cap and holding a sign that said *Señora Herbst.* He took them to a white Mercedes CLS Coupé, they got in and drove to the city centre.

Konstantin and Marna didn't talk very much during the journey, they were dwelling on their own thoughts.

The CLS pulled up outside an imposing urban villa that was reminiscent of a hacienda and had been spruced up with pillars and marble. It looked alien in the midst of the otherwise modern architecture of this district, all chrome, steel and iron.

'Stylish,' said Konstantin. 'Classic.'

'Like that cathedral in New York,' Marna agreed. 'Is it St Patrick's?'

Konstantin supposed Señor Hoya had already been offered

a lot of money to give up his villa and plot of land. 'That's definitely an old building.'

'I couldn't say. Before now I've only ever met him in one of his offices,' she answered. 'If we're lucky, there won't be any of his wife's pictures hanging up here.'

The chauffeur opened the doors for them, escorted them to the entrance of the villa and rang the bell.

Konstantin noticed a tiny lens that had been installed in a corner above the entrance. Señor Hoya had recorded his face onto a hard-drive with it. *Surveillance system.* Hardly surprising, if he kept his jewellery collection in this house.

The door was opened by a woman in a red dress whom Konstantin would have put around the fifty mark, but whose figure could have made a thirty-year-old jealous. There were gold chains around her wrists, and a round pendant with a figure looking into a mirror around her neck. If Konstantin was not mistaken, there was a skull looking back out of the mirror. *Classic Vanitas motif. I've come to the right place.*

'*Buenos días,*' she greeted them. Then she switched into unaccented English. 'Lovely to see you, Señora Herbst.' She held out her hand to Marna first and then turned to Konstantin. 'And you too are a very welcome guest, Señor Korff. I'm Carola Hoya, Ruben Hoya's eldest daughter. My father is expecting you in the library. Please come this way.'

She turned around and led the way. Long black hair fell down her back. She walked silently in flat shoes across the polished stone floor.

Konstantin and Marna followed her through the pleasantly cool entrance hall.

The walls were panelled with dark wood, and on them

hung paintings with Spanish landscapes: a Don Quixote was riding towards windmills, a bull was fighting against a toreador in an arena. Chandeliers with real crystals hung from the ceiling. It smelled of oranges.

Konstantin was impressed, and judging by Marna's face, she was equally so. Yes, somebody had a pretty penny or two.

Carola veered left towards a large set of double doors. She gave a quick knock and opened the doors. 'Our guests, Papa.'

They entered a room with ceilings six, or maybe seven metres high. A set of red-black mahogany shelves, one below the other, hung around the perimeter of the room, lined with spine after spine of books. Two narrow balustrades ran along the lowest and middle shelves, accessible from rolling ladders.

In the middle of the room there were several illuminated display cabinets. Open books lay inside, and in between them were rings, amulets and brooches as well as some loose stones. It smelled of oranges and paper, blended with a black note of old varnish and wood.

Ruben Hoya was standing behind a trolley table with a clutch of eclectic bottles of spirits. He had already put glasses out on the tray. His age was difficult to say. Konstantin would have put him at sixty at the most, but if his daughter was around fifty, he had to be at least seventy.

'My dear Señora Herbst,' he said in English with a strong Spanish twang and gave the suggestion of a bow. He wore a dark red shirt, aubergine-coloured trousers and black leather shoes. 'I'm pleased to be able to welcome you into my city residence. We have not been granted the opportunity before now.' He glanced briefly at Konstantin. 'Hello, Señor Korff.' His short, clipped, grey beard lent him even more of a fatherly air. He looked like a *don* through and through.

They all shook hands. Hoya's fingers were well groomed, strong and slightly damp.

He is anxious. Konstantin sat down in the leather armchair that Hoya pointed to that would have been just as at home in the smoking lounge of a gentlemen's club. He glanced around, looking at the old and new books on the shelves, which had been sorted by their publication date. He spotted a few books of fairy tales among them. *Interesting.* He couldn't make out the display cases very well from his seat, he could only see a black stone that had been set into a brooch.

Without asking them, Hoya handed them each a drink. 'A vintage port from 1977 for the Señora and a dry Palo Cortado sherry for the Señor,' he explained as he served them. He picked up a cognac glass and made the amber liquid in it swirl gently. 'I'm really pleased that you're both here.' He took a sip.

Sherry! And dry too.

Carola sat on a chair next to him. She opened the laptop she had picked up from the table behind them. That made Konstantin nervous, although he couldn't explain why.

'Thank you so much for taking the time to see us so quickly,' Marna replied. 'It's a particular issue that brings us to you, as I said on the phone. Señor Korff would very much like to sell a family heirloom and get to know you.'

'So that I know that the Harlequin's Death is in good hands,' Konstantin began. 'You have an interesting collection. Would you perhaps do me the favour of letting me—'

Hoya raised his hand to get him to stop. 'First I want to

raise a glass with you. After that we will have time for all that other stuff.'

Marna threw Konstantin a significant look and said cheers to everyone.

They drank in silence.

Hoya gently swilled the brandy around in his mouth before swallowing it and then took a seat next to his daughter, crossing one leg over the other. The Spanish man's pale green eyes scrutinised Konstantin, examining, committing every detail to memory.

'You know of my ring's reputation, Señor Hoya. I want to be sure that it will be well kept in your hands. And I have a few more questions,' he said, which earned him another admonishing look from Marna.

Hoya made a gesture inviting him to ask his questions. 'Shall we find out how I can help you?'

During the journey, Konstantin had pondered what he should say so that he wouldn't come across as a lunatic. But nothing quite right had occurred to him, so he decided not to beat about the bush. *Then I'll have the embarrassment behind me.* 'Since you collect jewellery of a certain reputation, Señor, I wanted to know whether you believe in the power of Reaper's Rings.'

Hoya's eyes narrowed, his pale brows lowered. 'Señor Korff, I'm a religious person, I'm hoping for the salvation of my soul through Jesus Christ on Doomsday, and I know that death does not signify the end,' he replied. 'The power of death is undisputed, Christ the Lord had to bow to it, and every being on earth will have to. Nobody escapes it. Not even with the help of trick, charlatanry, the power of Satan or alchemy.

And certainly not through what they call Reaper's Rings.'
Hoya lifted the hand with the glass and pointed to the display
cases. 'If I collect something, Señor Korff, then it's because of
the beauty and uniqueness of the thing and not the stories
that have grown up around it. I've been offered the most
peculiar relics and devotional objects before.' He smiled at
Marna. 'Señora Herbst knows what I want and keeps me well
supplied. I'm in your debt for that.'

Marna raised her glass to him.

Konstantin was watching the man carefully for signs in
his behaviour or in his eyes that he was lying. But the aged
Spaniard spoke with a dignity that ruled out any suspicion
of untruth in his words. *No, he really doesn't believe in this.* He
looked at Carola who was typing so quietly that you couldn't
even hear the keys clicking. *So why is Hoya anxious?*

'But you collect the legends about the jewellery, as I see
from the books?' he persevered.

'Certainly. They complete my collection. I essentially try
and get the original editions of the works where the pieces
are described. My favourite is the brooch made from plum
tree wood with the opal. Do you know the fairy tale and the
brooch?'

'No,' Konstantin conceded.

'The setting of the brooch is said to have been made from
a tree in which Death got stuck after being outwitted. This
fairy tale is told in various countries, from France all the
way to the Orient, sometimes it's an apple tree, sometimes
plum. But in the oldest version of the fairy tale, it's a plum
tree. Since you are here on the recommendation of Señora
Herbst, you are welcome to take a look at the unique piece.

But as I said, I don't believe in fairy tales, just in the exceptional nature of the jewellery.' He looked expectantly at his daughter, prompting her.

Carola got up and unlocked a display case by running her thumbs over a hidden scanning panel.

It clicked.

She opened the cabinet and came back with the brooch that Konstantin had noticed earlier. Meanwhile Hoya stood up too, took a book off the shelf, opened to the story and began to read aloud.

Godfather Death in the Plum Tree

There once was an old man whose small house was his pride and joy, in a village near a small river on the Ottoman border.

One evening there came three richly dressed men who were from the Turkic lands. They were passing through the village but the villagers were afraid of them. It was said that they were sorcerers and soothsayers. Since they did not have a place to sleep for the night, not even in the shabbiest tavern, they knocked on this old man's door.

The three sorcerers asked him for a place to sleep.

And the old man responded that they were welcome to lie down next to the oven where it was warm. But he could not offer them a bed.

Yet the Ottomans were satisfied. And they took off their turbans and lay down there.

The old man was preparing dinner. He had nothing but hard breadcrumbs and crab shells from which he was cooking himself a thin soup. He bid his guests eat with him, if it was to their liking.

The sorcerers thanked him. And they feasted together.

In the morning, as the sorcerers were preparing to set off, they asked the man to tell them what they owed him for the accommodation and meal.

The man answered that he did not ask for any coins, but he did own a plum tree that no longer bore fruit.

'If only the plums would keep hanging on these magnificent branches! They have hardly begun to ripen when they all disappear from the tree.'

The strangers ensured that from then until the end of days and the final judgement, the plums would no longer disappear.

One morning the old man went out and saw that his plum tree was full of small boys and there was also a grown man perched up there on the treetop.

The old man asked him: 'Tell me, how did you end up there?'

But the man did not reply.

Now the old man let the boys climb down from the tree, but he made the tall man sit and wait.

But the man began to beseech him, and so he let him climb down. And he was glad since he had so many plums that he beat them down with a stick and feasted on them.

Soon Godfather Death came to the old man. 'It is time for you to come with me.'

'Of course, of course,' said the old man and asked that Death allow him to take a handful of plums with him for the journey.

Death allowed him.

But the plums hung far overhead and the old man could not reach them.

'I don't have all the time in the world. The people are waiting for me, old man.' Thereupon, Godfather Death climbed up using his long legs and fetched the plums.

Yet when he went to climb back down, he was stuck!

He gave the tree a good shaking, but he could not get

to the ground. The magic of the sorcerers was too powerful, even for him.

Now Godfather Death pleaded with the man to let him get down.

'Only if you grant me some more years to live.'

Godfather Death promised him this. When he finally came down from the tree, he was upset over the old man's ploy and took to his heels.

World Fairy Tales, Lichtenberger Press, Hamburg, 1863

'Lovely, isn't it?' Hoya laughed quietly. 'Do you want to look at the other pieces?'

No. I would rather take them with me. Konstantin was not in the mood for more story time. He was looking for information about the rings, no, about *his* ring, not about brooches, buckles or other jewels. 'Later, thank you.' He sipped at his dry sherry again. Perhaps the alcohol gave him the idea he needed so that he could make headway. 'Señor, I take it you've read all of the stories about your rings?'

Hoya smiled indulgently, which was answer enough. 'I even know the stories about Harlequin's Death.'

'Assuming someone was a superstitious person and believed in the power of Deathgems, have you come across a method of how to . . . *deploy* a stone like that?' Konstantin could not think of the right word.

'Do you mean, how could you use the power of a ring? To protect oneself from Death's clutches the way the plum tree protected the old man? Or to summon Death?' Hoya was looking dismissively at him.

'Both. Do you have to turn the ring three times, bathe it in your own blood or just wear it?' he blurted out.

Hoya stroked his beard and swirled the brandy again. 'Ah, I get it. You're one of those people who believe in them.' He glanced at Marna without looking too reproachful and fixed his pale green gaze on him. 'Why are you afraid of Death? You should be familiar enough with it, in your line of work, Señor.'

Konstantin could almost have burst out laughing. *I only fear him because of the people around me.* 'For me, it's more about meeting someone who can speak with Death,' he replied.

Hoya raised his eyebrows. 'Señor Korff, I believe your work has influenced your reasoning too much. In my view you are far too concerned with the Grim Reaper. Yet . . . well, you're entitled to a bit of eccentricity. You can allow yourself that.' He took a mouthful of his drink. 'I heard from a close friend that you are an excellent thanatologist, Señor. He praised your craftsmanship to the skies. In my family, the farewell to the dead is an old tradition and we would find it very unpleasant if such an intimate moment were tarnished by a botched job. Would it be possible to secure your services for myself at this stage? During my lifetime?'

'That is . . . unusual, Señor Hoya. I'm flattered.' Konstantin struggled with his disappointment. Apparently the Spaniard did not want to tell him anything more about the rings. 'Who recommended me?'

'Marquis de Girardin. We've known each other since

childhood. I attended the señorita's lying in repose. A disgrace that she died so young. A beauty like that.' He looked at the display cases.

The world of the wealthy is even smaller than that of normal people, thought Konstantin.

'To come back to your question, Señor Korff: no.'

'No?'

'You wanted to know whether there is a method of putting a Grim Reaper's Ring into action. Supposing I believed that you could influence Death, who was sent to us by God so that we pass away and free up our places for our children, then I would have to assume that the stones work of their own accord. I'm not aware of any indications that would allow for any other hypothesis.' Hoya looked to his daughter. 'Or do you see it differently?'

Carola looked up from the screen. 'I do, Papa.'

Hoya laughed softly. 'Our old disagreement. My daughter shares my weakness for gemstones and books and all things rare. She is taking over the research and she establishes the initial contact with dealers. But unlike me, she has a penchant for anything mystical.'

Konstantin watched Carola, who was writing yet again. *Does she know more than she is allowed to say?*

Hoya put his brandy glass aside and leaned forward. 'Can I see the Harlequin's Death, Señor Korff?' he asked quietly. He rubbed his hands together, reached into his pocket and pulled out a pair of cotton gloves. 'So that we can get down to business.'

'Certainly.' Konstantin looked for the ring, which he didn't even keep in a jewellery box, and held it out to the Spaniard. *You can look, but I'm not going to sell it.*

His backing out might make Marna quite angry. A deal fallen through: no commission. But she was involved in dubious deals, she had to reckon with disappointing negotiations. At least he was still replacing her Audi.

Since Carola believed in the mystical, Konstantin wondered whether he should try to have a word with her on her own, away from her father's eagle eye.

Hoya took the piece of jewellery and his daughter brought him a magnifying glass without being asked. He examined the ring for several minutes as the Herbst siblings had done before; unbridled joy spread across his aristocratic don's face. He had confirmed that he was not holding a fake in his hands.

After all that, I probably only have to put the ring on and wait and see what happens. Perhaps nothing at all will happen because it's just a shitty ring and I'll never be free of the curse. Konstantin finished off his sherry and looked at Marna who was busy with her port and had her head tilted up slightly to look at the upper storeys of the library. He thought her profile beautiful and photogenic. *Like Iva.*

He turned away and let his gaze wander across the room. As he did so, he noticed a tiny camera in a corner, and thin sensor wires that ran along beside the floor-to-ceiling windows. Nothing escaped the Hoya family, which was understandable with the jewellery they stored. The alarm system would undoubtedly be directly linked to the police and to a security firm.

Their host finished his examination, but instead of giving Harlequin's Death back, he placed it on his desk. 'Thank you, Señor Korff. There are few honest finders like you,' he said with a friendly smile. 'I will see what I can do for you and Señora Herbst. I was thinking of double the fee for my thanatological treatment which will be due at some point and immediate payment in advance?'

First Marna looked at Hoya in astonishment and then at Konstantin. 'Señor Hoya, there has been a misunderstanding,' she corrected him. 'We wanted—'

'Señora Herbst, I know *what* you thought and I made you believe it,' he interrupted her in a businesslike manner and recrossed his legs. 'Otherwise you would not have come to me with Mr Korff and *my* ring.' He smiled and finished his cognac. 'Before you call me a thief, Carola will explain everything to you.' He got up, took the ring and went to the door. 'I'll be right back.'

My ring! 'Señor Hoya!' Konstantin leaped up. 'Give me my heirloom this instant—'

Then he felt Marna's hand on his forearm. 'Don't let yourself get carried away, Korff. Let's wait first,' she whispered.

'Wait for what?' Konstantin was distracted for a moment – the heavy door fell shut with a clatter. Hoya was gone. With Harlequin's Death.

Carola raised her head. 'I'm sorry, but I . . . You will understand in a moment.' She left the laptop on her lap. 'My father turns into a little boy very quickly, despite his age, when it concerns his collection. Please forgive him that.'

'I'm still waiting for an explanation,' growled Konstantin. The sherry on an empty stomach made him more relaxed and less inhibited. Marna didn't take her hand away as he sat down again. It lay soothingly on his arm.

'My father *is* the rightful owner of the ring.' She radiated conciliatory friendliness, the gold on her wrists jangling softly. 'Señor Bouler got in touch with us a few weeks ago with an offer to sell the ring. Without intermediaries.' She looked apologetically at Marna. 'I don't know where he found out that you sell his goods to us. We met with him, checked the ring's authenticity and then made a payment of 200,000 euro in cash. Monsieur Bouler took the ring with him, because he was demanding a further 250,000. We agreed and arranged to meet in Marrakech.' Carola looked back and forth between Konstantin and Marna. 'As you know, Bouler died before we could complete the deal. My father thought the ring was already lost.' She turned the laptop around.

There was a photo on the screen and in it, Konstantin recognised Bent Arctander. He bit back all that he'd wanted to say. The visit to the Hoya hacienda might still prove useful after all.

His tenseness hadn't escaped Marna and she glanced at him, silently asking for an explanation. He shook his head quickly.

However, Carola didn't notice anything and kept talking. 'This man came forward and claimed that he had stolen the gemstone from Señor Bouler and wanted to sell it. I met him at the Almudena graveyard, but it quickly became clear that he didn't have the ring at all.'

'Did you suggest the place?'

'No, he insisted on it. I was to bring a white rose with me and place it on a certain grave. As a signal.'

'And?' Konstantin was looking at the screen, where several photos of Arctander were alternating in a slideshow. 'What did he say?'

'He asked similar questions to you, Señor Korff. About the rings, whether they worked, whether you could not only keep Death away or summon him with them, but also see him. I found his behaviour very disconcerting, he seemed borderline obsessed. As if he believed he was personally being pursued by the Grim Reaper. He left very suddenly, because he wanted to get to the Real game. If he did make it, he must have died with the other 80,000 people.'

Photo after photo of Arctander rolled past. The shots must have been taken using a small camera at chest-height with an enormous wide-angle lens. Konstantin suspected a spy camera that Carola had carried concealed.

'Do you believe in the power of Reaper's Rings?' Konstantin probed, exploiting Hoya's absence.

'Let's just say I'm not as hostile towards the stories as my father is. Every legend hides a kernel of truth, and the accumulation of catastrophes surrounding some precious stones would be a very big coincidence. There is something more around us, Señor Korff.' She played with the little magnifying glass. 'People walking among us who can speak with Death, I don't find that far-fetched.'

Marna laughed out loud and covered her mouth with her hand. 'Sorry,' she said. 'I . . . right now, I'm just—'

Carola felt provoked by Marna's reaction. 'What's so funny, Señora Herbst? Just because you don't believe in it, doesn't mean that people like that don't exist.'

Konstantin's heart beat faster. The conversation was developing in the right direction. 'What do you mean by that?'

'Psychics lead police to sites where corpses have been left, mediums communicate with the other side, people know things it is impossible for them to know – there is so much that we cannot explain,' Carola said and placed the magnifying glass on the table.

'Because there is no scientific proof,' Marna argued.

Señora Hoya smiled haughtily. 'There initially wasn't any proof of dark matter or quantum particles either, until the relevant evidence was developed. Maybe it will also change for the supernatural in the years to come.' She fixed her gaze on Konstantin. 'Why shouldn't there be people who are unusual and who see Death and can speak to him?' She made a sweeping gesture towards the display cases with her right arm. 'Perhaps even these pieces of jewellery have hidden powers that we cannot measure nowadays. Perhaps, to put it in physical terms, they are catalysts: converters of energies we cannot yet comprehend.'

Marna stifled an objection by drinking her port, but Konstantin's hopes were fuelled by Carola's remarks. Which in turn meant that he absolutely had to have the Harlequin's Death back.

Carola turned to Marna. 'I don't need you to share my views at all, Señora, but neither am I going to budge from my standpoint; a standpoint that my father disparagingly calls *mystical*. I would rather meet these special people than anything else.'

Carola shook her head and went to stop the slide show – when Konstantin noticed a figure in the background.

'Stop,' he cried and sprang out of his armchair. He knelt down in front of Carola and placed his finger on the touchpad. 'There in the back, next to the tree. There is a bench there . . .' He didn't wait for her permission, zooming in on the photo.

The resolution may have been lost when he did so, the

picture pixellating noticeably as the zoom increased, but the man's outline was enough for Konstantin. The unusual clothes and the protruding lens he remembered well. 'Thielke,' he murmured without meaning to. *So he's in Madrid too.*

Carola turned the computer so she could see too. 'I didn't notice the man,' she said pensively. 'He was photographing me?'

'You and Arctander,' Konstantin corrected her.

'Arctander? Is that the name of the man I met? How do you know both of these men?' Carola cast him a mistrustful look, which she also cast in Marna's direction. 'What's going on here?'

'I have no idea, Señora Hoya!' Marna burst out. 'I'm hearing about this for the first time too.'

I have to call Jester. Madrid is a dangerous place. Konstantin went to the trolley with the bottles of spirits and poured himself a glass of cognac, from which he took a quick mouthful. 'Monsieur Bouler stole my ring and promised it to lots of people.' He spun his next lie for Hoya. 'A woman called von Windau tracked me during my search for the Harlequin's Death in Idar-Oberstein and almost killed Ms Herbst and me. Thielke is also after the ring and seems to be on Arctander's heels. That led him to you.'

The door swung open and Hoya rejoined them. He was carrying the ring in a little glass box, lying on a black satin cushion that showed it off even more. Judging by how the silver flashed, he had polished the parts made of precious metal.

His daughter explained to him in a nutshell what had been discussed. Meanwhile Konstantin tried to get through to Jester but only reached voicemail. A message and a text later, he turned back to the events in the library.

Hoya had sat down, his cognac glass freshly filled. Harlequin's Death sat on the desk in its magnificent new case and shone with an almost wicked beauty.

Marna was silent and clung to her port as she avoided looking at them.

'Who were you calling, Señor Korff?' Hoya wanted to know.

'A friend in the British secret service. But I only got hold of his voicemail. He is on the trail of Arctander and Thielke and will be pleased if I can tell him where he is highly likely to find them.' That was close enough to the truth. *Now comes the most difficult part.* 'Señor Hoya, I must ask you to give me back my heirloom,' he said loudly.

'I paid for it.' Hoya placed a protective hand covered in age spots on the box.

'You handed over a *down* payment. And on top of that, it was to the wrong person, a thief and robber who stole the ring from me.' He looked at the Spaniard. '*I* was in Marrakech, Señor Hoya, and *I* stood on Djemaa-el-Fna Square, surrounded by thousands of dead bodies. I am taking my ring back. *Mine!* Not yours! And do you know what? I don't believe in the nonsense about terrorists. Everywhere that Death has appeared, the ring was not far away. Did you know that Bouler was staying in Paris when the A380 crashed into the terminal?' Another lie, but it fit in well.

'No,' whispered Hoya and stared at Konstantin, stupefied. '*No sé!* But still, that's—'

Carola laid her hand on his. 'I always told you, Papa. They have this power. These pieces of jewellery are capable of more than sparkling prettily,' she murmured to him imploringly. 'Can you see what they can unleash?'

'Paris, Marrakech, Madrid. The Harlequin's Death is always in the vicinity. Don't risk dismissing its curse as a fairy tale, Señor Hoya. The other stones in your collection could be harmless, but this one is not.' He held out his hand. 'Give it back to me. As its rightful owner, it won't do anything to me. But I will solve the mystery of it, I swear it, by the late Lilou de Girardin. The ring has her on its conscience along with almost 100,000 other people. Do you want it to be your turn next, Señor?'

There was silence in the library – the tension in the air was virtually palpable.

Konstantin had planted himself in front of Hoya, his hand still outstretched, and looked down at the old Spaniard stubbornly defying his gaze, although he seemed to have shrunk down into the armchair.

Carola and Marna sat in their seats as if they were melded onto them.

XVII

Should there not also be a Death over there,
whose outcome would be earthly birth?
If a ghost dies, he becomes a person.
If a person dies, he becomes a ghost.

On the Secret World, Novalis

Madrid, Spain

Konstantin sat alone in his hotel room with his headphones on, listening to soothing music by the band Lambda on his smartphone while examining the Harlequin's Death. *You are beautiful, but do you possess the power that I require?*

Hoya had relinquished the ring to him without saying another word. Afterwards, Carola had led them to the door and instructed the chauffeur to drive them anywhere they wanted to go. Before they left, Carola wrote down her mobile number for Konstantin and pleaded with him to brief them on everything that he experienced with the ring so that she could write it down 'for my file', reminding him strikingly of Thielke. He promised her that he would, so that he could keep in contact and ask her for help in case of emergency.

Fortunately, Marna knew her way around Madrid and had them brought to a hotel not far from the airport.

Konstantin still didn't know what to do next. He was waiting for Jester's call. He had sent his friend a brief summary of what had happened in Almudena by email. That had been two hours ago.

Marna was in a bad mood and had barricaded herself into her room. Her job in the Gemstone and Diamond Bourse demanded that she be there. She couldn't leave his side until he had paid her for the Audi TT. She had only just about managed to assign the unproductive trip to Madrid to the business account. Expensing their other expeditions to the company would be more difficult to explain. Plus, she was angry that he hadn't sold the ring to Hoya. Instead of getting her commission, she had been fed a load of supernatural crap, which she – as she clearly told him – had no interest in. She now considered her reputation with Hoya as an honest broker damaged, which would in turn be passed around her circle of clients.

Konstantin stretched his fingers and pondered whether to slip the ring on. *What happens then? Will anything happen at all?*

His imagination conjured up images of the Grim Reaper lifting his head and looking straight into his soul with his bony mug, swooping downwards through space and time like a bird of prey to do away with an abhorrent Death Sleeper with a single, wildly violent blow and a loud cry of delight.

He felt a chill and was horrified when he looked at his hands. He had unconsciously slid Harlequin's Death over the crook of his index finger.

Another few centimetres and he would know more.

No. It's too soon. He couldn't just ignore the fear of becoming visible to Death and dying immediately. He wanted to go to Iva, experience stuff with her, have a *life* with her. And above all he needed to find Arctander and stop him. Carola's words echoed inside him, she had given him courage.

His smartphone caught his attention with a buzz. Jester's number was on the display.

Konstantin turned off the music and answered the call. 'Yes?'

'"Life is too important to be taken seriously," came the latest Wilde quote through the receiver. 'But in this case, old boy, I have to disagree with Oscar. Human life is too important to let the narco remain at large.'

'You're right there.' Konstantin placed the ring on the cushion, the opal shimmering pale blue on the black background. 'Were you able to do anything with my information?'

'Yes, thanks. I fed it to my department. As soon as the results are in, I'll be in touch.' Jester sounded relaxed in a way he had not done for a long time, as though he had lots of pieces of good news and he wanted to enjoy dropping them one by one. 'Are you still in Madrid?'

'Yes.'

'Where?'

'Hôtel Oro. I wanted to be near the airport, depending on where you send me.'

'Ideal, old boy. Brilliant! Just stay where you are. I've sent a team to Madrid. They will contact you. There are two Torpor's Men and two freelancers who will do what you tell them. Do you remember Johnny?'

'Yes. Is he one of them?'

Jester said he was. 'He's been getting on well in recent years and I thought your role as team leader would be easier for you if you knew at least one face.'

'You're not coming?'

'No. I am the spider in the web, as it were, and will provide you with the news that my hard-working hackers, wiretappers and satellite spies obtain.' Jester cleared his throat. 'Arctander is making unbelievable mistakes with his escape right now. He has used up almost all of his fake identities, so the next time he checks in or pays by credit card he will attract attention immediately. We are prepared.'

Konstantin lay down on the bed, contemplating the ceiling. 'So, why do you still need me?'

'Because you are a good man, Stan . . . I mean Konstantin. Oneiros. Whatever. Your past predestines you for the hunt for Arctander,' said Jester. 'You are the only person to have escaped me and my team more than once. And the Phansigar to boot. That makes you a legend, even if you've withdrawn from that life. Many people remember the name Oneiros very well.'

'While that's flattering, I still don't like it.' Konstantin sat up and opened the minibar to get out a bottle of Coke. He was tired, even though he had slept in the bath for an hour beforehand, the door locked so that room service would not happen to come in and die an unexpected death. He needed sugar and caffeine. 'On the subject of Phansigar, what are the Indians really doing? Are they any closer to him than we are?' *Let's see what you say now.*

Jester seemed surprised by the question. His answer took a little too long to come. 'Ah, the Phansigar. We've had sightings

of their people, in Constantinople anyway. We don't understand what they want there, but it won't be long until they
come to Madrid. The massacre was too clear a clue. But don't
worry, old boy. My team are well trained in firearms, unlike
you. Not everyone is as much of an amateur at shooting as
you are.' Jester laughed.

Konstantin shook his head in disappointment. *Still the same
old secret-service man.* He opened the bottle of Coke on the edge
of the bed. 'Jester, what's with the bullshit?'

'Pardon?'

'The Phansigar are not after Arctander. I've pulled some
strings and kept an ear out.'

Jester was silent again, then laughed sheepishly. 'I wanted
to get you going, and the most ruthless Death Sleepers are
now the chai-makers. I thought I could spur you on. Sorry, pal.'

Konstantin could see him now, with his boyish grin and
that 'busted' expression. *I knew it.* 'You don't need to use that
MI6 psycho-shit with me. That'll cost you a bottle of good
vodka! Russian.'

'Alright then. My friends from the FSB still have some
locked up from the last raid.' Jester sounded relieved that
Konstantin didn't hold the lie against him. 'It won't happen
again.'

'It's okay. I'll wait in the hotel, then. See you soon.'

'Cheerio, Konstantin.'

Konstantin didn't feel completely comfortable at the
thought of commanding a team. He was a solo player, and
with all of Jester's experience he would rather have had him
by his side.

There was a knock at the door.

Konstantin got up and looked out through the door's spy hole.

Marna was waiting on the other side of the door. She had put on a dark grey suit with a black blouse and her hair was pinned up. As if she had guessed that he was standing on the other side of the door, she looked straight into the lens. Their eyes met through the glass, in a way that they had never met before.

Konstantin felt a warm sensation spreading slowly from his core. *What was that?* He quickly snapped out of it and opened the door.

'Hello, Korff.' She smiled. Her anger at him had subsided. 'So, how are things looking? Got any plans?'

He struggled to compose himself. 'I ... have called my buddy ... and—' he said, and drank the Coke he was still holding to wash away the confusion and quench his thirst. 'He said—'

'Do we want to discuss this in the corridor?' she interrupted, and leaned sideways to look past him. 'Or do you have a woman with you who I'm not meant to see?'

'Rubbish.' Konstantin stepped aside so that she could come in. He tried to think of Iva. Her image lit up for him, flickered and was destroyed by the strange feeling he'd just had. *Nothing but mild confusion. I've spent too much time with Marna. That's all.*

Marna pushed past and looked at him in bewilderment, but didn't say anything about the state he was in. 'You spoke to your buddy and ...?' She propped herself against the wall and crossed her arms.

He quickly took another swig and suppressed the gurgling in his throat from the carbon dioxide. 'He ... is sending me a team of specialists. We are going to deal with Thielke and Arctander so that they can't do any more damage,' he summarised. 'I can't tell you anything more, Ms Herbst.'

'Understood.' She looked at the bed. 'And what now?'

'What—'

'The ring. What are you going to do with it? The commission you owe me is still tied up with the jewellery. You can trick Hoya into believing it's a family heirloom. I know better.' Marna beamed at him. 'I was impressed by your imagination, by the way. I would not have thought Hoya could be put off so quickly. All credit to mysticism. You engaged with Señora Hoya excellently. Well done.'

'Huh. Thanks very much.' Konstantin had finally overcome his confusion. 'I will probably carry out a few more investigations before I decide what to do with the Harlequin's Death,' he answered somewhat at random.

'More investigations? What else is there to find out, other than what you already know from me?' Marna was breathing hard. 'Ah, you don't want to tell me what you're planning.'

'I can't. A secret service matter. And it's also *mystical*, which isn't your thing anyway, as you've said.' *That dig was necessary.* He sipped from his bottle. 'That means you can fly home, Ms Herbst. You've had enough of an adventure.'

Marna didn't move. 'What about my TT?'

'I will pay you.'

'An IOU, Korff?' she suggested.

Konstantin laughed. 'You are persistent.'

'I work in a profession concerned with money and securities,' she retorted, pushing herself off the wall and making her way to the desk. She opened the hotel folder and drafted

Konstantin's happy smile froze.

Less than four metres away, a woman was turning towards him. A woman whose lungs he'd thought had filled with Nahe water. Her face was lined with scratches; he could make out a long plaster on her neck that disappeared under her clothes and probably hid stitches; her right arm was in a plaster cast as well as a sling-like brace.

But Baroness Kristen Sophie von Windau was alive!

And yet again she has found me. Konstantin frantically weighed up what to do as she slowly raised her uninjured arm in greeting – and stretched out the fingers of her left hand towards the hairpin.

Madrid, Spain

Martin Thielke gave himself a shot of insulin in the stomach and ordered a second slice of the divinely delicious Spanish cake almost entirely made of sugar, almonds and oil, held together by at most a teaspoon of flour. Alongside it he was slurping a *café bombón* – espresso with sweetened condensed milk. A combination that his body would barely survive without the insulin injections.

'Somebody had better come soon,' he muttered, lifting his Nikon to take a few snapshots of the villa he was sitting 500 metres away from.

Nobody had emerged yet, but he had been assured that the *señora* turned up at her father's city residence from time to time.

The café he was sitting in was the spawn of an ugly, modern

design that a bank had conjured up. In his country, outdoorsy look, he stood out among the suit-wearers like a chicken in a monkey house, but Thielke wasn't concerned about that. He was following a trail and it had led him to this fancy place.

The waiter brought him the cake and he started eating it immediately.

His stump had settled down, thanks to the painkillers he had taken. Some essential nicotine was making its way into his body via seven plasters on his chest. He felt nice and relaxed thanks to the lengthy snooze he'd rewarded himself with. Without any sleeping tablets at all.

He washed down the bite of cake with a mouthful of sweet espresso and looked back at the villa, which did not fit at all with the modern buildings on either side of it.

His impatience grew.

He toyed with the idea of simply ringing the doorbell and asking for Arctander. The time he was wasting here was time that innocent people might not have later; it could be the difference between life and death.

After Arctander had escaped from him in the stadium, Thielke had used the photographs from the graveyard to identify the face of the woman online. He was hoping to come across a name and with the name an address.

It was easier than he'd thought.

Carola Hoya was extremely well known in Madrid, partly because of her father and partly because of her work with charitable organisations. Her main residence was in Seville, but after a few calls he'd found out that she was staying in Madrid.

The city residence of Ruben Hoya, her father, functioned

as a hub for the whole family and so Thielke had got himself into position nearby. Now she just had to show up so that he could ask her what she knew about Arctander.

He scratched his head and straightened his sunglasses. His hunger for action was uncontrollable now, spurred on by the overdose of nicotine. He shovelled the cake into himself, tossed back the coffee and paid.

The bankers and lawyers scrutinised him with condescending looks, but it didn't bother him and he stayed sitting. Anyone with his wealth of experience could remain calm in a place like this. There was a black patch over his blind eye, which made him look like an old marshal from a western when he took his sunglasses off. Black elastic bands ran out from underneath the frames to the right and left of his head.

Thielke lifted up the Nikon again, shooting photos of the villa's windows. He picked out the home security system using the zoom.

Señor Hoya, the chief – no, the *don* – of the family was known for his passion for collecting. He maintained a private museum and acted as its patron. In light of the well-concealed cameras around the villa and other security measures, Thielke assumed that there were objects of not inconsiderable value in the house.

He mulled over what Arctander could have wanted from Señora Hoya. Did they perhaps know each other from before? He hadn't been able to find any connection between the Hoyas and the Death Sleepers so far. *Perhaps a connection to Arctander's Spanish relations?*

The mulling was no good. The *señora* would have to help him get to the bottom of the matter.

A Mercedes CLK drove up and a chauffeur got out and approached the villa.

Thielke photographed the number plate and stood up. He supposed a member of the Hoya family would soon emerge, potentially Señora Carola. Hopefully an opportunity to talk would present itself – voluntarily or involuntarily.

He left the café, walked along the pavement and approached the villa. He put his camera on his back as he did so, so as not to look like a psychopathic paparazzo, and took off his sunglasses.

He stopped on the curb. *Look right, look left, all clear.* He lifted his healthy leg and was about to take the first step in crossing the street when the aggressive roaring of a small motor made Thielke spin round.

A souped-up scooter carrying two people was hurtling towards him across the square. The mirrored visors on their helmets covered their faces. The guy riding pillion raised a silenced Heckler & Koch MP5, a fully automatic machine gun. *Clearly not your average handbag-snatcher.*

Thielke threw himself backwards. He crashed onto the ground hard.

The first burst of fire just missed him. Fragments of asphalt sprayed upwards and hit him in the face. The lens of the Nikon broke with a clatter. He drew the LeMat, pointed it at the driver and fired twice.

The heavy revolver discharged with a cracking sound, vibrating in his hand. The detonations of the propellant drowned out all background noise.

The projectiles from the LeMat hit the pillion-rider in the arm, which split open as it swung around, and the visor, which shattered into pieces. The back of the helmet exploded as if a hand grenade had been let off in there.

I missed the driver! What's wrong with me?

The gunman tumbled off the scooter and somersaulted several times, scattering blood and little grey-red lumps of brain. The dead man's fingers had cramped up around the trigger and the MP5 spewed its bullets at random into the glass frontage of an office building. Cracking and bursting, the shards rained down on the ground and covered the paved forecourt.

Thielke was still lying on the ground. He had felt a jolt in his leg. A glance downwards told him that the prosthesis was in tatters, his lower leg and foot now consisting only of the component parts. He pulled up his healthy leg; luckily it had escaped the enemy fire.

The scooter driver pulled up and reached underneath his windcheater to draw a weapon.

Thielke straightened up, the muzzle of his LeMat trained on the assailant. *This time I won't miss.* He aimed a single shot at the driver's throat, resulting in even more mess on the pavement as his life force spurted in a thick stream from the entry and exit wounds. With his head half ripped off, man and scooter fell to the ground.

Well then! Thielke got up awkwardly and hopped on one leg to a two-metre-long flowerpot for cover. *Where did these wankers suddenly come from?*

People were running across the square, crouching, fleeing into the buildings. Cars drove down the street; people goggled wide-eyed behind windows at the bodies and the blood. It wouldn't take long for law enforcement to roll up. The events in the stadium had put the *policía* on constant alert.

Thielke saw the bankers who had looked so condescend-ingly at him earlier crouched under the tables of the café. How quickly the arrogance and superiority of the moneyed elite could vanish.

Next to him dark soil flew into the air, little flowers were torn to shreds, sending their petals into the wind.

Thielke slumped to the ground and looked behind him. The absence of bangs meant that his enemies were shooting at him with silencers, indicating secret service or a career criminal. Since he hadn't messed with gangsters recently, that left the secret service.

A hundred metres away, he made out a man in an ice hockey mask and a suit standing in the open door of a dark blue van, training a long assault rifle on him. Judging by the shape, it was an AK-74.

Thielke hurled himself to the side, rolling over the Nikon again with a crunch and dodging the three bullets that struck the flowerpot, blasting pieces of concrete out of it.

I'll show you how it's done. The LeMat wasn't especially accu-rate at these distances and his first bullet tore through the metal of the car next to the gunman, the front windscreen colouring red from the inside; the second scraped past the man's gun, knocking it to the side, and just as he ducked down he took the third one in the stomach. His screams muffled behind the mask, he sank down onto the floor of the van.

Another masked man appeared at the rear of the van; he too raised an AK-74 with a silencer and brought it into position.

'Shit!' Thielke crawled quickly around the flowerpot as

it thrummed behind him and showered him with stone splinters. A shot grazed his right thigh, though he couldn't use the leg to walk anyway since the prosthesis had been shot to pieces. *The left would have been worse.*

Thielke heard the enemy advancing and changed his magazine, dropping the empty one onto the road with a clatter.

From a distance came the wailing of sirens, presumably from police vehicles. Thielke guessed it was a special task force; given the tense atmosphere since the incident in the stadium in Madrid, they would probably come in guns blazing.

He cast a hasty glance over the concrete rim of the flowerpot and saw the masked man less than thirty metres away.

Thielke pulled the trigger and the fire was immediately returned by the AK, forcing him back down. Covered in tattered plant stems and leaves, he made himself as small as possible in his hiding place. Having fired so many shots, the man had to reload again immediately.

Anticipating the clatter of the empty magazine landing on the street, Thielke leaned out sideways from behind the flowerpot. He aimed and fired twice at the masked man's upper body.

The man lunged backwards with each impact, dropping first the gun and then the replacement magazine before finally collapsing.

A bang rang out behind Thielke, followed immediately by a pain in his right hand. Screaming, he let go of the LeMat, pressed his hand against his chest and rolled around.

Two more assailants, also wearing suits and ice hockey masks, were approaching from the other side of the square, keeping their MP5s trained and rushing towards him at a run. Since they had held their fire after making the first hit, they probably wanted something from him. His hand was throbbing dully; thanks to the painkillers he'd gulped down earlier, he barely felt the gunshot wound, as if he had guessed that he would need them today – and not for the twinges in his leg stump either.

Thielke rolled himself over his revolver so that he could grab it with his left hand without being seen by his two attackers. With a dramatic groan, he stayed like that, waiting for his enemies to arrive.

The duo reached him within seconds.

'Stay down,' one of the masked men rasped at him. 'Come in, Homeboy,' he radioed.

No answer.

He looked at the van. 'What is it, Homeboy? Drive the banger over, we need to leave!'

Thielke thought about the red windscreen. His first bullet had found its way into the driver's cab and hit something. Homeboy was at the least seriously injured.

'Jeff, run over and check,' his partner ordered him. 'I'll ask the boss what to do if we can't drive him anywhere.'

They exchanged glances and turned away from him for a few seconds; Thielke whipped the LeMat up and let off a round of shot.

The tiny little bullets and shrapnel thundered out of the muzzle, hailing down on the masked men with enormous force and piercing through their clothing, tearing up the hockey masks and drilling through skin and flesh.

The men stumbled backwards screaming, shooting haphazardly at Thielke, who took another bullet in his injured thigh.

He let off a series of roughly aimed shots until his magazine was empty, and the men were out of action.

He quickly removed the empty cartridges from the barrel and slid in new ones from his jacket pocket. He left the shot barrel unloaded as it took too long.

Taking on stronger opponents with rapid-fire weapons, killing six and giving the bankers a thorough scare. Thielke considered that a good result for a shoot-out.

But his injuries were worrying him. He felt his blood pressure dropping and the effect of the shock was spreading, making him tremble uncontrollably. He was on the verge of losing consciousness and then bleeding out – or getting lynched by the Spanish *policía*, who would clock him as Igor from the stadium if the ballistics experts had done their job.

'Sleeper One, have you got him?' came a quiet but urgent voice in his ear.

Moaning, Thielke crept over to one of the men he had shot and found a bloody headset underneath the destroyed mask. He pulled it off the dead man's head and held it up so that he could use it. 'Sleeper One here. We have him,' he said tensely. 'He got me. Where should we take him? Come in.'

'Is he still alive?'

'Yes. Come in.'

'Then finish him off. We don't need the old bugger. I do not want him accidentally talking to Korff.'

The voice seemed familiar to Thielke, but he couldn't think of the face it belonged to. He needed to hear more, maybe then it would come to him. 'Copy that. Should we eliminate Korff too, boss? We have seen him in the vicinity. Come in.'

'Are you crazy?' The voice sounded surprised and angry.

'He needs to work for us before we get rid of him. Take care of Thielke, get out of there and bring me the LeMat. It seems the old idiot's knocked up a really good weapon for himself there.' A quiet laugh rang out of the headphones. '"I am not at all cynical, I have merely got experience, which, however, is very much the same thing." Over.'

That little MI6 wanker! Now Thielke knew whom he had to thank for the ambush.

Distracted by the conversation, he hadn't noticed the car doors closing or the footsteps behind him.

A blow to the back of the neck pushed him into unconsciousness, though it was already fast approaching. He drifted into the blackness.

XVIII

The desire to have a death of one's own
is becoming rarer all the time.
In time,
it will be just as rare
as a life of one's own.

The Notebooks of Malte Laurids Brigge,
Rainer Maria Rilke

Madrid, Spain

Konstantin stared at the woman he had believed to be dead. *How did she survive that?*

Von Windau's arm drifted upwards. But this time she did not reach for the hairpin that he had to thank for the hole in his hand, instead giving someone a signal.

At this, two men and a woman wearing suits walked up to her. One of them was Johnny. And with him standing coolly next to the baroness, that could only mean ... *No! This can't be true!*

The lift doors slowly closed.

Konstantin held a foot between them, activating the

photoelectric sensor, and the lift opened. He stepped out. 'Johnny?'

The short, wiry British man grinned widely, which made his narrow face appear disproportionately broad. 'Konstantin,' he said cheerfully, silently adding *Oneiros*, 'long time no see!' They shook hands. 'We're the team that Darling promised you.'

Johnny led him into a quiet corner of the lobby and began introducing his team. 'This is Anjelica Miller, codename Red, a freelancer the Deathslumberers sent us. The man next to her is called Rick Strong, codename Black, and he belongs to the Torpor's Men. You know Baroness von Windau and me. I'd appreciate it if you would call me Green, as soon as we—'

Konstantin seized him by the upper arm and pulled him a couple of paces away. 'You *know* who von Windau is, don't you?'

'I know, Konstantin,' Johnny retorted tartly and freed himself from his clutches with a jerk. 'She's here on Darling's orders.'

'Why?'

He shrugged his shoulders. 'He said that she's capable of putting Arctander out of action, and without weapons.'

Konstantin looked over at the baroness, who was looking out of the window, expressionless. She was just as unhappy as he was. *What kind of game is she playing? And how the hell did Jester get her to help us?* If that was even what she was planning to do.

He went over to her. 'I have a few questions and I wonder if you might answer them.'

Von Windau didn't look at him. 'Curiosity, in my opinion, is the mother of invention and catastrophe,' she replied calmly. 'Are you an inventor, Korff?'

'Your body was pulled out of the Nahe. How—'

She smiled almost imperceptibly. 'Th-th-that wasn't me. They fished a suicide v-v-victim out of the river whom they erroneously d-d-deemed to be the driver. That's how false reports develop.' Von Windau took a little vial of tablets out of her pocket. Two white pills found their way into her mouth.

A false report. Konstantin would have been all too happy to grab her and shake her, hit her to show his gratitude for that stunt in Idar-Oberstein. 'Why are you here? What makes you so special?'

She slowly lifted her healthy hand and placed it on the bridge of her nose. 'I could show you, Korff. But then y-y-you'd be dead.'

He laughed out loud. 'Oh, you can kill me with thoughts!'

'Not quite. With brainwaves.' Von Windau answered quietly without a trace of irony. Her stutter had disappeared, but her pupils seemed microscopically small.

'Explain that one to me.'

She was silent for several seconds before she countered, 'I don't need to, Korff. You wouldn't understand anyway. It's related to us, to sleep, to the various electrical waves that develop in the brain and attract Death the way blood attracts a shark. And to my insomnia.' The brunette slowly turned her face towards him. There was disdain and arrogance in her eyes. 'You chose the dead, I chose the living and life.'

'Is that why you're hunting Death Sleepers?'

'I don't know what you're talking about.'

'I know that you have a penchant for making members of

our kind disappear. That's what you were intending for me too, am I right? In Leipzig. And in Idar-Oberstein.'

She wouldn't allow herself to be intimidated by his menacing tone. Her posture remained relaxed, her arm hung down loosely by her side. She wrinkled her nose slightly and didn't reply.

'Johnny, come over here for a second,' Konstantin said. The MI6 agent obediently appeared next to him. 'What exactly is our mission?'

'Track down and eliminate Bent Arctander,' he answered straight away. 'Either with a bullet or with the help of the baroness.'

'Okay.' Konstantin couldn't imagine the baroness was taking part in the operation willingly. Jester was probably blackmailing her, or there was a secret deal. Immunity from prosecution in return for the release of the abductees. 'What's the plan?' he asked Johnny.

'We wait in the hotel until Darling contacts you. Then we head off. To wherever the mission might lead us.'

'Are there any leads?'

'Arctander still seems to be in Spain. That's as much as I know. We're monitoring all of his aliases and accounts. It can't be long now until he makes a mistake. With you, we'll manage to catch the narco.'

Konstantin nodded and thought about the potential repercussions of misjudging the narcoleptic. 'Great. Let's wait.' He pointed to an empty set of armchairs and the team went and sat down.

Strong lugged some suitcases across and put them down next to him before getting a book out. Johnny picked up a computer bag and took out a laptop, flipped it open and began working on it. Von Windau read a newspaper and Miller took out a smartphone from her jacket, studying the news.

The only one who didn't know what to do while they waited was Konstantin. He got out his phone and found an old message from Iva. *Call me!*

He dialled her number and stood up to get away from the Death Sleepers. He kept an eye on Kristen so that she couldn't sneak up on him and find out about Iva.

It rang several times, then there was a click. 'Yes?'

As soon as he heard her voice, he felt hot and his blood pressure rose. 'Hi Iva. It's Konstantin here. I wanted to—'

'Hello?' she cried. 'I can't understand you.'

The Spanish satellites didn't seem to want them to be together. 'Iva, it's me, Konstantin. I can't explain everything over the phone—'

'Hello? Who is this?'

This is making me feel sick. What Konstantin most wanted was to crawl through the line to her in Leipzig, to hug her, kiss her and show her how much he missed her. 'Iva! Iva, I have to see you again soon! Can you hear me? I—'

Toooot . . .

'Shit!' Annoyed, Konstantin looked at the screen. The reception bars weren't showing up at all; there wasn't even an emergency signal in the lobby.

He tapped the mobile nervously against his chin. On top of everything he now felt a rising fear and the desire to protect her from every possible danger.

Konstantin looked over at the suite of chairs, at his team.

He didn't want to go back to them. He had a hankering for a session of parkour to clear his head. That being out of the question, instead he prowled through the hallway, inspecting the leaflets on display and the prints on the wall, then sat down at a public computer and searched for any recent horrific news that could be linked to Arctander.

He found a report about a spectacular shoot-out that had taken place quite close to Hoya's villa.

Madrid (ed.) A gun battle in front of the RICO Bank building today has left the city in a state of shock. Six assailants armed with automatic weapons attacked an as yet unidentified person, who launched a robust defence. However, all six assailants lost their lives and the alleged victim vanished before police arrived. Analysis of CCTV cameras is ongoing.

A further seven people were injured due to ricochets and bullet fragments. The material damage amounts to approximately €120,000. According to an investigating officer, ammunition casings of an unusually large calibre were found at the scene. They are currently being compared with similar ammunition found at the Estadio Santiago Bernabéu. It is suspected that the alleged victim is a man named Igor who was in the stadium's commentary box at the time of the attack.

A witness described the man to this newspaper as fifty-five to sixty years of age. He was wearing an eyepatch and rural clothing, as well as a lower-leg prosthesis, which was destroyed by the assailants' bullets. A broken zoom lens was also found at the scene.

Any additional witnesses to the shoot-out are asked to come forward.

Konstantin leaned back in the office chair and used the ground to push himself so that he spun round on the chair's axis. *It must be Thielke*, he mused. He must have tried to glean more information on Arctander from Señora Hoya. The well-armed death squad that had been set on him was a surprise though. It would have fit with Bouler, but he was dead. Had Señor Hoya sent them?

Konstantin looked over at the group of chairs and his brow furrowed. *Does von Windau know the right people for something like that? Did Thielke annoy her enough to hire a gang of criminals?*

Johnny raised his head and looked at him, beckoning him over. His lips formed the word *information*.

He went over and crouched down next to the MI6 agent so that he could see the monitor. 'So?'

Johnny brought up an email with several attachments. The images had been taken from far away and above, and showed a figure standing at an ATM. Other photos showed him walking along a street.

'*That's* Arctander?' Konstantin couldn't have sworn on it.

'Yes,' said Johnny, and enlarged the next photo where the man was standing next to a puddle and was just leaning down to wipe a mark off his clothes. The reflection of his face in the pool showed very clearly that it was the narcoleptic.

'Did the photos come from a drone?'

'No. Better. The Americans gave us access to one of their spy satellites, thanks to the influence of the Deathslumberers.' He nodded at Miller with his broad grin, who returned it cheerfully. 'We noticed that Arctander had tried to withdraw money from one of the MI6 accounts. Since it's suspended, he didn't get anything, but we used the opportunity to track him.'

'Where is he?' Konstantin's gaze was fixed on the pale, exhausted face of their target. *Another catastrophe is looming.*

'In Zaragoza. He tried to buy a ticket online for a train to Barcelona, but we prevented that too. Without money it will be harder and harder for him to get away.' Johnny opened a browser window, which showed a city map of Zaragoza with a small, blinking spot on it. 'We linked up a satellite with facial recognition software and set it on Arctander. Now the city's cameras are working for us too.'

Konstantin looked at the glowing spot and thought about Arctander's white, shrunken face. *Dead man walking.* 'On your feet, team. We have a lead,' he said loudly to everyone.

'The helicopter is on standby,' Johnny interjected. 'Only the best for us.'

Yet another helicopter. Konstantin straightened up, his knees cracking.

One after the other, the four men and women got up. Suitcases were divided up, and they left the hotel, climbed into an extra-large taxi and drove to the airport.

Konstantin tried to get through to Iva again on the runway, away from the others. Still no reception. It annoyed him beyond reason that the satellites weren't able to produce a stable signal. He sent a text and hoped that she would answer soon.

Konstantin noticed that von Windau was also tapping away at the buttons on her smartphone with her forehead creased. Madrid didn't seem to be a good place for mobiles.

Madrid, Spain

Thielke opened his eyes, surprised that he was still alive.

He was lying in a comfortable bed, looking at a stuccoed ceiling with a chandelier hanging from it. Not exactly what you'd expect in a police station or a hospital. His injured leg was burning slightly.

His tongue was swollen, he was terribly thirsty and he felt woozy. His blood sugar levels were undoubtedly crap; he needed fast-acting carbohydrates or insulin, and nicotine and a cola chewing gum to get the disgusting taste out of his mouth.

With some difficulty, he sat up to work out where he was. His right hand had been professionally bandaged and as he threw off the thin sheet he saw that his injured leg had been treated in the same way. It seemed as though a medic had been taking care of him.

Thielke patted his face. The eyepatch was still there.

He turned to his right and on the side table he saw a syringe and infusion needles as well as several ampoules of insulin. A glass vial had already been cracked open and used. Someone must have realised quickly that he suffered from diabetes, which was admittedly extremely easy due to the documentation in his wallet and an emergency tag.

He was wearing a cream-coloured bathrobe, with nothing underneath, he noticed. He could see double doors that would have suited a castle or a palace. The sound of sirens came quietly through the windows and receded.

Talk about a gilded cage! Thielke clenched his teeth together and got up, sliding off the bed and hopping to the window, using some chairs, a table and a chest of drawers as a support.

Through the glass he saw the front of the RICO Bank, where he'd got into a shoot-out with those strangers earlier. Police vehicles were parked around the scene, the street was strewn with little marker flags to indicate empty cartridge shells and forensic workers in white protective suits were striding around the six corpses.

Camera crews were clustered around the extensive cordon, and reporters were shooting photographs from the windows of the surrounding multi-storey buildings. There was only one place with a view like this: the Villa Hoya.

At that moment, the doors behind him opened.

Thielke looked over his shoulder and recognised Carola Hoya. She was wearing a short whitish-grey dress with matching leather gloves. She had braided her black hair into a long, thin plait. 'Ah, Señor Thielke! Out of bed already? You're stronger than I thought!'

He turned round with small, hopping movements and sat down on the chest of drawers. 'I would never have thought that an old geezer like me would wake up in a beautiful young woman's bed like this,' he replied with a grin.

She smiled in a detached way. 'I'm not that young, Señor Thielke, and it's also not my bed. In my bed, you would neither fall asleep nor wake up, I can promise you that.' Carola stayed standing, two metres away from him. 'My father and

I would very much like to know what's going on. That's why I had you picked up before the police turned up.'

'What if I can't tell you anything?'

She pointed at the window. 'I'm sure the *policía* would be pleased to take you off our hands.'

'And how would you explain this?' Thielke pointed at the bath robe and the bandage on his hand. 'I broke in, and you caught me and treated me before turning me in?'

'Nobody will ask me any questions, Señor Thielke. I am a Hoya. They would simply take you with them, pleased to have caught Igor, the terrorist who killed 80,000 people.' Carola sat down in an armchair. 'My father and I initially thought you and Señor Korff, as well as Monsieur Bouler, were ruthless jewellery thieves, fighting over the Harlequin's Death for financial reasons and willing to go to extreme lengths. You took those photos of me in the graveyard, you know the man I met – as does Señor Korff.' She raised a hand, the index finger pointing at him. 'But everyone's asking me about the stone's effect on death. And I'm starting to ask myself whether it really is just about money. You are going to tell me what this hunt is really all about.'

He shifted his weight, his stump and the gunshot wound suddenly painful. It would probably be better if he hopped to the bed and lay down again. 'What will you do if I have nothing new to report?' He spread out his arms. 'I'm just a jewellery thief, as you've already said.'

Her smile became malicious. 'I'm not as patient as you might assume, Señor Thielke. We had your wounds treated, but we could also arrange it so that you wished you *had* been apprehended by the *policía*.' Carola leaned forwards. 'So that you understand the position you're in, Señor: nobody knows where on earth you are. Nobody will suspect you're here. If I so desire, your life will end here.' She tapped the marble floor twice with the top of her foot to make a clacking sound.

Thielke knew she was serious. Her eyes betrayed her determination. 'I understand. But how will you know that I'm telling the truth?'

Carola's gaze settled on the side table with the ampoules. 'Judging by the show outside my window, you love your life, Señor Thielke. Yet you are treating it in a reckless way, if the doctor has evaluated your blood results correctly. You know, detox is a painful thing. It brings even the strongest people to their knees. We will talk, I'll check your statements, and if you've lied . . . well, then, we'll see how long you last.' She leaned back and sat up straight in the armchair. 'That's how it will go, Señor Thielke.'

He mumbled his agreement, even if he didn't exactly like what he was hearing. The headache from the lack of caffeine and nicotine was already beginning. 'I'm happy for us to talk but I'm warning you, Señora Hoya, allowing me to go into withdrawal will put you in more danger than you realise. In your position, I would in fact be making sure that I was well supplied with coffee and cigarettes.' He hopped back to the bed and sank down onto it before his knee gave out.

'How come? Could you really be that aggressive?'

'No. I will fall asleep. Simply fall asleep, as I have not done in many years,' he replied. 'It will be fatal for you.'

Carola Hoya burst out laughing.

'Many different people have made that mistake before,' he murmured.

Zaragoza, Spain

In the evening, Konstantin and his team arrived at the airport in the city of Zaragoza, with the longest landing strip he had ever seen. Continuing immediately to the old town, they set about hunting Arctander on foot. They were wearing identical bluetooth headsets, which Johnny had given out along with their mobile phones and they looked like a group of workaholic bankers on a business trip.

The MI6 agent's smartphone was guiding them. They were following the red spot that represented Bent Arctander, which seemed to be wandering aimlessly through the narrow, slightly shabby alleyways as well as the large main roads. There was no pattern.

Konstantin knew hardly anything about the city of Zaragoza. Unfortunately, the only thing that came to mind when he heard the name was a hit band from his childhood, who were called Saragossa and had warbled a song about summer. On the plane, he'd read a few basic facts in the in-flight magazine, but he'd already forgotten most of them. He was left with the memory of an impressive image of a cathedral and the founding of the rock group Héroes del Silencio. But the most important information kept going through his mind: the city was home to 700,000 residents, of which an incalculable number were in danger from Arctander.

They moved through the old town, the *casco viejo*, as it said on the signposts. The historical city centre had ironically fallen into disrepair while also becoming the pleasure strip, with row upon row of bars. Konstantin supposed it was nicer to live in the more elegant housing on the outskirts of town. At most, the locals came to these areas to party at the weekend. Like today.

'So what is he doing?' Johnny asked as their target swung abruptly into a street. 'Is he looking for something?'

'Potentially a contact.' Konstantin pulled up the man's route so far on the little screen. Arctander was more or less walking in a circle, walking the same streets over and over with slight deviations. 'He's waiting for someone and doesn't want to linger in one place, I think.'

'He's begging,' von Windau remarked. 'They locked his accounts, he won't have any more money. He didn't get the online ticket to Barcelona either so he has to get the full amount for himself some other way.'

Very well deduced. Konstantin thought about it and exchanged looks with the MI6 agent. 'Possible, isn't it?'

Johnny nodded. 'Yes. If he sticks to his route, he's got to be heading our way. As long as we're right about him begging.' He looked at Konstantin. Clearly he was expecting an order from his team leader.

Konstantin watched the lively activity in the streets. *A narcoleptic fit and we have a hundred people dead. At least.* The group was equipped with tranquilliser guns, which would put the narcoleptic into an unnatural but harmless deep sleep. But Arctander would be intensely agitated; he would be feeling the noose closing in around him, expecting someone to step in any moment. And he was tired. *The best conditions for one of his involuntary naps.*

'We should wait and ambush him,' said von Windau, before

Konstantin could make the same suggestion himself. 'Two shots with the tranquillisers and I' – she tapped the tip of her right middle finger against her head – 'will stand by, to interfere with his wave signal if need be. So that the people in the vicinity are safe.'

'Good.' Konstantin looked to Miller. 'You get us a car. Without a driver. We need a way of getting Arctander to the airport without witnesses.' He waited for Johnny to protest that MI6 might have already prepared an alternative. But none came.

Miller nodded. 'All right. I'll head into the pedestrianised zone as soon as I receive your go on my mobile.' She walked away.

'Strong, Johnny, you're the shooters. Von Windau, you stay nearby. Make sure that Arctander doesn't notice you and only intervene if necessary.' He couldn't be bothered to use the colour codenames. He didn't see any point in it.

Both agents agreed curtly, while von Windau gave him a scornful look. That was as much as he got from her. She was her own boss in this enforced collective.

Konstantin would have liked to have known more about her skill and how exactly she was planning to interfere with Arctander's wave signal. As far as he knew, she was the only person with this ability. *And she won't tell me anything about it. Pity.* Perhaps she needed the Death Sleepers she abducted in order to practise her skills. He had better keep his distance from the baroness, despite his curiosity.

The men subtly primed their guns. Von Windau strolled to a stall of children's toys and pretended to look at what was on offer.

'And you?' Strong looked at Konstantin.

'I'm going to get a look at Arctander up close,' he replied. Konstantin wanted to get an impression of the man whose sleep could be as destructive as a small neutron bomb. 'We will only step in if I—'

'That will put the operation in danger. What if he realises we're onto him?' Johnny exclaimed, incredulous.

'Why should he? He doesn't know me, and with her powers, which I hope will work, von Windau should be able to block the Reaper. Worst case scenario, he notices me and runs away. Or he has a fit, von Windau interferes with his signal and we tranquillise him.' Konstantin broke away from them and walked through the streets, towards the narcoleptic. He knew that his explanation was somewhat thin, but he couldn't just order the attack on Arctander without looking him once in the eye. He turned off his phone so that it wouldn't ring at the wrong moment.

People swarmed past him, scraps of conversation in Spanish, English, French and German pressing against his ears. The warm air was filled with cigarette smoke, various perfumes and the smell of food. Moths danced around the street lamps and swallows darted over the heads of passers-by, chasing their dinner.

There are too many people here. He decided he would speak to Arctander and try to guide him away from the busy street. He was sure he could think of an appropriate pretext. *The most powerful Death Sleeper in history and he's about to be standing right in front of me.*

Konstantin kept an eye out for his face, so as not to miss him in the cheerful crowd.

Suddenly, he appeared in the middle of the idyll. Arctander was heading straight towards Konstantin, holding a paper cup in front of him and speaking to people at random. Most people gave nothing, others threw change into the container. Judging by the sound, the narcoleptic hadn't collected much yet.

Arctander looked even worse than in the photo; he had a tired, haggard face, dull eyes and a light film of sweat on his forehead. Most people would take him for a junkie, or otherwise think he was very ill – someone you wouldn't want too close to you. No wonder he wasn't doing very well at begging.

Judging by his rumpled clothes, he had been wearing them for more than one night. He was pulling a little trolley behind him, which looked well travelled.

Konstantin pretended to read a menu on display and waited for him to approach.

The jangling coins drew nearer, followed by the smell of stale sweat that had been sprayed over too many times with cheap deodorant. 'Excuse me, sir,' said Arctander in English. 'I got into some trouble through no fault of my own and need a bit of money to get out of here. Would you be so kind?'

Konstantin turned to him and stuck a hand in his pocket, looking for his wallet. The fugitive was looking at him with pupils like pinpricks, shivering slightly with cracked lips. 'Have you ever considered detoxing?'

Arctander laughed, his lower lip falling open. A thin rivulet of blood became visible. 'I wish it were something like that. I was unlucky. Everything went down the drain.'

'Well, where are you going? Maybe I can give you a lift?'

Arctander's face changed, brightening up with hope. 'Are you driving to Barcelona by any chance?'

'Yes. My wife and I are planning to go there tomorrow. Can you wait that long?' *Barcelona! His next target?*

The initial joy vanished from Arctander's expression, replaced by suspicion. That a stranger would make an offer like that seemed to give him the creeps. He scrutinised Konstantin and saw the tattoo "Do not fall asleep until . . ." on his upper arm. His eyes widened. He shrank back.

Konstantin seized him by the wrist. 'Listen, Arctander,' he whispered quickly and quietly. 'I'm not here to kill you.'

There was a brief rustling in his ear. 'Shall I step in?' Johnny's voice rang out from the headset, so loud that Konstantin worried the Swedish man would hear the question. He shook his head ever so slightly to decline.

'Who are you?' Arctander stood still, but his muscles were noticeably tense. 'Did Darling send you?'

'I'm not from MI6 and I'm not a member of any Death Sleeper organisation either—'

'Tell that arsehole that he's never getting me back again. He can do that shit by himself!' Arctander interrupted him, looking around frantically.

'Explain to me why you're fleeing and costing innocent people their lives instead of letting Darling help you,' Konstantin said stonily.

'*Help?*' Arctander stared at him. 'Are you crazy? He's the one to blame. He made me what I am! For his project.'

That can't be. Konstantin closed his eyes for two seconds. 'Why would he do that? Can you explain what happened? What project are you talking about?' He didn't know what to think. Jester was his friend, he'd known him so long. 'How come—?'

'Who the hell are you?' Arctander exclaimed and tried to loosen Konstantin's grip on his wrist. His sparse, light blond hair fluttered like candy floss. Then he froze for a moment. 'Hang on, I know you! You were there in Marrakech when Bouler caught me!'

'Now?' asked Johnny again in his ear.

He saw me. I never thought of that. Konstantin countered the Swede's movement with an aikido technique. A slight twist of the arm, some pressure on the elbow and wrist and Arctander had to hold still if he didn't want to hurt himself. The whole thing happened quickly and inconspicuously. Onlookers would believe the pair were chatting. 'My name is Korff and I—'

Arctander looked to the right, and screamed, shrinking away from Johnny, who was now in position for a clean shot. They seemed to know each other. 'You *are* from MI6!' he cried in a panic. 'Help! Help! I'm being abducted!' he shrieked in a high-pitched voice. Bystanders were looking at them now.

'Get down! Police!' Johnny whipped his gun out of its holster and shot at the narcoleptic twice.

Screams rang out through the street, people ducked, ran away or looked for cover under tables and in shops.

Arctander thrashed around desperately in Konstantin's grip, dodging the bullets by chance more than anything else. A moment later he threw the coins in Konstantin's face. He managed to break free and plunged into the throng of people rushing this way and that, ducking down.

No more massacres! Konstantin didn't let the narco out of

his sight. *How far do von Windau's wave signals reach? Can she still block them?* What had started out so well might swiftly end in catastrophe.

In the panic and confusion, he lost sight of his team. So he concentrated on Arctander, doing all that he could to keep the fugitive in his eyeline.

Time for parkour. Konstantin leaped onto the nearest table, launched himself off it and grabbed an awning to pull himself up, swinging onto a flat roof. He sprinted on, parallel to the alleyway and was reminded of his experiences in Marrakech. *It must not end that way again.*

He jumped down the other side onto the roof of a kiosk and saw Arctander around fifty metres ahead of him.

Konstantin bounded from one stall to the next, lunging over people's heads, then swung himself up onto a balcony by a street sign; he pulled his belt out of its loops and swung it over a gently sloping electricity line. Using it like a bracket, he grasped the ends and slid down the thick cable.

Thirty metres to Arctander.

He let go and leaped at full speed onto a dumpster, which absorbed the impact, then jumped onto the ground and kept racing after the surprisingly speedy Swedish man.

Konstantin would have found the chase quite fun if it weren't for the fact that the narcoleptic could have an attack at any moment. Stress was thought to be one of the main triggers. *Fingers crossed he's having a good day and has taken the proper medication.*

Where his team had got to, he did not know. He didn't have time to get out his phone and start calling round. *Hopefully von Windau is in the vicinity.*

Arctander looked back, noticed him and vanished round a corner.

Konstantin followed him and jumped onto a plastic dumpster just before the corner, using it like a trampoline to leap across the junction and push himself off the opposite wall on one leg.

Below him, he saw that Arctander had lain in wait for him, a bent metal pipe, frayed at one end, in his hand. The Swedish man followed him with his eyes, astonished, but his surprise didn't last long. He charged, while Konstantin, having barely landed on the ground, avoided the blow with a backward roll.

Konstantin dodged the second blow and used the third to redirect the narcoleptic's momentum, the pipe slamming into the wall. He combined his counter-attack with a light blow and a shoulder barge, slamming the inexperienced Swedish man into the wall.

Arctander crashed face first into the brickwork and lashed out blindly with the pipe behind him.

Konstantin avoided the haphazard attack by turning, but the sharp end slit his trouser pocket open.

The Reaper's Ring fell to the ground with a soft clink and lay between the two opponents.

Arctander turned around and stared at the glittering piece of jewellery. 'Harlequin's Death!' he murmured, dumbfounded, and slowly shifted his gaze to Konstantin. 'You believe in it?'

He recognised it immediately and knows what it means. 'I've heard there are rings that can make a Death Sleeper visible,' he said. 'Whether I believe in it or not, I don't yet know.'

Arctander threw the metal pipe away. 'So you want to get rid of the curse too?'

Konstantin couldn't shake the feeling that it was suddenly more complicated than he had expected, and that there were some things that Jester was keeping from him. *Be on your guard. It could be a trick.* 'I do. And I'll say it again: I don't belong to MI6. What did Darling do to you? What kind of project do you mean?'

Arctander patted the skinned cheek that he'd earned from coming into contact with the brick wall. 'I think there's a thing or two you should know. About me and Darling.'

Konstantin agreed. 'We have to take cover before the satellite picks us up. It might have lost us in the chaos just now.' He snatched up the Harlequin's Death and looked around.

'So what kind—'

'Later.' Sirens wailed in the distance. The police would be searching for the gunman who had been firing in the street. Johnny's nerves had got the better of him – or else he had acted on Jester's orders. 'It looks quite deserted in there.' Konstantin pointed right, towards a rundown factory building with ivy and other creepers growing over its glass façade.

They climbed in through a window left ajar, closed it behind them and sat in a corner of the empty, overgrown building, apparently once a small metal foundry. The light from outside shone in weakly.

Arctander dropped onto the floor, removed a dispenser from his pocket and pressed out two pills. He put them in his mouth and sucked them. 'What was your name again?' he asked incoherently. His breathing was fast; he was sweating heavily and couldn't suppress his coughs. His eyes darted back and forth as if in REM sleep.

This does not look good. 'My name's Korff. You stay awake, okay, Arctander?'

'For me it's not a question of willpower.' The narcoleptic's eyelids closed. 'Explain one thing to me, Korff: if you're not an MI6 agent and don't work for a Death Sleeper organisation, then why did you get involved with that arsehole Darling?'

'We know each other from before. I'm curious about what you're telling me about him,' replied Konstantin and sat down on an dirty upturned drinks crate covered with cobwebs. *I hope I'm able to wake him again if he falls asleep.* 'So you believe in the power of the Reaper's Rings?'

No reaction.

'Hey!' Konstantin gave him a light slap.

The man started and opened his eyes wide. 'Easy there! I was just thinking.' He smiled weakly. 'Yes, yes. The Reaper's Rings. They certainly have a function, but I still don't know what. I'm seeking out people who can speak to Death. Like Auro, but he's . . . no longer with us, unfortunately.'

Konstantin inhaled sharply. 'People who—'

'People who can speak to Death. I found Darling's research on death and a possible way out of our curse. I realised there really must be people who see him. The ring's trail led me to various people who I'd hoped might be capable of it. The first time I got it right was with Auro. Unfortunately I had a fit and—' He shook his head in frustration.

The news report from Roccastrada. The hopes that had been raised at the narco's few words had been dashed again.

Bent Arctander was fleeing from Jester and was looking

for someone who could help him. Who would free him from Death's curse. *He had the same plan as me and was actually closer to achieving it.*

Why hadn't the MI6 agent helped him? What better solution than to defuse Arctander?

Obviously Jester needed Arctander. *But for what? It can't be for anything good. Didn't Arctander also say that Jester had made him into what he is? Into a Death Sleeper? What else could he mean?* 'Let's start from—'

'Apparently he also found a woman who is a Death Seer. A doctor,' Arctander interrupted him, exhausted. 'Auro told me her name before he died. She lives in Barcelona. Come with me, Korff! I have to get to her and she . . .' He had been growing quieter and quieter as he spoke and now his head sank down onto his chest. He was falling asleep.

Into a deadly sleep.

Since Konstantin didn't know what exact restrictions Arctander's Death-summons was subject to, he did the first thing that occurred to him: he picked up a stone from the floor, quickly wrapped it up in his jacket and knocked the narcoleptic out with it. The Reaper didn't come when someone was unconscious. Zaragoza was safe.

Konstantin watched Arctander slump down, his words still echoing in his head. *He found a Death Seer!*

He could barely wait to learn more. So they did exist, these legendary, extraordinary people who saw Death, who spoke to him without him killing them. *Carola was right!* His heart was beating loud and fast.

Perhaps he really did have a chance now of going back to Iva as a free man and leading a normal life, albeit with an unusual job. A little nap in the park, a little snooze on the deck of the *Vanitas*. In Iva's bed. Provided she still wanted him.

Not so fast, he said to himself, trying to lower his expectations of meeting the doctor. So far he had nothing more than Arctander's word that she really was a Death Seer. And even if she were, it was possible that the Grim Reaper would not want to negotiate at all. Maybe what awaited him at the end of the meeting was the greatest disappointment of all: the end of all hope.

Konstantin looked out the window, past the lamp post to the moon that lay bright against the night sky. *I have a chance. The fairy tales show us that Death is prepared to bargain. You just shouldn't screw him over.*

Konstantin wondered what role Jester had in this game. It would be difficult to check the narcoleptic's story, but Konstantin wanted to hear it. His friend had already lied to him several times about the Phansigar. To spur him on, as he said. He didn't entirely believe it any more.

He got out his smartphone and turned it on.

Not a text or an email or a missed call. His team had made no attempt to get in contact. On Jester's orders?

Konstantin lowered the phone. *This is not a good sign.*

XIX

Are you afraid of death?
Do you wish you could live eternally?
Live fully!
When you are long gone, it remains.
A good departure is worth practising for.

Friedrich von Schiller

Madrid, Spain

Thielke lay in bed contemplating the stucco on the ceiling. He had to hand it to Carola Hoya, she knew how to pry information out of people: with a tenacious smile and the withdrawal of essential medications.

They had talked for two days. About Death Sleepers, about what had happened in front of the villa and the links between the dead in Paris, Marrakech and Madrid.

And constantly about his role: the lone wolf who kept watch over Death Sleepers, selected them, instructed them in his sleep method or hunted them. To keep them away from normal people insofar as that was possible. He contented himself with putting their bodies beyond use. He wasn't interested in what happened to the men and women's souls.

Initially, Thielke could clearly tell from her face, Carola Hoya didn't believe him.

But after the first day, he had suddenly been allowed to smoke so that his nicotine levels rose. His tetchiness did vanish with the first cigarette, but the neurotoxin was much more important for his truly unusual trait. Nicotine was the reason he could go to sleep anywhere at any time without causing disasters.

There was a knock, and the door opened straight away.

Carola Hoya was back. Today she was wearing a knee-length, black dress with a white silk wrap over it, flat shoes and her hair down. Two long, silver hair-clips stopped any strands of hair tumbling into her face. She had a laptop with her, which she used to record her interrogations.

'Hello, Señor Thielke,' she said amicably. 'How was your breakfast?'

'That *café bombón* is dynamite,' he replied, 'even if I have to give myself a shot of insulin for it every time.' He took a cola bubble gum from the bedside table, peeled off the paper and stuffed it in his mouth. 'Another interrogation?'

'A conversation, Señor Thielke.' Carola sat down in an armchair next to the bed, flipped open the computer and turned on the recording programme. The built-in camera was recording his face, Carola stayed outside the frame. 'Is there anything else I can have brought for you?'

'Freedom would be nice. Laced with a pinch of clothes,' he replied. 'My time in this golden cage is going on a little long for me. For the record,' he spoke into the camera, 'I'm not doing this voluntarily and what's more, I'm of unsound mind. I don't believe in either Reaper's Rings or in personified Death or . . . in . . . oh yeah, Death Sleepers.' He grinned and blew a bubble with the bubble gum, which burst with a pop. 'I made all of that up to please the sick *señora* here. I hope the police take her in.'

'You've already said that. Maybe I'll make you famous, Señor: Thielke's fairy tales, recorded by Carola Hoya.' She laughed and made herself comfortable. 'So, Death Sleepers summon Death as soon as they sleep. Because Death wants to avenge himself because he is angry and feels provoked by their invisibility. There are various reasons for this,' she summarised, 'which ultimately can only be speculated about. Correct?'

'Correct. That's how I imagine it.'

She clicked her tongue. 'Various organisations exist, you say?'

'Yes, although I have nothing to do with them.' That was a lie, because he wanted to see whether she would be able to tell. She had demonstrated a remarkable perceptiveness and awareness of human nature over the previous two days. He put it down to him being easier to figure out than usual due to the withdrawal of insulin, nicotine and caffeine. 'I only know them through hearsay.'

She nodded. She hadn't noticed this lie. 'Now explain to me again why you can sleep without Death coming and causing a massacre, like in Estadio Santiago Bernabéu.'

'Did you not understand the first time?'

'I did. But the recording was poor.'

Thielke grinned. 'All right then. Once more from the top.

You close your eyes, you fall asleep and your brain does too. Completely. Both halves of your brain go on standby and process what you experienced during the day. The dream factory's recalibration.' He sat up, crumpled up his pillow and crammed it behind his lower back. Carola corrected the position of the camera. 'As soon as Death Sleepers fall asleep, things get unpleasant for the surrounding area, as I described to you. So I looked for a way to prevent that.'

'Permit me to interrupt with a question. Why do you not use any sleeping pills? You did say that an unnatural sleep protects against an attack by Death.'

He sighed and shook his head. 'If only it was so simple. It ought to be an anaesthetic like narcotics or roofies. Since it's not particularly healthy to use these kinds of substances on a long-term basis, I wanted to find a better way to get to sleep than always getting myself clobbered with a baseball bat, without killing people in the process.' Thielke looked at her. 'I found the answer in the animal kingdom.'

'Animals sleep differently to humans?'

'Some animals. There is a special way of sleeping called unihemispheric sleep. It was first discovered in dolphins. The scientific world hypothesises that they have developed the ability in order not to drown. Pulmonary respirators, you see. In unihemispheric sleep, as the name indicates, only one side of the brain succumbs to sleep, the other remains active. This has the unbeatable advantage that only one eye is closed during it, so that you can still keep an eye on your surroundings.' He pointed to the patch on his left eye socket. 'That was tough luck for me of course. The whole thing is quite stressful when you've lost one.'

'And you decided on the spur of the moment to equip yourself with the same skills as dolphins, Señor Thielke? Explain to me how it works. Suppose I went on one of your courses.'

'Well, first I would say to you that you might die during it. Then I would pump you full of nicotine, until you were close to being poisoned.'

'Nicotine? Why?'

'It gives the brain the necessary kick. Adrenalin, dopamine and serotonin are released by it, the psychomotor performance increases, you can concentrate better and the memory works better too. Since the effects only last for a short time, you need to keep taking nicotine. Then we follow up with a few energy drinks so that you really get into gear. Until you think your heart is exploding,' he listed everything off with a smirk. 'If you survive that, we will experiment with more pills that help to minimise the need for sleep. Then we top off this cocktail with strong sleeping pills. Afterwards I'll write down for you which medicines I'm using.'

'What effect does this mixture have?'

'You will be wide awake, yet still want to sleep. You feel the madness within and try everything to reconcile the contradictory signals from your mind and your body – and either you crack up and die or it goes *click*. Practice, that's all it is, if you can work up the necessary courage, or are desperate enough to put yourself through all that. At some point you get the hang of how it works. Nowadays I only need nicotine in my bloodstream and not pills. I read it also works for killer whales. Unihemispheric sleep. Without nicotine. It would be difficult to smoke underwater. But does anyone know what pollutants are floating in the sea that they're addicted to?' He assumed that Hoya had understood. She was shrewd enough. And that in turn made it difficult for him to outwit her and escape from her.

'I researched a bit more yesterday and found even more animals, apart from marine mammals, who have mastered unihemispheric sleep. Birds for example,' she remarked.

'I see myself more in the tradition of dolphins and less in the tradition of ducks.' Thielke blew another bubble with the bubble gum.

Carola merely nodded. 'One more thing. You mentioned that every Death Sleeper has a different radius of effect. Could you speak a little bit more about that?'

'Of course. Sometimes the Grim Reaper rampages only in a closed space, no matter what the dimensions, no matter whether it's St Peter's Basilica or a broom cupboard. Other times the area is spherical in shape and not hindered by walls.'

'And for you?'

'It's already so long ago that I can't remember.'

'Ah, ought you lie to me, Señor Thielke?' she admonished him with feigned reproach. 'I'll take you off your insulin, if you don't behave yourself.'

That put him in a tricky situation. If he revealed his secret to her, she as good as had him over a barrel. 'I'm practically harmless. It's not particularly far and depends on various factors anyway, so that the distance is difficult to put a number on.'

Carola looked at him patiently, folding her hands in front of one knee and crossing the leg over the other. This meant: I can wait.

'About 300 metres,' he said with a sigh. 'Because I don't sleep in the traditional sense any more, the distance has remained the same. Imagine that I emit a signal in my sleep that is inaudible to humans and approximately ninety to a hundred decibels. If I'm in a room like this one, the walls absorb the sound. But in an open space, for instance on a mountain, I'm quite powerful as a Death Sleeper.' Thielke had painstakingly investigated his trait. 'Above all, it's unpredictable with me. Supposing I fell asleep here, and the right-hand window was open, then the Grim Reaper would advance further on the right because the signal resounds further there. Do you understand?'

Carola nodded. 'What about the echoes?'

'Because I mentioned the mountains?' Her question surprised Thielke. 'I don't think there is such a thing.' *Wow, she really is giving me something to think about.*

'Let's come to the final question of the day: how many Death Sleepers do you know of and how high would you estimate their total number to be worldwide?'

'Huh, that's difficult.' Thielke would have liked to lie again and say 'two or three'. But he wouldn't have got away with that, he could tell from looking at the Spanish woman. He cursed himself for having brought up the organisations, which had led her to work out that there were more of his kind. *Dependency and a survival instinct really could bring out a lot in someone.* 'There are around thirty that I'm sure of. The total number . . . honestly, I don't know.'

The organisations were constantly looking for Death Sleepers to recruit and direct along their own paths, but most of the younger generations came from their own ranks.

Finding new Death Sleepers turned out to be difficult if they weren't just obvious mass murderers like Arctander. Plus, there were simply too many deaths and not all of them could be investigated.

'Would you agree if I were to say that your kind is very uncommon?' asked Carola. 'A sort of mutation?'

He took the empty wineglass from the bedside table. 'Can I have a bit more?'

'Sure.' Carola ended the recording and flipped the laptop shut. 'I'll have some brought to you.' She contemplated him with a look he'd seen before, although not from her. From her father, yesterday, during his excursion to the library from his sickbed. Señor Hoya had been looking at the rings and almost self-combusting with pride at being their owner. He saw that same strange glow in Carola now. 'You are a very rare, mystical being, Señor Thielke and you care so little for yourself and your health,' she said reproachfully. 'We'll keep you here a bit longer until you're better, agreed? The new lower leg prosthesis will be ready soon. After that you can go out into the world again and look for Death Sleepers to change or kill. But out of gratitude for my care, you'll tell me more about yourself and your life, for as long as you're here, okay? I want to know everything.'

Thielke agreed.

Carola got up and left the room.

The expression in her eyes unsettled him.

She is absolutely obsessed with me and the Death Sleepers. She knows by now that I've been telling the truth, no matter what I might have claimed.

Thielke supposed that she was very keen to keep him as a

guinea pig, to find out everything about the Death Sleepers. The prospect of freedom was probably just meant to keep him quiet.

He might have been including many lies to disguise the truth, but he had had to talk to get his medicine. He didn't want to die. Not in this place. The villa definitely had enough ghosts already.

Thielke checked the wounds in his hand as well as in his right thigh. The holes had closed up, but those areas were incredibly itchy. He had deliberately kept *this* theory from her: that Death Sleepers regenerate more quickly during their sleep. It seemed to work for him anyway, even though he didn't actually sleep properly.

From tomorrow, he decided, he would not impose on their hospitality any longer. The Hoya family's urge to collect things gave him a thorough dose of the creeps.

Zaragoza, Spain

Kristen saw Arctander disappearing into the pandemonium and Korff taking up the pursuit.

It was evening and there was absolute uproar in the alleyway; the panic tearing people apart. As soon as their instinct for self-preservation kicked in, they forgot respect for fellow humankind and other such virtues of social cooperation. People who fell were left lying there, stalls and tables were knocked over to provide cover from the man with the gun.

Johnny put away the semi-automatic and dived into the

fray, shedding his jacket as he did so. To Kristen's surprise he approached her. 'Retreat,' he said as he reached her.

'But ... wh-wh-what about the narcoleptic?' The bloody stammering was coming back, she was too agitated. The drugs' effect wore off too soon. She quickly tossed back two pills.

The MI6 agent looked at her in disbelief, as though it were absolutely unthinkable to question an order. 'Retreat, I said! The instruction came from Darling.'

'B-b-but I also have m-m-my instructions f-f-from D-d-darling.' Kristen didn't intend to give up her two most important targets just because the mission wasn't going to plan. She wanted to have Arctander and Korff no matter what, and nothing was about to stop her. *Tick, tock*, her time was running out. 'We're going a-a-after them.'

'Certainly not, von Windau. You'll do what I tell you.' Johnny turned away from her and pushed his way through the people fleeing down a street, which was bordered by the walls of houses. Strong materialised behind them.

Cursing, Kristen followed the agent and drew her hairpin. She would rather have taken him and the other members of the team with her to Minsk as test subjects, but the situation made it impossible to overpower them all, so she'd have to concentrate on the two most interesting targets only – of the ones that were left, anyway. What a waste of resources.

Kristen shoved Johnny into the dark entrance of a court-yard, out of view of the people. In the same movement she stabbed him in the back of the neck. 'You are an expendable idiot,' she murmured.

Johnny was fully unprepared for the attack. The sharp

point pierced the skin and went past vertebrae into the cerebellum.

Kristen shook the needle once, hard, to cause the greatest possible damage, before she pulled it out again. There was nothing visible other than a small red spot.

Johnny collapsed without a sound, tumbled down a dark, well-worn set of basement steps and came to rest, prone on the ground.

Kristen leaned out of the entrance to the courtyard and beckoned to Strong who was already looking around for them. The street had emptied in the meantime, fear sweeping people away. 'Green fell,' she said into her headset and pointed to the stairs. 'I won't be able to get him up by myself.'

'Understood.' Strong reached her and set one foot on the first step to get to Johnny. 'How did it happen?'

'A bit like this.' Kristen stabbed with the needle again, hitting the same spot as on the MI6 agent, killing the Torpor's Man in under two seconds. He fell down the stairs too.

Kristen followed him quickly, drew Johnny's gun, swapped the tranquillising ammunition for live ammunition and shot them both in the back of the neck to cover her tracks. Then she put away the gun, hurried upstairs and ran into the narrow street that Arctander and Korff had disappeared down. She put the needle into the inner pocket of her coat because she had lost her leather clasp.

There was no way she was following Darling's orders, not so long as there was still an alternative. The alternative in this case meant one lie and two people dead.

Kristen called the commander. 'Arctander got away. Korff helped him do it,' she said curtly. 'He killed Johnny and

Strong when we were retreating. I think it was a mistake to rely on Korff being stupid enough to believe you.' No more stammering, the drugs were working again. And she had calmed down.

Darling cursed loudly. 'Okay, follow them both. The satellite has lost them.'

'Give me phone coordinates on Korff.'

'Won't work. His smartphone is switched off.' Darling shouted something incomprehensible: an order to an underling. 'Keep looking,' he instructed her next. 'I'll let you know as soon I hear where the phone is.'

'Understood.' Kristen ended the call. She didn't trust Darling. She trusted him just as little as he trusted her. Both of them were used to playing both sides. The commander was sure to be dispatching a new team to check up on her. He would probably find out soon that she had already broken their agreement. Although she hadn't felt bound by the deal anyway. Not given the circumstances under which it had been struck.

The wail of sirens sounded like the plaintive call of a whining animal. Hardly any passers-by were hurrying past her, the people were holing up in their houses. The images of the attacks by the unknown terrorist group were too fresh. Nobody wanted to be one of the next victims of the deadly gas.

Kristen looked around carefully as she roamed through the abandoned streets, searching for traces of the fleeing men. Minutes passed. She ran and ran until finally she realised it would be impossible to find Korff and Arctander this way. Luck would not come to her aid, so she contacted Darling again. 'I've lost them.'

'Call Miller and wait with her until I have news,' he said irritatedly.

Kristen agreed, ended the conversation, called Miller and ordered her to come to her. She used the waiting time to get rid of Johnny's gun, in case it occurred to Miller to doubt her story and frisk her. The gun disappeared into a sewage shaft with a clatter. She didn't need anything apart from the needle anyway.

Kristen looked at her watch. Every pointless wasted second pained her, getting deducted from her valuable lifetime, from the single year still left to her – as long as Smyrnikov was not mistaken. She absolutely had to speak to Eugen. Her son, her anchor, her greatest treasure, her greatest achievement.

There was very little that she was really proud of, and everything good in her life paled in comparison to the things that she had done since her initial diagnosis. But Eugen saved her balance sheet. Cheerful, lively, shrewd and good-looking, the best of herself and her ex-husband in one person.

The fact she couldn't exactly be proud of her actions hadn't changed even now that she had started acting with the blessing of MI6. The deal that she had agreed to was essentially blackmail: Darling would leave her in peace so long as she delivered Arctander to him unharmed. She did not want to know anything about what the agent had planned for the narco. He certainly wasn't acting for the good of mankind.

Her encounter with the troop of agents at Minsk Airport should have been warning enough. Then it happened in France: Darling had stood in front of her in his designer suit, described to her exactly where the Life Institute was and which doctors and scientists had travelled to Minsk most recently. Although he had denied that the little troop of agents she'd encountered had been under his command, he had grinned the whole time. Kristen had had no option but to accept his offer, to defect to his team and support him with her powers, should the need arise. But that didn't mean that she couldn't be quietly preparing a counter-attack all the while.

Yet another reason to come to an arrangement with her ex. An attack from that quarter would come at Darling as if out of nowhere. MI6 definitely didn't have Anatol on its radar.

She could not allow Darling to destroy her life's work. Not Darling and not some authority or other, a state, a person – nobody! Her ex-husband would help her.

The unintentional waiting time gave rise to trains of thought that she otherwise rarely gave in to. Normally, she didn't have the peace and quiet for it. She knew that a person's soul was in the head not in any other part of the body. At first this conclusion had sounded almost ridiculous, but she had produced the proof. One of humanity's mysteries – solved.

The Death Sleepers whose brains she had successfully transplanted behaved as though they were in their old bodies, provided the effect of the trauma had been kept at bay and countered with chemistry.

Even though the deceased Patient 22 had been the most promising for long-lasting use of a stranger's body, Smyrnikov and his team had achieved some short-term successes.

The mind played a huge role. So long as you didn't allow the transplanted person to know what had happened to them, they would only be surprised about the bad state they were in: bandaged eyes, fake mirror images, they had tried many things to keep the subjects in the dark. Most of them believed the tale of an accident. They made an effort to resist the paralysis, the altered feel of the body and more blackouts. But they soon died due to the intense strain placed on the organism.

The really ground-breaking successes would happen eventually.

Eugen was just eight years old. Even if Kristen got into the cryotank soon, to preserve her mind, the doctors would still have years left to enable her son to have a sublime life. A life that surpassed everything else and could last a very long time.

She even assumed that science would make further progress in a hundred years. In her best case scenario, Eugen simply lived forever, transplanting his brain from body to body. She had prepared the path for him to do that. Her legacy to him: a new, revolutionary way of life.

At last a pair of headlights approached and slowed down.

A car emerged out of the darkness, a Seat Leon, black and used, probably stolen. Miller was sitting behind the wheel and pulled up next to Kristen.

She got into the back. 'I lost them. Korff has killed Strong and Johnny.'

'Shit.' It didn't sound entirely sympathetic. Miller drove off, using side streets to avoid running into a police checkpoint, and left the old town. Eventually they parked the car in a parking bay at the side of the road.

The wait for Darling's call began.

Kristen spotted the neon sign of an Internet café not far away. *Perfect! A chance to talk to my son!* 'B-b-be right back,' she said and got out. 'If anything happens, just c-c-call.'

She crossed the street, went through an alleyway and did a loop to approach the Internet café from behind. Miller mustn't see what she was doing.

The side entrance to the shop was unlocked and Kristen walked into the main room from the passageway that led to the toilets. 'Hello,' she said to the surprised member of staff in English. 'I need a PC with a webcam. Preferably somewhere where I will not be disturbed. Will that b-b-be okay?' She put a fifty down on the counter and pointed wordlessly to one of the bottles of vodka in the display case behind him.

'Sure.' He looked past her into the passage to the side door and patted his utility belt as though to make sure that he still had the key on him. 'Seat fourteen.' He stood up, handed her a bottle and went back to lock up.

Kristen took the vodka and sat down in the quiet corner, away from two gaming teenagers, a mid-forties man downloading something, and a babbling Indian man who was consulting with his family loudly in his native tongue. It would drown out her own conversation.

She opened the lid, drank two large gulps of vodka to help the stuttering and went online, activating the Internet camera, the speech programme and the chat programme, and then looked up Eugen.

His status said that he was busy, but there was a little green symbol illuminated after her ex-husband's username.

One click on it and she was writing to him that she needed to speak to him.

Even more vodka.

A face came into view on the screen. He had set up a lamp so that the camera was in its glare and he was barely recognisable. Every so often a part of his face, an eye, a bit of mouth or the chin emerged out of the darkness, like in the amazing shot in the film *Apocalypse Now* with General Kurtz speaking from the darkness. Her heart immediately began to beat faster at the sight of him. Her feelings for him were undiminished, still strong, her love for him not extinguished. Unfortunately the feeling was not mutual. Not any more. Not since the truth had come to light – or what he thought was the truth about her.

'Anatol,' she whispered in Russian, entranced. She drank some more of the vodka, then pushed the half-empty bottle aside.

'I'm listening, Sophia,' he spoke quietly and dismissively. He found it hard to have a conversation with her, but he did it nonetheless, for the good of the child they shared. In the background there was the soft sound of men's voices, accompanied by the clink of glasses. 'Where are you? Eugen is waiting for you.'

'I . . . am in Spain. On business,' she choked out in a whisper. *Sophia.* From the beginning, he was the only person who had called her that. An ice-cold hand burrowed into her insides, seized her heart and held it in a vice. In her mind's eye, she saw her son at the window with longing in his eyes, keeping watch for her. And she wanted to take him in her arms just as desperately. 'I'm . . . having problems,' she confessed and rested her head in her hands.

'Who?' The camera caught a section of his broad torso. He was wearing a tuxedo with a black bow tie and white shirt.

'MI6.'

Anatol's mouth came into view. The small scar to the right

of it was dark red, the memento of a knife wound. The person who had inflicted the injury on him had been fed to the dogs in little pieces. Kristen had never liked the Dobermans. The fact that they ate human flesh increased her aversion. But Eugen loved them and the dogs obeyed his instructions to the letter. 'Names?'

'Timothy Chester Darling, MI6 commander,' she whispered and connected her smartphone to the computer, uploaded a photo that she had taken of Darling and sent it to her ex-husband. 'He knows a lot about the institute, about my scientists. He could put my research at risk, Anatol, and therefore our son's health!'

His powerful hand appeared, straightening up the bow tie. A gold signet ring flashed, as well as a ring that had been a medal for bravery before being reworked. It was just one of many military achievements that he had battled to win in his first career. Literally. 'I'll take care of it. Anything else?' He spoke softly and coolly, impatient and contemptuous.

'I need more money, Anatol. For my research. I've got to have the institute moved, even if you are taking care of Darling.'

'Do you have an alternative location?'

'I was thinking of Orscha.'

The camera showed his right eye, the pale blue iris glinting like a precious stone. The firm expression from it was directed right at the lens. 'Don't you think it would be better to just drop the whole thing?'

Kristen felt a red-hot stabbing in her middle. 'Drop it?' she cried out louder than she'd intended. 'You are talking about our child's life! If I'm not successful, then he'll get this insomnia and . . . worse. You know that!'

'Yes, I know, Sophia. But there has to be an end to it,' he countered. 'You're not just putting yourself at risk with this.'

'I can't stop! This is about Eugen,' she whispered breathlessly. 'He has to be given a chance! A chance that I don't have. I'm not doing anything objectionable. In fact, I've already saved many innocent people from sudden death. Look at the victims in the stadium. If I had caught Arctander, 80,000 men, women and children would still be alive. I hunt and execute killers.' Kristen was trembling with emotion. Her ex-husband was about to betray his own flesh and blood. 'I cannot stop, Anatol. This has got to happen.'

'You are putting a lovely spin on your motives.' He turned his head to the side, the eye disappearing into the blackness, his short, brown hair appearing instead. 'You and your scientists are no better than concentration camp doctors.'

'You're hardly in a position to make moral accusations against me! You don't earn your money selling baby food,' she retorted caustically. The icy hand inside her crushed her heart more. 'Please, Anatol! Help me!'

Her ex-husband was silent. Glasses clinked in the room behind him again, his name was being called loudly by a woman.

Kristen was familiar with these events, which took place several times a year in one of his houses. There were oligarchs at the table, international millionaires, discreet representatives of political personalities from various countries. They sat there, in tuxedos and cocktail dresses, in a dress code that would have been a credit to a reception for a president.

They spoke about innocuous things, using codes all the while to conduct business, eating delicacies and deciding upon the deaths of rivals, listening to classical string quartets and typing orders on their smartphones to dispatch firing squads or detonate bombs.

Anatol couldn't go round playing the better person compared to her. They were both criminals, only their motivations were different. She actually felt superior to him, because the insights her work gained would be used by the whole of humanity. Her methods might have been questionable or morally reprehensible, she acknowledged that. But they were producing fresh insights for medicine and these would, in turn, save many lives one day.

Anatol's legal–illegal dealings, on the other hand, didn't bring about any improvements, apart from for him and his small circle – so long as you were loyal, otherwise you were fed to the dogs. That's how it went, the ruthless, selfish game that she had once participated in.

'Good,' he said in a quiet, deep voice that gave her goosebumps. 'I can transfer ten million to you immediately for the move. I'll send you the number of a transport firm that doesn't ask questions and supplies all the necessary papers.'

'Thanks,' she murmured and stared at the screen.

She was hoping to see his whole face again. Because she missed him, missed him desperately. His smell, his touch, the hours they spent together. Most of all she felt the pain of not getting to hear his laughter any more. He had taken it away from her. For ever.

'I want to expand my team of doctors,' she added.

'Even more money?'

Anatol's left hand became visible, along with a small spot between two fingers. An inconspicuous tattoo. But the spot stood for ten years in prison. The three spots between his thumb and index finger meant respectively: believe no one, have no fear of anyone, do not ask for anything.

'Please. For our son!' Kristen knew every symbol that had been etched into his skin.

The stars on his knees meant that he never knelt for anyone and served no one. The tiger on his back stood for the Siberian prison he had done time in. A compass across his chest and a cross behind his muscular shoulders said: *vory v zakone*. Thieves by law, a union of criminals who enjoyed a high level of respect. Anatol was a criminal with a good reputation as he himself said, an enemy of politics and a proudly conventional man.

She remembered a summer's day when they had been travelling in St Petersburg. Anatol had been wearing a short-sleeved shirt so that everyone could see the quotations on his arms. On the front of his right forearm it said: *'Please let everything I've experienced be a dream!'* On the back of his left arm he flaunted, *'Where are you going?'* and on the right the relevant answer: *'What the hell does that have to do with you?'* His favourite tattoo ran across the inner part of his right arm: *You should not wait for the first strike.*

Smart people had crossed the street, customers in a local bar had stood up and left, even though they didn't know Anatol.

Kristen realised that these tattoos signified a reputable thief who did not accept any authority. Among *vory*, there was only respect for people who rejected the state's authority.

Her ankhs had a different meaning: for every Death Sleeper that she had executed, a cross was added. The symbol stood for the eternal life that she had taken from a man or a woman, half memorial, half trophy. After Johnny and Strong, two more would be added.

'As soon as the move is complete, get in touch with me,' Anatol said quietly. 'Then I'll see what I can do for you.' He straightened his cufflinks, which were former medals of naval merit. 'I'll let Eugen know that you don't have any time.' His right hand thrust forward out of the darkness and moved towards the touchpad. He wanted to break the connection.

'No, wait! I want to talk to him at least!'

'You had your chance to visit him,' he replied stubbornly. 'You're not here, so you won't see him.'

'Don't be so horrible to me!' she said and felt her eyes filling with tears. 'I was looking forward to seeing him!'

'He was looking to forward to seeing you too, Sophia. Imagine what is going to happen to him when I tell him that you didn't have any time.' Now the deep voice was sharp like the cold steel of a knife. His punishment for her absence.

'Please, Anatol!' she sobbed.

'Be punctual next time. In two weeks, that is.' His tone was aloof, the camera showed his mouth and chin. 'You will have to come to Moscow. St Petersburg is not safe at the moment.'

'Why?' she asked in shock. 'What have you—?'

'Not *me*, Sophia. *You* have attracted the attention of MI6. Maybe they've taken a photo of Eugen and know more about him than I approve of.' Anatol's right cheek appeared, the muscles under the skin twitched briefly, an expression of his irritation. 'I'm checking it out, as well as dealing with the MI6 commander. Until then I'm going to use extreme caution. This is about the safety of our child. I cannot take your self-centred needs into account.'

'You're right . . . but . . . let me speak to him!' cried Kristen and gripped the monitor with one hand, as if she could stop what was happening on the other side of the camera.

But Anatol placed his hand on the touchpad – and the screen went black. The status message went red, for both his and Eugen's usernames.

Kristen slumped onto the countertop and hid her face in the crook of her arm, crying soundlessly, one hand on the edge of the screen.

She forgot the time as she sat there and shed tears of longing, tears at the pain of being separated – until she felt a hand on her shoulder.

Kristen leaped up, yanked the hairpin out of her jacket and held it out, ready to stab.

Miller was standing in front of her holding up her hands defensively. 'Easy, easy. It's me.' She looked quickly at the dark monitor. 'We've got to get going.'

'How did you find me?' Kristen lowered the needle and looked around. Nobody had taken any notice of them. The other patrons were gaming, downloading and chatting; the clerk was looking at his laptop, headphones in his ears and nodding to a beat that only he could hear.

'Mobile geolocation. Darling called. We have Korff's position.' Miller pointed to the door.

'I'm coming.' Kristen left the vodka bottle behind and followed her. She cursed herself inwardly. How could she have been so careless? She would have to kill the agent to make sure that she hadn't seen anything and told Darling about it. But at least she had the chance to tranquillise the Death Sleeper this time and use her for her own purposes, as the next test subject for her laboratory. Wherever this would be after the move.

But the Death Sleeper and Darling were not her biggest problem. She didn't trust Anatol any more, was no longer sure that he was going to stick to their deal and let her see Eugen. He considered her research pointless. How could he when their son's life was at stake?

She would call Brian as she flew to Minsk, and take a detour via Ireland on the way.

XX

He who fears death
has relinquished his life

Apocrypha, Johann Gottfried Seume

Zaragoza, Spain

Konstantin could be a very patient man when he wanted to be. But not right now. After half an hour, he shook the Death Sleeper until he woke up out of his faint. He wanted information at last. About the Death Seer, about the rings, about Jester and the role the Scandinavian had in this.

Arctander stretched, felt his face and the bump, but didn't say anything. He knew why Konstantin had done it. 'Do you have anything to drink with you?' he asked in a scratchy voice.

'No. We'll buy something on the way.'

He cleared his throat. 'By the way, you don't have to knock me out, so long as I have an attack somewhere indoors like this factory. I thought I'd tell you that before you accidentally beat me to death.'

'Do I not?' Konstantin's voice was icy. 'I wasn't sure whether all of the windows were closed properly.'

Arctander gestured towards the empty building. 'My curse expands throughout any enclosed space. A car, toilets—'

'A stadium . . .' Konstantin couldn't help saying.

Arctander steeled his jaw. 'Yes. Only people inside with me die. Nobody outside does.'

Like with me. 'Okay, I'm up to speed.' Konstantin stood up and did a few half-hearted stretches to get rid of the stiffness in his limbs. The journey to Barcelona where the Death Seer lived would take a long time. *Jester might figure out that I've bailed in the meantime.* 'Before we get going, Mr—'

'Would you mind calling me Bent?' he cut in.

'Can do. I'm Korff to you.' Only his friends called him Konstantin – or at least people he was sure he wouldn't kill. 'Can you explain to me what's going on?' He braced his hands on his hips. 'Why did you run away from the Torpor's Men? What project were you talking about Darling wanting to conduct with you?' There was one lone champion inside him who came to Jester's defence and recollected the good times. *But there were those lies that Durga had demolished. How many other times has he lied to me? But, can I believe everything Bent says, either?*

Arctander threw him an appraising look. 'How well do you know your mate Darling?'

'I thought I knew him well. What I don't have right now is enough information to get an overview of this whole confused situation.'

'I don't have that either.' Arctander sighed, still holding the place on his head where the bump was.

'Let's find out together.' Konstantin hunkered down and looked the narcoleptic in the eye. He wasn't looking so incredibly exhausted any more. Although he could have done with a shower and fresh clothes. 'What was going on?'

'Darling came to see me after . . . the thing with my family happened,' he recounted hesitantly. 'I'm from Idre Sameby, a Samian village in southern Sweden. We earned a living from reindeer breeding . . . until the day . . .' He sighed heavily. 'The narcolepsy was never truly dangerous. I had an attack once or twice a year and it lasted seconds at most. Cataplexy, yes, that did happen sometimes, but we had it under control. It was because of the cold that it wasn't that bad, I reckon. But on *that* day, it was a severe attack. I fell off my snowbike at full speed. We were driving the herd further south at the time because the tourist season in the skiing area . . . whatever. I was lying in the snow, couldn't move and was still thinking: excellent, now the herd on my side will escape and we'll have to start again. Then I suddenly felt more tired and fell asleep.' Arctander leaned his head back. You could tell that he was ashamed of what had happened. 'I thought I could hear a cracking, like a sheet of ice splintering. When I woke up, it was dark. Silent.'

Konstantin could well understand how he had felt. He knew the cracking sound from his own gift. It came as soon as he fell asleep: Death hurtling towards him to kill every living thing.

Arctander swallowed nervously. 'I found my skimobile, it had crashed into a birch tree a few metres on . . . and . . . my brother-in-law was huddled next to it. I ran over and realised that he was dead. I . . . looked for my torch and shone it around me to look for his skimobile so that . . .' The Swedish man's breathing quickened. 'They were lying around me,' he whispered, eyes wide. 'My sister, my wife and both my sons, and everywhere around them dead reindeer. The animals lay in a perfect circle, wrenched from life, and I had slept in the centre. I'm like a death magnet.' He gasped out and covered his face with his hands.

Konstantin was afraid the next attack was looming, but he wanted to hear everything. 'Then Darling came?'

'Yes,' he mumbled into the hollow of his hands. 'The incident spread through the local press, but MI6 stopped the news attracting any more attention. Darling introduced himself to me and revealed to me what had happened and what I am: a Death Sleeper.'

Konstantin thought about it. He would have put the Swedish man in his mid-forties, but it was hard to believe the death of his family had taken place more than a few years ago. *I have never heard of the curse emerging at such a late age before.* 'How old were you then?'

'It happened three years ago. I was . . . forty-two then.' Arctander let his hands drop, his fingers drawing patterns in the dirt on the factory floor. Dust and soil stuck to his damp fingers, coating them in grey and reddish-brown.

'Did the curse not have any harbingers of any kind?' Konstantin felt sympathy for the Swedish man. It wasn't uncommon for a family member to be among the first victims of a Death Sleeper, but the whole family straight away, including the children. *Poor sod.* 'Dead insects in the bedroom or—?'

Arctander looked straight ahead. 'I don't know. No idea. If there were any, what was I meant to infer from that?' He breathed deeply in and out. 'Darling took me to England, put me up somewhere in the countryside near London. In the months that followed there came a medical history, investigations with electric and electronic equipment, probes on my head, MRIs and everything you can think of. I thought the Torpor's Men wanted to get to the bottom of the curse, to switch it off and give me my life back.'

A car drove past the front of the factory. It slowed down, stopped, reversed and the engine was turned off. The headlights went out.

Konstantin signalled to Arctander to stay silent and got up to look out the window.

It was a truck with a couple inside. Right now, they were climbing into the small back seat, kissing passionately by the looks of it.

Yes, desire. He grinned and thought of Iva. The night with her, making love and the overwhelming feeling that neither of them could resist. They probably would even have done it in a fully packed tram, their feelings were that powerful. 'False alarm,' he assured the narcoleptic. 'Keep going, Bent.'

'It . . . Darling got me to drift into an attack more quickly over the course of the tests. It soon became clear to me that, for him, it was about having me fall asleep suddenly. I pretended to be oblivious. One day I eavesdropped on them. They were openly talking near me about how strong I had become and all that was possible with me. And then I realised that they had never intended to take the curse away from me.' Arctander also got up off the ground and wiped his dirty hands on his trousers. The mixture of stale deodorant and stale sweat hit Konstantin. 'They were working to strengthen the curse. Now and again they let the name Oneiros slip, but I couldn't figure that one out.'

My old codename. Konstantin had raised his arms and placed his hands on the back of his neck. He recalled his fake friend's hard sell for him to join the Torpor's Men very well. *Would they have done the same thing to me that they did to Bent? Let me fall asleep and woken me up again straight away, over and over again, to intensify my curse?*

With a narcoleptic it was of course simple to produce a Death Sleeper of enormous power in an extremely short amount of time. Arctander was perfect for that kind of training.

What does Jester have planned for him? He knew that the Torpor's Men meted out vigilante justice to criminals – but criminals rarely turned up in one place in the kind of numbers that made a Death Sleeper of Arctander's calibre necessary. That was a mystery. For now.

From outside came the couple's muffled groaning sounds. They had plunged even deeper into their passion.

'What happened next?'

Arctander moved his shoulders in circles, moistening his dry lips with his tongue. 'I stuck to the strategy of pretending to be grateful and naive, and snooped around the house. I found Darling's notes on the Reaper's Rings and Grim Reaper's Stones while snooping. Since I'd never dreamed there could be such a thing as Death Sleepers before I myself became one, I assumed these rings existed too. I researched, in secret, and found many clues. It occurred to me that people who see Death might exist. For more than a year I read the most awful rubbish on the Internet, checked every online forum, looked for miracles where a person had been snatched from the jaws of death. I made a list of doctors, faith-healers, preachers and other figures who are meant to have brought about supernatural things.'

'That was your travel itinerary.'

'Yes. The doctor in Roccastrada and a faith-healer in Venice who ran a pharmacy and promised salvation for the terminally ill. I'm just getting started.'

'How did you hit upon Marrakech?'

'Ah, it had to be there, with the Reaper's Rings and the stones. Thanks to MI6, I could use the databases of the secret services, the police and Interpol. The name Bouler appeared many times in relation to auctions of historic jewellery. He was suspected of dealing in stolen rings and recut precious stones. And he's also meant to own two stones that, based on their provenance, fit into the category of blood diamonds. I travelled there to ask Bouler specifically about the Grim Reaper's Stones. I had hardly begun when he wrongly took me for an errand boy for Ruben Hoya. I played along and had him show me the Death Rings. When Bouler told me about Harlequin's Death, I could hardly believe my luck and assured him I was picking it up for Hoya and would bring the money to him that same evening. I still had enough money from the MI6 accounts in the hotel. I went and got it and returned to the shop. But then . . . everything descended into chaos. Somebody shot at me. Bouler pursued me, then you turned up.' He shook himself. 'Then the attack . . .'

Konstantin nodded. He could see the shoot-out as well as the dead in Djemaa el Fna in his mind's eye. *It wasn't his fault. Jester turned him into this. That stupid arsehole!*

Arctander needed a few seconds to regain his composure. 'Since Bouler was dead, I travelled to Madrid, met up with

Hoya's daughter and I pretended I wanted to sell Harlequin's Death in order to get to speak to Hoya.'

'But what on earth would possess you to go into a packed football stadium?' Konstantin tried to put his question as calmly as possible and yet couldn't stop himself sounding critical.

'I just had to go there,' Arctander replied in a hoarse voice. 'Please understand! All kinds of characters are on my trail and the quicker I could be rid of the curse the less interesting I would be. To Darling . . . and that guy with the revolver.'

'His name is Thielke and he's a Death Sleeper, he—'

'I know. He was in the stadium and tried to shoot me.' Arctander moved his left leg. 'Two graze wounds. If I hadn't had any cover, I would be dead now.'

That would be better for everyone. Konstantin was immediately sorry for the thought, but quite frankly it was true. It *would* have been better for the 80,000 visitors to the stadium. *He can't help it*, he told himself again. 'Why did you have to go there?'

'The doctor. A Death Seer. She was there. She's a Barcelona fan. I found out that she would be sitting in the VIP lounge and . . . I thought, I . . . the tablets—' Arctander burst into tears. 'I was so sure. So sure! And now all of those people are dead! She wasn't even there. It was pointless. I went . . .' He sobbed and suddenly crumpled in front of Konstantin. He fell silent, falling to the floor of the factory with ramrod straight limbs.

A cataplexy attack. Konstantin placed his jacket underneath Arctander's head so that he was lying more comfortably, and waited. There was nothing else he could do.

He wondered how Arctander knew that the doctor was a

Death Seer. Did he have legitimate reasons for his assumption, or was he indulging a false hope? Again, Konstantin had to wait for answers that only the narcoleptic could give him.

The couple's soft moaning noises had become a loud groaning, man and woman trying to outscream each other, she in Spanish and he in a language Konstantin couldn't place.

Whatever they're doing, it sounds good. He looked at Arctander who opened his eyes wide then lowered his eyelids and went limp. The cataplexy had turned into a narcoleptic attack.

Konstantin heard Death careering towards them a moment later. There was a crackling and rustling around him as though he were standing on a piece of ice as it split to join an ice floe. *Here he is. Filled with rage, angry, vengeful. Looking for us and for every life that he can destroy.* The sound gave him goosebumps, the fine little hairs on the back of his neck stood up.

The sounds of passion in front of the factory suddenly broke off. The couple had probably reached their climax and were now in a post-coital haze. The rustling stopped too. That meant that Death had gone away again because there was nothing to kill in the vast space.

Or else ... no! A terrifying suspicion struck Konstantin. He looked at Arctander, did a visual sweep of the factory to check all the windows really were closed, then looked back at the pick-up truck – there was a dead pigeon lying in front of it. *Shit, no!*

He climbed down quickly, went to the truck and tried to open the door.

Locked.

He tried to peer in, listening intently, but there was no sound coming from inside. *This cannot be happening!* He caved in the passenger door window with his elbow, unlocked it and looked into the truck bed.

The couple was lying on a blanket, him behind and slightly on top of her. The cab smelled of steamy bodies, of passion, of faint perfume and car tyres. The couple's eyes were closed. They looked like they had nodded off in the middle of sex.

Konstantin swallowed. He refrained from scrambling over to them and feeling for their pulses. The Grim Reaper knew no mercy. *Bent's usual limit no longer applies.* With the narcoleptic sleep-wake experiments, Jester had made him pass beyond the conditions of the curse. Walls and enclosed spaces no longer mattered.

He went back to the factory, appalled, and contemplated Bent Arctander, the most powerful Death Sleeper in the world.

What is capable of stopping you now? You are worse than any bomb, gas, poison or radiation. Konstantin's eyes fixed on the stone that he had used to knock the man out earlier. *Can I even risk travelling with you through residential areas? How many people are going to die just because of you?*

There was a simple, effective alternative to meeting the doctor and the precious hope that it was possible to speak to the Grim Reaper.

Konstantin stooped down and picked up the lump of rock, weighing it in his hand.

Madrid, Spain

Thielke felt that the day for departure had come, irrespective of his missing lower leg prostheses. Carola Hoya was being nicer to him every day, but the interviews and the occasional detox were still happening. He felt he was being stalled. He had to stop Arctander.

He leaped out of bed, hopped forwards on his left leg and made his way to the wardrobe, where clothes had supposedly been left for him. Right now, he was wearing nothing but a surgical gown.

When he opened the door and found nothing but a hospital vest, he felt vindicated in his theory: there was no plan to release him any time soon.

That won't stop me. Thielke looked around. The windows were locked and secured, and on top of that there was the video surveillance. He didn't know whether there was a camera in his room, but he would soon find out. Hopefully nobody would think a cripple capable of preparing an escape.

It's time for lunch, so . . . He positioned himself next to the door and waited.

Footsteps were approaching on the other side and then stopped. There was a knock and the door swung open.

Thielke saw Señora Hoya coming in – and with his balled up fist, he punched her in the middle of her pretty face. He had always been in favour of gender equality.

She fell to the floor with a quiet squeak. The food tray went with her, the vegetables, pasta and brown sauce splattering her dark grey-blue patterned dress and white jacket. She lay there on the marble tiles, her eyes closed.

'That hit home,' he muttered and dragged her into the room, examined her and took every key he could find, along with her wallet and the mobile. He tied her up with strips torn from the bed sheet and placed her in the corner of the room with a blindfold on.

Thielke hopped out of the room, locked it and set off on the hunt for clothes. He didn't want to waste much time. He looked through the rooms. One turned out to be the butler's room. He found a black suit in it that more or less fit him – only the missing lower leg and trouser leg dangling down looked strange.

Thielke checked Carola Hoya's set of keys and found the car key: a BMW, something expensive. 'I hope it's an automatic,' he muttered as he went looking for the way out. He vaguely remembered the route to the library, but the villa proved to be full of winding corridors.

Hopping was also extremely strenuous. He wished he could find a wheelchair or at least an office chair that he could use to move down the corridors.

After passing through a set of high double doors, he finally made it to an outside staircase.

Thielke was just about to slide down the banister when he heard Señor Hoya's voice. He was making a phone call in English, the sound was coming from one of the rooms below. *When I'm so nearly outside.* Thielke ducked down behind the balustrade.

'. . . I can only say it again, my friend. I . . . yes, I swear it to you.' Footsteps sounded, Hoya was moving up the stairs. 'The Harlequin's Death is responsible. It was at the place where the accidents happened every time.'

He was speaking to someone about the Reaper's Ring that Arctander and Korff were after. Was there really something to that story? Thielke peered around the corner.

Hoya was standing on the steps, the mobile pressed to his right ear and leaning against the banister. He was listening carefully to the person on the other end, his face showing the stress he was under. He was drumming a rhythm on his lean chest with the other hand. Finally, he went on slowly, annoyance etched on his face. 'Well, nothing can be done about that. I'll let you know as soon as the thanatologist gets in touch.' He lowered his arm and ended the call without saying goodbye, hurrying up the remaining steps.

At first, Thielke had wanted to let him simply go by, but there was one item missing that was vital to his happiness: *I want the LeMat back.*

Just before Hoya got to the last step, Thielke sprang up and barged into him, so that the Spaniard lost his balance. He screamed as he fell backwards down the steps.

Thielke slid down the banisters after him and even reached the ground before Hoya did. '*Hola!* as they say in your neck of the woods,' he greeted him mockingly. The man in front of him was bleeding through the nose, his right arm at an unnatural angle as though it were either broken or dislocated. 'I asked your daughter to let me go many times. Since my wish wasn't granted, my departure became more unceremonious.' He pulled the dazed man to his feet and dealt him a punch in the mouth. 'Where is my revolver?' Another punch knocked out two of Hoya's teeth. 'I swear, I will get every single—'

'Study,' mumbled the groaning Spaniard.

'With the ammunition? And my papers?'

'*Sí.*'

'Then let's go.' Thielke turned him around, placed his arms on the Spaniard's shoulders and hopped after him to the study. There, Hoya really did give him back the LeMat, as well as the ammunition that was still left. Twenty bullets and a full barrel, and the round of shot had been replaced too.

'Sit down,' Thielke commanded, pointing at him with the revolver as he jumped onto the desk.

Hoya sat down in an armchair, slowly took a handkerchief out of his pocket and dabbed the blood off his lips with it, then pressed it against his lips. 'Piss off,' he muttered in a hiss.

'Ah, the fine Spanish way.' Thielke grinned broadly.

Hoya turned his head and looked stoically out the window, holding his arm.

'Tell your crazy daughter to leave me alone. If I see her anywhere near me, I will shoot her immediately. And that's about it. In farewell, I'll give you something for the pain. Always helps, but gives you a headache later.' Thielke raised his hand and dealt Hoya a blow on the temple with the butt of the LeMat. He slumped in his seat with a wheezing sound.

Thielke left the room quickly and grabbed a broom leaning against the wall as he passed. He flipped it so the bristles pointed upwards and used it as a makeshift crutch. He could walk much more easily and quickly with it.

Thielke went out through the front door. The *señora*'s BMW was parked right in front, but unfortunately the car wasn't an automatic. *Huh.* He hobbled on and threw the keys down a storm drain in the street. He kept an eye out for anyone that might want to stop him as he hurried to the closest metro station.

The Hoya interlude had used up days. Important days. Arctander might be long gone.

The leads and clues to the narcoleptic's travel itinerary that he had so painstakingly worked out weren't worth anything any more. He was back at zero with no knowledge of what Arctander was planning next.

Thielke found a bus stop before he reached the underground station. One of the lines went to the main train station. There would be ATMs there and, above all, a pharmacy to buy insulin and also nicotine patches. *If the pill-pushers refuse to give me anything without a prescription, I have the LeMat.* Without the symptoms of the detox and with sweet things in his belly he would be able to think better than he could now, feeling as edgy, hypoglycaemic and hungry as he did.

The moment he reached the train station he bought and smoked a cigar, and wolfed down his first hamburger followed by a 99 ice cream. Once under the influence of nicotine, sugar and fat, an idea formed in his head.

With a bit of luck, his plan would put him back on Arctander's trail.

Zaragoza, Spain

'Slow down,' said Kristen. Looming up ahead of them was the factory where the most recent geolocation showed Korff to be. An old pick-up truck was parked by the side of the road.

She noticed the dead pigeon next to the wheel. On the alert now, she looked around more carefully.

She spotted more pigeons and crows on the pavement, on the streets, on the roofs, and three dead cats too . . .

'Looks like one of our friend's attacks,' Miller concluded.

'In a public street?' Kristen thought about Marrakech,

about the stadium. 'Why are the police not here yet?' She opened the door. 'And why did Korff stay in the factory?'

Kristen got out, went over to the pick-up truck and cast a glance through the broken window. Two dead bodies. She drew Miller's attention to her discovery and then climbed into the factory through a window.

The enormous room lay empty before her.

She prowled around, finding evidence of two different pairs of shoes. In one corner she saw a bloodstain and drag marks on the floor that led to a door that was ajar. The smartphone was there too, the one that Darling's specialists had homed in on.

Korff had shaken them off and, what's more, had gone with the narco. If Korff had killed Arctander, the body would still be lying here. She could judge the thanatologist pretty well by now: it was significant that he had fled with the target.

Miller bolted across to where she was standing. She had drawn her Beretta 93R, a fully automatic pistol. She obviously feared an ambush. 'Is he gone?'

'Looks like it.' Kristen stepped through the door into a backyard lit by stars that opened onto a street. 'Yes, they're gone.' She turned to her comrade. 'I have a question. Why is Korff suddenly protecting the narcoleptic from us?'

Miller looked her directly in the eye. 'I have no idea what he has planned for him.'

Someone untrained would have believed her. 'That's not quite true, is it?' Kristen pointed at her. 'You know things that Korff only found out in conversation with the narco. So he vanished with Arctander instead of meeting up with us.' Her eyes narrowed. 'What does Darling have planned for the narco?'

'I think you're getting carried away by an *idée fixe*.' Miller took subtle little steps backwards to put some distance between the baroness and herself. 'And you ought to have asked Strong or Johnny that. They were working for the Torpor's Men and MI6. I'm just a—'

Kristen followed her, a predatory smile on her lips. 'You think I wouldn't find out about the people I'm supposedly working with? You and Darling were together for a year and you definitely still like him enough to help him. That's why he wanted you as a representative of the Sleepers in this group, a confidante who would act in the way he wants.' She raised her arms, despite bandages and sling. 'Look! I'm unarmed. Do you know why I go without a firearm?'

Miller raised her arm, training the Beretta on her. 'Stop!'

'You've seen the crows, pigeons and cats. The dead couple in the pick-up. And there will be more corpses in the flats and houses around this factory because Arctander fell asleep.' The agent's eyes were locked on Kristen. Like a rabbit in front of a snake. 'Up till this point his gift has only worked in closed spaces. Why is that changing?'

Miller's face went blank, the finger on the trigger twitched.

'Ah! You're meant to shoot me if I ask too many questions?' Kristen's arms were still raised. 'Did Darling order that or the head of the Deathslumberers?'

Miller fired. The Beretta spat out a volley at Kristen.

She dropped with a loud scream – even though the bullets had missed her. She landed in the dirt and lay there as she heard her opponent's footsteps approaching to give her the fatal shot.

Kristen spun over and flung the hairpin that she had drawn as she fell.

The thin piece of metal sped forwards like an arrow, boring into Miller's right eye socket. She shrieked and shot at Kristen again, the bullet missing its target. She grabbed the hairpin and yanked it out. Blood and a murky fluid oozed out of the wound and ran down her cheek and chin.

Kristen kicked her opponent's legs out from under her and rammed her heels down on the fallen woman's chest, neck and head until her fingers let go of the gun's handle. She immediately threw herself on Miller, grabbed her by the throat with one hand and pressed her forehead against her opponent's temple. Her altered gift kicked in, a tingling spread through the front part of her skull. 'Quiet or you'll be dead in a second,' she snarled. 'I'm making you visible to the Grim Reaper and I bet he's looking forward to coming for you.'

Miller could feel what Kristen was unleashing and went stiff as a board. 'It was an order,' she whined. 'Please, I—'

'From Darling?'

'Yes! He said that I was to shoot you if you snooped too much.'

Kristen congratulated herself on having already spoken to her ex about Darling. At least that problem would soon be solved. 'What does Darling want with the narco?'

'I don't know.'

Kristen intensified her gift and Miller whimpered. 'Then tell me what you *think* you know!'

'Oneiros,' she stammered. 'He set up a project called Oneiros. He and other select Death Sleepers were working on it.'

'What is it supposed to be? Who is involved?'

'There are a good dozen of us, we didn't include the Thugee. Project Oneiros is meant to ensure greater power and influence for us,' she explained timidly.

'So the organisations don't know anything about it?'

Miller shook her head. 'No. Timothy approached me a year ago. He thought we were doing our governments' dirty work without really standing a chance against crimes and corruption. He wanted to set a more drastic example than a few select murders of gangsters. Something that would prevent humanity from committing crimes for ever.'

Kristen laughed cheerlessly. 'Darling, the world's saviour? And for that he needs a narcoleptic Death Sleeper of all things?'

Miller closed her eyes, she was panting more than breathing. 'It's a question of killing the dirtiest swines in politics as well as in the ranks of organised crime. The proof that nobody is a match for us and nothing can guard against us. No bunkers and no money in the world, no prisoners, no entourage.'

'And you call yourselves Oneiros.' Kristen believed the woman. It fit with Darling, the ambitious MI6 agent for whom it was never enough to eliminate one criminal after the other. He wanted all of them and he wanted to be at the top of the Death Sleepers.

At the same time, Kristen assumed he had told Miller a fairy tale to draw her to his side. To dissuade humanity from crime through a kind of shock therapy was a lovely idea, but nothing more. It couldn't work. She thought of Mexico, of the cartels. The bosses wouldn't give a shit about how many of their people snuffed it. And if the bosses themselves bit the dust, new ones emerged.

Kristen suddenly hesitated as a surprising thought occurred to her: the only way to stop people committing crime for the rest of time was to wipe them out. But surely Darling wasn't that crazy. But how far would Arctander's Death summons reach once he had been hounded from one narcoleptic attack to the next, day after day for a year or two?

'Can I stand up please?' Millers asked, choking. 'My eye—'

'Quiet.' She shuddered. In the end only Death Sleepers would be left, the new and sole inhabitants of earth. Kristen shook her head. This idea was too insane, too over the top, too terrible. Surely Darling just wanted to do something relatively harmless, like blackmail governments using Arctander. Oneiros was probably nothing more than a criminal gang made up of Death Sleepers who wanted to make a real profit out of the gift.

Miller was crying, motionless. Her injured eye had stopped bleeding, but it was watering constantly.

Kristen felt no sympathy, instead contemplating how to proceed. Should she track Darling down and beat the truth about Project Oneiros out of him? Or should she keep chasing Arctander and Korff?

'We're going to the airport,' she said to Miller. 'My jet is waiting.' She removed her forehead from her opponent's temple and stood up. She picked the hairpin up off the ground and put it away, then took the Beretta.

'We?' echoed the woman and rubbed her head hard. Her face was distorted with pain. She sat up, took a handkerchief out of her pocket and pressed it against her injured eye. 'I have to go to a doctor, the—'

'You're coming with me.' Kristen positioned herself above the woman, the barrel of the gun pointed at her. 'I will show you things that you'll feel enthusiastic about.' She smiled. 'Darling is not the only one running projects.'

XXI

If death is just a sleep,
how can you fear dying?
Have you not felt it before,
when you slip away at night?

Poems, Friedrich Hebbel

Barcelona, Spain

The car shot across the motorway towards Barcelona. Konstantin sat at the wheel. Bent Arctander lay slumped in the passenger seat with a makeshift head dressing on.

Actually, it's dangerous to bring him into the city. But there's no way round it. After the first blow with the rock, he hadn't been able to kill the Death Sleeper. For one thing, he was in no position to condemn him, and for another, Arctander held the key to Konstantin's own redemption. So he had stolen a car, dragged the Swedish man into it and set off.

Arctander groaned, opened his eyes and vomited in the footwell. Konstantin's blow had given him concussion. He felt his head dumbly, flipped the sun visor down and looked at himself in the small mirror. 'What did you do, Korff?'

'It happened while we were getting out of there,' he lied. 'I carried you out of the factory, you fell off my shoulder and banged into an iron ledge. Sorry.' He pointed to a road sign flashing past. 'We're already in Barcelona, the exit for the inner city is just about to come up. Where do we find the doctor?'

Arctander retched, vomiting out the window as they drove this time. Behind them there was the noise of agitated beeping and headlights were turned on full beam in protest.

It's my own fault that I have to endure this stink now. Konstantin put on his indicator and turned off for the city. Barcelona. 1.6 million residents. Thousands of streets. And no satnav.

Arctander coughed and spat out the window one last time. 'She's called Isabella Dolores Sastre and she's a professor,' he explained. 'She has a general medicine and homeopathy practice in the Carrer dels Esports.'

'I suggest we buy a city map first.' Konstantin pulled in at the next petrol station. 'Something to eat or drink?'

Arctander nodded and looked at what he'd vomited up at his feet. 'A new car would be good too. It stinks here.'

Grinning, Konstantin got out to pick up some supplies in the petrol station shop, plus two air-freshener trees and a map of the city so that Arctander could guide him through Barcelona. The news programme on the television above the till was reporting a mysterious mass death in Zaragoza, around an abandoned factory. According to the authorities, the bodies of 211 people had been discovered in an area near the inner city. All animals in the region had died from the same unknown causes.

I'd better not tell him. He's giving himself enough of a hard time as it is.

The newsreader was speculating about terrorists and a possible connection to the other attacks. The police were not making any comment on it, but were requesting assistance in the search for several people involved in a shooting incident in the pedestrianised zone that had left two people dead. The identikit pictures of the suspects that were flashed up luckily didn't look like him or Arctander. When they showed the faces of Johnny and Strong as unidentified victims, his surprise grew. *Has the baroness already ended her collaboration with Darling? That was quick.*

He went back to the car, drove on a few metres to the vacuum cleaner machine and simply hoovered up the vomit before unwrapping the air-freshener trees. Meanwhile, Arctander was studying the map and looking for the shortest route as he ate and drank a little. Although, even this didn't put much colour back in his face, he looked like he might keel over any moment. The concussion had not exactly improved his condition.

'You should clean yourself up. They have a shower for long-distance drivers here,' Konstantin advised him. 'You look like a tramp.'

'I haven't got the nerve to shower.'

'And you *smell* like a tramp. Do you want Sastre to turn green when she gets a whiff of you?'

Arctander looked over at the petrol station, then down at himself and lowered his head to smell himself. 'Are there clothes in there too?' He slipped two tablets out of his dispenser and put them in his mouth, washing them down with lemonade.

Konstantin nodded and threw a few banknotes to him over the car roof. 'I'll wait while . . . or should I come with you?'

'No. I'm feeling pretty good,' he replied and pushed the map over to Konstantin. 'I've marked the route with a pen.' Arctander went towards the petrol station and disappeared around the corner where the toilets were.

Konstantin watched him go and had to fight the urge to follow him and make sure that he didn't get an attack – or turn the attack into a blackout with a well-aimed smack to the head. *At some point that's going to do him lasting damage.* He would ask the doctor for chloroform or something similar.

Konstantin took a look at the route. A small ring marked Isabella Dolores Sastre's practice. Arctander must trust him, considering he had let him have the address before he himself went to take a shower. They had around five kilometres to go.

In less than half an hour it would be clear whether he and Arctander had been chasing a false hope based on fairy tales and legends. Or whether the Grim Reaper really did reveal himself to the woman and it was possible to negotiate with him.

God, what I wouldn't give for that! Konstantin got out his mobile wanting to call Iva – but decided against it after all. He would see her face-to-face soon, hold her hand and perhaps even spend nights with her without having to creep away afterwards. *I will lie next to her, hold her in my arms and fall asleep.* The thought was overwhelming. *I'm looking forward to it so much!*

His mobile beeped, he had a text message.

It was from Jester:

YOU HAVE ABUSED MY TRUST. BRING ME THE NARCO, OLD
BOY, AND I WILL FORGET WHAT YOU HAVE DONE.

Definitely not. I'm freeing your plaything from his curse. Konstantin
didn't reply.

He took the battery and chip out of the smartphone and
put everything into his pockets separately. He had almost
forgotten he could be geolocated.

Arctander came back, his hair still wet, dressed in an FC
Barça tracksuit. 'They didn't have anything else. But I'm sure
it will get us bonus points with the doctor.'

Konstantin thought about the dead in the football stadium.
He found it disconcerting that the narcoleptic was wearing a
football kit, of all things. He got in without a word, Arctander
sat next to him and they drove off, following the route they
had chosen.

They got lost twice, but after a few dodgy U-turns they
made it to their destination. Konstantin was so worked up
by then that he forgot to ask what made Arctander so sure
that Sastre was a Death Seer.

The practice was in an old building in the north west of
the city.

It looked like a hotel from the outside. According to a
Plexiglas sign in the front garden, in addition to Prof. Dr. Med.
I.D. Sastre, General Practitioner & Homeopathist, there was
also a massage parlour, gym and management consultancy
in the imposing building.

Konstantin parked in one of the gym's spaces. His heart
was beating faster and faster. 'All okay, Bent?'

'I'll do my best,' Arctander replied uncertainly. 'Just about everything that I can take to combat the illness is in my bloodstream. But I can't promise anything.' He breathed deeply in and out. 'If needs be, you will have to intervene.'

Konstantin didn't like the sound of that last part. 'Pull yourself together.'

They got out and crossed towards the main entrance. Walking through the lobby, they came to a glass lift, which brought them to the fourth floor where Sastre had her practice.

Countless thoughts were racing through Konstantin's head, he could feel his hands getting clammy. It was about to become clear whether all hope had been in vain – or not.

'Where do we start?' Arctander whispered to him as they stepped through the door and into the waiting room with a reception on the left hand side.

'With the truth.' Konstantin nodded to the receptionist behind the counter and went up. 'Hello. My name is Karl Schmidt. My friend, Hans Müller,' he pointed to Arctander, 'has an urgent problem. An emergency. His heart. Can the professor listen quickly to see if everything is okay?'

The young woman looked at the narcoleptic and noted his weakened state, which neither the brand new tracksuit nor the overpowering smell from the air-freshener trees could cover up. 'Come with me. I'll take you to Treatment Room Two. The professor will be right with you.' She led the way. 'Do you have an overseas health insurance document?'

'No. We'll pay cash.' Konstantin handed her 200 euro. 'That should suffice, I think?'

'I'm sure you'll get some of this back. I'll sort it out with the professor.' She opened the door to a room with high ceilings and dark wood furniture, along with a treatment bed. 'Please strip to the waist, Señor Müller. Then I can put the electrodes in place. For the ECG.'

Arctander hesitantly obeyed the request.

'Would you please wait outside, Señor?'

'No. We're partners, and I don't want to leave him alone,' Konstantin replied.

'I understand, Señor Schmidt.' The receptionist wired Arctander up and switched on the ECG, then left the room.

The *beeeep, beeeep, beeeep* sound started at 120 beats per minute.

Arctander's heart rate was fast, which Konstantin could understand. *Same here.*

It was taking a while for the doctor to come, and both men put up with this silently and impatiently. Arctander's heart rate was rising, reaching 165.

'Breathe in, breathe out,' Konstantin instructed him, placing a soothing hand on his shoulder. His pulse slowed down.

Five minutes later a woman in a white coat came in, whom Konstantin estimated to be around fifty. Underneath the white coat, he could see a grey blouse and grey skirt, her feet in comfy white slip-ons. She had tamed her black hair into an up-do, and she had round, rimless glasses on her narrow nose.

'Hello, Señores.' She shook them by the hand one after the other, looked at the ECG and the regular deviations on it. 'Well, it's in great shape. A little fast, but on first impressions, nothing that I would worry about.' She took the stethoscope out of her pocket. 'I'll listen to your heart, Señor Müller.'

The truth. Konstantin stepped closer to her, to prevent her escape, if needs be. 'Professor, we're not here on account of his heart,' he began. He was in an indescribable emotional state: hope, fear, disgrace and foolishness crowded together. 'My name is Korff, his is Bent Arctander. We are suffering from the same problem, and you were recommended to us as a specialist.' This is the moment. A brief hesitation, a deep breath, before he really came out with it: 'Apparently you can speak to Death.'

Sastre had placed the end of the stethoscope on Arctander's bare chest. For a moment she didn't move, blinking twice before regaining her composure. 'I don't know what you mean by that, Señor.' She looked politely at Arctander. 'Your heartbeat is—'

'I was at Professor Auro's. In Roccastrada,' the narcoleptic said in a low voice. 'I wanted to ask him for advice, but he referred me to you. Before he could tell me why you—' He pressed his lips together. His pulse had quickened to 150 again and was still rising.

'The chlorine gas accident,' she said and pressed some buttons on the ECG machine, and a different diagram showed up on the small screen. 'My poor colleague. I was shocked when I heard.'

'It was not an accident. You know that.' Konstantin nodded towards Arctander. 'It was him. In Paris, in Marrakech, in the stadium in Madrid. Where he wanted to meet you, Professor. You're only still alive because you weren't there. Does the term Death Sleeper mean anything to you?'

Sastre remained remarkably calm and turned her gaze to Arctander. 'What did Auro tell you about me?'

'That you can see Death ... and ...' The narcoleptic faltered. 'That you can talk to him.' He took her hand and his heartbeat went up to 180. 'I . . . please! You've *got* to speak to him. I want to be rid of this curse and be a normal person.' The despair distorted his tired face, tears burst over his lower eyelids and rolled down his stubbly cheeks. 'I want to fall asleep without fear, I want to be uninteresting, Professor. I want . . . to go back to my life, back to Idre Sameby and . . .' He broke into uncontrollable sobs. 'Nobody else should die because of me,' he gasped. His pulse had levelled off at 190.

At first, Konstantin wanted to cut in, but he swallowed hard. He felt for Arctander, whose desires were the same as his own. The man's despair made more of an impression than anything else Konstantin could have said. *I can tell that she knows exactly what he's talking about.*

Sastre lifted one arm and cautiously placed her hand on his. 'You are a very, very disturbed man, Señor.'

Arctander's eyes widened in surprise. 'But . . . I'm not making this up!'

'I have colleagues who can help you.' Sastre smiled and took a step back. Konstantin kept an eye on her movements. 'To be on the safe side, I'll prescribe you a little something for your nerves. Something homeopathic. It can't do you any harm.' She went over to her desk and pulled open a drawer. 'Ah, I still have a packet of zincum metallicum here. Take—'

Arctander leaped up. 'I'm not making this up!' he shouted, beside himself with despair, and rushed towards her. The cables came loose from the probes and sprang off. 'Professor, I—'

'Wait, Bent!' Konstantin stopped him pouncing on the woman. Sastre was denying her gift, and there was sure to be a reason for that. And it wasn't that she simply had no gift. Maybe she didn't believe them, or had had some bad experiences. *She's afraid that what happened to Auro will happen to her too!* 'Listen, Professor. Whatever proof you need that two Death Sleepers are standing in front of you, we'll produce it for you,' he swore to her.

Sastre fixed her grey-blue eyes on him. 'Apparently you need the same medicine as your friend,' she replied coolly, handing him the piece of paper on which she'd written some names. 'These are good psychiatrists. It would be best if the two of you left now.'

Arctander was just about to dive across the table with a scream, but he couldn't get out of Konstantin's grip.

Suddenly his body went limp and soft as jelly; he was collapsing. His eyes closed, his head sank onto his chest.

No, not here! Not in the middle of Barcelona! 'Professor, he's having an attack!' Konstantin shouted in a panic, laying Arctander on the carpet. Bent was already asleep and summoning the Grim Reaper. *He will bring death in the thousands. Sastre will snuff it first.* That long-held hope, now within his reach, was in danger. He felt hot and was sweating.

The menacing rustling was already audible.

I cannot let this happen. I brought him to Barcelona, I'm responsible for this. Konstantin looked around for a heavy object and found nothing, nothing at all. *If I can't knock him out . . .* He let out a desperate scream and reached for the desk where he grabbed a pair of scissors. *My fault!* He raised the long, blunt blade with both arms above his head to stab hard. Through the chest, into the heart. *I've got to . . .*

'Wait!' Sastre lowered her eyelids and spread both hands out on the tabletop. Her lips formed soundless words, her body was as stiff as a poker and her upper body was ramrod straight.

And the high-pitched rustling stopped.

How . . . does that work? Konstantin got up and watched. All that could be heard was a gentle whispering.

A minute went by.

Konstantin didn't know what to do. He looked back and forth between the narcoleptic and the doctor, glanced at the door and hoped that nobody was going to come in.

Another sixty seconds of her constantly uttering inaudible words went by.

Konstantin was spellbound, shudders ran down his spine. He thought he could detect a faint smell of flowers. *Lilies. How appropriate.* He wondered whether she was triggering the phenomenon or whether Arctander's curse was changing.

Finally the tension in her subsided and she sank, panting onto the table.

Arctander opened his eyes at the same moment, groaning and looking around, disoriented.

Konstantin helped him to his feet and looked at Sastre. 'What . . . did you do?' he said in a hoarse voice. *She can do it! She really can. She put a stop to the Reaper!*

The professor coughed and straightened up uncertainly, staggered to a cupboard and opened it. There were bottles of mineral water and vodka inside. 'Now I understand why Massimo sent you to me.' First, she drank two big gulps of alcohol, then some of the water. 'He knows you both very well,' she said quietly.

'Death?' Konstantin wanted to confirm.

'Yes. And he hates you. He especially hates Arctander,

to such an incredible degree that I've never seen anything like it.' She knocked back more vodka, supporting herself with one hand on the cupboard. 'Never,' she murmured and shuddered. 'Never before. Massimo would not have been able to handle the rage.'

Konstantin brought Arctander over to an armchair and then went over to her. 'What did you discuss with the Reaper?'

Ashen-faced, she placed the bottle to her lips again. 'I don't *speak* to him. I soothe him.'

'That means he's gone?' Arctander was clinging to the arm of the chair.

She nodded, exhausted. Another swig of vodka. She had already emptied the bottle by a third. It didn't look like this was her first time.

'Nobody dead?' Konstantin tried to wrest the bottle gently from her.

But she held onto it tightly and threw him a reproachful look. 'No.'

'Then ... are we rid of the curse?' Arctander placed his hands together as though in prayer and looked pleadingly at her.

Sastre walked past Konstantin, the bottle in her hand, and threw herself down in her office chair. 'No. I can't do that.' She looked at the men, one after the other. 'Neither I, nor the Grim Reaper himself can take this gift away from you. All that I can do is placate him.'

All for nothing ... Konstantin could have screamed.

Arctander curled into a ball and buried his face in his hands.

Shannon, Ireland

Kristen was sitting in the passenger area of the jet, drinking a glass of sparkling wine and looking at the selection of pills that she had lined up in front of herself. Most of them were white, some red, some greenish, some were capsules with little multi-coloured balls rattling around inside.

She needed every single one to combat the effects of the insomnia, blackouts, dizziness and sight problems. The sparkling wine helped with the stuttering.

Her laptop was on the table in front of her, the messages piling up in her email inbox. From Darling, from Death Sleepers, from Smyrnikov, from friends that she had been trying to contact.

Kristen didn't have the time or inclination to answer them.

Miller was groaning in the background. The Death Sleeper lay tied on the floor, with a gag in her mouth so that she couldn't scream. There was a piece of gauze stuck to her injured eye. Every two hours, once she'd woken up, Kristen had anaesthetised her so that she didn't lapse into a real sleep and attract attention.

Kristen took the first tablet and swallowed it. Then the second, the third and so on until she had choked down all nine. A full meal, you could say.

She had sent Darling a text saying she and Miller were on their way to Ireland because she had found evidence that Arctander and Korff were trying to get there. Which was, of course, a lie: she was just making a stopover in Shannon to pick up people who had nothing to do with Darling or Death Sleepers.

In the task bar at the bottom of the laptop, the little green status light for Eugen's chat came on.

Kristen was surprised. Anatol had forbidden Eugen to chat online without his express permission, no matter who it was with. And they hadn't arranged anything today.

She activated the camera and waited excitedly to see her son. And there were Eugen's features materialising on the screen. 'Hey, champ!' she greeted him cheerfully. 'Did Papa let—'

'Mama! I miss you!' he whispered. Judging by the background, he was sitting in a box or in a wardrobe. 'I miss you so much!'

She could tell that he was agitated and afraid. 'Does Papa know that you have the computer?'

He shook his brown mane.

'What's wrong? Did something happen?' Her throat was closing as she looked into his brown eyes and realised how distressed he was.

'Papa said he doesn't want us to see each other,' he blurted out. 'He said that you don't deserve it because you didn't come the last time.' He began to cry, snot running from his nose. 'And he also said that you don't love me.'

'Oh no, no! You mustn't cry, Eugen. You've misunderstood Papa,' she tried to soothe him. 'I really wanted to come, believe me, but . . . the weather was bad. My jet wouldn't start.'

He nodded, sniffling and wiping his tears away with his right sleeve. 'So we'll still see each other?'

'Of course, Eugen! You're my son, aren't you? I always want to see you, you've got to believe me.' Kristen forced herself to smile as she dug her fingers into the tabletop with anxiety and fear. 'When did Papa say this?'

'The day before yesterday.'

'To you or—'

Eugen gave an exaggerated shake of the head, the way that children like to do. 'No. On the phone. To a man that he called Tujev.'

'Oh right. No, that was Tugurjev. An old friend of Papa's. I'm sure they were talking about something else.' Kristen longed to take him in her arms, to hold him and stroke him so that his fear subsided.

But right now she also wished someone would come to take away her fear. Her heart had almost stopped at the name Tugurjev: a lawyer, the best that you could get in Russia and someone who knew lots of judges personally. The cases he took always ended in his opponent's defeat. It looked like Anatol wanted to set his mate on her. Custody. Visitation ban. Separation. Definitively. If Anatol were to go underground with the little boy, she would never find him again.

'So it's not true, Mama?' Eugen clarified again.

'No, champ. We're going to meet. It's all scheduled for two weeks' time.' She had to suppress her tears when she saw him laughing with joy. 'And we'll do a lap in the jet. You can even pilot it.'

'Great!' He clapped his hands, then quickly placed an index finger on his lips and curled up in his box.

The microphone transmitted the sounds from Eugen's world to her. She could hear her ex-husband's voice calling

Eugen, heard his steps in the heavy shoes he was wearing. He walked past the hiding place.

'He's gone,' Eugen whispered and grinned. 'This is our secret, Mama.'

'Yes. It is indeed.' Kristen beckoned him closer with her index finger and she moved nearer to the camera too. 'We'll play another trick on Dad.'

Eugen grinned. 'Oh yes!'

'I'll send some of my friends to you. They'll pretend they're kidnapping you, but in fact they'll be bringing you to me. When it starts you'll have to be very good and do everything they say. Do you promise me that?'

'Yes, I'll do that.' Eugen looked into the camera seriously. 'But Papa won't like it. Or the bodyguards.'

Kristen waved it off. 'Oh them! They know. I let them in on it, and, just like my friends, they'll make it look really authentic. My friend is called Brian. You'll stay with him when you're playing, won't you? And you can't talk to anyone about it. Do you understand?'

Eugen nodded enthusiastically. He was pleased at the thought of being involved in a safe adventure. 'So when are we playing?'

'I can't tell you that. It's meant to be a surprise for you too.' Kristen gave the camera a kiss. 'And now out you go. And don't tell Papa anything,' she stressed to him again.

Eugen gave her a virtual kiss too and terminated the connection before she could tell him that he should delete the browser history. She hoped that he would work that out by himself.

There was a knock on the hatch of the aircraft.

Kristen switched seats and looked out one of the narrow oval windows.

Inside the hangar, a white van had come to a stop in front of the jet. Two men had got out and were waiting for her to open up. One of them was Brian.

She flipped the door open, which turned into a ladder, and signalled to them both to climb on board the plane. She could see four more people through the window of the car, as well as four large aluminium cases.

'Hello,' she said, throwing an energy drink from the minibar to each of the two men. 'I'm glad you're on time.'

'If we're paid to be on time, then we'll be on time,' Brian retorted with a grin. Like his companion, he was wearing jeans, a simple dark shirt and a leather jacket. The freckles on his distinctive face looked strange, they didn't quite suit his dark hair. 'We've brought the equipment with us.'

'How did you manage that?'

'I have friends at the airport who are married to a couple of my cousins and owe me a favour.' Brian laughed. 'How do we get the stuff off the plane after we land?'

'I have friends in Minsk, Brian. Admittedly they're not married to my relatives, they just like the money that I give them. Unfortunately the airport in St Petersburg would baulk at a gift like that, otherwise it would be easier.' Kristen opened one of the cupboards next to the minibar and lifted out a bag of cash. 'This is another 50,000. Your second installment.'

'That wasn't even settled,' Brian replied in surprise, but took the money. 'We haven't achieved anything yet.'

Kristen smiled. 'I'm doing a little something for your crew's motivation.'

Brian let out another booming laugh, which his friend joined in with this time. 'Excellent! Then I'll have everything unloaded and brought on board?'

Kristen nodded. 'The sooner we're in Minsk the better.' She pointed to the corner where Miller was tied up. 'Leave the woman alone, please.'

Brian and his companion turned around at the same time. 'Ah, I didn't even see her. Is that another task for us?'

'No. She's coming with me to Minsk.' Kristen stood up to walk into the cockpit. 'So, gentlemen: load up, make yourselves comfortable, raid the bar. We leave in an hour.' She entered the cockpit and went through the checklist, reviewing the maintenance work undertaken by the ground crew on the jet.

If Anatol thought he could take Eugen away, he would soon see he was mistaken.

The men she had hired for the abduction were Ulster Freedom Fighters who accepted missions as soldiers because of a lack of money. They were raising funds for their own battle in the north of the island.

For Kristen, the cash-strapped terrorists were a happy coincidence. She was now in the Mexican drug cartel Los Zetas' bad books, although there was no evidence against her. Officially speaking, the jet was missing. So she had asked around and acquired a replacement team. Irish people with their Caucasian appearance were less conspicuous in Russia than a group of Mexicans tattooed to the gills anyway.

Brian and his men knew what they had to do and the resistance they had to expect. The UFF veterans were not afraid of a shoot-out.

Kristen had just finished her checks when Brian knocked on the cockpit door and reported that everything was stowed away. Timing-wise, this worked out perfectly.

Now that night had fallen, she let the turbines start running and guided the jet out of the hangar to the airport where private planes and cargo were processed for take-off.

Kristen was allocated a runway and the clearance for take-off followed immediately. With engines screeching, the plane sped over the asphalt and lifted up into the air.

She was filled with a curious mixture of joy and tension. Minsk was waiting for her. Brian's team would go to St Petersburg by train and bring her son to safety. To his mother, where a son belonged.

She should have done this long ago. Not now, when they wouldn't have much more time together.

Roccastrada, Italy

Thielke drove into the tranquil village just as the sun was going down. This was where the unfortunate Professor Massimo Auro, who made the mistake of venturing too close to a Death Sleeper, had his sanatorium. Just because you were aware of a danger didn't make you automatically immune to it.

It's nice here. Not bad for a holiday. The GPS showed him where via Balzina was. He had quickly found out that Auro had a flat there.

Following all the rules of the road so as not to attract any attention, Thielke pulled up outside the building where Auro had lived and got out. *I hope there is something to find.*

The new prosthesis, a temporary solution, felt pinched and fake, which his old one had not. But he didn't want to fly to Germany to be fitted with a new artificial leg. The cheap version from an Italian medical supplies shop would have to do for now.

Thielke limped past a group of men who had sat down in front of a *trattoria*. As a stranger, he was definitely conspicuous here. *I should get a move on with my break-in.*

Thielke entered the apartment building, trudged through it floor by floor and looked at the nameplates next to the doorbells until he had found Auro's apartment.

The lock was still firmly in place in the door and there was no seal, no signs of it being forced open. The police had released the flat following their investigation. The heirs must already have come here to secure their share.

As far as I'm concerned, it doesn't matter if they've taken the expensive vases and all of the junk with them. Thielke was only looking for information. He drew out the electric lock-picker, threaded the thin tips into the keyhole and pressed the 'on' button.

There was a hum, and after a few seconds a *click*, and the apartment stood open before him.

He slipped inside and took a small torch from his jacket.

The flat smelled clean, like a faint trace of aftershave. A clock was ticking somewhere. In the torch's delicate beam, he saw pictures and prints on the walls that the professor had collected. Originals, by the looks of them. *The lucky heirs hadn't been up to anything after all. Or else they couldn't agree.*

Exactly what it was he was looking for would become clear just as soon as he'd found it. It sounded paradoxical, but that's how it was.

He was interested in clues to the possible whereabouts of the Death Sleepers, whatever form these clues might come in. Since Arctander had been at Auro's, he thought the likelihood of finding something that might give an insight into his plans was very high.

Thielke hadn't been able to wait in a hotel for the next horrific report of a massacre, for which a sinister terrorist group and its ringleader, Igor, would be held responsible. He needed to act in order to assuage his conscience. To feel like he was doing something.

He began his investigation in the study.

Thielke forced drawers open, rummaged through sheets of paper, shaded in notepads and sifted through every corner of the study but found nothing that would help him make progress. He looked out of the window at the *trattoria* from time to time. The men in front of it seemed to have forgotten him. They were chatting, smoking and playing a board game that he didn't recognise.

When he took the paintings and prints off the wall, he found a safe hidden behind a sketch of a landscape.

Well then.

It was a small safe, fitted into the wall, and it didn't take up much space. Instead of a little cog wheel, it had a complicated lock.

This will take me at least an hour to crack.

'Don't have anything else on today, though,' he muttered and set to work. At intervals, he lit up a cigar, put a chewing gum in his mouth, replaced his nicotine plasters and searched in vain for sugary drinks in the kitchen.

Thielke poked around with his break-in tools, including

the electric lock-picker, all at the same time, pushing and pulling, working at the safe.

After forty minutes, there was a *clack*.

'Bloody hell, that took a while,' he grumbled and opened the hatch – only to find another one behind it with a modern number keypad. Massimo Auro was obviously a person who liked to play it safe.

'Yeah, well, you can kiss my . . .' Thielke puffed quickly on the cigar. He had nothing with him to open this second obstacle. His good equipment, which would have meant he stood a chance against the electronics, was in Germany. Maybe he could cobble together an explosive device to blow the safe open. With the right household chemicals, that really wouldn't be that hard.

But can I get them quickly? Not in Roccastrada, in all likelihood. There was the sanatorium of course—

Click.

The overhead light snapped on, tearing him out of the safety of darkness.

Thielke looked over his shoulder in surprise and drew the LeMat. He trained it on the woman who was marching very coolly into the dead doctor's apartment – until she spotted him and came to an abrupt stop in the doorway of the study. 'Whoever you are, you've got bad timing,' he said in a voice hoarse with smoke.

'It would appear so,' replied the woman, who was almost as tall as he was. She was wearing boots, jeans, a long white shirt and a cropped black jacket. She wore her long, chestnut hair in a loose plait, which emphasised the casual impression of her outfit. Pausing on the threshold, she regarded him uncertainly.

'I'm glad that we understand each other. What do you suggest?'

'That you put down the revolver and raise your hands?' she retorted, smiling. 'I don't suppose you'll have a permit for what you're doing here, will you?' She straightened her rimless glasses, which suited her extremely well.

Thielke found her behaviour annoyingly calm for a woman looking down the barrel of a LeMat. 'What do you want here?'

She pointed to the safe. 'To retrieve property.' She tapped her coat pocket. 'With the permission of the heirs and the assistance of the Italian authorities.' The woman took a step backwards and two *carabinieri* in bulletproof vests appeared in the door, berettas drawn.

Thielke swore loudly.

XXII

Whoever loves life
And does not shy away from death
Will pass happily
Through the waning time

Schifferlied, Theodor Körner

Barcelona, Spain

There was silence in Isabella Dolores Sastre's treatment room.

She screwed the bottle of vodka closed after one last swig while Konstantin tried to digest what he'd heard. Arctander was sitting in his armchair, curled up with his face buried in his hands.

The sound of children's laughter drifted in from the street, the receptionist was running back and forth outside the door, speaking softly to other patients; the scent of freshly brewed coffee crept through some cracks to them. Around them was . . . life.

A small miracle. Konstantin looked at the doctor, who had put her hands together and propped her chin on the extended index fingers. *The Grim Reaper came and didn't strike.* But she had also said that she couldn't help them to escape the curse. And he didn't want to accept that. Not this close to a release from the curse. 'You soothe Death,' he repeated her words from just now, hoping that this would elicit a more precise explanation.

Sastre nodded slowly. 'I can feel it as soon as he comes or if he is present. It's not a case of seeing. If he really does have a form, I don't know it. For me, it's as if it gets colder, as if the colours pale and the noises fade while a low hum sounds. Like pulsating electricity. That's the general rule.' She looked at him. 'If he comes because a Death Sleeper summoned him, the sound changes. It was a rustling just now.'

'How did you make him leave?'

Sastre picked up the telephone and requested three double espressos for herself and her guests instead of answering him. She also asked that all patients be sent home. 'We only had routine tests scheduled for today anyway,' she explained. 'Nobody I urgently needed to see.' She took a pencil and drew a pattern on her writing pad with it before continuing with her explanation. 'I know when someone is doomed to die. As soon as one of my patients gets an illness or suffers an injury that will end their life, they bear a mark that I recognise. Depending on the size of the mark, I know how quickly it will be over.'

'What does the mark look like?'

'It's a kind of stain that spreads over people. The closer Death is the more they lose their own skin colour, to me. They look like they're dusted with flour. And before you ask, this mark varies depending on skin colour. But you learn to detect it quickly.'

'What do people get out of visiting you?' He thought about the fairy tale *Godfather Death*. 'Do you save them?'

'I don't presume to do that. Death knows what he's doing. I look at their stories, at their lives. When the day comes for Death to approach them, I request a deferral. Or not.'

'So you do speak to—'

She shook her head 'I speak, he understands. But there's no answer. We don't enter into a dialogue.'

There was a knock.

The receptionist brought the espressos. There were biscuits on a small plate, along with three mini cupcakes. Apparently she had classed Arctander and Konstantin as important guests, since her boss had cancelled all appointments because of them. But she did seem bewildered by the gloomy atmosphere in the treatment room. She barely noticed the vodka bottle. It seemed to be normal for her boss to be drinking. She put the tray down and disappeared again.

Sastre herself cannot decide who lives and who dies! But she is damn close. Konstantin took the espresso and drank some, Sastre did likewise. Arctander wasn't moving any more, he didn't seem to care about anything. Konstantin put the tracksuit top around Arctander's bare upper body.

The doctor looked at him over the rim of the cup. 'I can practically feel your thoughts, Señor Korff: how can I presume to pass judgement on the sick, to plead for one person and not someone else?' Sastre emptied her espresso in one mouthful. 'The answer is this: because I *can*. I make an effort to keep people alive if they're useful to society, if they have a future and are important for the future of other people. The only condition that counts for me is that the survivors and the dead have to be equally balanced at the end of a year.

'And if they aren't?' Konstantin would rather not have asked whether she herself made sure there was a perfect balance, or in other words, whether she killed people in order to offset the account. He preferred to assume that Death, at his discretion, and somewhere else, eliminated more lives than originally planned. He thought of natural disasters where hundreds or thousands of people died. There were so many possibilities for Death. *Did it bother Sastre that she had innocent lives on her conscience?*

'Then Death helps himself to me, Señor Korff. For every dead person out of balance, he takes a year from me. There's no escaping him – apart from for you and your kind. But even that, the Reaper doesn't just accept, as you know.' She picked up one of the chocolate biscuits and took a bite.

Konstantin was fascinated by her tale. 'Where did you get your gift?'

She laughed bitterly. 'I don't know. It's in our family. All of my ancestors were doctors and none of them lived beyond sixty. That's the price we pay: anyone who gets involved with Death dies sooner.'

'Not quite.' Konstantin thought of Ars Moriendi and his employees. Undertakers don't die earlier than other people.

'It could also be because they were all drunks. Like me. And that they had a penchant for drugs. Also like me,' she added. 'How else are you meant to bear it?' Her face hardened, her gaze riveted on the vodka bottle. She was visibly suppressing the desire to reach for it. 'Because of my family's reputation, we have always been sought out by people like you two.

Supposedly, we talk to the Grim Reaper for you and make him lift the curse.' She ate the rest of the biscuit. 'As I said already: I can't do that. Nobody can.'

Konstantin sat down in the chair in front of her desk and took another mouthful of strong coffee. 'I understand that now. Can you explain to me the significance of the Grim Reaper's Stones? I came across them numerous times during my search.'

'The stones.' Sastre nodded. 'I can do that. My family of course pitied the Death Sleepers. Besides, they were a danger to the public, as is clear from Señor Arctander.'

'If you know all this, why did you not want to help us at first?'

'Self-preservation.' She could no longer resist, reaching for the vodka bottle, opening it and pouring a shot into the espresso cup. 'We devised a system. Massimo was a kind of spokesperson for us, someone who deliberately attracted attention to himself. When someone came to him, he decided whether this person had a legitimate concern. If that was the case, he issued a letter of recommendation, as a message. Without it, we don't admit to being people who can communicate with Death. Only occasionally is it sensible to show your special quality openly. Some of my ancestors fell victim to the Inquisition, as you can imagine. That friendly institution doesn't exist any more, but the machinery behind it still does. The Catholic Church is extremely vigilant when it comes to unauthorised miracles. I've already had a visit from two exorcists who made it clear to me what I was allowed to do and what I was not.' She pushed up the sleeve of her white coat, revealing cross-shaped burn scars on her arm. '*Ego te absolvo*. Those arseholes!' she hissed.

'On that front, I understand your holding back.' Konstantin was surprised by this news. *Does the church know about us too? They must do. Surely the Inquisition became just as aware of our ancestors.* He leaned back in his chair. 'Let's get back to—'

'The stones, yes, I know.' Sastre drank some vodka. 'As I say, for us it was a question of trying to find a way of making normal life possible for the Death Sleepers while also protecting people around them from harm. Experiments began very early on. In the late Middle Ages they were expanded, especially by alchemists, whom my ancestors collaborated with. Coincidence and patience ultimately led to a result. At first, a particular alchemical mixture was thought to be the reason why a Death Sleeper suddenly became visible to the Grim Reaper, a drink made up of different elements, including ground gemstones. But after a number of serious setbacks, it turned out that gemstones alone were responsible. When a Death Sleeper wears a Grim Reaper's Stone, he can be perceived by Death, and the Grim Reaper is placated and doesn't rampage around any more, because he knows that he can find and fetch the Death Sleeper any time. The holy order of death and life is thus established.'

'The opal,' he interjected and looked over at Arctander who was slowly lowering his fingers. Hope had returned to the room.

'Yes. But that's not the only one. A stone must display a certain purity to produce the phenomenon. On top of that there are more physical qualities and specifications that can only be identified in a lab. It would go over your heads if I were to go into detail. Suffice to say, a stone is suitable only if these criteria are fulfilled. We have every nuance checked before we buy it.'

'Do you have some?' Arctander whispered longingly. 'What do they cost? How—?'

Sastre straightened her white coat. 'No. I had requested new ones from Massimo.'

The narcoleptic became slightly paler than he already was. 'Did you not say they were in his safe? Then I would have been close to my redemption without having a clue.'

'I don't know. Thanks to you, he can no longer help me. That really goes beyond gruesome irony, doesn't it?' She laughed bitterly and reached for the bottle. Her tongue was getting noticeably heavier, the effect of the vodka was impairing the language centre in her brain.

I would have been lying hammered under the table long before now. Konstantin wrenched the vodka from her with a firm tug. 'Why did Auro want to send Bent here if he had the stones at home in his safe?'

'Because I'm the stronger one out of the two of us,' she responded angrily and looked at the bottle. 'A stone has to be bound to a Death Sleeper by a Death Seer. The stronger the curse the more difficult it is to produce this bond between stone and Death Sleeper. Since I have a lot of experience, Massimo wanted to leave it up to me, I think. For safety reasons.'

Konstantin and Arctander exchanged glances. 'How do we get hold of new opals for Bent?' He thought about his own ring, which he was carrying around in his pocket, and of Marna. *I'm sure I could arrange something. But first let's see what Sastre says. I don't want to drag Marna into it unnecessarily.* He wondered whether the brunette dealer had put on an act for him and knew exactly who he was. *No, I would have noticed that. She specialised in the rings.* 'You're aware that this is urgent.'

'Yes, I know,' she replied acidly. 'What happened in the stadium should never happen again. It was difficult enough to convince Death not to give free rein to his hatred when Señor Arctander had his attack just now. Almost too difficult. I doubt I will be able to do it again.' Her gaze became vacant. 'It would be the first time in the history of my family that the curse of a Death Sleeper had been too strong.' She turned in her chair and switched on the computer. 'Apart from Massimo, I only know two other people with the same skills as me. A Chi-healer and a Chinese man who has devoted himself to traditional Chinese medicine. I'll write to them and ask whether they still have stones.'

'Will that be quick?' Arctander asked 'I— it has to stop!'

'I assume I'll have answers by this evening. Given how angry the Grim Reaper was, the stone has got to be of extreme purity.' Sastre wrote out her messages.

By this evening. That sounds good. 'How quickly can the stones be brought here?'

'They would be coming from Sacramento or Shanghai. With express deliveries and a few delays included, let's say . . . a week. Approximately.' Sastre obviously knew what he was trying to get at. 'Don't worry. I'll put you up safely. I have a small cabin outside Barcelona, in the countryside, isolated in the woods. It was built especially for Death Sleepers. You can stay there until I have the stones and can bring them to you.'

'A week?' groaned Arctander.

Sastre looked at him, and there was sympathy in her eyes

for the first time. 'Calm down, Señor. You will be absolutely undisturbed. Relax for a week, by a nice pond, in a peaceful cabin where you can live without fear. Señor Korff will keep you company and the seven days will go by more quickly than you can imagine.' She stood up. 'Agreed?'

Konstantin nodded and Arctander followed suit.

'Good. Let's go.' She took off her white coat as she walked, going past them towards the door. 'Come on, Señores. I'll take you to your holiday home which I'm sure is going to surprise you. And I don't want anyone falling asleep on me on the way. The world has had enough catastrophes thanks to Señor Arctander.'

They followed her through the surgery, took the lift down and went outside. Sastre brought them to an old Land Rover Defender.

They got in and the journey began.

On the way, Konstantin tried to phone Marna, to ask her whether she had been able to get hold of the stones in the end. Sastre could of course send the exact specifications. *Smartphones are quite a useful invention.* The only thing that annoyed him was that he had to turn off the phone he had saved her number on straight after he called her, to make sure that MI6 couldn't locate him.

Marna didn't get in touch immediately, unfortunately.

Well, she'll get in touch later then. By the pond.

The journey took them out of Barcelona, across the motorway and further north. They were silent most of the time.

Konstantin was not in the mood for a conversation. He went over all of the new information in his head, hoping to draw his own conclusions. According to Sastre, there was only a limited group of people who could sense and influence the Reaper. *Were there as many as there were Death Sleepers?*

The area around them was getting more barren. They were leaving the popular tourist spots and were taking narrow roads that led from one sleepy village to another. It would have been dangerously tiring, but Sastre's breakneck driving style and the sharp bends that hurled them about in their seats stopped them falling asleep.

'Do you happen to know a doctor called Bloem?' Arctander asked the doctor.

'No,' she answered without hesitation. 'What speciality?'

'Neurology. A Dutchman.'

Konstantin looked at him. 'Why? Is there something we should know about before we get into even more trouble?'

'No, no. I don't know the man at all, and he doesn't know anything about me. I just read that he is part of the research team that has discovered that narcoleptics don't regulate their body temperature properly. Not just in sleep,' he explained. 'That would still have been something to go on if I hadn't got any further with the stones.'

'How does this contribute to combatting the illness?'

'In the article it said that a narcoleptic has a body temperature of around thirty-seven degrees throughout the body. In healthy people the thirty-seven degrees is only recorded in the torso, the limbs are colder. Van Den Bloem's theory says that this consistently high temperature interferes with the nerves in the hypothalamus, which is responsible for regulating the sleep-wake cycles. I showed Darling the article at the time and he promised me he would set up a meeting with the Dutch doctor.' Arctander let out his breath. 'That arsehole.'

Konstantin remembered that Bent had put the low number of attacks down to the cold in his Swedish homeland. 'You would need a thermosuit, wouldn't you? An external regulator.'

'If the theory is correct. Supposedly these bloody sleep attacks only happen because my cooling system is faulty and my brain is overloaded, if you like.' Arctander nodded. 'That would be heaven for me: the curse disappears because of the stone and special thermal underwear stops me from just falling asleep. Maybe it would be enough if I could just go back to Sweden. Without killing people.'

Arctander lost himself in his dream as they left the proper roads and continued down a narrow, overgrown path running parallel to a rusty railway line.

The 4x4 passed a lake and as they approached a bridge Sastre clipped up the Defender's mirrors. Then they trundled onto a concrete square framed by leafy trees that towered above them, casting shadows. Sastre navigated the car through an entrance hidden by the trees, which led into a hill. She steered the car inside.

The Defender's lights came to life, revealing a tunnel seven metres high, where railway lines had once run.

Sastre came to a stop in front of a large gate, got out and pulled a key from her pocket. She slid it into a modern-looking lock, pressed it in hard and turned it.

There was a click.

A siren sounded its warning and the gate slid open with a hydraulic screech. On the other side, lights flickered on.

'I can't drive you any further. You just go through the gate and through the corridor beyond it and you'll get to the plot of woodland on the other side. A little to your left there's a small stream that leads to the lake, and that's where the cabin is that I told you about. You'll find underwear and food supplies in the cupboards. There are some games too. You won't be bored, I'm sure of that.' She looked at her watch. 'I've got to get back.'

Arctander held out his hand to her, but to both Death Sleepers' surprise Sastre took him in her arms, just for a moment. Then he went through the gate.

'Did you have this double door system built into the hill?' Konstantin was impressed.

'No. That was Franco. At one point this complex was going to become something special, a kind of dictator's bunker and treasure trove. But he ran out of money and then his dictatorship was ended for him before he could steal any more. I bought it along with the hill and the land. The upkeep was too expensive for Spain.' Sastre pointed to the entrance. 'Enjoy, Señores. I'll see you in a week.' She stuck the key in the lock again.

The acoustic warning sounded again, the hydraulics sprang into action.

She also hugged Konstantin, who was keeping all of his other questions to himself for now. In the coming week he had enough time to answer some of them himself and put the rest of them to her. 'See you then, Señora. And thanks very much for everything.'

Konstantin walked into the corridor, as the bulkhead, more than a metre thick, closed centimetre by centimetre.

Arctander was on the other side and was already heading around the curve – only to turn back with a horrified look on his face. 'Stop!' he shouted and pointed to the gate.

'What's wrong?'

'She tricked us! There's no exit here!'

Konstantin spun around and was forced to watch as the bulkhead smoothly closed.

It locked with a click. The sound of a ventilation system hissed very softly in the silence, otherwise there was nothing to be heard, nothing at all. Even the engine noise from the Defender didn't penetrate steel or concrete. *What the hell is going on?*

Arctander came to stand next to him, rattling the handle on the gate. 'Shit!'

'Are you sure there's no exit?'

'Of course I'm sure! You know, I can—' His eyes rolled and he collapsed, stiff as a board.

A narcoleptic fit? But the rustling wasn't there. So Konstantin concluded it was catalepsy that paralysed Arctander and made him lapse into a stiffness that only eased off minutes later. There was nothing he could do.

He went off to the far end of the tunnel and saw four beds, several lockers of different sizes and a television with a cable connection. To his right there was a door with the word TOILET in different languages. There was no exit.

I won't have reception here, will I? Konstantin reached into his pocket.

His smartphone was missing. Sastre had done more during her hug than just give him a squeeze to cheer him up.

A quick investigation of the unlocked lockers showed him that the professor hadn't lied insofar as that he and Arctander had enough food and drink supplies.

What Konstantin did not like was the fact that they were enough for more than seven days.

What does she have in store for us?

Roccastrada, Italy

If there was one thing the *carabinieri* had not counted on, it was that Martin Thielke would shoot without warning: with a loud crack, the round of shot flew out of the revolver.

The little bullets flew at the police officers, ripping wood splinters out of the doorframe and shredding the roughcast on the wall. The woman let out a high-pitched cry.

The *carabinieri* fired back, missed him and went down, bleeding from lots of small wounds. The bulletproof vests had definitely protected them from fatal injuries, but the shock from so many small shots had been enough to take them down.

Thielke was holding the LeMat trained on the police officers and watching the woman, who had fled to the window in the room next door and was attempting to climb through it. 'Come back,' he snarled at her and gave each of the prone police officers a powerful kick to the head to knock them out. 'I have no problem with shooting you in the back.'

She stayed still, one leg on the window ledge.

'I want the number combination for the safe,' he said. 'I promise I'm only interested in certain things. If you're lucky, I won't be interested in anything you want to have.'

She turned round to him and slowly took a piece of paper out of her pocket. 'The combination is—'

Thielke pointed to the safe. 'You do it. I don't like being taken for a ride, you know.'

She walked past him, scrutinising him carefully as she did so, climbed over the unconscious, wounded *carabinieri* and stood in front of the safe. She pressed various buttons on the keypad and it beeped and clicked promisingly.

'Now, hands off and step aside,' he ordered and limped closer. He couldn't spend too long on this. In a small Italian village like this one, every resident probably had their own gun in the wardrobe, for hunting, poaching or because they were in the mafia. He wanted to be gone before a neighbourhood militia could be formed.

He opened the second, larger door to the wall safe and looked inside, the LeMat pointed at the woman.

Papers, confidential documents, some letters.

Well okay. Let's see what I find there. He stuffed the letters into his jacket.

Then he spotted the tiny little box, right at the back in the reinforced compartment.

He took it out and shook the contents onto the desk.

Gemstones rolled across the wooden tabletop, in polished form, in their raw form, even two rings with large and small opals.

Thielke saw the woman tense. 'Aha. That's why you're here.' He picked up the first ring, which was decorated with a stylised skull made from silver with diamond chips. 'Looks expensive. Everyone has been going mad for these Death Rings recently.' He laughed softly. He was on the right track. Massimo Auro shared a weakness for Reaper's Rings with Hoya and Bouler.

He tossed the ring back onto the table and held the other one up in front of his working eye: small opals arranged in a cross shape, surrounded by symbols etched into silver. 'So who are you acting as debt collector for?' he asked her.

'Why should I tell you?'

'Because otherwise I'm going to pocket the lot and you'll be fired by your boss,' he replied, taking the stones and going towards the exit, the revolver still trained on her. 'And careful. Don't lie. I'll notice.'

'For the Gemstone and Diamond Bourse, Idar-Oberstein,' she answered, grinding her teeth. 'Everything that I do is legal. Herr Auro was behind in his payments for the stones. Before the heirs can suddenly no longer recall ever seeing stones in the safe, I came to retrieve them.'

'And where did you get the combination? From the heirs?'

'No. I got in touch with the manufacturer of the safe. There is an emergency code that always opens the safe. The number is at a—'

Thielke waved this away. He didn't want to know this much detail. Since he had seen the permit and the *carabinieri*, he believed her story. *I could keep the stones as bait for Arctander.* He reflected quickly. *No, that makes it too complicated. Surprise is my greatest advantage. Arctander won't allow himself to be trapped by me.* He threw the rings and stones to her. 'There you go. I don't believe in their power. But be careful, because other people do. And commit murder for them.' He turned around and went to the door.

'Do you mean Baroness von Windau?'

Well, look at that. Thielke looked back over his shoulder. 'For example. Apparently you're well informed at the bourse.

Take care of yourself and think about Bouler's fate.' He briefly considered taking her with him and interrogating her, but he didn't want to tie himself down with a hostage who would cause him trouble down the line. 'What's your name?'

'Sybille Quandt.'

'I may only have one eye like a cyclops, but I can see very well all the same, petal. Show me your ID.'

At first she didn't move, but when he pointed the LeMat at her face, she took out her ID: Marna Philomena Herbst.

'Thanks. Have fun with the stones.' He limped out of the apartment and down the stairs, holding the LeMat hidden and primed for action underneath his jacket.

When he stepped out onto the street, he noticed with surprise that the men were still sitting and playing in front of the café, chatting and drinking wine. Presumably they assumed the gunshots in their little village could only be related to the mafia and preferred to pretend they hadn't seen anything.

The best protection against trouble. Thielke grinned. People thought he was a mafioso. He looked up to where the woman was standing at the window of Massimo Auro's apartment and watching him. She was holding a mobile in her hand and probably calling in the cavalry.

He kept walking until he reached his rental car, got in and drove off. Only once he had left Roccastrada behind him and was in the next biggest city did he pull into a side street to look through his haul.

There were innocuous letters from a doctor called Isabella Dolores Sastre. Although he could make out fine pencil markings over the letters that had definitely been made by Auro.

Little secret messages?

He got out a fresh piece of paper and sketched out the marked letters and syllables. This resulted in a new text about ordering new stones.

Sastre had used up her stocks in recent months and needed new supplies: two opals, raw, along with two polished ones. It didn't matter what they looked like, the message said. As always, it was about the function, not the value. *I didn't expect that. The stones really do help fight Death!*

Arctander was trying to get rid of his curse with the help of the stones.

That was to the narcoleptic's credit, but it didn't make him any less dangerous or bring back to life any of the dead he had killed – and would continue to kill so long as he was at large.

Thielke looked at the envelope. Sastre lived in Barcelona, her address was his next destination. Soon he would find an airport with flights to the famous Spanish city. *Onwards.*

He wanted to warn Sastre, to lie in wait for Arctander and see what happened. If it were possible and one hundred per cent safe to switch off the death curse with a stone, he wanted to give the Swedish man a chance.

If not, twelve millimetres would end his natural life.

XXIII

I have no terror of Death.
It is the coming of Death that terrifies me.

The Picture of Dorian Grey, Oscar Wilde

Near Barcelona, Spain

Konstantin felt as though time passed more slowly in the bunker than it did outside it.

He and Arctander mainly spent the time reading, watching television and DVDs, wondering about Sastre's behaviour and speculating, as well as eating and drinking.

Arctander enjoyed sleeping without having to worry about the surrounding area even more than Konstantin did. But the days dragged, stretching out like they had rarely done before in his life. On top of this there was the uncertainty about the end of their imprisonment.

Konstantin was sure that Sastre didn't intend to kill them. He assumed that, for her, their imprisonment was about securely accommodating two dangerous Death Sleepers whom she didn't want to spend a long time debating with.

He admitted that it was perhaps the best solution for everyone until she came back with the stones. *If.*

She was the only person who knew the tunnel and had the key to access it, he supposed. If she were – for whatever reason – to die, it would be very bad for them, surrounded by metres of concrete and a hill. Konstantin had estimated that the supplies were just enough for one year.

Instead of considering horror scenarios, he imagined a future without the curse instead. He longed to see Iva again. Relaxed, without a curse, without excuses.

Konstantin thought about her eyes, about her lovely long blonde hair – and especially about her smile. He recalled the first glances of longing they had exchanged in the Gewandhaus before they had even spoken to each other.

He wanted to see her again at last, to look into her eyes. And if he found that what had been there before was still there, then everything would be okay. Then he wouldn't need to explain anything. He would simply take her in his arms.

He was just coming out of the shower wearing nothing but a towel around his hips when the warning signal sounded: the hydraulic jack was starting to move, the bulkhead swinging open.

'She's coming! She's coming!' Arctander called and stood up from the table where he had been working on a jigsaw puzzle.

Konstantin slipped into a black tracksuit at his locker, pulled the zipper up and ran his hands once through his wet hair. *What is going to happen?* He rushed to the entrance, only one thought in mind.

The round steel gate had opened. Sastre paused uncertainly

in front of the threshold and looked in at them, slowly raising one hand in greeting. She was wearing a T-shirt, jeans and trainers, her hair down.

Arctander, standing less than four steps away from her with a breadknife in his right hand, moved towards her. He was openly showing his distrust. 'What the hell was that? Couldn't you have just told us that you were locking us up for safety? What are you planning next? Where are the stones?'

Konstantin saw her hesitation and the strange expression on her face. Something wasn't right. 'Stop,' he warned the narcoleptic.

Then a man's arm appeared from the side and shoved Sastre in the back, flinging her into the bunker.

Thielke stepped out from behind the bulkhead, the LeMat trained on them. A fizzled-out cheroot cigar hung from the left corner of his mouth. With the eyepatch and his country look, he looked like the forgotten hero of a western who had only stumbled into a bunker from the Second World War by mistake. 'Nobody is trying any kind of martial arts, heroics or God knows what other tricks, okay?' he said calmly. 'The shot cartridge in my revolver will shred Professor Sastre's skull into tiny pieces if any of you make any false moves. And I hear you two still need her smart, pretty head.' He threw quizzical looks at the Death Sleepers and waited for them to nod reluctantly. 'Good. Let's sit. We have things to discuss. I think you'll be surprised.'

Konstantin walked backwards slowly. For now, he was obeying the instructions so as not to put Sastre in danger. *The man is a plague.* He saw the gate key in Thielke's left hand.

To his relief, Arctander, who was shaking with nerves,

didn't try anything either. The three of them squeezed onto the corner bench together.

Thielke stayed standing at a safe distance, the muzzle of the gun swivelled towards the group. 'This is one for the books.' He sounded relieved. 'Bent Arctander, a murderer a thousand times over and the most powerful Death Sleeper in the world, together with his comrade Korff who, as a former sinner, is trying his hand at normal life,' he characterised them in a nutshell. 'Great company, isn't it?'

Konstantin looked over at Sastre who was uninjured. 'How are you?' he asked softly, ignoring Thielke. 'Did he do anything to you?'

She shook her head. 'No.'

'No,' Thielke confirmed. 'Why would I? She's not one of us. In fact she is the exact opposite to us. It would be stupid to harm the good doctor. After all, she can help you to become practically normal people.' However, the LeMat wasn't lowered. 'I only need her here as a means of exerting pressure so you don't make any trouble and pounce on a half-blind, lame cripple like me.' He laughed. 'The *donna* and I had a bit of a chat and I learned some new things. Exciting things. Since I don't want to be a monster, I will risk an attempt with the stones. If it becomes clear that the Grim Reaper is in fact content to know *where* you are, that will be enough for me. It would save me a lot, no, a *huge* amount of work.

That sounds good. Konstantin relaxed slightly. 'Tell us what game you're playing, Thielke. I understand you're a Death Sleeper. But why did you follow me?'

Thielke tilted his head to one side, drew a petrol lighter out of his pocket and lit his cigar, puffing and spewing clouds of smoke out of his mouth. 'You're right. I should tell you a little bit about myself so that you understand that, by and large, I'm not an enemy. If the thing with the Grim Reaper's Stones works, I can retire anyway – as long as the Death Sleepers go along with it.' He sucked on the cheroot several times. 'I was a member of the Sleep's Brothers, but I didn't want to do it any more. Like you, Korff, I didn't want to kill any more people, no matter whether they were good or evil. Their fate should determine their death, not me or another Death Sleeper. We behaved like gods.' He pulled up a chair for himself and sat down, massaging his right leg with his free hand. 'I did research, I hit upon unihemispheric sleep as the solution to not summoning Death as soon as I dozed off. We can talk about the details some other time, it would take too long now. I understood that it's our electrical signals, the theta waves, that summon Death. As soon as we send them out, he's there. So I worked on a device that functions as a scrambling transmitter with an electrician friend of mine.'

'You monitor Death Sleepers and intervene if they want to kill someone,' Konstantin put it together. *A scrambling transmitter. A crazy idea.*

'Yes. I eliminate all Death Sleepers who belong to organisations and whom I catch exploiting their power. I disturb their theta waves beforehand, which I need to do in order to get close to them, so that they don't cause any deaths. The battery power is usually enough to block the waves for several seconds.' He tapped the revolver. 'An extremely large calibre because we don't die in the true sense of course, and so I need to cause as much physical damage as possible.' He was silent for a moment. 'I don't like doing this, Korff. But what choice do I have? Can I allow Death Sleepers to commit murder because they see themselves as guardians of the law or as their own moral authority? Since my answer to this is a *no*, I act accordingly. I eradicate those of us who have become megalomaniacs.'

'Isn't what you're doing the same thing?' Sastre interjected. 'You're setting yourself up as the judge of the judges. The highest authority.'

Thielke bestowed a gentle smile on her. '*Donna*, I'm not debating with you. I'm explaining my motivation.' He pointed at Arctander with the revolver. 'It was clear to me that I couldn't let him live.' He looked around pointedly. 'Although this would be suitable accommodation which I could make an exception for. Nothing can happen here. But would he willingly allow himself to be locked in?' He fixed his gaze on the narcoleptic. 'I know you're a poor sod. But more than anything you are a weapon that mustn't fall into anyone's hands.' He slid the bolt back.

'No,' stammered Arctander. 'Korff, you can't let this happen! You know that I—'

I can't do it. Konstantin wouldn't be able to cover the distance quickly enough to throw himself on Thielke. The old man would shoot at him first, and probably hit him, then at Arctander. 'Wait! I have to tell you something about Arctander and Timothy Darling! He got him—'

'I've found you, narco. Your time on the run should really end here, with one shot,' Thielke interrupted him. 'But after the professor told me what you can achieve with the Deathgems, I decided *not* to kill you, but to wait and see for the time being.' He looked at Konstantin. 'Now you can tell me about Darling. What does he have to do with it?'

Konstantin breathed a sigh of relief. 'Thanks,' he said. 'I would find it beyond unfair. Bent can't do anything about it.' He told Thielke about his conversation with Arctander, about MI6's experiments and that Darling had worsened the unremarkable Death Sleeper's attacks. As he spoke, he could feel the anger brewing inside him. The man whom he had considered a friend had been using him in the most nasty way – and now he was hunting him.

When he finished his report, Thielke looked very pensive. 'So, Darling built himself a weapon of mass destruction,' he summed it up. 'It fits with his deviousness. Now I'll tell you what I heard from the commander when his MI6 idiots were trying to shoot me down.' He gave Konstantin a detailed account of the radio message in which he had clearly heard Darling's voice. 'I swear this to you by the ashes of my amputated lower leg: I'm not making any of this up.'

Konstantin clenched his fists. *Jester, you swine.* 'Leave him to me, Thielke,' he said, hoarse with fury.

Thielke lowered the revolver and put it away. 'Good thing we're swapping stories. Nobody has anything to fear from me for the time being. I swear it.'

'What,' whispered Arctander anxiously, 'happens if the stone doesn't work on me?'

Thielke pursed his lips and didn't respond.

Konstantin swallowed and wondered how to calm the Swedish man down, but Sastre placed a hand on his shoulder and said, 'It will work. I promise.'

'I hope so,' Thielke added. 'Great. Let's start. Where are

the stones?' He looked eagerly from one person to the next. 'What do you have to do with them?'

Konstantin pointed at Sastre. 'She's our expert.'

'Yes. But—' She clicked her tongue glumly. 'My friends didn't have any suitable stones.'

'What?' Arctander's eyes opened wide and he looked at Thielke as if he feared that the man would draw his LeMat and immediately open fire.

'Why didn't you tell me that before we set off?' Thielke asked.

'You had a gun and wanted to see them both. I didn't want to contradict you unnecessarily in that situation,' she replied. 'My life may be shorter than others', but I'm quite attached to it.'

Thielke reflected. 'When I broke into Auro's in Roccastrada, there were some stones in the safe. Polished and uncut.' He was getting annoyed.

'But you didn't take them?' Konstantin cursed. Their suspicion had been correct: Massimo Auro had had in his possession the stones that were going to help Arctander. Death had come for him before he could give them to Arctander and send him to Sastre.

'No, I decided against it. Huh, I can't change that now. A woman called . . .' he pulled his mobile out of his jacket and pressed a few buttons on it, 'Marna Philomena Herbst was there with two *carabinieri* and took the stones for the Gemstone and Diamond Bourse in Idar-Oberstein. Auro hadn't paid his debts.' He waved his smartphone. 'I have her address. Maybe—'

Konstantin stifled any response that would give anything

away. If Thielke had hurt her . . . 'Oh, that sounds like you were friends when you parted ways?' he said instead.

'Let's say I'm in the police officers' bad books. But nothing happened to the lady. I'm not a psychopath.' Thielke looked warily at him. 'You're interested in women you don't know? If Iva were to find out . . .'

Konstantin would only be fully reassured once he'd spoken to Marna. 'She's not a stranger, she's a . . .' he faltered briefly, 'a good friend. She and I escaped from von Windau together.'

'Oh, right. She mentioned something along those lines. *That* explains why Herbst stayed fairly calm, she's definitely used to worse than a burst eardrum.' Thielke put the mobile away. 'I'm sure you have her number.'

'But I'll call her from your phone anyway. Darling could locate mine if I spend too much time on it.' Konstantin looked at Sastre. 'While we're on the topic: can I have *my* mobile back? I saved Herbst's number on it.'

'Sure! Sorry. And I'm also sorry that I had to lock you two in. I felt it was safer not to say what I was planning in advance. Señor Arctander is just too—'

'Lethal,' the narcoleptic ended her sentence. 'Still, I resent it.'

Sastre gave Konstantin the component parts of his mobile and Thielke handed him his own handset. 'You'll get reception straight away at the exit of the tunnel.'

'All right. Where should I ask you to go, provided she can get us the stones?' Konstantin walked over to the open bulkhead.

'Tell her I'll pick her up at the airport. It would be better if you stayed here,' Sastre suggested.

Arctander nodded. 'No problem.'

'Agreed.' Konstantin left the bunker, walked past Sastre's 4x4 through the darkness and towards the bright tunnel exit. It looked as if it had been carved out of the darkness.

He breathed in the fresh air, the earth, the trees, the sweet scent of fruit and blossom. The world greeted him with a symphony of sensations, which were all the more intense after a week in a concrete tomb.

He took deep breaths and switched on his phone, found Marna's number in the phone book and dialled on Thielke's phone. Before he turned off his phone, a series of texts downloaded. *There will be time to read those later.*

Theilke's phone rang.

Once, twice, several times . . .

Click. 'Herbst?'

'Hello, it's Konstantin Korff here.'

'Korff! Do you even exist any more?' Marna sounded relieved and cheerful. 'I've already called Ars Moriendi and asked about you. Even your secretary is wondering where you've got to. What are you up to? Are you well?'

She really is glad. 'It's a bit complicated,' he said. 'I have to ask you for a favour.'

'Forget about it! I've just bought a used car because you still owe me money. For the Audi. Remember our race in Idar-Oberstein?' Then she laughed. 'I'm listening?'

'Because of the debt?'

'No. Because of the favour. What's wrong, Korff?'

Konstantin looked up at the trees in front of the tunnel, the sun shining through the treetops and making him squint. 'I need the stones that Massimo Auro kept in his house in

Roccastrada, in the safe.' It was finally becoming clear to him how the connections worked: from Bouler, via the bourse with the experts in gemstone analysis, to Auro. Konstantin could see more and more things were coming full circle; the coincidences made sense.

'How do you know that?' Marna took a breath to ask more questions.

'It was in a letter that Auro wrote before his death. I need those stones, Ms Herbst. They are vitally important. Could you bring them to Barcelona?' he pleaded.

She was silent for a moment. 'Well, now you're seriously making fun of me, Korff,' she blurted out. 'The stones belong to the bourse. They don't do loans.'

'Tell them they have a buyer.'

'Who is that supposed to be?' she demanded, quick as a flash. 'My superiors will want to know.'

'Choose Hoya.'

'Absolutely not. That's easy to check.'

'Then ... Professor Sastre,' he said, without thinking too much about it. 'Her first name is Isabella.'

'Address?'

He gave the address with a sigh and hoped that he wasn't creating difficulties for the doctor. 'Tell your bosses it's a—'

'I know what I need to say. Promise me that I will either take the stones back home with me or will receive the equivalent value?'

Konstantin hesitated. 'I ... think so. If needs be, I'll sign Ars Moriendi and everything that belongs to it over to the bourse.'

Marna hemmed and hawed. 'I should really just say no,

Korff. You're getting me into yet another tricky situation. I don't suppose you want to give me the lowdown on your request?'

'Afterwards. Please, Ms Herbst.'

'Great. I'll do it. In return for you signing your business over to me,' she gave in.

I must be crazy! 'Done. As soon as you've landed, send a text to . . .' he gave her Sastre's mobile number. 'You'll be picked up, details to follow. And please hurry!'

'Of course, Korff. For you, always. But if I don't get the transferral papers from you at the airport, I'll fly away again.' She hung up.

I must be crazy. Mendy is going to kill me.

Konstantin took the time to read the texts now.

Iva wrote several times that she absolutely had to see him and wanted to speak to him, which he was pleased about. Jester also demanded in several messages that he get in touch immediately and explain what was going on. His one-time best friend didn't make threats or tell him off, but the style in which the texts were written made it clear how pissed off he was. This was not the genteel English way.

You bloody . . . His anger at Jester made him dial Jester's number on Thielke's phone, although he had the sense to set it to withheld number first.

The MI6 commander picked up after the second ring. 'Is that you, old boy?' he heard the cheerful voice, but the jolliness in it rang false.

'You bastard! No matter what your plan was, you can forget it!' Konstantin screamed at him, and it did him so much good! *I'd love to punch his face in.* 'I've found a way of neutralising the curse and I'm going to offer it to all Death Sleeper organisations.'

'Calm down, calm down—'

'And do you know how I managed that?' he bellowed. 'With the clues that you gave me! With the help of precious stones that make us visible to Death.' He took a deep breath. 'You can stop looking for Arctander. He's not worth anything any more. Stand your people down and leave me in peace too, as well as him.'

Konstantin ended the call without waiting for a response. He took the phone apart, separating the battery and SIM card from the casing. He hadn't used it for more than half a minute. *I'll buy Thielke a new one.*

That still left Project Oneiros, Jester's allies and their plan with its unknown aim. The MI6 commander was guarding secrets from the Death Sleeper communities and they wouldn't tolerate that.

I will inform the organisations. Arctander will come with me before he's allowed to slip into obscurity. Jester and his people must be exposed. Afterwards, Thielke will not be the only person to go hunting. I'm seriously going to enjoy seeing Jester get what's coming to him for his betrayal!

Konstantin headed back to the bunker. He touched the frame of the steel bulkhead before climbing into the luxury tomb, which would probably withstand a nuclear strike. One more day, two at the most.

From then on he would be a doubly free man. Free of this prison. And free of his curse.

Near Barcelona, Spain

Konstantin was in the tunnel waiting for Sastre to come back from the airport. His fingers touched the ring in his pocket. He listened to the rustling in the trees, the birdsong and the sighing of the wind. He took a deep breath of the pure air. *Free!*

Thielke and Arctander were sitting and talking in the shelter. Sastre had left them the key. An immense act of faith.

Konstantin was mentally recapping the astonishing developments of recent days. Enemies had become men who respected each other. They had talked about their experiences, shared their suspicions and developed them further. Darling's operations, von Windau's activities, Minsk, the Life Institute, the cooperation between the baroness and the MI6 commander, the Oneiros venture. Yet more secrets that Thielke wanted to get to the bottom of.

Arctander had already announced that he didn't want to have anything more to do with it. His modest dream was to return to breeding reindeer, to solitude and the cold of his homeland.

Konstantin had emphasised the importance of informing the organisations soon. The solution to the mystery of the Death Sleepers who disappeared in von Windau's vicinity had definitely had something to do with the hospital in Belarus. The experiments she was carrying out, or rather, had others carry out on her behalf, were beyond Konstantin's powers of imagination, but they would be neither legal nor humane for the people involved.

Thielke didn't like the fact that Konstantin wanted to call in other Death Sleepers, but they were hardly going to be successful by themselves.

Konstantin hadn't yet decided whether he would go with Thielke or join one of the organisations to catch Jester. Thielke was just as much of a murderer as the members of the Deathslumberers or Torpor's Men, although he justified himself by protecting normal people. *That guy is just not someone I want to ally myself with for very long.*

There was the sound of an engine: a heavy car was navigating its way down the path.

Konstantin's excitement grew. *The problem of Bent Arctander is going to be solved bloodlessly and safely any moment. And she'll free me next.*

Sastre had confirmed that the opal in Harlequin's Death was a Grim Reaper's Stone and she was about to bind it to Konstantin. *The fulfilment of my greatest wish!*

As Sastre's Defender rounded the tree trunks, driving towards him in the tunnel and coming to stop, he could hardly stand the suspense any longer.

Marna got out first, followed by the professor.

'Ms Herbst?' Konstantin was shocked at the sight of her. She had been given the transferral papers for his undertaking business by Sastre, along with the message to hand over the stones to the professor. He didn't want to put her in the firing line again. It seemed Marna had not felt like going back to Germany. *The mistrustful business woman. I might have guessed.*

'I didn't know that you ran your own mines too, Korff.' The gemstone expert came over to him. She had refrained from an expensive suit and put on jeans and a T-shirt. Her chestnut-coloured hair was tucked underneath a peaked cap, her laced-up boots came to the knee. They shook hands. 'Thank you for signing over Ars Moriendi. Professor Sastre gave me the letter you signed, but you can't seriously believe that I would let the stones out of my sight, when I haven't received any money for them?'

He looked to Sastre who was just walking past him. She shrugged her shoulders. 'I'm sorry, Korff. She wouldn't be dissuaded.'

'Correct. Let's see if we can top our little adventure in Idar-Oberstein. I'm sure you'll show me what you're planning to do with the stones now?'

'You're not afraid that we'll attack you, Ms Herbst?' Konstantin grinned at her. 'Who would hear your screams out here anyway?'

Marna smiled confidently. 'Who says I'm unarmed? I could also be carrying a tracking device on me that shows the bourse exactly where I am and where they should send the rescue team. Oh yes, I put your hand-over in an envelope and posted it at the airport. I won't reveal the address to you. You're rid of your company, even if you do anything to me. But you're much too nice a man to pull off something like that.' Marna pointed to the entrance. 'In here?'

Konstantin bowed. 'After you, Ms Herbst.' She strode past him and, without meaning to, he drank in the perfume she wore so well. Her tight trousers emphasised her bottom and long legs.

They joined the rest of the group.

Marna saw Thielke and immediately stopped walking. 'Korff, perhaps you aren't so nice after all!' she cried. She took a step backwards. 'That's the guy from Roccastrada—'

'He's on our side,' he said, trying to calm her down.

'It was nothing personal, gorgeous,' Thielke interjected with a grin.

'You shot at police officers!'

'It was just shot, and they had bulletproof vests on. Nothing was going to happen,' he replied. 'I'm one of the goodies. Ask Korff.'

Marna threw Korff an accusatory look. 'I want to get out of here, Korff. This is too messy for me.'

Konstantin shook his head. 'I promise I'll explain everything later, but we need the stones now. Please, Ms Herbst!'

Something in his eyes or voice seemed to convince her. Marna slowly took a strongbox out of her bag, opened it and shook the contents onto the table. Several polished and uncut stones, as well as two rings, rolled out, and threatened to fall off the table before Thielke caught them and pushed them into a pile.

'The contents of Massimo Auro's safe,' she remarked. 'I've had the stones analysed, for value and composition.' She drew some folded pages out of the side pocket and spread them out. 'The total value comes to 180,000 euro.'

'I'll see if there's something suitable for Señor Arctander among them.' Sastre had taken a seat at the head of the table. She picked up one stone after another, closing her eyes and rubbing them. She did the same with both rings. She cast an occasional glance at the results of the analysis.

They were in suspense, waiting to see which stone she would choose.

Even Marna didn't ask questions. She had crossed her arms over her chest and was watching the doctor's every movement, fascinated. But after five minutes she touched Konstantin on the arm and pulled him to the bulkhead.

'So. I've done you a favour, got into a stranger's car and let myself be carried off into a bunker. I'm getting the feeling that I'm among people even stranger than Hoya. And that's still an understatement,' she whispered to him. 'What does she mean by *suitable*? What's happening here, Korff?' She looked solemnly at him.

This was inevitable. Konstantin returned her gaze frankly. 'I can't explain in such a short time. Really I can't. We have less than four or five hours now to get you—'

'Korff!' yelled Thielke. 'Shit, get over here! Help me with the narco!'

Konstantin and Marna turned towards the table.

Arctander was lying on the floor, his arms and legs tensed up. He was wheezing heavily and trying to say something. The cataplexy prevented him from being able to express himself. Thielke was trying to shift him into a more comfortable position, but his disability made it difficult.

He's having an attack! Konstantin looked at Sastre, who had closed her eyes and was holding an unpolished, raw stone in her fingertips. He took Marna's hand and dragged the surprised woman after him, pulling her right behind the doctor. 'You stand here,' he said, hoping that Sastre could protect her. Attempting to take her out of the reach of the Reaper could only go badly. The power of Arctander's curse might extend hundreds of metres by now. He preferred to trust the calming effect that Sastre had already shown evidence of in her surgery.

Marna let go of his hand. 'Why should I?'

'Just do it if you don't want to die!' he shouted at her and bent down to check on Arctander. 'Bent! Bent, pull yourself together! Where are your medications?'

Arctander whimpered and rasped incoherently.

'Leave him,' Sastre said softly. 'He ought to summon the Reaper. Then I can bind him and the stone.' She opened her eyes, got up and came over to them, pressing the opal against Arctander's forehead. 'Give in. Give in to sleep and call your brother into our midst.'

The man's eyelids fluttered and closed—

And the shrill rustling sounded!

Konstantin's face distorted in disgust. The sound became more intense each time, boring painfully into his head. He was ice cold, he could feel panic rising inside and a blackout approaching. The lamps flickered, even light fled from Death.

The stone on Arctander's forehead glowed dimly, seeming to suck up the last of the room's brightness. His veins shimmered under his skin, the blood inside them pulsating. His skull became more and more transparent, like an X-ray image, until even the narcoleptic's brain was visible. Death, it seemed, not only saw him but was taking in every last detail.

The hairs on the back of Konstantin's neck stood up, and goosebumps spread over his body. Through the creaking and cracking of millions of ice floes, he could hear Marna's piercing screams.

Where is she? He looked to his right where she stood.

The young woman sank right to her knees, her mouth wide open and her chalk-white face a mask of pain. She struggled for air, clasping at her chest.

She's dying! Sastre was using her gift to bind the Reaper and

Arctander. Protecting the surrounding area was less important to her right now. *Sastre needed to . . .* 'Hurry up!' he cried over the rustling. 'Herbst is going to be a goner if you don't!' He looked at Thielke, whose horror was clear. Such hatred from Death was like nothing he had known before.

'Put on the ring,' Sastre replied. Her exhausted voice was barely audible.

'Which?'

'Harlequin's Death,' she groaned. 'Now, Korff. I won't endure this again. It's now or never, I know that.' She closed her eyes and reached out a hand towards him, while the trembling fingers of her right hand lingered on Arctander's forehead and the stone. Her dark hair turned lighter from the roots, going greyer and greyer. Her face was gradually becoming shrunken, the skin taut and leathery.

Konstantin slipped the ring onto the middle finger of his left hand.

The rustling in his ears became overwhelmingly loud, a scream forced through his lips. Every cell in his body seemed to be exploding, black sparks danced in front of his eyes. He swayed, driving away the blackout thundering towards him by sheer force of will.

Sastre caught hold of his hand and held on tight, tighter than a woman of her stature should have been capable of doing. His fingers hurt under the pressure, he could feel a bone break, but he didn't flinch away from her.

A hot beam swept his arm upwards, a mixture of electric shock and acid ate through him as the world disappeared in an exploding fireball.

Konstantin could smell melting plastic, piano varnish and

warm felt, followed closely by mint and metal dust. His mouth felt like it was full of stones – and then came the images from the past.

He saw the faces of the people he had killed; they were piled into a mountain of corpses and slowly rotting. The flesh was disintegrating and ran from the limbs in a stinking slime, creeping towards him, enveloping him.

He shrank backwards and into a grave that was filling with the vile-smelling liquid. He screamed and the corpse juice filled his throat, his eyes and ears.

Konstantin howled – and found himself back in the bunker.

He was kneeling next to Arctander and had vomited all over the floor, blood streamed from his bit-open lip. The hand bearing the ring burned like fire. His veins stood out, bloated and engorged underneath the skin, as if twice the usual amount of blood was straining through them.

Sastre was crouched in front of him, her arms resting on her thighs. She was struggling to breathe. Her hair was snow white and falling out in clumps. Konstantin looked at the careworn features that seemed to have aged by years in the last few minutes. *What did this effort cost her?*

Konstantin spat and wiped his mouth, looking around. Arctander was sleeping contentedly with the stone on his forehead, Thielke lay with his upper body on the table and was just heaving himself up with a long groan as though he were a freshly awakened zombie.

'Herbst?' He checked for Marna quickly.

She was lying less than two metres away from him, crumpled up like a foetus, her fists clenched. Blood was running from her hands, where her nails had cut through the flesh.

He crawled towards her, turned her onto her back and patted her pale cheeks. The unusual reddish grey eyes were open, she was looking right through him at the ceiling.

'Herbst, don't die!' He felt for her pulse. It grew weaker by the beat underneath his finger. Until her chest sank – and stayed still.

But her eyes weren't unseeing, she hadn't become lifeless yet.

Without hesitating, he put his lips on Marna's, blowing air into her lungs, and then thumping rhythmically on her chest, the way he had learned. 'Hey, Herbst,' he called at intervals, feeling himself starting to sweat. There was a crack. He had broken one of her ribs. He didn't give up. *She didn't deserve this. Not her.* 'Herbst, stay here!'

He lowered his mouth to hers to give her breath again. Then Marna's lips moved. She lifted her arm and touched him on the shoulder.

Konstantin straightened up at once and smiled at her. 'There you are.'

She coughed and held her side. There was fear in her eyes. She looked at him, distraught, trying to grasp what had happened to her. 'I . . .' Marna coughed again and tried to get to her feet. 'Korff . . .' Konstantin carried her carefully to the sofa, put her down and braced himself against the wall as he stumbled. He staggered over to one of the lockers to get some water.

His broken finger was painful, as was his middle finger where Harlequin's Death sat. Konstantin felt like he'd been boozing for ten nights, he was seeing stars and had double vision. His blood flow was making it unmistakably clear to him that he was on the verge of collapse.

When he turned back from the lockers, Herbst, Sastre and Thielke were sitting at the table in silence. He put the bottles of water on the table and fell heavily into the free seat. He could barely get his bottle open, and when he drank, water ran down his chin because his hand was shaking so much.

Apart from Arctander, they sat awake, panting, drinking, staring.

'What was that?' Marna whispered, holding her ribs and groaning at every movement. 'What just happened?'

'Death came and left again, without being able to take any one of us. He doesn't like that,' Sastre answered her with the cracked voice of an old woman. 'Señor Korff, always carry the ring with you from now on. It's best kept on your finger, but otherwise always close to your body. I'll emphasise that to Arctander too. If you put it aside for more than half a day and fall asleep . . .' She had to close her eyes. 'The Reaper will rage worse than ever before. You will be like Arctander.'

Konstantin nodded. His mouth was dry, his throat tasted of blood and corpse water. Happiness wouldn't come, he was struggling to pull himself together too much for that. The images of the dead, Herbst's brush with death, his weakness. He looked at the ring. *I . . . cheated the curse.*

Thielke gulped down his water and tried to light up a cigarillo. 'I . . . felt him,' he croaked. 'The Reaper was—' He pushed up the sleeve of his jacket. 'I thought he would hit me.' His shaking hand wasn't able to keep the flame still long enough to light the cigarillo. After several attempts, he gave up. 'Sastre, you are a miracle-worker.'

The doctor burst into tears. Black-red blood flowed from the corners of her eyes, which made Marna flinch. The bloody tears rolled down her aged face, dripping onto the table and forming little pools. She was crying convulsively, her body shuddering.

Konstantin put a reassuring arm around her and held her tight. 'I can't tell you how grateful I am,' he told her gently. 'You've given me a new life.'

As he was saying these words, the realisation finally sank in. *I'm visible to him! I'm mortal! The Reaper can see me and knows where I am.* This thought, which would have terrified anyone else, made him smile.

Sastre gradually calmed down. She broke away from him and he handed her some tissues to wipe away her tears. 'Thanks,' she choked out in a whisper. Black-red streaks clung doggedly to her cheeks, so she got up and limped to the bathroom.

'Take good care of the stones.' Thielke put Arctander's opal in his pocket so that he wouldn't lose it and then patted him on the shoulder. 'I'm so glad,' he said, 'that I've found my own way of cheating death.'

Konstantin's forehead creased. 'You don't want a stone?'

He shook his head and gave him the finger. 'After seeing *this*? Never. I'll stick with my trick. Unihemispheric sleep.'

'I don't understand a word of this.' Marna got up, staggering. 'I need fresh air. And you, Korff, are coming with me and explaining to me what has happened, for fuck's sake! Or else I'm going to go mad.'

'Thielke, you look after Arctander.' Konstantin stood up too. 'You're right, Ms Herbst. I'll explain it all to you, although I don't expect you to believe me. But everything that I'm going to say is the truth.'

They were striding through the tunnel towards the bright sunlight.

Konstantin immediately noticed the silence; there were no sounds of birdsong.

'I'm intrigued,' she replied and groaned softly. 'My rib is done for, I think.' Marna held him tight, turned him towards her and gave him a kiss on the lips. 'That was my thank you for saving my life.' Then she continued on her way.

They reached the end of the tunnel and looked out.

A dead squirrel lay on the path underneath the trees and next to it two blackbirds in the withered leaves, their wings outstretched. Grass drooped, shrivelled; petals fell from dried up stems; stinging nettles and ferns lay decaying on the ground; the trees had shed their leaves, branches had broken off. The air was heavy with the scent of rotting wood, of putrefying plants – of mortality.

A muggy wind lifted up the leaves and blew them about. They played around their shoes with a rustling sound and rushed into the tunnel.

'My God.' Marna looked around in horror. 'What—?'

Konstantin ran a hand through his dark hair and took some deep breaths.

The Reaper had harvested what his scythe was capable of cutting down. *How do I explain all of this to her?*

XXIV

*To me, it's as though one
does not know all of life
if one does not take Death
into account to some extent.*

Wilhelm von Humboldt

Barcelona, Spain

'This doesn't mean it's over.' Bent Arctander looked around at the small group that had retreated to a quiet corner of a tapas bar. There were a number of empty wine bottles on the table. The Swedish man had clearly not had any alcohol for a long time, because he had not drunk more than the others, but he looked like he had. He was grinning and giggling the whole time, in high spirits and laughing about everything.

Nice to see him so relaxed. Konstantin put down his glass of red wine and waited for the other man to continue. Marna, Sastre and Thielke were watching him expectantly too.

They had been sitting there for a few hours, guzzling various Spanish nibbles, drinking quaffable rioja and putting the events of the previous days behind them. Sastre was wearing a headscarf. She'd had the grey-white hair cut off because she was hoping that it would grow back dark.

'Darling.' Arctander flapped his hands around to quiet them. '*Pssst.* Let me finish, okay? The *arsle* knows that I exist. He won't be interested to know that I have a stone that makes me visible to the Reaper.' He topped up his red wine. 'But I'm not afraid any more. I'm going north, to my homeland and he won't find me among my thousands of reindeer. That *arsle*.'

Konstantin's head felt rioja-addled. His thumbs kept rubbing Harlequin's Death the whole time, as if to check the Reaper's Ring was still there. 'No worries, Bent. I'll speak to the Deathslumberers and the Torpor's Men. They'll take Darling out. He's a megalomaniac back-stabber who abused his power and wanted to make you his tool. They won't let him get away with it.'

'I will confirm everything,' Arctander muttered, hiccuping and stuffing an olive in his mouth. 'That *arsle*.'

'What does *arsle* mean?' Marna asked.

'Arsehole,' the Swedish man explained, emphasising every letter of the word. '*Arsle*, Arsehole.'

She grinned and raised her glass to him.

'It's the best solution. We're no match for Darling and his people by ourselves,' Konstantin took up the topic. 'Especially since we don't know who his allies are.'

'Who knows how many people belong to Darling and his Project Oneiros?' Thielke interjected acidly. 'It will be something new for the Death Sleepers.'

'What do you mean by that?' Sastre was eating some of the pickled, stuffed vine leaves.

'Normally they like to play jury, judge and executioner of

human society. Now suddenly they have to clean up in their own ranks: Darling, and von Windau with her institute. That will absorb their energy for a while, that's for sure.' Thielke picked up the bottle of red wine and realised that it was empty. He ordered a new one with a wave. The seventh.

'A war between brothers,' Marna said pensively. She was watching Sastre. 'You have a mark on your cheek. Looks like mascara.' The professor ran a hand over her skin, but Marna didn't look happy. 'Nah, still there. It's probably nothing, or something to do with the light.'

Sastre agreed. 'Or it's a new age spot.'

'Not a real war,' Thielke corrected hesitatingly, and started to warm to his subject. 'Some people strayed out of line. It will be possible to clear it up, it will simply entail time and effort. A war between brothers, more an open dislike that unites the Europeans with the Indians, the Phansigar. And in South America there are—'

That's enough classified information. Konstantin cleared his throat. 'But it's all the same to us. This is about Darling and von Windau.' He cast a reproachful look at Thielke to get him to be quiet. Sastre and Marna, and even Arctander, had been listening to him in fascination. 'Professor, can you make more of us visible to the Reaper?' He tried to return to the problem at hand. 'And what about the other Death Seers? Would they help too?'

'It's not all that simple. It begins with sourcing the suitable stones. Then the Death Sleeper has to be freely willing to—'

'Unless I plant the stone on them,' Thielke muttered into his glass.

'Sorry, sorry, but at this point I'd like to remind you that one of the gentlemen still owes me about 20,000 euro for the uncut opal that Bent is carrying,' Marna said with mock gravity. You could hear that the red wine had not passed without leaving its mark. 'I know a collection agency that collaborates with a gang of rockers. Just to warn you.'

'I'll sell Ars Moriendi,' Konstantin reassured her with a grin.

'That belongs to me anyway!' Marna stuck her tongue out at him and grinned back. Her eyes shone.

Sastre chose a dried tomato and spread it with a thin layer of tapenade before biting off a piece. She seemed to be the only person who was still sober. 'Apart from Massimo and my two friends, I knew two other Death Seers. But one of them died and the other one was abducted during an aid project in Colombia.' She laughed uncertainly. 'It's difficult to recognise the gift in other people, let alone bring up your suspicion to turn it into a certainty.' She pointed to her aged, wrinkled face. 'People who look older than they are don't necessarily have to be Death Seers.'

'So we just have you.' Konstantin ran one finger round the rim of his glass and then licked the red drops from it.

'Yes. But right now I don't feel strong enough to dare to make another attempt. This last meeting with Death ...' She sighed and reached for her red wine. 'I need a break, otherwise he will kill me next time.'

'Shouldn't he be grateful to you for making the Death Sleepers he hates visible?' Marna asked in surprise. She had got up to speed on the topic astonishingly quickly, in Konstantin's opinion. During their long conversation in front of the bunker, amid the dead plants and animals, she had asked many questions, which he might have wished had come from Iva's lips. She accepted what had happened, although it would be another while before she truly grasped it. 'Why is he punishing you, Professor? He should give you some extra years of living for your work.'

'It just doesn't work like that,' Sastre replied glumly. 'Being in contact with him saps my energy, he damages me. Like workers who have to contain the danger after a nuclear accident. They are doing a good thing, but they are being exposed to radiation and pay for their actions with a lower life expectancy.' She raised her glass. 'Ingratitude is just the way of the world, Señora Herbst. What's that nice way of putting it: someone's got to do it.' She drank hastily and poured herself some more.

An awkward silence set in, punctuated by Arctander's giggling as he enjoyed a cartoon on the wall. His concentration left a lot to be desired at this stage.

The waiter brought the seventh bottle, opened it and placed it on the table.

'I think it's time for me to go to bed. Every bone in my body aches.' Sastre got up, swaying slightly, which had less to do with the alcohol than with her exhaustion. 'Señor Korff, let's speak on the phone. Can we agree that you will keep my identity secret from the Death Sleepers? We will do the sessions for those interested in carrying a stone only under my terms.'

'Of course. Did you have your bunker in mind?'

'Yes. My way or not at all.' She shook hands with everyone, wished Arctander all the best and disappeared out the door.

Thielke looked pensive as he watched her go. 'What a waste,' he murmured.

Konstantin didn't probe what he meant by that. 'You'll keep your mouth shut too, understood? You promised Sastre,' he said quietly, but sharply.

'Of course I will.' Thielke remained nonchalant as usual.

Konstantin could tell that he was brooding. *Is he pondering an alternative to his scrambling transmitter method? What did he say just now about planting stones?* 'Count yourself lucky you've escaped the Death Sleepers this long, Thielke.' His tone was urgent. 'I'd advise that you—'

Thielke laughed and stood up. 'Have a good evening, all. My bed is waiting and my sugar levels are so high that I could sell my blood as a sweetener.' Turning towards Arctander, he said, 'All the best, Bent. If you lose your stone, and I have to read about the next catastrophe in the paper, we'll be seeing each other again.'

Arctander grinned broadly and murmured, *'Arsle!'*

Thielke pointed to his healthy right eye, then at the Swedish Death Sleeper. 'I only have one of these, but I see everything with it.' He winked at Marna and Konstantin. 'You two too.' He limped out.

'That guy is a cross between Captain Ahab and Rooster Cogburn,' said Marna and reached for the wine bottle.

'Rooster who?'

There was a *plock* sound. Arctander's head had suddenly hit the table and he was snoring loudly. The other customers in the tapas bar were grinning over at them.

Marna shrugged her shoulders, 'More for us.' She topped up their glasses. 'Rooster Cogburn is a one-eyed law enforcement official from an old western.'

Konstantin declined too. 'Thanks. That's enough for me. I still need to haul Bent to the hotel.'

'A few metres. That's no bother for a strong man.' Marna stood up, took the bottle and went to the counter. 'I'll pay.'

'No, wait! I—'

'Leave it. The bourse will cover it. Business meal. I'm still getting 20,000 euro from you anyway. Oh yeah, and 50,000 for my Audi. Remember that I have your Ars Moriendi as security.' She kept walking.

I need to win the lottery very soon. Konstantin heaved Arctander up from the bench and threw him over his shoulder. It was true, what she'd said. The issue of payment for the stones remained unresolved. He hoped that the organisations would step in and take on his debts.

Amid friendly laughter from the remaining customers, he carried Arctander through the bar to the exit. There, he turned, grinned and waved as though he were a matador after a successful fight. *I'll be so happy if I can eventually do my work again.* He pictured his thanatological workshop. He was looking forward to seeing Mendy, Jaroslaf and his other colleagues; he'd texted them that he was coming back tomorrow.

And of course he was thinking of Iva.

He and Marna reached the exit at the same time. She opened the door and with a collective '*olé*' from the tapas bar, they left the place laughing.

The hotel was not all that far away. Arctander happily snored the whole way, and farted once, which made Konstantin curse loudly and Marna laugh loudly. They shared the bottle of wine on the way and had emptied it by the time they reached the hotel foyer where they got into the lift.

How lovely not to have to worry about anything. Konstantin closed his eyes and leaned his free shoulder against the lift wall. The world spun like it used to do on the cup-and-saucer ride that he'd loved as a child. I can just sleep. *Eyes closed, dreaming for hours on end.* He grinned – and suddenly felt Marna's lips on his.

She tasted wonderful, and a tingling spread from his mouth throughout his body.

Almost automatically, he reciprocated the passionate kiss, but then he pulled his head away. He had almost dropped Bent.

Marna looked at him and stretched out her left hand to his face.

'No,' he said softly.

'But I *want* this,' she replied in a breathy voice. 'Let's do it. Tomorrow we can smooth it over by saying we were smashed.' Marna kissed his neck, which gave him fresh tingles. She dropped the empty rioja bottle and it shattered with a crash on the floor of the lift.

The lift stopped.

'Eleventh floor. We have to get out.' Konstantin pushed her backwards out of the lift. 'Bent is getting too heavy for me.' He trudged along the corridor looking for the narcoleptic's room. The numbers on the doors swam in front of his eyes, the walls rocked like on a ship, which he found funny.

It took them several minutes to find the right room and almost as long again to open the electronic lock.

Konstantin staggered into the semi-lit room and threw Arctander on the bed who muttered briefly and then rolled onto his side without waking up. 'Do you hear that?' Konstantin asked, finding it difficult to speak.

'The snoring?' she asked, giggling. She was still standing at the door, which she now closed.

'No. There's . . . silence. No rustling. No Reaper. He can give in to Death's brother like any normal person. He can sleep.' Konstantin touched Harlequin's Death. *Sleeping. In a bed, not in a bathtub or in a shower or cubbyhole.* 'I'm looking forward to it so much,' he murmured.

There was the whisper of material. 'Me too,' whispered Marna, and Konstantin turned round to her. She came towards him. The light from the metropolis fell through the window and illuminated her naked body. 'I want you, Korff.' She pressed herself against him.

Konstantin could feel her full breasts, her warmth.

The scent of her hair and her perfume penetrated his nose. His hands rested on her back, then slid down. Her skin was velvety, lightly tanned and tempting.

She lifted her arms, placed them around his neck and pulled him towards her, holding herself against him with a low moan and kissing him. She licked his lips with her tongue. The taste of red wine mingled with her own flavour.

Konstantin could feel his desire, his erection growing by the second. 'We're drunk,' he said hoarsely and stroked her bottom with one hand, while the other hand went up and caressed her neck gently, making her gasp. Iva's image faded in the haze of red wine and lust.

'We are ridiculously drunk,' Marna breathed and opened

his shirt, kissed his chest, then drifted downwards and stripped off his trousers. She already had his hard member in her mouth, letting her head glide back and forth, gripping the shaft with her hand and rubbing it.

Konstantin stroked her head, then gave her a gentle shove so that she lost her balance. But before she could fall, he grabbed her under the arms and lifted her onto the stool behind her. He sank between her splayed legs and kissed her sparsely haired mound of Venus. She was already wet and writhing with desire.

Marna moaned and grabbed his hair, pulling him closer to her.

He licked her hot gash, which made her pant. The taste of her increased his lust and he drove her more and more crazy with his tongue.

Then he flipped her onto her stomach. She pushed her luscious bottom out to him, her upper body sank downwards in a gentle arch. She spread her legs expectantly for him. 'Wrap up,' she whispered and pushed a condom towards him over the carpet. Konstantin was not drunk enough to leave it. He slipped the condom onto his cock and leaned forwards to kiss Marna's bottom. With one hand, he touched her gash, slipping a finger inside and pulling it out again immediately. She was more than ready for him.

He grasped her hips and pulled her, along with the stool, towards him, pushing himself slowly inside her and enjoying the warmth that surrounded his cock. Marna groaned with pleasure, tensing up her muscles. Moisture ran down her thighs, dripping onto the stool and carpet.

Konstantin pulled his member out halfway and plunged it

in again as far as it would go, and repeated the movements, getting faster and faster as Marna braced against him and adjusted to his rhythm. He stroked her back and as he did so, admired the play of her muscles in the dim light. He touched her bottom, her thighs and finally clutched her long, chestnut-coloured hair to pull her upper body upwards.

His arms were around her, his hands massaging her soft, firm breasts. He panted as he thrust faster and harder into her, heard her gasp and sink into a whirl of sensation – before he came with a loud cry and thrust jerkily into her until he collapsed.

When he opened his eyes again, he was surprised that he was suddenly lying on top of her and in her arms. He hadn't noticed that they had changed positions.

Marna's skin was coated in a film of sweat, just as his was. He pressed his face into the back of her neck to take in her arousing scent more intensely as she gently kissed his throat and stroked his back.

Konstantin had been sure he would be seized by feelings of guilt that would make him ashamed because of Iva. But they failed to materialise. His solar plexus was glowing, his flushed body slowly cooling down. But he wanted her again. *What is going on here?*

When the loud sound of snoring came from the other bed, they both laughed.

'I forgot about him.' Konstantin levered himself up and sat up, as did Marna. They grinned at each other and Konstantin detected real affection in her reddish-grey eyes. *My eyes won't look any different.* He gave her a long kiss on the mouth and ran his hand along her neck, caressing it at the nape.

'I think it's great,' she whispered, 'that we're drunk.' She leaped astride him and pressed her hot, wet gash against his cock, which was already getting hard again. Her breasts lay on his skin, her nipples pointing forward perkily.

Konstantin pushed himself up off the ground, lifting her with him. She slung her legs around his hips and kissed him tenderly. Then they disappeared into the bathroom in case Arctander did wake up after all.

Barcelona, Spain

Konstantin heard the ringtone as though from very far away. Quiet enough for him to ignore and try to drift back to sleep.

But the tinkling came closer and closer until the sound was coming from right next to his ear.

Since when can my phone walk? And when did I even turn it on?

When he opened one eye, he saw a woman's hand, Marna's hand, holding out his smartphone to him. They were in his hotel room, but he had no idea how they'd got there. *Yes, we were* seriously *drunk.* 'Thanks,' he murmured and took the phone.

On the screen it read *Iva*.

Cursing, he shot upright and accepted the call.

'Hello, Iva,' he said croakily. He had cried out so often in the passion of the night before that he was hoarse. His head swam with confusion, he kept reminding himself that he and Marna had been drunk. 'I'm sorry that I went off the radar for so long,' he spluttered out. 'I'm coming to Leipzig soon. We have a lot to discuss.'

Next to him, Marna curled up with a plaintive noise and pulled the covers over her head; her chestnut-coloured plait peeked out from underneath it. Light was falling into the room through a narrow gap, too bright for someone suffering from a hangover.

He could see the outline of her body beneath the sheet and thought about her full breasts . . . *Residual alcohol*, he told himself. 'Iva?'

'"A true friend stabs you in the front,"' came a voice from the speaker. Jester laughed softly. 'I thought to myself it was time to declare another of Oscar Wilde's truths, old boy. By now you'll have understood that the rules of our game have changed.'

No! The temperature in the room dropped suddenly. He froze.

'Konstantin?'

'Yes,' he croaked. 'Yes, I'm here.'

'Ah, I can see I have your full attention. I'm pleased. And thanks very much for your motivational speech about Bent Arctander and the new developments. Lovely to hear how committed you can be. I've always admired that.' Jester was pacing up and down as he spoke; judging by the sound of his footsteps he was walking through a high-ceilinged room with a floor made of stone. His voice echoed slightly, there was silence in the background.

Konstantin fought back his hangover and panic and tried to marshal some clear thoughts. 'Leave Iva alone,' he said, uninspired. It was unoriginal, but nothing better occurred to him and it was the truth.

'Why should I? I'm not one of the good ones, Konstantin.

I want my narcoleptic back and you are going to bring him here.'

'He doesn't have his gift any more.'

'Bring him here. I'd like to see it for myself.'

'I can't be responsible for doing that.'

'I wonder if Iva sees it that way too? Or Professor Sastre?' Jester responded cheerfully. 'You will be the first to die, old chap. I'll happily keep killing until you deliver my narcoleptic to me. I found him, I saved him, I trained him. He belongs to me!'

'You're planning to make him into a tool. You couldn't care less about Bent!' Konstantin shouted, getting up and going into the bathroom. He hastily drank a mouthful of water and splashed his face. The cold chased away the effects of the alcohol. 'What do you want with him?'

Jester stopped walking. 'He is one of a kind. There has never been a Death Sleeper with narcolepsy before. I need him to carry out my aims.'

'And what are they?'

'Why do you need to know that? You wouldn't join in anyway. I know you too well for that, old boy.' Jester sounded full of regret.

Marna appeared in the door, naked and with a look of concern on her face. She looked fantastic and the small scar on her lower abdomen didn't take away from that at all. Konstantin hadn't noticed it yesterday. 'Trouble?' she asked flatly.

Konstantin nodded.

Jester walked on a few paces. 'Ladies, do say hello to Mr Korff so that he knows I'm hosting you as my guests.' Two women shouted out in confusion. Konstantin recognised Iva and Sastre's voices. 'I could have the hotel you're in right now stormed, but that would be too much effort when there is a much simpler way. So, here's the deal: you bring Arctander to me, I give you your darling and Sastre. Alive. By the way, I've spoken to the doctor a little. You know how valuable the doctor is. To avoid any misunderstandings: I welcome her. She has a unique gift and I would only kill her with reluctance. Why should anyone prevent a Death Sleeper becoming visible to the Reaper if he wants to be?' He laughed scornfully. 'They can all go ahead and be weak. I, on the other hand, *like* my special power and am happy to use it. For the good of the general public.'

'And the fact that Arctander wants to be normal doesn't count, does it?'

'We all have to make sacrifices for the public. I trained him and made him into the weapon I need to make governments do what's best for their people, and not what's best for the companies they've signed contracts with. No state in the world will dare to act against its inhabitants if the powerful people know that the hand of Oneiros can reach them anywhere.' Jester sounded excited about his own idea. 'Arctander is the best thing I've ever created. For mankind. Can't you see that?'

'And how often do you want to demonstrate how strong Oneiros is? How many people must die before it's enough?'

'The unintentional demonstrations in Paris, Marrakech and Madrid are enough, I should think. Soon I'll send some polite letters to the world's governments and it will become clear whether they have understood.' He laughed again. 'Oh yes, and I'll have money transferred to me of course. I have to finance my research after all. I'll introduce von Windau to you quietly when I get a chance. She and her scientists are working on fascinating things that could revolutionise the future of mankind, just like my project. Right now I'm thinking about how synergistic effects might be achieved. Now, she doesn't know anything about the partnership that I'm looking for yet and she's not going to be keen, but I can be *very* convincing.'

He's mad. Konstantin didn't even try to figure out whether Jester was lying to him. His behaviour was sheer nonsense. If Jester decided one day that some head of state had offended him, or somebody didn't carry out his demands quickly enough, or if he simply wanted a nation for himself, he would take away Arctander's stone and have him sleep in the middle of a city. *The number of victims would run into the millions.*

'Konstantin?'

'Yes, yes, I . . . just needed to think about how quickly I can find Arctander.' He looked at his watch which read 11.32 a.m. If he was unlucky, Arctander would already have left. Konstantin covered the receiver. 'Ms . . . Marna . . . Herbst,' he said, and he felt odd addressing her by her full name. *I'm too confused.* 'Go to Arctander and stop him leaving. We need him.'

'All right, Korff.' She disappeared through the doorway.

'Brilliant, old boy! I see we do still understand one another.' Jester laughed. 'I am, as you can imagine, with my people in Barcelona. Let's meet—'

'I have to fetch Arctander first. He has already left,' Konstantin interrupted him abruptly. 'But I know where he's going.'

'I'm very glad to hear that. I'll give you until this evening. Eight o'clock, at Plaça de Catalunya. You and Arctander. Nobody else. If I find out you're double-crossing me, I'll have two of my people go to sleep. It would be a pity about all the innocent people. Like Iva. And the doctor.'

If Jester chooses the meeting point, we're done for. The bunker would be perfect. Maybe . . . 'No, I'll tell you where we'll—'

There was a loud bang and Iva shrieked in pain.

'Whoops! I did fire a shot there after all. But it doesn't look that bad, Stan. Just a flesh wound in the right thigh. Good thing Doctor Sastre is here,' said Jester as Iva sobbed and begged him to spare her life. 'Sorry, did you contradict me?'

'No,' he replied and slammed his fist against the shower panel, which cracked under the pressure. *I'll kill him, even if I have to wait years to do it.*

'Will you repeat the time and meeting point to be on the safe side, old boy?'

Konstantin swallowed, looking at the ruptured skin on his hand. Blood was running down and dripping on the tiles. 'Eight o'clock, Plaça de Catalunya.' *Filthy swine!* He was inwardly boiling with fury and hatred. He had never been so betrayed or deceived in all his life.

'Well, well. See you this evening, then. I'm looking forward to seeing you again. I'm sure Iva is too.' Jester hung up.

The hotel room door opened. 'It's us,' called Marna. 'I dragged him out of the taxi.'

'Thank you. I might already have been on my way to the airport,' grumbled Arctander. He put his bag down with a clatter. 'So what's wrong?'

'I'll be right there.' Konstantin slipped into a bathrobe and wrapped a towel around his bleeding hand. He must have switched his phone on in his drunken state, some time after the sex with Marna. To call Iva and apologise? To take photos? *I'm never drinking rioja ever again!*

He came into the room. Arctander watched him with a chilly expression. Marna was only wearing a blouse and trousers, she had been going around barefoot. He noticed that it smelled of sex and rioja in the room. An empty condom packet crackled beneath his toes, which he slid quickly underneath the bed. 'We have a problem,' he began. 'Darling.'

Arctander's expression changed immediately and he got anxious. 'Is he here?'

'He's in Barcelona, yes. He has just called me to tell me that he has taken Sastre and another person hostage. He wants an exchange.'

'Forget it!' cried Arctander indignantly. 'I'm definitely not going back to that arsehole!' He tapped his trouser pocket. 'He will take the stone away from me and then it's . . . all been for nothing, what we . . . what I—' He was becoming more and more worked up, more desperate. He shook his head and picked up his holdall. 'I'm sorry about Sastre and the hostage,' he said quietly and looked at the floor. 'But I'm not getting involved.' He turned towards the door and walked past Marna.

Konstantin watched him go. *I might have an idea. But I need him for it no matter what. Otherwise there's no way I can trick Jester.* 'Bent, you have that woman to thank for even having a chance at a normal life!'

'But if I go to Darling, thousands of people will die. Besides, he's going to kill them anyway. I don't think he sticks to his bargains. And you don't think he does either.' He placed his hand on the doorknob. 'You're going to have to come up with something else.'

That's exactly what I have in mind. Konstantin lunged across the bed, leaped past Marna and grabbed Arctander by the shoulder. 'You're staying. I want to get you—'

'No!' The narcoleptic lashed out with his bag in a panic.

Konstantin's martial arts reflexes kicked in automatically. Using an aikido hold, he threw Arctander against the wardrobe with his own momentum. As the impact made a crashing sound, he let go of the bag. While he staggered backwards, Konstantin picked him up again, hurled him onto the bed and punched him in the right cheek so that the Swedish man passed out.

Marna had retreated to a corner and was watching the brawl. She put her hands in her trouser pockets, looked at the unconscious man and then at Konstantin. 'I'm keen to know what you're planning, Korff. Bent won't be your friend any more when he opens his eyes.'

'I know.' Konstantin tore a sheet and bound Arctander's arms and legs, then gagged him. Even after a night like that, Marna was addressing him by his last name and acting as though the night of passion had never happened. *Fine by me.* He got out his phone and called Thielke to ask him to come to the hotel. He promised he would.

'You have a plan?' Marna asked curiously.

'Yes. Could you arrange for us to have the room for a day longer?'

She nodded and reached for the room telephone. 'Do I get to find out what you're planning?'

'Sure. As soon as Thielke is here, Ms Herbst. And I'm afraid I'm going to have to run up more debt to you and the bourse.' He ignored her sceptical look, stripped off his bathrobe and went into the bathroom. 'I'm taking a shower and freshening up. That night was . . .' He broke off in the middle of the sentence. *But I've got to say something.*

'I don't remember anything,' Marna replied quickly and turned away. 'Must have been the rioja.' She gathered up the last of her things that were strewn about. 'You'll call me as soon as Thielke is here?'

'Yes.'

She nodded to him and hurried out.

Konstantin started up the water in the shower and removed the towel from his injured hand.

He could remember the previous night with Marna very well. Her skin, her smell, her laugh, her desire. All of the confusingly intense feelings that he had experienced.

What would have happened if I had got through to Iva sooner, if I had spoken to her in the last few days? Her life is in danger now because of me.

He got under the shower. But the guilt couldn't be washed away by all the water in the world.

XXV

Now, no one can divine
that he'll not be missed.
Your death or mine
leaves no abyss
in the world.

Eduard von Bauernfeld

Barcelona, Spain

Konstantin hauled the large, aluminium suitcase into the circular Plaça de Catalunya a little before eight o'clock in the evening. He was sweating; despite the evening drawing in, the temperature had not changed since the afternoon. He came to a stop next to a drinking fountain, took a mouthful and wiped his face with damp hands.

Swanky neo-classical buildings surrounded the square; rustling fountains sent their cascades shooting into the sky. The foliage in a small, park-like strip of green muffled the sound of the never-ending stream of traffic that ran around the square in multi-lane streets.

The place must have seemed idyllic to its many visitors.

That would change if they knew what kind of people were here.

Konstantin's heart beat loudly: he wasn't just playing with the lives of Sastre and Iva. Barcelona had more than a million and a half residents and here he was in the centre of the densely populated city.

The wind changed and blew a refreshing cloud of spray from one of the fountains across Konstantin's face. He looked around; along the edge of the Plaça winked the logos of banks housed in the square's majestic buildings. The reinforced concrete façade of a modern shopping centre was the exception to the rule, and it belonged to a Spanish chain.

He had posted Marna on the roof and she was using binoculars to monitor the square, resplendent with a large star made of multi-coloured cobblestones. They had bought pre-paid mobiles in an electronics shop, along with small bluetooth earpieces so that he, Marna and Thielke could remain in constant contact. The jack was only visible if one looked carefully.

Inside the suitcase next to him was a tied up Bent Arctander, who still hadn't been prepared to contribute willingly to the rescue of Iva and Sastre after a long discussion and abject pleading. In the end, Konstantin had forced him to cooperate. Air holes in the aluminium casing of the suitcase prevented the narcoleptic from suffocating.

The plan that Konstantin had come up with entailed an increased risk.

Here, in the middle of Barcelona, innocent people were packed into the cars and buses that drove bumper to bumper, in the many houses, cafés, bars and restaurants, and, directly beneath them, in the junction of two metro lines and the express train line.

Nobody knew the scale of Arctander's curse, especially now that they were cheating Death if he were to take off his ring. Even an ordinary Death Sleeper could cause a monstrous disaster here.

Darling was well aware that Konstantin would investigate the Plaça de Catalunya before the handover and realise the potential of this meeting point.

He will think that I wouldn't dare to make a stand. Konstantin pushed the suitcase further, following a wide, red line that led to the star in the middle. *He's mistaken.*

Jester was standing there, dressed as a tour guide, with a small group of people. It looked like a few couples who were friends with each other had booked a private tour. Apart from Iva and Sastre he counted five people who belonged to Darling and his Project Oneiros. 'Ah!' the MI6 commander cried across the square. 'We've been expecting you, Señor. Come on. We want to get started.'

Nobody took any notice of them, the scene couldn't have been more ordinary. People were strolling around, sitting at the fountains, talking, jogging, taking photographs, children were splashing around, while their parents tried to make sure they didn't get too wet. A normal evening at a popular tourist destination.

'Here we go,' Konstantin said to Marna and Thielke.

'Copy that,' she reported. 'I can't see anyone else acting suspiciously in any way.'

'Same here,' Thielke added. He had taken up a position at one of the fountains. His new Nikon camera with a powerful zoom function gave him a good view of what was happening. Thanks to his lip-reading abilities, he would know what they were talking about. The LeMat could certainly come in handy.

Nothing must go wrong. Konstantin pushed the luggage forwards and joined the group.

He nodded to Iva who looked anxiously at him. Her eyes were red from crying. He had pictured their reunion differently. Romantic, intense, just the two of them. Instead their lives were in danger and the fact he had cheated on her with Marna while soused only made the situation worse. His feelings for her were different, more tenacious and hesitant, probably the result of a guilty conscience. *I'll make up for it, I swear!* Sastre seemed more worried than yesterday evening.

'Here I am,' he said to Jester and placed a hand on the suitcase. 'Arctander is inside here.'

'I thought so, old boy.' Jester looked pleased. He ran his fingertips over his carefully styled hair. 'What a magnificent evening! Take a look at how many people are gathered peacefully around us.'

'You're putting them all in danger with this meeting.'

'Me?' asked Jester, feigning surprise. 'No, I've got myself under control. I think it would be terrible if anything were to happen to these people. After all, the only thing I want is for them to live under better conditions.'

'What a do-gooder you are.' Konstantin could not stop the disdain creeping into his voice.

Jester ignored it. 'A new era is dawning: the world will be led by honest politicians in the foreseeable future. Thanks to me and Oneiros.' He smiled smugly. 'My partners and I will be modest as far as our compensation goes. In fact, our efforts cannot be repaid with money at all.' He smiled gently. 'Do you actually know why von Windau wanted to abduct you back in Leipzig?'

'No.' Konstantin could barely contain his impatience any longer. *This narcissistic arsehole!*

'Just imagine: she is on the search for genuine immortality for us. She rips Death Sleepers' brains out of their skulls and implants them into new bodies.' Jester tapped his ring finger against his dark hairline. 'Sounds mad, doesn't it? But the progress she is making is impressive. That's where I come in, to help her progress. I want to grace the world with my presence for as long as possible.'

Konstantin laughed incredulously, but his stomach turned at the same time. *Hopefully that's nothing more than crazed ranting. The idea that . . .* 'I've listened to you long enough,' he said gravely. 'I want Iva and Sastre and then I want to get out of here.'

'I want my narcoleptic. It's lovely that we were able to bring everything to a happy conclusion.'

'Are we doing that? Or are you going to kill us as soon as you have Arctander?'

Jester's smile was indulgent and paternal, but there was a malicious glint in his eye. 'What for? I have everything I want. Oneiros won't be directed at you or anyone who is a victim.'

I can't make any mistakes. Konstantin sat down on the suitcase. 'What guarantees do I get?'

'My word. I cannot offer you more than that. Have I complained that you posted a woman on the roof of the shopping centre and Thielke is loitering over there by the fountain? How did you even get him to participate?'

'It wasn't all that difficult. He hates you and is looking forward to bringing you to justice.'

'My fear of a one-legged, half-blind man is limited.' Jester's smile died. 'Nothing gets past me, Stan. And now get off that suitcase and open it!'

The group changed positions, forming a circular shield from the numerous passers-by.

He spotted Marna and Thielke quickly. A shade too quickly. Konstantin got up and tipped the suitcase onto its side, undid the locks and flipped the lid open. Arctander lay inside, bound and gagged, his gaze full of accusation. 'There he is.' He slowly put his hands in his pockets. He looked at Sastre and tried to make her understand with one look that something was about to happen.

She nodded imperceptibly and her gaze fell on his fingers – and she went pale. Sastre had noticed that he wasn't wearing Harlequin's Death any more. She shook her head, but this time it was he who nodded, although only slightly.

Jester leaned forwards and checked the narcoleptic's binds. 'Were those bed sheets?' he asked in amusement. 'You're still able to improvise. Brilliant.'

'He didn't want to come with me,' Konstantin replied offhandedly. His right hand closed around the bag of powder in his pocket, his left drew out Thielke's signal scrambler.

'No, Korff,' whispered Sastre anxiously. 'No, don't do it.'

Jester looked at Konstantin in alarm, then at the little box. '*What* shouldn't you do?'

'Hand Arctander over to you. She knows how dangerous he is,' he lied. 'I've put explosives underneath the narco's shirt.

If you try to mess with me while I disappear with Sastre and Iva, he'll blow up. Along with you and your friends.'

Jester's face distorted with understanding. 'Ah, now I understand what the girl on the roof is about. She has the trigger. Clever.'

Arctander let out a groan and pulled at his binds. Some fibres audibly ripped, but the material held fast. He was agitated and trying to say something.

'I'm also holding a detonator with a dead man's switch. If I take my finger away, Bent will turn into a red firework straight away.' Konstantin looked at the Swedish man. 'Sorry, but you should have come willingly.' He took a step backwards. 'The ladies are to come to me, if I may be so bold.'

Jester straightened up slowly and gave his companions a signal. The two women were let go.

Sastre went to him, along with Iva, who didn't look at Konstantin, but stared at the ground in front of her. Jester's people shifted sideways until the MI6 commander and his agents were standing close together.

Konstantin threw Iva a long look, but she didn't raise her eyes. *I deserve her contempt.* Especially since he wished he could see Marna again, who was waiting in the building behind him once more. If his plan didn't work out or if the timing went badly, they would be dead. Without a chance to say goodbye.

Now! Konstantin wrenched his hand out of his pocket and tossed the crystalline powder out of the bag at his enemies. Glittering, it scattered over their hair and shoulders. 'Give it all you've got. I only need a few seconds,' he muttered to the doctor, then he shouted at Arctander. 'I'm going to kill you, you piece of shit!' At the same time, he made as though to draw a gun. 'You're not going to help Project Oneiros!'

Arctander moaned loudly in fear of his life – and drifted off into an attack.

Sastre screamed out, 'No!' but already there came the sound of the rustling that announced the Reaper's arrival, even louder, more angry and destructive than in the bunker.

The light around the square was fading, a flock of pigeons rose up in panic, a bird plummeted, then all of the birds crashed onto the Plaça, dead.

Please! Please, it's got to be quick this time! Konstantin held the scrambling transmitter and kept a close watch on his surroundings.

The gemstone dust that he had scattered over his enemies flashed . . .

Jester let out a shrill scream and fell onto his back, his hands pressed against his chest. He rolled from side to side, groaning frantically. His minions collapsed screaming, clutching their throats, heads, hearts. They were dying at Konstantin's feet.

The sight filled Konstantin with grim pleasure. The Reaper had recognised them as Death Sleepers in a split second and had caught them before they became invisible again. An unbelievable opportunity: a Death Sleeper called him, but here were other Death Sleepers whom he was finally able to see. And kill. The people on the square were forgotten, but the Reaper could still sense the presence of another Death Sleeper who was defying him.

Please let this work! Konstantin pressed the button on the scrambling transmitter and hurled himself down next to

Bent Arctander, holding the generator against the man's head – and the rustling sound ebbed away. But it didn't vanish completely. Instead it sounded as if it had only withdrawn a little way.

In a frenzy, Konstantin picked up the injection containing a mixture of extreme stimulant and adrenaline, and drove it into the narcoleptic's arm.

It took four seconds, which seemed like an eternity, for Arctander's eyelids to open.

Suddenly the rustling disappeared. The light ventured out again and a blazing sunset bathed Barcelona in dazzling gold.

'It's over,' Konstantin tried to soothe the panic-stricken man, loosening his binds. 'It's over, Bent. We're rid of them. Darling is dead.' He quickly pressed the Reaper's Stone he had taken away from him earlier into Arctander's hand and took his own ring out of the inner pocket of the suitcase, and slipped it onto his finger. With terrifying uncertainty, he checked on Iva and all of the other people in the square.

Dead pigeons bobbed in the water of the fountain, and there were even more lying on the pavement. Dogs and stray cats had collapsed in the square, flowers had wilted and lost their blossoms. Parched bushes had dropped their foliage. But the people were still standing, looking at each other in confusion and fear.

It worked. Konstantin breathed a sigh. The Reaper had only rampaged in a small, jagged area, without unleashing his full power. *Was Death more merciful than usual, or simply confused because we let him take the Death Sleepers' lives?*

'No casualties,' he heard Marna's relieved voice in his ear. He was very glad to hear it. 'Nobody went down.'

'There are two grannies who are just about to be helped to their feet again,' Thielke reported, 'but no bodies.'

The dog owners examined their lifeless pets, children pawed at the lifeless cats and pigeons. There rose a tumult of voices speaking over each other, as people were loudly giving vent to their shock at what had happened.

Konstantin got up and went to Iva, taking her in his arms. 'It's over,' he whispered to her and held her close to him. She didn't return his embrace. 'You're not in danger any more.'

'Korff! Take cover!' Marna screamed in his ear.

A gun went off behind him with a crack. Several shots were fired which would certainly have hit their target had the warning come a second later. But he threw himself to one side in time and pulled the shrieking Iva with him.

People were wailing. The LeMat boomed dully from the other side of the square amid people's voices. Chaos erupted.

'Stay down!' Konstantin rolled on top of Iva and looked around for the attacker. He was fully expecting to see von Windau, fresh from firing in ambush. *He said that she was a partner* . . .

But instead he looked up in time to see Jester crumple a second time, bleeding from gaping holes in his chest and throat. The jacket still bore shimmering traces of gemstone dust, but it seemed Jester had shaken it off just in time to evade the Reaper's full power. In his right hand he held a gun with smoke rising out of the muzzle. Jester looked stunned. Red spit and foam was running over his lips, but he was crooking his finger to fire another shot as though in slow motion.

No! You escaped Death, but you're not going to escape me.

Konstantin leaped up, bent the arm holding the gun upwards as the trigger finger pressed down.

The bullet travelled upwards through Jester's chin and shattered his skullcap. Brain matter, blood and scraps of flesh splattered everywhere. The LeMat banged again a tenth of a second later and tore the right hand side of his face off.

Your just deserts. Konstantin let go of the arm and the corpse fell backwards. *As far as I'm concerned, your soul can stay here on this square forever. It's actually better than getting taken out by the Reaper. You will never have a sense of release.*

The Plaça de Catalunya was completely empty of people when Konstantin looked up again. Tourists and locals had fled across the streets, diving behind trees as cover. A cry of 'terrorists' spread and the first sirens sounded.

Sniffing, Iva hauled herself to her feet, with difficulty. As Konstantin went to help her, she waved him off with a sob. 'Leave me alone!'

Konstantin looked at her in consternation. He was confused and hurt, blood whistled in his ears. 'I'd like to—'

'Well done, Korff. Check on Sastre. She hasn't moved yet,' Marna advised over the mobile phone line.

'I'll be right back.' Konstantin crouched down next to the doctor who had sat down as though to meditate. Her face had aged again, now weathered like rock.

'Stand up so that I can smack you in the jaw!' Arctander stormed over, seething with rage and winding up his arm. 'You owe me that, *arsle!*'

'In a moment.' Konstantin held out his arm, gesturing for him to be silent. 'Professor?' He felt for her pulse. The thin skin was warm and dry.

Nothing.

'What's wrong with her?' he heard an agitated Marna asking.

'The police are approaching,' Thielke said at the same time. 'Get out of here, Korff. We'll meet at the hotel.'

This was not part of the plan. Konstantin felt responsible. He touched Sastre on the shoulder in farewell, got up and linked arms with a reluctant Iva to guide her away from the Plaça de Catalunya. 'We'll go to my hotel,' he told her. 'I'll explain everything to you there. I'd like you to know what has happened.'

Arctander followed them at a distance.

At first, Iva hobbled, sobbing and limping along beside him, but once they had crossed the street she broke away and took a step backwards, away from him. 'I said, leave me alone! I don't want to know anything,' she spluttered, pointing at him. 'I don't want anything else from you either. Nothing at all, do you hear me? I had already written to you to tell you that.'

Konstantin thought his knees were about to give way. And yet he didn't feel what he would have expected to feel at her words. Incomprehension and shock, yes, but also relief. *No. She's confused . . . like me. It was too much for her . . . for us.* His head was spinning.

Tears flowed from her eyes and down her cheeks. 'This is all too . . . weird for me. Too crazy. These people, the abduction, and I don't even know what they've done with Thorsten.' She clapped one hand to her mouth and placed the other on her stomach. After a deep breath she said falteringly, 'What if they've done something to him? Oh

my God, what if they've done something to him? Then ...
I wouldn't know ...'

He remembered that one of the cellists in the orchestra
was called Thorsten. 'Who is Thorsten?'

She glanced at him, awkward and uncertain. 'My boyfriend,' she answered finally.

Konstantin braced himself against the wall. *That was it.* His
feelings were too chaotic for him to comprehend what was
going on. In any case he didn't feel plunged into despair or
any acute pain, the way he might have done.

'You walked out on me after a garbled story about fairy
tales and ... I was sorry that I had laughed at you, I wanted
to apologise. But you disappeared, I didn't hear anything at all
from you and I was feeling more and more rotten. Thorsten
was there for me. We talked, we got closer.' Iva ran a hand
through her blonde hair. 'I tried to get hold of you to tell you
that, and ... then these people turned up. This MI6 agent—'
She hunched up her shoulders. 'Do me a favour and stay
away from me. I don't want anything more to do with you.
Whatever is going on with you, it's too insane for me. Look
after your corpses and be happy.' Iva looked around as she
wiped away the tears with one hand and hobbled towards
the entrance to the metro. Without a word of goodbye she
disappeared down the escalator.

Konstantin sighed. *That was it,* he thought again. He couldn't
grasp any of the thoughts racing through his head. There were
too many of them and they disappeared just as quickly as
they came, but Marna cropped up in most of them. Following
Iva's revelation he was feeling shocked, relieved, confused,
bewildered, surprised, calm ... 'Marna, are you still on the—'

'As I said, I owe you this,' Arctander suddenly planted himself in front him and lashed out with his fist, '*arsle!*'

Konstantin had completely forgotten about the Swedish man. Despite the ambush he could have easily dodged the weak blow. But he didn't.

The fist hit him, his jaws crunched and the taste of blood filled his mouth. He had underestimated the lanky narcoleptic's strength. Stars twinkled in front of Konstantin's eyes and he fell to the floor. Everything went black.

Minsk, Belarus

Kristen walked into the university building that housed the Life Institute and stopped short: nobody was manning the reception. There were no armed guards, no telephone, no monitors. Loose cables hung out of sockets and in the corners where there had once been cameras.

The Institute's move was in progress and she had already visited the new site when she had dropped Miller off there, but the moving company had not been scheduled to work so quickly or so thoroughly. Still less had she ordered the guards to stand down. Large parts of the research equipment were still in the building and basement. Most importantly: the cryotanks and the cold chambers.

Kristen looked at the clock on the wall, listening carefully for noises.

She didn't like the silence. The lift wasn't moving, the generators weren't humming, the students who usually had lectures on the ground floor had fallen as silent as mice.

She drew her semi-automatic, went to the lift and pressed the call button.

The display remained dark.

Kristen cursed and went to the door that led to the stairwell. The combination lock had been removed, anyone could go upstairs and downstairs from here.

She raced up the stairs to the first floor. Even on the stairs there were chemical stains and blood spatter on the greyish-blue-painted concrete floor. Two used bullet casings lay in one corner. The door to the first floor was decorated with bullet holes and even more red marks.

The institute's relocation had not gone to plan.

She stormed into the corridor and switched on the light.

Two overhead lights snapped on and lit up the whole floor, which contained nothing more than wires dangling down and the lights on the ceiling. The machines, the beds and even the outlets for oxygen lines in the wall were missing. Kristen could have been standing in any abandoned factory building.

Her stomach contracted, her throat constricted. The equipment from the first floor hadn't been at the new site. She would have noticed that.

Something had gone terribly wrong.

'Shit!' Kirsten sprinted out and down the stairs. Sweating and panting, she kept running despite the muscles burning in her legs. She raced down, leaping across entire landings to get to the basement as quickly as possible. She fell down the last steps and went head over heels, landing hard on the ground. Dazed, she got up, and when she ran a hand over her forehead there was blood on it. It was warm and running down her face.

It was just as silent down here as it was on the floors above. The machines were quiet, the CT and MRI scanners had disappeared.

Sheer panic rose up within her. She hurried onwards and tore open the door to the cryotanks.

'No,' she gasped.

In the light of the construction lamps there was a single container, just one where there had once been five. A ladder leaning against it led to the opening in the tank. On an overturned beer crate next to it there was an open laptop connected to the mains.

Kristen had barely taken a step inside the room when the screen lit up.

She put away the gun and watched the screen where a film was playing. It had been shot with a wide-angle camera and showed a group of masked gunmen skulking in front of a house.

Kristen recognised the men straight away: Brian and his troops.

A convoy of three limousines was approaching. They stopped and the doors swung open. To the Irishmen's surprise, heavily armed men leaped out of the cars and opened fire. Only two of them managed to return fire at all, the rest of them went down in the hail of bullets. Barely a minute later, the battle had been decided and Brian's squad obliterated.

One of the Russians turned to the camera and gave two thumbs up. The film stopped and a still image appeared: Brian's bloodied face, deformed and barely recognisable after three bullet wounds.

This image vanished too and was replaced by the silhouette of Anatol's shadowy head. He still opted not to show her his features. His way of punishing her, denying her the beloved face. The *vory v zakone* was silent, expectant.

Kristen knew that he was watching her. 'Y-y-you would have tried to do the same,' she said firmly.

'Of course I would have, but I would have been successful,' he replied coolly. 'You can see that in your toy laboratory. I won't have anyone tricking me.'

Kristen looked around. 'W-w-what is all this? What have you d-d-done?' She cursed her stuttering, which made her feel weak and stupid.

'What I should have done two years ago: taken the research away from you and taken care of it myself,' Anatol replied. 'Your scientists work for me now. They have been taken to a new hospital in a place you will never see. The procedure and aims have changed slightly, Sophia, but the well-being of our son remains unremittingly the focal point.'

'C-c-can I . . .?'

'*You?* You cannot do a thing!' he interrupted her icily and moved his head so that his mouth and nose came into view. 'You risked our son's life with those Irish bastards! Those arseholes could have killed him. A stray bullet and he would have been dead! I cannot forgive you for that.'

Kristen was seized by a terrible fear of loss. 'W-w-where did you have my f-f-father taken to?'

'The new hospital. He survived the transportation in his cryotank well,' said Anatol.

'W-w-when can I-I-I see Eugen—'

'Do you see the ladder, Sophia?'

'Yes.'

'It's for you. Take off your clothes, climb into the cryotank and close it. As soon as you are inside, it will activate.' Anatol spoke without emotion. 'The doctors said that your insomnia is too far advanced to be able help you any more. Not with how the research currently stands.'

'B-b-but . . .' Kristen's confusion grew. 'I still h-h-have another y-y-year.'

'No, you do not have that. *I* am taking this year from you. It's punishment for what you almost caused.' Anatol hit the table with his fist. The bang made her jump even though the sound was only audible through the shoddy speaker. 'If you refuse to climb into that tank, I will have your frozen father cut into slices with a bandsaw and you will never see Eugen again for the rest of your life. I promise you that.'

She had struggled for too long. Against her body, against time, against other people. Suddenly it was tempting to simply give up. She was wracked with dejection, with utter mental surrender. 'W-w-when do I see him then, i-i-if I have myself f-f-frozen?'

'In the future,' he replied pitilessly. 'Pray that your research-ers reach the goals that I've set for them. If God is merciful, you will wake up some time and hold Eugen and his children and grandchildren in your arms.' He drew back from the light, only one ear and his temples still visible. Anatol waited, enjoying his triumph.

Kristen bit her lip. She wanted to scream, wanted to point the gun at the computer and shoot him to pieces, wanted to hold Eugen tight and never let go – but instead she stood there helplessly in the basement of the cleared out building where she had worked on her dream of eternal life.

Pride, defiance and fear filled her. And desperation, which was increasing with every second and pushing everything else aside, right down to her last scrap of confidence that there would be a sudden turnaround in her favour. She couldn't get anywhere any more. Her ex-husband had her in his grip.

'I'll d-d-do it,' she whispered. 'I'll d-d-do it for Eugen. S-s-so that I can hug him again one d-d-day.' The fear was cutting off her air.

'Is there anything you want to say to him? I'll note it down and show it to him when he's older.'

She shook her head. 'I w-w-will tell him w-w-what I have to tell him myself. Whether that's in a hundred years or a thousand.' Kristen slipped her clothes off and threw them on the floor.

'You have my word that I will take care of your frozen body and I'll raise Eugen to be a good, upstanding man. A *vory v zakone*,' Anatol was saying goodbye. 'He may carry your curse in him, Sophia, but we will break it. I'll find ways and means. He will have a good life.'

Naked, she revealed her athletic body with its numerous ankh tattoos to the camera. 'W-w-what should I d-d-do?'

'Climb into the tank and close the lid. There are sense electrodes on the floor that you should affix to yourself: the small ones to your chest, the two larger ones to your temples. Men will come and operate the machine.'

'I d-d-don't s-s-see anyone.'

'They're there. Trust me.' Anatol raised his hand in farewell and fell silent.

Kristen climbed up the ladder and swung herself over the edge of the tank, letting herself slide down the smooth walls with their many small openings. In the weak light that penetrated through the opening from above, she stuck the electrodes firmly to herself. Then she went up on tiptoes to close the lid.

It clicked as she pulled it down and it locked into place.

Kristen sat down on the cold vulcanite floor, drew her legs in close to her body and placed her head on her knees. It was lonely in the metallic darkness. It didn't smell of anything.

She didn't know whether Anatol had seriously meant what he'd said. She thought he was capable of anything. He could freeze her and really have her cut up with a bandsaw; give her to a plastinator; not move her research forward; feed her to pigs and his dobermans; take care of her and have her thawed in fifty years. Nothing was impossible where Anatol was concerned.

In her overwhelming fear she concentrated on Eugen's lovely face. In case you dreamed in the frozen state, she wanted to set off with good images in her mind. She imagined how he would look when he got older. Eugen would have lots of girlfriends as a young man and treat them well. She was sure of that.

Kristen smiled.

There were several clacks above her head. The professionals had arrived and were preparing for her hibernation, which would happen with the help of liquid nitrogen and a few other tricks.

Icy air streamed out of the many tiny nozzles in the metal wall of the tank with an aggressive hiss and quickly made the temperature fall below freezing.

Strangely, she recalled a line from Jean de la Bruyère. 'A death that forestalls frailty comes at a better time than a death that puts an end to it.'

In her case, she was choosing neither death nor frailty.

She was cheating the Reaper. Not truly and eternally dead, and yet not alive.

Kristen's pulse was slowed and she shivered, her teeth chattering and fatigue setting in. She was freezing very gradually. As soon as her heart stopped, the men would pump in the liquid nitrogen which would then flow around her and flash freeze her down to the smallest cells.

'Eugen,' Kristen whispered, anticipating the moment when she could open her eyes again and look into his face.

Then her heart stopped . . .

Barcelona, Spain

When Konstantin came round, he was lying in a white hospital bed.

Oh my God, or whoever else: don't let me have ended up in von Windau's institute! He looked quickly around the single room.

Marna was sitting on a chair next him, a laptop on her knees. She was wearing a business suit again, grey and white. Her chestnut brown hair was pulled back tightly and there were glasses on her nose. He cleared his throat.

'Just a moment, Korff,' she said without shifting her gaze from her screen.

'Sure.' He raised a hand to his painful, swollen face. His fingers bumped into a mask. *What is this then?* 'Do you have a mirror, Ms Herbst?'

Marna typed one last letter and looked at him. 'No, but I've got a built-in camera.' She turned the laptop around.

Konstantin saw himself sitting in the bed. A mask that the hospital appeared to have nicked from the *Phantom of the Opera*'s prop store was on his face. 'What's this about, then?'

'Bent broke your cheekbone and two other bones,' she explained. 'The doctors thought it was best, to protect the fractures.' Marna smiled. 'He has flown back to Sweden. Thielke has gone with him. He'll be in touch as soon as they've arrived safely.'

'A new dream couple, it sounds like.' Konstantin laughed, then groaned. It was painful. 'The one time I don't put up a fight, and this is the result.'

'It would probably have been smarter to dodge the punch. But you also fell awkwardly.' She leaned forwards. 'Besides, you deserved it, Korff. You've got to admit that. It wasn't nice, what you did to him.'

'It wouldn't have worked otherwise.' Konstantin saw the Plaça de Catalunya in his mind's eye, he saw Sastre, who had sacrificed herself. *Whom I sacrificed.* He still believed that Death had shown leniency that day and contented himself with a warning to the surviving Death Sleepers by only killing plants and animals. Konstantin interpreted it as a reminder never to take off his Reaper's Ring. He stroked the ring with one thumb. 'How long have I been here?'

'Exactly a day. I told the doctors everything they needed to know. My Spanish is good.'

'And the doctors went along with it?'

'Since I'm your *sister* of course, Korff. With my charm I even made them leave you the ring,' she retorted with a wink. 'Nobody asked for my ID. Barcelona's got other things to worry about right now.' She turned off the laptop's camera and pulled up a news website.

There was speculation about the curse of the Plaça de Catalunya. By this point, some experts excluded the possibility that the incident had been caused by the Russian gas, since the people would have been just as affected by it as the animal and plant life. Others claimed the reason the catastrophe didn't happen was a flawed gas mixture.

As for verified facts, there remained six dead foreigners, of whom one seemed, according to initial findings, to have been shot by Igor, as well as one local who had died kneeling on the star in the very centre of the square. Mystics and other weirdos talked about cosmic rays that had come together in the Plaça de Catalunya's star. There were no logical explanations and the investigating authorities suspected a fight between terrorists.

Konstantin still felt relieved that everything was over, but the pangs of guilt were still there. 'I have Sastre on my conscience,' he said haltingly. *She could have helped lots of us.*

Marna touched his hand encouragingly. 'She wouldn't have lived much longer, Korff.'

'What makes you think that?' He looked at her in surprise. 'Did you hang out with the female Death Sleepers?'

'No, but women go to the loo together. In the tapas bar.

I came out of the cubicle and saw her swallowing tablets. Morphine. She had bowel cancer and was in the final stage. She wouldn't have had more than three months.'

'I didn't know.' Konstantin was reassured to some extent. He was reminded of Iva going downstairs in the metro. To Thorsten. His guilty conscience over the night with Marna was fading. He no longer felt confused – relief had come to the fore. Much as it astonished him, the loss of Iva didn't bother him.

'You're acquiring 100,000 euro as soon as possible for me to send to the bourse so that I can claim I sold the opals absolutely legally and officially.' An unruly strand of hair fell into her face and she blew it back. 'I take it you can arrange that? Some of your friends will surely be glad about Darling's death, if I understand it correctly. Friends who are solvent?'

Konstantin nodded. He would approach the remaining Torpor's Men, the Sleep's Brothers and the Deathslumberers. 'It's possible you'll get lots of orders soon,' he said and raised the hand with the ring adorning it; there were IV lines stuck into his other arm.

He thought about informing all the organisations about the connection between the Death Sleepers' curse and the Grim Reaper's Stones. The Dream Dragons, Kali's Thoughts, the Thuggee Nidra and the Dream Wind Catchers – there were certainly some in their ranks who wanted to do a deal with the Reaper. Thielke could then use his LeMat to eliminate those who declined the option of a normal life. *They have the choice.* Konstantin was still not in absolute agreement with Thielke's methods, but the man could not be deflected from his mission. 'The Death Sleepers will need opals. You know what matters of course. As someone in the know.'

'I'm glad of that. I could buy myself a proper new car with the commission.' She laughed. 'Oh, and I'm the owner of Ars Moriendi. Maybe the car thing will work out even sooner.'

'True,' he murmured. 'You have a point.'

'Feel free to call me *boss*, Korff. But don't worry. As soon as I have my money, including the 50,000 for my Audi, you'll get the business back.' Marna stood up and stowed the laptop away in her shoulder bag. 'You're not getting shot of me, Korff. And as you say, I'm an expert on the topic of Death Sleepers. They'll need me. So I reckon I'm just as unlikely to be shot of *you*.' She lifted her hand in parting. 'By the way, you've got to stay another week for observation. Make sure you get some rest.' For a few seconds, her gaze became softer and filled with affection before the professional distance returned to her reddish-grey eyes. 'I'll see you tomorrow. I've put a mobile in the drawer for you.' Marna wanted to leave the room.

'Ms Herbst?'

She stood still. 'Yes?'

'Shall we not call each other by our first names?'

Marna considered it, picking up the bag containing the laptop with both hands. 'Can do, Korff.' She grinned, turned on her heel and left.

Konstantin grinned too. *Yes, you're right. I will still have a lot to do with you.*

Then he took the mobile phone out of the drawer. He had to make several phone calls. It was a question of money and gemstones and the search for new Death Seers. They were the greatest hope for people like him to have a normal life.

A nurse came in before he had even dialled the first number. Balancing a lunch tray on one hand, she rubbed at her neck with the other, as if she was trying to get something off. '*Holà*,' she greeted him. 'Here comes your food. But it's a light meal and easy to chew, so it won't hurt, Señor.' She removed the cover, presenting mashed potato with peas cooked practically into mush. 'Listen, do I have a red mark here?' She leaned forward and showed him her neck.

Konstantin couldn't see anything. 'No. Nothing.'

'Your sister was mistaken then.' She smiled and put the tray on the small table. 'Bon appetit, Señor. The doctor will come by later and explain what you should be avoiding in the coming weeks, for as long as you are wearing the mask. Wish me luck: I'm completing my first parachute jump today.'

'Best of luck. And thanks for letting me know.' Konstantin waited until she had left the room before he picked up the phone again and made the first call. The harlequin opal flashed in its silver carnation setting. *As soon as I can stand up, I'm going to visit Sastre's grave.*

There was a click and the call was answered. '*Namaste*,' said a man's voice.

Konstantin faltered. He had been expecting Durga. He could hear her laughing in the background.

In fact, why not? He might as well speak to one of his enemies first, although he would have been happier to speak to the Indian woman. He was going to introduce himself as Korff, but then he changed his mind. *Shock tactics.* 'This is Oneiros.'

A brief silence, then: 'I haven't heard that name in a long time.'

'It wasn't easy to find out the number for a Thuggee Nidra.

Fear seals even your clients' lips. Most of them anyway,' he lied, so that Durga didn't come under suspicion of being in contact with him. 'There's news, Yama.' He looked out the window, glimpsed the sun and closed his eyes as he breathed in a faint trace of Marna's perfume. Memories of that night with her crept incongruously into his thoughts. 'What would you say if I were to describe to you a method of making Death Sleepers visible to the Reaper and enabling them to have an almost normal life?' Konstantin waited eagerly for a response.

'I would assume that it's a trick and decline.'

'And if it *wasn't* one?'

Yama, the chief of the Thuggee Nidra, hesitated before answering cautiously, 'I'm afraid I wouldn't be pleased at all. It would spread unrest in the ranks of the Thuggee, there would be advocates and opponents. A war could break out between brothers and sisters and that is far from ideal. And I would be even less pleased if there were someone who knew of such a method and could make me into a normal person against my will. I'm one of the chosen ones and want to stay that way.'

Konstantin clutched the phone, listening carefully with a pounding heart. *He sounds anything but enthusiastic.* He had picked up on the Indian man's threat.

Yama's deep voice took on a sharp undercurrent. 'I would think it clever if you were to say to me that it *is* in fact a trick. Then I could decline, reassured, and everything would be all right.' He paused for a moment, as though he wanted to give Konstantin time to think it over. '*Are* you clever, Oneiros?'

The Fairy Tale of the Reaper and Sleep

The two very different brothers, Reaper and Sleep, were fighting over who was the stronger of the two.

'I end every life,' the Reaper bragged and placed a bony hand on the chain of Deathgems that he wore around his neck.

'I help people recuperate, send them dreams that cheer them up, frighten them, rouse them, inspire them, show them new paths,' Sleep argued and placed a slender finger on the chain of dreams that adorned his chest. 'You are capable of killing people, but I give them so much more. I'm more powerful.'

'And yet in the end they come to my kingdom. They can sleep and dream there as much as they like,' sneered the Reaper harshly. 'I can kill sleeping people, but you cannot bring dreams to the dead. I outrank you, brother.' He hurried away with long strides to pursue his mission.

Sleep was angry and wanted to pay his brother back.

So he secretly selected people from all over the world to make them invisible to Death with a spell. He linked his incantation with a gemstone he had stolen from his brother's chain.

But Sleep was a joker into the bargain.

So that his brother would be constantly reminded of the humiliation that Sleep was the stronger of the two of them, he granted his protégés the ability to ridicule and insult Death in their sleep. Choruses were to ring out from all countries on earth to make fun of Sleep's brother.

And that's how it happened.

When the Reaper heard the laugher for the first time, he was surprised.

When he heard the abuse, he was angry.

When he took in the insults, he went on the rampage.

The Reaper raged around the world and looked for the voice who dared to mock him. But no matter how hard he tried, he could never find them. He could come close to them, but he could not see them.

'Where on earth are they?' he roared. 'I can hear them! There are people who laugh at me. I need to punish them for their impertinence!'

Sleep was full of glee. 'I created them, my dear brother. Their sleep should always remind you that I have more power than you.'

'What foolishness! Your chosen people may live, my dear brother, but all living things around them will die and never be able to dream again,' growled the Reaper. 'Their death will always remind you that I have more power than you.'

So the brothers parted on the worst terms.

And so long as the chosen ones laugh at Death in their sleep . . .

. . . the Reaper and Sleep will not settle their argument.

Konstantin Korff

Closing Credits

As I had promised in so many lectures in the lead-up to this book: no vampires, no werewolves, no demons.

I'm not ruling out a return to the familiar mishmash of spooky characters; I enjoy them too much for that.

But it was about time I tackled something new. A complete change was needed.

And I found the idea of a person being immortal *without* the clichéd advantages fascinating. Not forgotten by Death, but invisible to the Reaper.

With *Oneiros* I wanted to demonstrate that you can show the classic subject in a new light and that it can be surprising for readers – or at least I very much hope so.

I was inspired by old fairy tales and the idea in them of the living interacting with the Grim Reaper, bargaining with him, tricking him – but sooner or later they can't escape him.

Out of this came a book that might prompt you to think about your own life. Life can come to an end sooner than people might like.

My thanks to the test readers Tanja Karmann, Yvonne Schöneck and Sonja Rüther who paradoxically helped me to stay hot on the heels of Death and immortality in equal measure.

I also want to thank reader Anne Rudolph whom I occasionally confused and surprised. With her notes she in turn ensured that the readers were spared the confusion and only the surprise remained.

In order that the descriptions of thanatological terms are correct, I asked Kuckelkorn Undertakers in Cologne to check those scenes. My thanks to Christoph Kuckelkorn for his suggestions and improvements!

Speaking of technical information: thank you to the Saarland University Medical Centre in Homburg, especially Roger Motsch from the press office who organised the interview with Professor Joachim Oertel, Director of the Neurosurgery Clinic.

And of course a special thank you to Professor Oertel himself that he didn't see me as a lunatic at the beginning with my questions about brain transplants. I don't know what he thinks now, but I'm hoping for the best!

Anyone interested in Lambda's music, which Korff listens to in the novel, will hit the jackpot here: www.lambda-band. de. Their second album, which came out in May 2012, includes wonderful vocals from Mareike Greb.

It has been mentioned and recommended: a group out of the ordinary, both live and on CD.

It's important that there are artists who interpret music and lyrics in their own way, although they've got to assume they won't be discovered by the masses.

Keep it up!

I've been busy too and have put a few little pieces together, my amateur soundtrack to the novel, you could say. Don't worry, I don't sing . . .

The songs can be found online at MySpace under the name The_Mahet's. Enjoy!

Producers are very welcome to get in touch.

What will come next?

Werewolves, vampires and demons again?

I haven't planned a sequel to *Oneiros*, although you should never say 'never'. In any case, Korff's answer in the phone call at the end of the book is still pending.

Since I'm sometimes accused of not being able to write a book with a proper ending (which isn't true, because the stories have been told to the end), I could reveal here how the answer turns out.

But I won't.

But it is an ending. Korff must see for himself what happens next before I potentially return to the world of the Death Sleepers one day. I think the unresolved ending to the film *Inception* is superb. Novelists should have the same freedom, which I gladly exploit here.

Perhaps I'll make an excursion into the world of the thriller and put my own spin on it?

The ideas will show me where the journey will go.

... ah yes, the Drinks for the Book

Please remember: Drink sensibly, as the adverts advise. These drinks are strong stuff and not for people under the age of eighteen. All right, maybe the Mata Hari. That could be poured out at a children's birthday party. But be warned: chai will bring you to life!

The delicious Red Russian *(Korff style)*

- Pour 300 ml each of vodka and kirsch into a glass.
- Add three ice cubes. Crush three mint leaves with a pestle or spoon, so that the essential oils are released and place them in the glass.
- Stir briefly. Done.

For the alcohol-free contingent:

Mata Hari *(Kristen style)*

- Place 200 ml of unsweetened chai tea in a shaker, along with 2 tsp. sugar, 200 ml grenadine syrup, 200 ml lemon juice, a dash of rosewater and ice cubes.
- Shake hard.
- Strain into a cocktail glass and garnish with dried rose petals.

The ultimate Fresh Death (or Mahet's)

- Place 400 ml each of lime juice and vodka (not the cheapest kind and no aromatic kinds) into a shaker with ice cubes. Stir for a moment so that the ingredients blend and chill.
- Cut a large piece of orange zest and put it into the shaker. Shake well.
- Strain into a glass with two ice cubes and add fresh orange juice.

For anyone who wants to round things off by listening to another funny song on the topic of death, I would recommend the group Knorkator and the song 'Wir werden alle sterben' or 'We will all die'.

They are right!

But there are still many more experiences to be had before then.

Wohlsein, Cheers to the Lost and *Nastrovje!*

Markus Heitz
Autumn 2011

Brief interview with
Professor Joachim Oertel

Professor Joachim Oertel is Director of the Neurosurgery Clinic at the Saarland University Medical Centre in Homburg, Saarland. The central focus of Professor Oertel's work is developing and establishing new and innovative operating techniques. Within that, he particularly concentrates on minimally invasive procedures. Oertel has received numerous prizes for his scientific work.

Markus Heitz: The experiments in the novel that are carried out by Kristen von Windau's team are based on papers by the doctors White and Demikhov, who performed tests on dogs and apes that are extremely gruesome by today's standards. They justified it by saying that these transplant procedures could be used on victims of accidents to allow them a new life in a new body.

Are these doctors or their experiments from that time still discussed during training these days?

Prof Oertel: During my studies I had never heard of either of them. Their experiments and theories were not a topic in lectures; I didn't come across their work in everyday life as a doctor afterwards either.

But having said that, now that you ask, I remember having seen clips of the transplanted apes. That's a long time ago now. I don't think any of my colleagues know the film.

Markus Heitz: I don't suppose the two doctors' ideas are even partially under consideration by modern medicine?

Prof Oertel: Generally speaking, when it comes to this topic, we can say that the more complex an organ is and the more specialised its function, the more likely it is that an artificial replacement is being developed. That is the route that the research typically takes to minimise complications through transplant or repair. Even if the artificial replacement is much worse than the original.

Great progress has been made in hearing and the eye. At the moment there is research being done into restoring the sense of smell.

But there is extremely dubious research in Europe where paraplegics are injected with stem cells in return for paying huge amounts of money. Their hopes for a complete recovery are raised. That is indefensible.

However, it's true that huge developments have been achieved in the area of prosthetics and this was through the use of stem cells.

Markus Heitz: If you walk across the Homburg campus, you spot rather mysterious sounding signs that say 'experimental surgery' and 'experimental neurosurgery'.

As an author writing in the horror genre, images flash up almost automatically – but what is actually being done there?

Prof Oertel: Experimental neurosurgery has been on campus for about thirty years. We are concerned with investigating new operating techniques or restoring nerves such as auditory or cranial nerves. Experiments on this are performed in cell culture or on laboratory animals.

With our research, we are interested, among other things, in how to bring brain haemorrhages under control. In our modern society, many people pop blood-thinners as a matter of course, which becomes a big problem during brain surgery. We also replace, for example, parts of the cranial bone of a rat with Plexiglas in order to be able to observe directly what is happening in the brain after administering a drug. In this way we obtain information about the processes and effects.

Markus Heitz: Assuming there really were ruthless doctors like the ones the anti-heroine of the books surrounds herself with, doctors who would do anything for money and mistaken ambition: what would they be capable of? With today's capabilities?

Prof Oertel: At the moment, the transplantation of a brain as such or a head is not possible; a person's mind, or rather their head, cannot simply be transplanted into or onto a donor body. The overall structure is too complex for that and the allocative functions of the nerves are too comprehensive. That was the main error in the doctors' theories back then. Neither communication nor senses would function after a transplant like that.

But what would be very easy to imagine is this: assuming that one has an intact brain plus the corresponding spine and spinal cord – it would be possible to enable the control of muscles via direct connections between the spine and these muscle groups.

Besides this, there is a trend in the US of freezing dead people directly after death, in order to be able to thaw them at a later date and bring them back to life with modern methods. But some people confine themselves to the head.